P

"Many thanks ... series sexy and uniqu ... *Reader at Heart*

MASTER OF SWORDS

"Fabulous . . . A terrific romantic fantasy that spins the Arthurian legend into a different, unique direction."
—*Midwest Book Review*

MASTER OF WOLVES

"Grandmaster of the paranormal romantic suspense."
—*Midwest Book Review*

MASTER OF THE MOON

"Packs in tons more passion, danger, and sizzling sensuality . . . Scorchingly hot." —*Romantic Times*

MASTER OF THE NIGHT

"A terrific paranormal romantic suspense thriller that never slows down until the final confrontation between good and evil. The action-packed story line moves at a fast clip."
—*Midwest Book Review*

continued . . .

WARRIOR

"A wonderful science fiction romantic suspense."
—*Genre Go Round Reviews*

"The character chemistry is gorgeous; the sex is searing hot; the world fascinating and a joy to explore. All in all, a great book!"
—*Errant Dreams Reviews*

JANE'S WARLORD

"What an awesome, scintillating, and sexy book! *Jane's Warlord* is intriguing, extremely sensuous, and just plain adventurous. A star is born."
—*Romantic Times* (Top Pick)

"Chills, thrills, and a superhero and heroine will have readers racing through this sexy tale. Take note, time-travel fans, the future belongs to Knight!"
—Emma Holly, *USA Today* bestselling author

"[Angela Knight's] world is believable and her plotting fast paced. Knight's fictional world seems to have a promising future."
—*Booklist*

"Solid writing . . . sexy love scenes and likable characters. I look forward to [Knight's] next book."
—*All About Romance*

"Amusing . . . Exciting . . . Anyone who enjoys strong women kicking butt . . . will enjoy this."
—*Midwest Book Review*

"A fantastic story of a love that never died."
—*A Romance Review*

"Exhilarating . . . Delightful."
—*The Best Reviews*

MASTER
of
SMOKE

ANGELA KNIGHT

BERKLEY SENSATION, NEW YORK

THE BERKLEY PUBLISHING GROUP
Published by the Penguin Group
Penguin Group (USA) Inc.
375 Hudson Street, New York, New York 10014, USA
Penguin Group (Canada), 90 Eglinton Avenue East, Suite 700, Toronto, Ontario M4P 2Y3, Canada
(a division of Pearson Penguin Canada Inc.)
Penguin Books Ltd., 80 Strand, London WC2R 0RL, England
Penguin Group Ireland, 25 St. Stephen's Green, Dublin 2, Ireland (a division of Penguin Books Ltd.)
Penguin Group (Australia), 250 Camberwell Road, Camberwell, Victoria 3124, Australia
(a division of Pearson Australia Group Pty. Ltd.)
Penguin Books India Pvt. Ltd., 11 Community Centre, Panchsheel Park, New Delhi—110 017, India
Penguin Group (NZ), 67 Apollo Drive, Rosedale, North Shore 0632, New Zealand
(a division of Pearson New Zealand Ltd.)
Penguin Books (South Africa) (Pty.) Ltd., 24 Sturdee Avenue, Rosebank, Johannesburg 2196,
South Africa

Penguin Books Ltd., Registered Offices: 80 Strand, London WC2R 0RL, England

This is a work of fiction. Names, characters, places, and incidents either are the product of the author's imagination or are used fictitiously, and any resemblance to actual persons, living or dead, business establishments, events, or locales is entirely coincidental. The publisher does not have any control over and does not assume any responsibility for author or third-party websites or their content.

MASTER OF SMOKE

A Berkley Sensation Book / published by arrangement with the author

PRINTING HISTORY
Berkley Sensation mass-market edition / January 2011

Copyright © 2011 by Angela Knight.
Excerpt from *Master of Shadows* by Angela Knight copyright © by Angela Knight.
Cover art by Phil Heffernan.
Cover design by George Long.

ISBN: 978-0-425-23916-2

BERKLEY® SENSATION
Berkley Sensation Books are published by The Berkley Publishing Group,
a division of Penguin Group (USA) Inc.,
375 Hudson Street, New York, New York 10014.
BERKLEY® SENSATION and the "B" design are trademarks of Penguin Group (USA) Inc.

PRINTED IN THE UNITED STATES OF AMERICA

10   9   8   7   6   5   4   3   2   1

ACKNOWLEDGMENTS

As always, it took a team to help me get this book whipped into shape, and I want to thank those people for all their hard work. My editor, Cindy Hwang, gave *Master of Smoke* her usual care and attention to all the things that make a romance work. My critique partners Diane Whiteside, Kate Douglas, Shelby Morgen, Camille Anthony, and Stephanie Burke were an invaluable help and source of ideas. I also want to thank beta readers Virginia Ettel, Linda Kusiolek, Wingednike, Marteeka Karland, and Ani Stubbs for making sure the book doesn't suck.

Berkley has a wonderful team of people who work very hard on our books. My thanks to Berkley's Cover Gods, also known as the art department. Then there's Cindy's assistant, Leis Pederson, who is always willing to help me with whatever questions I have.

And last but certainly not least, I want to thank my wonderful agent, Roberta Brown, who is a constant source of encouragement.

I would also like to dedicate this book to my new grandnephews, Charles, William, and Richard Patterson, and my grandniece, Naomi Looper. I envy my sister all her beautiful and brilliant grandbabies!

ONE

Boom!

The psychic rumble seemed to vibrate Eva Roman's skull. She jumped. "What the heck was that?"

Her father glanced over at her. "What? I didn't hear anything." Bill Roman was a bear of a man with a broad, handsome face and a gray-shot black beard that blended with the salt-and-pepper bristle of his hair.

The customer he was talking to shook his head and slid his hands into the pockets of his jeans. "I didn't hear anything either."

Eva hadn't either, but she still felt as though she were sitting next to the amps at a rock concert. Her chest vibrated as if from a deep bass note, and ripples of ice crawled along her spine.

What *was* that?

Something that isn't making you any money. Unpack the boxes, Eva. Dragging her attention back to the job at hand, she used a box cutter to slice open the cardboard box at her feet, pulled out a stack of books, and started counting. It was Wednesday, and the week's shipment had arrived, so she needed to check the contents.

Yep, fifty copies of *Amazing Spider-Man,* just like the shipping manifest said. She put a check on the list and propped the books up at their assigned spot on the New Releases display rack.

Ruuuumble. Despite her instinctive jolt, Eva tried to ignore the vibration as she started pulling copies of *X-Men* out of the box.

"It was completely out of character." Her father leaned an elbow on the counter, settling in for his favorite pastime: debating his beloved comics. "Deathrage would never torture anybody, not after what Psicopath did to her in issue 28. It's like Batman using a gun or Superman beating somebody to death."

"The writer's just trying to take the book in a darker direction." A tall, handsome blond, Joel Harmon had intense opinions and a love of comics almost as deep as her father's, which was why Bill loved to argue with him.

Eva had fallen in love with him for basically the same reasons. At least until she realized what she was doing to him. Or worse, going to do.

"Darker? Her name's Deathrage, for God's sake. How much darker can she get?"

Rummmmmmmble. Something about that sound gnawed at Eva, gave her the nagging feeling that something was deeply wrong. Something she had to do something about. Stop. Fix. Fight. Something.

And she had to do it *now.*

Dropping the stack of books back into the box, Eva looked over at her father. "Mind if I take off, Dad?"

He turned around and examined her face. Whatever he saw carved sudden lines of worry around his hazel eyes. "Hey, are you all right?"

Eva rolled her shoulders uneasily. "I just don't feel well." She had to find out what the hell was causing her Spidey sense to tingle.

She hadn't even known she *had* a Spidey sense.

"Go. I've got this." Bill took the box cutter out of her hand and went to work on the next box of books.

"Thanks." She gathered up her purse and headed for the

door, striding past massive wooden display racks stacked with comics. "See you tomorrow, Dad."

"Bye." He pulled out a stack of books. "I'm telling you, Deathrage wouldn't have laid a finger on that guy . . ."

The bell attached to the door jangled merrily as Eva stepped out of the Comix Cave. It was dark, the moon riding the stand of pines that bordered the strip mall's parking lot. In the distance, dogs barked in a hysterical chorus. Probably at the same thing that was making *her* crazy.

She could head into those trees, transform, and go investigate. Might be better to take the car, though. Especially if she needed a quick getaway from whatever was doing . . . whatever the hell it was doing. Eva dug her keys out of her purse and clicked the fob to unlock her dark blue Ford Focus.

Curiosity might have killed the cat, but she hoped it didn't do anything to werewolves.

Greendale, South Carolina, was a New South town, which meant it was one big suburb and a small city core that included one or two tall buildings with skyscraper pretensions. The Comix Cave lay on the western outskirts, among ranch houses, subdivisions, and so many trees you had to drive carefully to avoid hitting Bambi. It was mating season, and amorous deer and speeding cars made very bad mix.

But there was something out there that definitely wasn't a deer. Driving toward the psychic rumble, Eva tightened her grip on the steering wheel. *Should I be doing this? What if it's dangerous? I could be getting myself in real trouble.*

On the other hand, what if somebody else was in trouble? It certainly *felt* like trouble, and Eva could handle threats other people couldn't. If, that is, she could figure out a way to do it without scaring the crap out of the innocent bystanders. Most folks found the sight of a seven-foot werewolf seriously disconcerting.

That included rapists. There'd been the incident last year when Eva had heard a woman screaming near the shop late one night. When she'd gone to investigate, she'd found four drunken frat boys trying to rape a seventeen-year-old girl.

Eva was strong enough and fast enough to knock all four of them out before they even knew what hit them. Their victim, however, did see her; in fact, she'd screamed louder at the sight of werewolf Eva than she had during the attack. Eva had told her to shut the hell up and hand over her cell phone. She had, shaking.

She'd looked thoroughly astonished when Eva simply called 911, handed the phone back, and growled, "You never saw me, right?"

Not surprisingly, Eva did not make the papers, though the kid did tell the cops a very thin lie about a big guy with a baseball bat who'd rescued her from her attackers.

To Eva's satisfaction, all four little bastards had gone to jail—after a stint in the hospital.

Go, Team Fluffy.

Too bad somebody hadn't been able to do the same for Eva five years ago.

The rumble was coming from the left now. She turned into a neat little middle-class development and drove down the darkened street, following the sensation. The vibration had grown so powerful, she could feel it in her back teeth. Howling instincts insisted something evil was up ahead.

Not just bad. Mwwwwhahahah *evil.*

Looking through the trees bordering the yard just ahead, she saw something glowing blue. Eva pulled over and parked, staring through the windshield at the light. Could be a police car. Except police cars didn't go Mwwwwhahahah.

"You are such an idiot," Eva muttered, swinging the car door open. She was starting to feel like the dumb blond baby-sitter investigating the mysterious sound in the basement.

Don't be a wuss. If you run into a knife-wielding psycho, you can always eat him. There was a certain comfort in being able to kick a grizzly's ass.

Unfortunately, that sense of Mwwwwhahahah—whatever the hell it was—made her think it was something a hell of a lot worse than a grizzly bear. And that she'd do well to be a lot more careful than she'd been with those rapists.

Still, she had just as strong a sense that she had to investigate. So one way or another, she was going in.

Time to pop the claws? Eva started toward the glow, her running shoes padding quietly on the pavement. Deciding her chances of scaring an innocent bystander were a little too high, she veered into the trees for whatever cover they could provide instead. If she'd still been human, she probably wouldn't have been able to see where she was going.

Eva slipped through the woods until she found a good view between two trees. She promptly wished she hadn't.

There in the driveway of a brick split-level, a man in armor writhed five feet off the ground, suspended in a globe of shimmering energy. Blue bolts of force snaked in and out of his helpless body as the globe grew brighter. He grunted in pain as the energy licked at him.

Eva stared in sickened horror. *It's torturing him!* As if that wasn't bad enough, a huge, white-furred shape stood bathed in the blue glow. Another werewolf, one even bigger than Eva was when she got fuzzy. He'd plugged his fingers into the globe's shimmering surface, and streams of energy flowed into his claws, as though he was capturing them.

A vicious grin stretched his thin black lips, displaying a mouthful of very white, very sharp teeth. His eyes glowed feral and orange. He looked even bigger than the monster who'd attacked Eva five years ago, easily eight feet tall, as brawny as a polar bear. Like the bear, his fur was white, though flecked with crimson splatters. She realized it was the man's blood.

All of which made him a fifteen on the Furry Badass scale. Eva considered herself a seven on a good day.

I've got to do something. She flexed her hands nervously, cold anxiety drawing her muscles into quivering knots. As soon as the werewolf got tired of torturing his victim with . . . whatever the hell he was doing, he was going to start ripping the poor bastard apart. She couldn't just sit back and watch.

Claws digging into flesh, fangs slicing into her belly, jerking bloody mouthfuls, the spreading cold of death as her life drained away, the black horror of being eaten alive . . .

Eva swallowed hard, trying to keep from tossing the burger she'd had for dinner. Squaring her shoulders, she started to reach for the magic.

No, shrieked a mental voice, hitting a note that would have made a chalkboard cringe. *That thing will come after me . . .*

But if she did nothing, the armored man was dead. Spider-man's mantra flashed through her mind: "With great power comes great responsibility."

Like Dad always said: just because you read it in a comic book, that doesn't mean it isn't true.

Eva breathed deep again, shoving aside her howling terror and stuffing the memory of pain and blood back into its scarred psychic box. *Time to Change.*

But just as she reached for the magic, the armored man did . . . *something.* Mystical energy surged around him, swirling hotter, brighter inside the force globe, streaming into the clawed fingers the werewolf had dug into the magical field.

What the hell is he . . .

Before she could even finish the thought, the magic detonated. Eva yelped and threw up a hand to shield her eyes from the blinding blast. Another silent psychic rumble shook her skull. Every dog in the neighborhood howled. She damn near joined in.

When she could see again, the werewolf lay on his back, smoke rising from singed claws, muzzle—even his closed eyes. He'd been knocked cold. Both the energy globe and the man were gone.

Jesus, he blew himself up!

No, wait—there he was, running toward her. Actually, it was more a drunken stagger. The man's face looked white and blank, stunned, as if he was moving on blind instinct. And he was naked.

Really, really naked.

His powerful broad-shouldered body gleamed in the moonlight, sweat slicking his skin as he raced across the neatly trimmed suburban lawn for the shelter of the trees.

Eva blinked. What had happened to his armor?

Not that it mattered. He was hurt. She had to help him.

Even as she ran to intercept the victim, she shot a wary glance at his hairy attacker. He hadn't moved, apparently still unconscious on his back on the cement driveway, curls of smoke wafting from his body into the spring night.

Why the hell hadn't the neighbors called the cops? Nobody had even stepped outside to investigate. Had the monster cast some kind of spell to keep them from noticing what was going on?

Though the idea of a magic-using werewolf was just *wrong.* Wasn't it enough being eight feet of fangs and bad attitude? Did he have to be the love child of Darth Vader and a yeti?

Really, White Fang? Really?

Meanwhile, White Fang's former victim wasn't letting any grass grow under his bare feet. He ran into the woods as if he could see in the dark, long, black hair flying, every step shouting of a grim determination to put as much distance as possible between himself and his attacker.

Then he stumbled over a root, slammed a shoulder into a tree trunk, and fell on his face.

Shit. Eva slid to her knees beside him. "Hey, are you okay?" She took him by one brawny shoulder and rolled him over. He was heavy, massive with bone and muscle. Back in her human days, she probably wouldn't have been able to budge him at all. He stared up at her, dazed and shocked. She tried again, enunciating, "Are you hurt?"

His pupils snapped into thin slits against crystalline blue irises, and his lips peeled back from fangs. One hand flashed out to clamp around her wrist in a grip like forged steel.

And he snarled right into her face.

Startled, she tried to jerk back. With her strength, she should have pulled free easily, yet his grip didn't break. "Hey! Let go! I'm trying to help, dammit!"

He stared at her, something profoundly alien in his blue eyes. Abruptly the hostility faded, replaced by a hot male interest. She tugged again, but he dragged her down and breathed in deeply, as if drinking in her scent.

Just as she drank his. Damn, he smelled good. Pure male musk, tempting despite the sweat, rage, and fear lingering in his scent.

Eva frowned. There was blood, too, smelling of copper and pain as it rolled from the cuts and scratches marring muscled ribs and brawny arms.

"It's you." His voice was incredibly deep, as dark and soft as black velvet. "At last."

"Me?" She swallowed. "What are you talking about?"

"We have waited for you for so very long," he rumbled, his gaze searching her face with a passionate intensity she'd never seen in a man's eyes. "We've hungered for your love—for your simple company. And now here you are. At last."

As she stared at him in helpless fascination, his nostrils flared and his pupils expanded. With a tug of her wrist, he pulled her right down into a kiss, possessive and deliciously sexy.

For a minute, she was stunned still. Then arousal hit her in a wave, so incredibly hot, it was all she could do not to skim down her jeans and mount him on the spot.

Oh, hell, it's that time of the year, Eva thought, and kissed him back.

Most of the time, she felt relatively normal. Being a werewolf didn't give her any desire to kill, and she controlled when and where she fuzzed out; the moon had nothing to do with it. But for one month a year, generally around springtime, Eva's hormones went nuts. It was like PMS with a nymphomania chaser. She got incredibly bitchy and incredibly horny, all at the same time. Even the skinny geek customers at the shop started looking pretty good, except, given the bitchy thing, they pissed her off.

In the back of her mind, she'd known she was getting close to That Time for a couple of weeks. Now Tall, Dark, and Naked seemed to have triggered a full-blown attack of raging hormones. Eva dragged her mouth away from his to gasp as a wave of heat rippled over her body from hairline to heels. Desperately, she fought to think. *I can't do this. I don't even know this guy.*

Having lost access to her mouth, TDN started working on her neck, right under her ear, licking and kissing and—*oh, God*—biting her pulse with delicious little nips. One hand found her breast, cupping her in long-fingered heat through her Comix Cave T-shirt and Victoria's Secret bra, thumb flicking back and forth over a hard nipple. Squeeze. Flick.

Oh, holy God.

Somebody was making a tiny moaning sound. With a jolt, Eva realized it was her.

Somebody else was making a low rumbling sound. That was him.

It wasn't a growl, but it was loud, coming from deep in his broad chest, a rhythmic in-and-out rumble in time to his breathing. She'd never heard a human make that particular sound before, but something else had . . . Wait, the cat she'd had as a teenager.

TDN was *purring.*

People didn't purr. Books said they did, but humans weren't capable of making that sound . . . and *who cared*? He had amazing hands. The other one was exploring the curve of her butt through her jeans, squeezing and stroking.

There was some very good reason she shouldn't make love to him right now. Damned if she could remember what it was, though. *Oh, yeah—White Fang. We really need to . . .*

TDN tangled a fist in her hair and dragged her head back down so he could kiss her some more, his mouth surprisingly gentle despite its searing heat.

With a heroic effort of will, Eva jerked back far enough to talk. "We can't," she gasped in desperation against TDN's hot, soft lips. "We've got to get out of here. When that werewolf comes to, he's gonna eat us. That happened to me once, and believe me, it's not fun."

The purr cut off, and TDN stiffened against her. "You are right. We must leave."

"I've got a car." She dragged herself off him despite the protests of her lust-crazed body. "Right over here."

"Good." He rose easily to his feet as she scrambled to hers. "We will go to your home, away from my enemy."

"Yeah, I've got an apartment a few miles away. We'll be safe there."

He nodded, flicking a long lock of silken black hair over his shoulder. "Yes. Then we can have sex."

Eva stopped and stared at him. He was easily six-four or -five and built like an NFL quarterback, all broad shoulders and long legs, power and speed in one yummy package. He had hair like the hero of an eighties' Native American romance, long and straight, reaching halfway to his waist. The bone structure of his face was stark and sharply chiseled, with a broad, square jaw, a generous Roman nose, and a sensual mouth that definitely knew its way around female real estate.

Actually, sex with him sounded pretty good.

The heat abruptly drained from his eyes, replaced by confusion. "Who are you?" He looked a little lost. "I know I want you, but I don't know who you are."

Oh, now that was flattering. "I'm Eva Roman. And a werewolf wants to eat us, so we really need to go."

"Yes." He squared those amazing shoulders. "That I remember."

"Good. My car is that way. You go. I'll follow along when my ego stops twitching."

"What? I don't . . ." He blinked at her, still white around the mouth.

She sighed. "Come on."

They called her La Belle Coeur. It wasn't her real name, but after so many centuries, that scarcely mattered. She was Belle even in her own thoughts now.

Davon's cock felt like a length of stone, thrust to the balls inside her as he rolled his hips, grinding deep. She braced her palms on the hard rise of his muscular chest as she rode him at a fast, hard jog. Belle always made a point of being on top the final time. It was safer if things went wrong.

His velvety skin looked as dark as expensive chocolate under her pale hands, striking and beautiful. Davon was a handsome man, with his high, stark cheekbones, full mouth, and broad, regal nose. At thirty-three, he was no boy, yet he seemed very young to her. They were all young to her, unscarred and innocent in a way she hadn't been a long time.

A stinging pulse of power suddenly rolled from the soles of her feet to the top of her head, and Belle shuddered. Her magic was gathering, preparing to trigger Merlin's Gift, buried deep in Davon's DNA.

Triggering the Gift was a court seducer's job, and Belle hated it. Unfortunately, she was also a very good court seducer, and her sense of duty was too acute to permit her to quit. Still, it hurt, and the effort reminded her far too much of giving birth. Which in a way, she was.

Like giving birth, it was dangerous for them both. If she'd misjudged Davon, if the Majae's Council had erred in sending her to him, he could kill her.

If he got very, very lucky. More likely she'd kill him, as she'd killed sixteen of her Latent lovers over the past thousand years. She loathed killing, and every one of those boys haunted her, but none of them had given her a choice. The Gift brought insanity to those not strong enough to handle it. Usually she could spot the ones who were too weak to make the transition, but everyone made mistakes.

Belle didn't think she was making one now, though. Davon was as intelligent and determined as he was handsome. Which was no surprise: wimps didn't become surgical residents specializing in trauma at Chicago's Mercy Hospital.

Merlin's Cup, she hoped she hadn't called it wrong. Killing Dr. Davon Fredericks would be a tragic waste. He didn't deserve madness and death because she'd screwed up.

Another pulse rolled over her, hot and burning. She ignored it, concentrating on the handsome face lost in delight as she ground down on him. Yet even as he rode the breath-taking build of his climax, he worked to pleasure her, one hand flicking a hard nipple, the other thumbing her clit, each tiny motion sending another sweet jolt through her body.

As her power built, the magic started coming in rolling waves like the contractions of labor. She caught her breath, recognizing how close she was from all the times she'd brought men to the Gift. And then . . .

The spell exploded out of her to lance into Davon like a solar flare. Merlin's Gift ignited in his DNA, and he turned into a glowing thing of pure, blinding magic, his cock pulsing inside her as she came, screaming out her release, screaming out the magic.

Too late to stop now, we're committed, please God, let him keep his sanity . . .

Belle rode out the spell like a woman in a hurricane, clinging to Davon's blazing body with all her strength. Until the glow faded some endless instant later, leaving her half-blind and deaf, feeling seared to the bone. She collapsed across his sweat-slicked body, sides heaving like those of a horse run too hard. His heartbeat galloped in his chest, a wild thudding, and she listened to it, praying she wouldn't have to kill him. He groaned.

Then Davon put his arms around her. It wasn't a grab for prey, but a tender lover's hold, light with affection and gratitude, perhaps even a little love. Belle closed her eyes in relief.

But there was one more test they had to get through. And it was the trickiest part, the one that determined if he'd really made it—or if insanity rose out of some dark cave in his soul and turned him into a monster.

They really should start, but instead Belle lay listening to his heartbeat slow as his abused body adjusted to its magical transformation.

Until she could put it off no longer.

Lifting her head, Belle met his eyes and forced a smile. "Hey, you."

"Hey." Davon smiled, dazed and happy and clueless.

She'd warned him about the risk of blood-madness, but she was fairly sure he had no idea how much danger he was in. "God, that was . . ." He blinked big brown eyes. "Surprisingly painful, actually. I've never been hit by lightning, but it'd probably feel a lot like that."

"Yep, that's the Gift." *He sounds good. So far.* "Are you hungry?"

"Yeah, now that you mention it." Another blink. Dazed delight slipped into discomfort as he processed the implications. "You mean . . . ?"

"Your body needs blood to complete the transformation." Rather a lot of it, more than the cupful vampires usually took. Which was what made this so damned tricky.

"Now?" He looked queasy and apprehensive, though nowhere near as scared as he should be.

They never were.

"Now. I'll show you what to do." Belle slipped off his limp cock and eased up his torso to reach his mouth. Unable to resist his worried expression, she gave him a quick kiss. "You'll be fine." *I hope.* She tapped a forefinger at the point right under her jaw where her pulse thumped. "Bite here. It's better if you do it fast. And for God's sake, don't gnaw."

"One clean stroke, like with a scalpel." He frowned. "But won't it hurt you?"

"Don't worry about that. You'll learn how to give pleasure during the bite later." She leaned down, carefully bracing her left hand on his upper arm, the other on the center of his chest. She eased up her right knee until it was next to his left arm, ready to clamp down and pin his hand if she had to.

Angling her throat right over his fanged mouth, she waited, doing a little praying while she was at it.

Davon hesitated a long moment, as if working up the courage. Then he bit, quick and stinging.

Both of them froze, nether so much as breathing. Until he finally began to drink. First one swallow, then another, then another. He moaned in startled pleasure at the taste.

Belle swallowed at the lush sensation of his mouth working at her flesh, delight seeping through her dread.

She lifted the right hand she'd braced on his chest, angled it. And conjured a knife, its blade thin and sharp, its point bare inches from the underside of his jaw. Ready to drive into his brain if he lost it and began to rip.

She'd have only the blink of an eye to decide if he'd gone blood-mad. If she stabbed too late, she'd be dead before her knife broke the skin. If she stabbed too early, she might murder a sane man who could have been a warrior Avalon needed.

Merlin's Cup, I am so sick of this. The thought flashed through her mind, cold and heavy as lead.

Davon opened his mouth and tugged his fangs free of her throat with exquisite care, so as not to tear her skin any further. "I think I've had enough." He was breathing hard, but as she lifted her head, his dark gaze met hers, sane and intelligent.

The knife vanished from her hand as she gave him a grin of pure, dizzying relief. "That's good. That's very good."

But as he wrapped his arms around her in a hug, the thought came again: *I am so very sick of this.*

TWO

There was something extremely disconcerting about driving with a naked man in the passenger seat. Even the coat didn't help.

Eva had found a jacket in the backseat and given it to Tall, Dark, and Naked. He'd looked at it askance. "I do not think it will fit."

Since it was her jacket, it sure as heck wouldn't. "It's to put in your lap while we drive."

He'd shot her a look of pure puzzlement. "But why?"

"To cover up your . . . umm." She gestured below his waist.

His lips quirked. "But why?"

Jackass. "To keep the other drivers from running off the road." *To keep* me *from running off the road*.

So he got in the car and draped the jacket over his lap as if humoring a crazy person.

Unfortunately, it wasn't helping. Her memory was way too good, and TDN's naughty bits weren't really bits. More like hunks. Of hunk.

Really, really naked hunk. Eva fought to keep her eyes from sliding sideways while she tried to drive. Meanwhile,

TDN filled the passenger seat with lots and lots of delicious bare muscle.

She couldn't keep calling him TDN. For one thing, she intended to get him dressed as soon as possible, if she had to wrap him in a sheet like a refugee from *Animal House*. "What's your name? I'm Eva Roman."

There was a pause that went on entirely too long. Either he was thinking up a lie and wasn't bright enough to do it fast, or he didn't know. And she didn't think he was dumb.

Eva flashed him a look and had to drag her eyes back to the road. Her inner werewolf was drooling again. "That question is not supposed to require so much thought."

"I . . . do not seem to know."

Oh, hell. She really hated amnesia plots in comics. Living one would be even worse. "What *do* you remember?"

"You."

Something about the velvet purr in those words made her nipples tingle. Eva turned to stare at him again, then had to whip around when the car swerved, and drag it back onto the road. She was going to get pulled over for DUI if this kept up. "What else?"

"My enemy." TDN paused. "He has a great many teeth."

"No shit."

TDN looked at her, puzzled.

"That means . . . never mind. Do you know why he was after you, other than he thought you'd make tasty kibble?"

The puzzlement intensified.

"That means . . . Oh, forget it. Why. Is. He. After. You?"

"You do not have to enunciate like that. I am not stupid," TDN said with vast dignity.

"I know that!" The other bad part about That Time of the Year was that her temper went straight to hell.

"I do not remember why he wishes to kill me." He paused. "That is bad."

She opened her mouth to say "No shit," then closed it again. "What would you like me to call you?"

He looked at her, and his lips curved. "Whatever you want." That was definitely a purr, deep and rumbly and . . .

"Cut it out!" Hearing the snarl in her own voice, she winced. "Sorry. This time of year, I get a little bitchy."

"Why?" He looked honesty interested.

"I don't know." Eva took a deep breath. She had to tell him. He needed to know, and anyway, he was pretty damned weird himself. "It has something to do with me being a werewolf."

TDN turned to look at her. He didn't seem in the least frightened. More interested, like she'd said she was a fire-fighter or a doctor or a comic book artist. "Like my enemy?"

"Yeah, only I'm not going to eat you."

"Too bad."

"Please don't." He blinked, and Eva drew in a breath, wrestling her inner werewolf for control. Fluffy just loved to take over. "Look, like I said, this time of year is difficult for me. I get very . . ." Horny. ". . . Short-tempered."

"Why?"

"You're like a two-year-old, you know that? You keep asking questions I don't know the answer to."

His lips twitched. "I can see how that would be annoying. But how do I know which questions you cannot answer?"

"Take a wild guess." He was making Fluffy crazy, and Fluffy was making Eva incredibly bitchy. Okay, bitchier. "I'm sorry."

"I accept your apology." He let several seconds slip by before adding slyly, "Would you like to make it up to me?"

"Would you like to share this car with seven feet of pissed-off werewolf?"

Honest to God, he seemed to consider the question. "I do not think so."

"Trust me, it wouldn't be any fun. Fluffy has the anger management issues of the Hulk."

"Who is . . . ?"

"Never mind, comic book reference."

He looked confused. Even that looked good on him. "Fluffy?"

"Oh. No, that's not from a comic book. That's what I call my werewolf."

TDN blinked. "You have a different name for your werewolf?"

"Well . . . yeah."

"*Fluffy?*"

"It kind of fits."

"I sincerely doubt that, if you look anything like my enemy."

"Well, she's definitely not as big as *that* guy."

"Why do you talk about your werewolf form as though it's someone else?"

"Because she is. Kind of." Eva sighed. "It's a little hard to explain."

"Apparently."

"Let's just . . . drop that subject. What do you want me to call you?"

He looked as if he was considering saying something outrageous.

"Give me a serious answer, dammit." She really needed to dial back the bitch. "Please."

"I have no idea. What would you like to call me?"

Clark? Bruce? Peter? And what did it say about her that all the names that sprang to mind belonged to comic book characters? *I am such a geekizoid.*

Maybe David. She couldn't think of a comic book character named David. And he did look like something sculpted by Michelangelo—big, hard, and very, very naked. "How about David?"

He gave it some thought and a regal nod. "That will do."

"Glad you approve."

The Drayton Apartments were a cluster of six beige three-story buildings surrounded by azalea bushes and Bradford pear trees, all of which were currently in gorgeous bloom. Its residents included college students, new families saving for a first house, and one or two assholes.

And a werewolf.

Eva parked in her assigned spot in front of Building Five. "Wait here. I'm going to go get you something to wear up the stairs." Before he could ask—and she knew he would—she explained, "Kids live here, too. I don't want one of them to look out a window and see you walking around nekkid."

David frowned, but before he could question her further, she opened the car door and bolted up the wooden stairs.

Eva lived in a two-bedroom on the second floor. Fortunately, her ex-boyfriend Joel had left behind a pair of ratty jeans and ancient running shoes he'd never returned to collect. He was a couple of inches shorter than David, but with any luck, the pants would fit. Probably not well, but they just needed something to cover that gorgeous ass until they could buy something better.

Though Fluffy liked his gorgeous ass just the way it was—buck naked so she could eye it lovingly. And drool a little. She'd especially been looking forward to watching him walk up the stairs. Preferably in slow motion with George Michael crooning "I Want Your Sex" in the background.

Fluffy had never grasped the concept of shame.

Eva found the jeans and shoes in the back of a closet and rounded out the set with an oversized Comix Cave T-shirt she often slept in.

She trotted downstairs with her prizes and handed them through the passenger window. David shot her a lifted eyebrow and started trying to squeeze his big body into the clothes. Eva turned her back and directed her gaze elsewhere.

Fluffy gave her a disappointed mental grumble.

Finally the car door opened. Eva turned as David got out to stand oddly hunched. "They do not fit," he gritted.

Frowning, she looked down the length of his body. As she'd expected, the hem of the jeans fell well short of his ankles, but Joel was a fairly muscular guy. The jeans were certainly very tight, but . . .

Oh.

David glowered at her as he tugged at the crotch of his pants. The fabric clearly outlined three large, interesting shapes that looked more than a little squashed. "They are digging into my genitals."

She bit her lower lip to keep from snickering at his disgruntled expression. "I'm sorry. We'll head to Wal-Mart in the morning and buy something that fits better. But you can't go around naked. You'd scandalize the neighbors and get arrested."

He growled, sounding more like a very large, wet cat than anything human. Turning, he limped up the stairs. Apparently Joel's shoes didn't fit him all that well either.

Eva clattered after him. She tried, she really did, but she just couldn't keep herself from watching his ass in those skin-tight jeans. It was a view to make a nun hyperventilate.

Fluffy started humming "I Want Your Sex."

The only thing David knew was that he wanted her. Otherwise his mind felt as blasted as a bombed-out building—nothing but dust and mental rubble. When he contemplated the aching gaps in his memory, panic rose. He didn't care for panic.

Much better to contemplate Eva's lush little body. As they reached the top of the stairs, she slipped past him to unlock a door with a musical jangle of keys. He followed her into her home, admiring the roll of her tight little derriere.

Tearing his gaze from her backside, David scanned the apartment, searching for exits and vulnerabilities. A glass door lay off to the right, across the small living room. He glowered at it in disapproval. His enemy would go through that like a bear ripping into a shrink-wrapped steak. Along one wall near the worrisome door sat a bright red couch crowded with fat yellow pillows. A bowl-shaped chair occupied the opposite corner, a red pillow in its bright yellow seat. A large black rectangle he somehow recognized as a flat-screen television hung from the facing wall.

The remaining walls were covered with posters of people in heroic poses. Their clothing was very colorful, and so tight it showed every muscle. He frowned, staring at one. It appeared the man had no genitals at all, judging from the lack of bulges below the waist.

Odd. Why would she have pictures of people who had suffered such a terrible injury?

Statues of similar figures stood here and there on the coffee table and inside a tall, narrow display case. Both those pieces of furniture were made of oak, with clean, simple lines.

He breathed deeply as he inspected. To his pleasure, the only male scent belonged to a young child who seemed to visit quite frequently.

"Are you hungry?" Eva asked, walking into the kitchen area that was separated from the living room by a long island. His stomach growled, and she grinned. "I'll take that as a yes."

"Combat sharpens my appetite." And not just for food, though he decided not to mention that. She didn't seem to like double entendres. He followed her around the oak island into the small efficiency kitchen, drinking in her scent as he went. His eyes shuttered in pleasure.

Sex. Distilled femininity, pure temptation. He really had to get her into bed.

"Do you like lasagna?" She opened the freezer door and withdrew two packages wrapped in aluminum foil.

"I have no idea, but I would be happy to eat it."

Eva laughed as she unwrapped the packages and put them in the microwave. "Enthusiasm. What more can a cook ask?"

David studied her profile as she moved over to open a drawer beside the stove. Her face was delicate, but there was strength in the line of her nose and the stubborn angle of her jaw. Her eyes were large, a velvety brown so deep as to be almost black. Her hair was the color of dark chocolate, falling around her shoulders like a straight, gleaming curtain that framed her face in shorter wisps.

The microwave pinged, and she took out the two containers. Picking up a spoon, she scooped their contents onto a couple of plates. He watched intently as she brushed past. She moved well, with a lithe athlete's grace.

And she smelled delightful—citrus and femininity, with

the faintest hint of fur. And under it all, the rich, fizzing scent of magic.

David realized he was purring and made a conscious effort to stop as he prowled after her to the kitchen table. Settling into a straight chair with red cushions, he watched her return to the refrigerator and pour drinks for them both.

Absently, he picked up the fork she'd placed beside his plate and dug in as he watched her carry their drinks back to the table. The "lasagna" was delicious, tasting of tomatoes, spicy beef, and at least three different kinds of cheese. "This is very good."

"Thanks," she said with a pleased smile as she put the glasses down. "I love to cook. Taking a bunch of ingredients and combining them to make something special—it's a lot of fun."

He listened to her talk about cooking as he ate, watching her full lips shape words like kisses. Until he could stand it no longer. Grabbing the arm of her chair, David pulled her closer. Her eyes widened in surprise as he leaned forward and took that tempting mouth in a long, erotic plunge into heat. The moment he tasted her, he wanted more. She moaned softly against his lips. He reached across, scooped her up, and pulled her into his lap. She wrenched her mouth away. "Wait—we can't . . ."

"We can," he growled back, and swooped in for another kiss. To his satisfaction, she hesitated only a moment before she threaded her arms around his neck and started kissing him back.

Which was when someone began pounding on the front door in desperate slaps. "Eva! Miss Roman! Help!"

It was unmistakably the voice of a child.

Warlock jolted awake with power singing arias in his veins and the Demigod's memories howling in his brain. The storm of power and alien recall sent him staggering to his feet.

Thousands of years. The cat had lived thousands and thousands of years.

All that experience and power seared Warlock's consciousness like a blowtorch. He could feel his mind cracking under the strain, and panic rose. *It's going to destroy me!*

He realized he had only seconds before his mind shattered. Reaching for his magic—it answered with a pounding fire-hose force—Warlock wove a spell to contain those alien memories. The spell took hold with blessed speed, sealing away the banshee shriek of the Demigod's life. He'd be able to access it, but only if he chose to.

He slumped in relief, knowing he'd come within seconds of destruction.

And then a new thought sent his fear shooting into an even higher spike: *Where is Smoke?*

Warlock stared around wildly, looking for his enemy. The last he'd seen of the cat, Smoke had been sealed in the force globe Warlock had created to drain his powers.

Yet somehow, the godling had outsmarted him. Instead of fighting the drain, Smoke had rammed the full force of his memory and power right down Warlock's throat, damn near frying him in the process.

And now the cat was nowhere to be seen.

Well, Warlock would just have to find him. Smoke had no power now, nor any of that incredible wealth of experience. It should be a simple thing to find and kill him.

Warlock shifted to four-legged form, the better to track his prey. He picked up Smoke's scent at once and began following it across the lawn to the edge of the trees that bounded the yard.

Where it blended with the scent of *another Dire Wolf.*

Who *dared*? He snapped his jaws in rage, wanting to rend the werewolf into rags of torn flesh. Instead he wrestled his fury back under control, reminding himself that his existence was a secret from all but a handful of trustworthy Chosen aristocrats. No doubt this idiot thought he was protecting some poor human from a rogue werewolf.

No, not he. She. He could tell as much from her scent. His lips drew back from his teeth. The little bitch would pay dearly for her error.

Nose to the ground, he followed the scent through the

trees to the yard beyond. The trail stopped on the edge
of the road. Throwing back his head, Warlock howled in
frustrated rage. The idiot wolf had put Smoke in a car and
driven away!

Perhaps he could track them with his strengthened
powers . . . He cast a spell with a flick of his mind and sent
it questing after the Demigod.

Nothing.

He snarled. The Direkind were resistant to all magic,
even his. Spells slid off them like water beading on an oiled
griddle. Only he and his descendants did not have that ability; otherwise they would not be able to work spells. If this
she-wolf was too close to Smoke, the aura of her power
would block Warlock's magic.

No matter. The moment she left Smoke alone, Warlock
would be able to pick up his magical scent.

And then Smoke was a dead Demigod.

Eva jerked the apartment door open to reveal a small boy
standing on the other side. He was shirtless and barefoot,
dressed only in a pair of flannel pants covered in tiny
white ducks. Flinging himself against her thighs, he wailed
out something, crying so hard she couldn't understand a
word.

Eva dropped to her knees and wrapped her arms around
him, stroking the disordered white-blond silk of his hair.
"Terry! Calm down and tell me what's wrong, honey."

"Mommy!" A bruise covered one entire side of his
small face. His bastard father had hit him again. Eva was
seriously considering catching Ronnie Gordon in the parking lot some moonless night and showing him what it felt
like to get beaten up. "Mommy's sick! Daddy hit her in the
head, and now she's on the floor, and she's not movin'!"

Oh, yeah. Ronnie definitely needed quality time with
a certain werewolf. As Fluffy put it, "With great power
comes a great responsibility for asshole education." Swallowing her rage, Eva forced a smile for the little boy. "It's
all right, Terry. We'll take care of your mother."

She started to rise. Terry's big blue eyes fell on David, and he cringed against her legs. "Who's that?"

"He's just a friend, baby." Eva stroked Terry's head and looked at her houseguest. "This is likely to get very messy. You should probably stay here."

"I'm coming with you." David peeled his lips back from his teeth. "I will take care of this 'man,'"—she could hear the sarcastic quotes—". . . while you deal with the boy's mother."

"Eva!" Terry tugged at her sleeve to regain her attention. "Please! Mommy needs you!"

"All right." She lifted the boy into her arms, then looked over her shoulder at David. "Just try not to start a fight in front of Terry."

David said nothing and followed, his hands balling into fists despite her instructions. A man who harmed his own mate deserved a beating—at the very least.

Terry's apartment was two doors down, a mirror image of Eva's, except for the furnishings. Unlike her bright color scheme, everything in this one was some shade of brown—dark brown couch, brown leather easy chair, beige carpet. Instead of posters, the walls were decorated with photos, most of them of Terry at various ages.

Shelly Gordon was sprawled in the floor by the kitchen table, surrounded by spilled food and the shards of a broken plate.

"I gather Ronnie didn't like the menu again," Eva growled, her full mouth drawing into a thin, pale line of rage.

David knelt and started to scoop the woman into his arms.

"Don't lift her," Eva said sharply as she dropped to her knees. "She may have internal injuries. Shelly? Shelly, honey, wake up. Terry needs you."

At those words, one swollen hazel eye opened a crack. "Ronnie?" She sounded dazed. No wonder, considering the beating she'd taken.

"It's Eva. And my friend, David. We're going to call an ambulance . . ."

Shelly's battered eye tried to widen in alarm. She was a pretty woman, but you'd never know it now with all the bruises distorting her delicate features. "No!" she rasped, her voice barely louder than a whisper. "Ronnie won't like it."

"I don't care. You're hurt, and you need help." Eva brushed the bright blond hair back from the woman's forehead to reveal a huge knot. "Looks like you've got a head injury. And you were unconscious, so you definitely need to be seen."

"Who the hell's here?" a male voice slurred from somewhere down the hall.

David rose to his feet as the voice's owner staggered around the corner. He was a massive man, his bearded face flushed red from drink. Enormous hands flexed and fisted as his gaze came to rest on David. His head lowered like a bull about to charge. "What the fuck are *you* doin' here?"

David gave him a smile that wasn't in the least pleasant. "Taking care of the wife and child you abused."

Ronnie's booze-reddened face flushed even brighter, and his small eyes narrowed to slits. "Get the hell out of my house!"

"Not until we're sure you haven't killed your wife."

He sneered and lurched closer. "What, are you trying to get into her pants?"

It would be profoundly satisfying to beat the bastard as badly as he'd beaten his woman. Unfortunately, the cretin was so drunk, he'd be no proper contest. David stepped forward, knocked aside Ronnie's clumsy punch with his left arm, and plowed his right fist into the man's nose. There was a highly satisfying spray of blood, and Ronnie toppled like a felled tree.

"Daddy!" the boy cried, running to his father's side. He shot David a glittering, betrayed look. "You hurt my daddy!"

David stared at him, nonplussed. The bastard evidently made a habit of brutalizing both the child and his mother, yet Terry was furious at David for one soundly deserved punch.

"He's brainwashed them," Eva explained tightly as she

pulled her cell phone out of a jeans pocket. "They think they deserve anything he does, while he can do no wrong. Nine-one-one? I need an ambulance at Apartment E-7 at the Drayton Apartments. A woman's seriously hurt. Her husband beat her pretty badly."

As she talked to the dispatcher, David watched the boy pat his father's face anxiously until the man began to stir.

"Get the hell away from me!" Ronnie pushed his son roughly aside. Shooting a glare at David, he scrambled to his feet and reeled back down the hall.

David curled his lip at the man's back and moved to crouch beside the women again.

". . . time to go to the women's shelter before he hurts you and Terry any worse than he has," Eva was saying.

"But he's not always like this." Shelly licked blood from her swollen lips. "He just had a really bad day, and then I overcooked the steaks, and they were so tough . . ."

David stared at her. "He beat you because the meat was tough?"

"Well, they were really expensive steaks. And his boss had raked him over the coals today . . ."

"I notice he didn't beat up his boss." Eva sighed and gently touched the woman's bruised shoulder. "Look, you've got to face facts, Shelly. Ronnie *could* control his temper—after all, he never attacks anybody at work. He takes it out on you because he's a bastard, and he can."

Shelly winced, but she didn't deny it.

David heard a heavy step in the hallway, and his jaw clenched in rage. Ronnie, coming back for another round. David rose to his feet and stalked into the hall.

To find the man holding a .22 pistol pointed right at him.

Ronnie gave him a sneering yellow smile. "*You're in my house*—and this is South Carolina. Which makes you bought and paid for, motherfucker. I can blow your ass away."

David backed up a pace, watching Ronnie's hands as the man stalked him, gun pointed right at the center of his chest. One more step, and Ronnie would be in range for a spinning kick . . .

Then there was a growl and a blur of motion. Eva's hand clamped down over Ronnie's gun and wrenched it upward. Before the man even knew what was happening, she'd jerked the weapon out of his hand as though he were an errant toddler. Even in human form, she must have enormous strength.

Ronnie swung at her, but she evaded the clumsy blow with a twist of her torso that made the bastard's fist shoot right past her head. Before Ronnie could try again, David grabbed him by one arm, half-lifted him off his feet, and hauled him toward the door.

Reading his intention, Eva dodged around them and opened the door, then slammed it behind them as David shoved the man hard against the outer wall. The big man's feet swung several inches from the floor as David pinned him with a hand wrapped around his sweating throat.

"Let me go!" Ronnie howled, his eyes rimmed with white. The flood of astonished terror at David's strength had evidently sobered him. "Get off me, you son of a bitch!"

"No!" David snarled, shoving his face an inch from the drunk's. "You will listen now. A man cares for his woman. A man cares for his child. He does not hurt them. One who does is no man at all."

"Fuck you!"

"Shut. Your. Mouth!"

"Your eyes!" Ronnie froze, staring at him in horror. "You ain't human!"

"No." Opening his mouth, David felt his incisors lengthen into fangs. "Now you will listen." He drew back and slammed Ronnie against the wall again to make sure he was paying attention. "Are you listening?"

"Yeah! Fuck, yeah!" Beginning to purple, Ronnie clawed frantically at David's arm.

"Your woman is going to leave you." Slowly, David began to squeeze until the drunk gagged. "Which is no more than you deserve. And you will do *nothing*. If I see one bruise, one scrape, hear one cry . . ." The human was definitely purple now, and his eyes rolled in terror.

". . . You are dead. I will take my time killing you, and then I will see to it that you are never found. Do you understand?"

He released his grip, letting the human fall. Ronnie staggered, gasping until he managed to wheeze, "Yeah! Yeah, I won't touch her again. I swear!"

Coward, David thought in satisfaction. *There will be no more trouble from this one.*

In the distance, sirens wailed, drawing closer. "Now. You will confess to the police exactly what you did to your wife and child." David displayed his fangs again. Ronnie stared at him with hypnotized terror. "Make sure they lock you away—away from *me*."

"Yeah." Ronnie blinked at him and sidled away. "I'll tell 'em everything."

THREE

Satisfied that the human was suitably cowed, David caught his arm and hauled him back into the apartment. Eva looked up when he entered, as she knelt next to Shelly. Terry crouched beside his mother in a small, miserable knot.

David dragged Ronnie over to them by one arm. "Apologize to your wife, and tell her that she will come to no more harm at your hands."

The man licked his lips. "I'm . . . uh, sorry, Shelly. I shouldn't have hit you."

"And?" David prompted, his tone cold and warning.

Ronnie's eyes rolled toward him, and he blanched. "And if—when!—when you go . . . I ain't gonna hurt you."

Shelly blinked at him in dizzy surprise. "Uh. Okay."

Grimly satisfied, David hustled Ronnie to the bedroom, shoved him inside, and slammed the door.

As he returned to the kitchen, he heard Shelly tell Eva, "I guess you're right. We'll go to the shelter." She sounded tired and depressed. "I can't let him go on hurting Terry."

David smiled at her carefully, trying not to show his

fangs. He did not want to frighten the human or her child. "That is wise."

Belle cast the shimmering magical gate in the center of Davon's living room. The doctor stared at the swirling portal with eyes gone wide and dark. "And this thing leads to another dimension?"

"Right," she said patiently, beginning the spiel she'd repeated until she could recite it in her sleep. "It leads to the Mageverse. That's an alternate dimension where magic is one of the universal forces. We all draw our power from it. Now that you're Magekind, you'll need to live there at least part of the time in order to survive."

"So I'm supposed to just walk through this . . . door?" He eyed the gate dubiously.

"Yep. Want me to go first?"

He shot her a cool look, his manhood evidently offended. "That's not necessary." Davon squared his broad shoulders and stepped through the gate.

Smiling faintly, Belle followed to find him standing on the other side, staring around in awe. All around them, the city of Avalon lay sprawled under the star-flecked night sky. Castles, mansions, and châteaus glowed with magic, their high stone towers reaching for the quarter moon. Magekind witches and vampires wandered the cobblestone streets, some in twenty-first-century jeans and shirts, others in medieval velvet glittering with gems. A few wore garb from other times and countries: kimonos, saris, flowing robes in shimmering silk, even feathers or fur or leather. It all depended on the wearer's magical whims.

Belle watched Davon as he turned in a slow circle, his lips parted in astonishment at the sheer, exuberant beauty of the ancient city. "And this is where the Magekind lives?" he asked at last. "Including King Arthur?"

"He's not a king anymore, but yeah." Deciding he'd had enough time to sightsee, she caught him by the arm and turned him toward a sprawling Mediterranean villa with walls of cream stone and tall, arched windows. "You'll be staying here. I call it Joyous Guard . . ."

He looked at her. "After Lancelot's castle?"

Apparently Davon had been doing some research. "Right. Lance used to be a Magus court seducer before he got married a couple of years ago. I built this place to house all the recruits, male and female. Most of them live here until they build a place of their own," she explained as they started up the stone walkway. When she'd conjured Joyous Guard years ago, the intricate spell left her feeling drained and sick for more than a week. But it had been worth it to ensure the recruits had a decent place to live.

"And I'll be sent out on missions." He looked dazed.

"Yes, once you've had some training. The original knights and ladies of the Round Table swore an oath to Merlin, promising to protect humankind against its self-destructive impulses. We've been doing that job ever since." Belle grimaced. "And judging from what's been going on lately, we've got plenty of job security."

Davon gave her a sharp look. "So you're basically a recruiter."

"Exactly." They walked through the building's double doors.

A tall Native American almost ran into them as they turned into the main corridor. His handsome face lit in a dazzling smile. "Belle!" He gathered her into a bear hug as Davon watched in surprise. "How are you?"

"Fine, Richard." She hugged him back and accepted his hearty kiss. "How are you? Settling in?"

"Yep. Reece Champion says I'm making real progress on my combat skills. He said I should be ready to go on my first mission in a month or so."

"Belle?" A broad-shouldered Iraqi emerged from his apartment to join them, a brilliant smile lighting his dark face. "It's great to see you. And with a new recruit, I see."

"Davon Fredericks, Mohammad Hasan." As the men shook hands, Belle gestured to Richard, who offered his own with a broad smile. "Richard Spotted Horse, Davon. Davon just completed his transformation."

"Welcome to the club," Richard said, pumping Davon's hand. "If you like, I'll be happy to show you the ropes."

Davon returned the big man's smile. "Hey, thanks. I need all the help I can get."

"It is not as intimidating as it seems," Mohammad added in his exotically musical accent. "The Magekind has a pretty good system for easing you in. Would you like a tour?"

"I'd appreciate it," Davon told him.

Belle smiled, knowing she could surrender her new recruit into the capable hands of the older ones, just as she'd been doing for hundreds of years.

Half an hour later, Belle found Morgana Le Fay on the city's practice grounds, a manicured expanse of grass dotted with combat circles of carefully raked sand. Low bushes separated the circles, bursting with a variety of white blooms that perfumed the air with sweetness.

Morgana watched Tristan and Arthur batter each other in one of those circles, blunted swords swinging in flashing arcs. The two men wore suits of magical armor that glittered in the moonlight as they circled, attacked, and retreated in a dazzling display of agility and strength.

Despite the complicated rhythms of combat, Tristan was simultaneously carrying on a spirited argument with Morgana.

"What about Delfina?" he demanded. "She's worked with me before."

"Which is why she doesn't want to work with you now," Morgana said, an edge of impatience in her voice. "She said, and I quote, 'Tristan may be a Knight of the Round Table, but he's also an arrogant prick. "Model of chivalry," my rosy pink arse.'"

"I'm extremely chivalrous," Tristan said, deeply offended. He spun, his blade flashing right at Arthur's helmeted head. "And I need a witch for this mission."

Arthur blocked the blow, then counterattacked, driving Tristan backward with a rain of blows. "Prick or not, Morgana, I want him in on this hunt."

As Belle joined her, Morgana met her gaze and rolled her eyes. "Then he needs to quit being such a jackass. I can't get anybody of the necessary power and experience to agree to work with him. And I don't dare send one of the younger Majae. Not against Warlock."

Vampires—who were always male—could not work spells, though they could shapeshift. Only female Majae like Belle and Morgana had magical abilities. Which meant if Tristan wanted a dimensional gate opened, he needed a Maja partner to do it for him.

Why Merlin had divided magical abilities along sexual lines, nobody knew. It was just the way things worked, at least for the Magekind. The rules were different for dragons, werewolves, and Sidhe warriors like Smoke.

But then, Merlin hadn't created them.

"So order someone, dammit," Arthur snapped, as he circled the knight, blade clanging on blade as each tested the other's guard. "I want that bastard found. He killed twelve Latents and damn near blew my son to hell, along with a whole bunch of mortals. And we still haven't found Smoke, which strongly suggests the Sidhe's dead, too. If he's not, I want him found. Either way, Warlock needs to pay."

"I'll go with him." Belle blinked in appalled surprise as the words left her mouth. *What the hell did I just say?*

In his astonishment, Tristan dropped his guard. Arthur's blunted sword clanked hard against his helmed head, and he staggered. Shaking off the blow, he flipped up his visor and glowered at her. "Forget that."

Instantly offended, Belle glared back at him. "I have more than enough experience."

"In the sack, perhaps . . ."

"*Combat* experience, jerk," she snapped, stung. "Arthur said I acquitted myself well in the Dragon Wars." Belle gave the former king her best demanding stare. "Didn't you?"

"She did," Arthur said, bracing his blunted weapon on the ground. He flipped his visor up, revealing his bearded face and dark, acute gaze as he studied his friend.

"I don't care," Tristan snapped. "I don't want her." He turned and lifted his sword. "Let's try that again."

Furious at his cavalier dismissal, Belle balled her fists and took a step toward the field. "I'll show you combat, you arrogant . . ."

Morgana caught her by one shoulder and dragged her to a halt. "Not a good idea, darling." She dropped her voice. "What's this about, Belle? You've never evinced much interest in going on field missions before."

"Maybe I'm sick of being the Whore of Avalon." She glared at Tristan, now in an intense low-voiced argument with Arthur.

Her friend stiffened in outrage. "Who would dare call you such a thing?"

"Spare me, Morgana. I know you've heard it before. They rarely say it to my face, but they do say it."

"I assure you, nobody uses that name in *my* presence. Maja court seducer is a difficult and dangerous job, and you're the best at it we've ever had. How many others have we lost to blood-mad vampires? You know how to handle them. And every man you've Changed adores you still."

"Only because they don't know how ready I was to kill them." Belle lifted one shoulder in a half shrug. "Trouble is, I've stopped caring. The next time one of them goes blood-mad, I may not bother to conjure a knife."

Morgana's head rocked back as if she'd been slapped. She stared at Belle a frozen moment before she turned toward the two men and lifted her voice. "Belle goes with you, Tristan. Or no one does."

The knight jerked around, and he stared at her, disbelief on his handsome face. "What? I'll not . . ."

"You will if you want magical assistance."

Tristan turned toward his friend. "Arthur . . ."

The immortal lifted both big hands in a warding gesture. "Morgana is the liege of the Majae, Tristan. I don't tell her how to assign her women, and she doesn't tell me how to assign my men. You know that."

"But . . ."

Arthur shot Morgana and Belle a look, then turned

deliberately back to Tristan and squared his massive shoulders. "You also know that I am your liege. And I'm *ordering* you to work with La Belle Coeur."

The knight snapped his mouth closed on whatever argument he'd been about to make. He gave Belle a glower, then swept a courtier's bow. "As you will, Sire."

Before Belle could decide whether she'd just won or gotten herself in a great deal of trouble, Tristan stalked off the field to catch her by one arm. "Come on, *partner*. We're going to have a little talk."

And he hauled her after him.

It was two in the morning before David and Eva returned to her apartment. Shelly's mother had arrived just before the ambulance crew, announcing she was going to take the pair to her house after they got checked out at the emergency room.

But it was Ronnie who had David's undivided attention when the police arrived. Under his ice-blue glare, the man had confessed to beating Shelly and hitting his son.

Eva kept a close eye on the cops the entire time, afraid they'd notice the way David's pupils contracted into vertical slits when he was pissed. She figured if anybody commented, she'd just claim he was wearing special contacts.

Hopefully the cops wouldn't realize nobody made contacts that reacted to light.

Luckily, the police were far more interested in Ronnie's confession than in the two neighbors who'd called the cops. They asked Eva and David a few questions, then let them go.

Too wired to sleep, Eva decided a trip to Wal-Mart was in order. The store was open all night, which gave her a good opportunity to replace David's pants before they gelded him—a fate he insisted was imminent.

She and David left the store half an hour later with three pairs of jeans, four knit shirts in different colors, socks, underwear, and running shoes, along with a toothbrush, razor, and male deodorant.

"I've got to get some sleep," Eva told him as they walked

into her apartment carrying their purchases. "I'm supposed to open the shop in a few hours."

"What shop?" David asked, following her back toward the guest bedroom.

"My father and I own a comic book store," she explained. "We share the chores of operating it. It's my turn to open tomorrow." Eva frowned. "I'm just not sure what to do about you while I'm working."

His eyes narrowed as his pupils contracted into slits. She really should have bought him a pair of sunglasses. "What do you mean, you are not sure what to do about me?"

"Uh—" Oh, shit. Might as well brazen it out. "I don't know if I should leave you here while I go to work. What if your enemy tracks you down?"

David stepped in so close to her, she became instantly aware of his size, his heat, his scent. "What if my enemy tracks *you* down?"

"Ah . . . yeah." She stared up at him, half-hypnotized. "Maybe we should stick together."

"Yes," he purred. "It's best if we are together."

David lowered his head and kissed her. She froze, stunned by the feeling of his lips moving on hers. Slow. Hot. Exquisitely seductive. His tongue stroked across her lower lip until she opened for him with a helpless moan. His fingers found her chin, cupped gently. His hand felt warm, just slightly rough with calluses.

The burning heat within her had been waiting for just this chance. It blazed up, hot and savage, searing her self-control to a black cinder.

And she was lost.

Eva's mouth tasted rich, female, intoxicating. The gentle power of it maddened him, made David want to roll in her like a cat in catnip. He contented himself with kisses— gentle bites, licking passes over her lips, before stealing inside to trace her teeth and tease her tongue. She moaned and kissed him back: delightful pressure, soft lips that gave against his, a nibble of his lower lip.

His arms slid around her without his conscious intent, hands slipping down to explore the shape of her: the lush curve of her hip, the dip of her waist, the rise of her rib cage. Her breasts seemed to call his hands, and he answered, first with careful brushes of fingertips that explored soft cloth and the intriguing contours beneath. What was she wearing under her shirt? And he found one nipple, jutting hopefully beneath all that fabric, a tight little bump that hardened even more as he cupped her, thumbed her, strummed the pouting button like a lute string. Eva's hands fisted in his shirt, as if she were holding on to the only stable thing in a whirlwind.

David kissed her some more, getting rapidly drunk on her as he slipped a hand under her shirt to find out what she wore beneath it. Something silky covered the full lower curve of her breast, turning to something a little rougher—lace?

Well, of course he had to find out. David grabbed the hem of her shirt and pulled it upward. Eva raised her arms, giving silent permission, and he drew the shirt off over her head and dropped it heedlessly on the floor.

Then he simply gazed at her. Her breasts were lovely handfuls, pale and round, cupped in thin lace and black silk. *Bra*, his memory whispered, and he wondered how he knew that.

His attention zeroed in on her nipples. They jutted beneath the silk, the rosy shadow of her areoles peeking past the delicate web of black lace.

David looked up to find her watching him with a trace of anxiety in those big dark eyes. As if she was afraid he wouldn't adore the sight of her.

"You are beautiful," he told her. Pitiful words, he instantly decided, and tried again. "Your skin is so pale, like fresh, sweet cream."

"I've been so busy I haven't had time to lie out in the sun," she said, as if his words were a criticism. "And they say it's not good for you, since it can cause . . ."

He slid his hands up and cupped her breasts, and she stuttered to a stop, those gorgeous eyes huge, eating light.

"Your eyes are so dark. Like a moonless night in a deep forest."

"I've always wished they were blue. Like yours." She stared into his face as if he'd hypnotized her. "You know, when you feel strong emotion, they almost . . . glow. And the pupils do that slit thing. Like a . . ."

David thumbed one nipple, and she apparently forgot what she was going to say, her head tipping back to show him the elegant line of her slender neck framed in the gleaming darkness of her hair. A pulse throbbed there, rapidly thumping, and he had to put his lips against it, feel its leaping bound. He tongued it, tasting her skin, trace of salt, female perfume, and the tinge of wild musk that was her wolf.

Fluffy.

He smiled against her throat, remembering the whimsical name. What did she look like when she changed? He wanted to see her, imagined her regal strength, her silken fur. She'd be as beautiful in that form as she was now.

He was purring again, but he didn't bother trying to stop.

David purred, a deep rhythmic rumble Eva could feel against her rib cage as he pulled her close. Her eyes drifted closed so she could concentrate on the kisses he was stringing down the curve of her throat. His warm lips felt impossibly soft, especially compared to the hard strength of the rest of him.

She wanted to see him naked again. Sliding a hand down his hard body, Eva grabbed handfuls of shirt and tugged upward. He lifted his brawny arms, and she managed to drag the tight shirt off. It hit the floor with a soft thump as she went for the snap of those tight, tight jeans.

He sucked his breath in as she started unzipping them, revealing his cock, which had somehow managed to get hard despite the skintight denim. Its head was a lovely dark rose, with a pearlescent drop of arousal trembling on the curve. Eva thought about tasting it, but she really had to get his poor dick out of those murderous jeans.

The zipper hissed in complaint as she pulled it down. His big hands joined hers when she started dragging at his waistband.

"Good God," Eva muttered, tugging, "I've worn panty hose that weren't this tight. No wonder you bitched."

"You have no idea," he growled, wiggling in a way that seemed so out of character she had to stifle a giggle.

David finally planted his butt on the carpet while she tugged and jerked, trying to work the skin-tight jeans down his muscled legs. The fabric clung like a determined—and very jealous—lover. Eva started giggling helplessly. When they had to stop tugging to pull off his shoes, David joined her, first with deep chuckles, then in booming laughter that made her giggle harder.

But when they finally got him naked, Eva's laughter died a very quick death. She stared at him as he sprawled on the floor like a pasha, all long legs, his cock curved over his tight belly. His biceps bulged as he braced back on his elbows, and his hair fell around his shoulders like a river of ebony silk striped in silver. He wasn't going gray; the stripes cut horizontally across his hair like the smoky markings of a cat. As she stared in fascination, he reached up and flipped back a lock of hair.

"Your ears are pointed." They formed curving, elegant tips that reminded her of the elves from the *Lord of the Rings* movies. What the hell was he, anyway?

Then he rose up onto his knees with a powerful flex of his body, and she found she really didn't give a damn. Whatever he was, he was most definitely male. And he wanted her. A lot.

David dropped to all fours and crawled up her body to unzip her pants and start working them down her hips. Eva lifted her pelvis and watched his eyes heat as he contemplated her tiny lace panties. She was suddenly very glad she hadn't worn her usual plain white cotton. He paused to pull off her shoes, then dragged the jeans the rest of the way off before going after her underwear.

And God, she was wet. Slick and swollen and ready for him, zero to sixty in two seconds flat.

He'd taken the panties off, and now he spread her, taking her legs in his big hands and parting her knees with delicious male greed. He edged his big shoulders between them, and lowered his head, and—*Oh, God*—he started *eating* her, licking her like a really juicy peach, long passes of his clever tongue while one finger worked inside her swollen entrance. Sensation seemed to blind her for a moment. She fell backward on the floor, staring helplessly at the ceiling, and *felt*. Felt that tongue, felt that finger, sliding and stroking and driving her insane.

Eva heard herself moaning. She knew she should hold it down because the walls were thin, but she didn't care. She let it rip, yowling like a cat in heat.

Lick. Lick. Thrust. Lick.

Holy God.

She couldn't move. Pleasure-stunned, she sprawled on the floor with him between her legs, using his tongue in delicately merciless flicks.

His hands found her breasts, thumbs strumming her nipples lazily, raking back and forth while he licked. Delight rolled over her like waves of heated honey, sweet and slooow, and she lost her mind by inches.

Then he drew away, and the loss of that hot tongue made her blink in stunned disappointment. Where was he going . . . ?

Oh. On top of her. Crawling up the length of her body, his hair and his warm, hard skin brushing along her flesh. He settled down lazily, his hips nudging her thighs wider. She watched him reach down and grab that cock, and aim it, and then . . .

Oh, sweet God in heaven.

As if he had all the time in the world, David filled her, *stuffed* her slowly with inch after inch of stone-hard shaft. Eva shuddered helplessly and rolled her head back. His lips found the pulse in her throat, kissing and biting as she quivered. Somehow she managed to lift her heavy hands and slide them along the width of his shoulders, feeling him under her hands, warm and strong.

Had she ever made love like this? Ever? With *anybody*?

The answer to that was a big, fat *no*. Nobody had ever touched her like this, taken the time to drive her out of her mind before he even thought about his own pleasure.

So she lay under David and quivered, stunned stupid by every sweet, hot wave that rolled over her head.

Eva entranced him. The smell of her skin at her pulse, the taste of the wet flesh between her legs, the long, straight silk of her hair in his fist.

The way she gripped him, slick and snug around his cock, a maddening delight.

He could feel the climax gathering in his balls, hot and heavy, ready to pound its way to his skull.

Gods.

Breath caught, David pulled out, forcing himself to go slowly, fighting to make the pleasure last. He wanted to hang on to every second of this incredible, soul-searing delight.

And, ooh, the way she *looked*.

She had her eyes closed, her lashes like sable feathers against her creamy cheeks. Her mouth parted as she moaned, lips flushed dark rose with passion, a blush painting those high, exquisite cheekbones. Her hair spread across the floor around her head in a dark halo of shining silk.

Every time he thrust deep, he felt her belly against his abdomen, her thighs sliding against his, her hips rolling to meet his grinding pelvis.

She slid her hands down, ran her fingers over his hips as if looking for a good grip. Found it, nails digging into his skin, the tiny pain sending him jolting deeper, harder, faster.

Lost and flying.

Her eyes opened, met his. Dark as the reflection of a moonless night on a still mountain lake. Drawing him in, pulling him down.

Her pupils flashed red, like fire igniting from a lightning strike, canine teeth lengthening into fangs as she came. Her scream spiraled into a deep-throated roar. Her nails lengthened into claws, but he barely felt the pain as he roared back at her.

Coming.

Pleasure like a firestorm raced along his nerves, searing his consciousness to ash as he shoved all the way to the balls.

Coming.

She writhed beneath him, her legs twining around his, tightening until his bones creaked. His teeth became fangs.

He raced along a forest trail on four big paws, alien trees all around. And she ran beside him, a streak of black wolf fur and flashing fire eyes, tongue lolling between white, white teeth.

Not human. Either of them.

Together. Finally. After so many uncounted centuries of longing.

Together.

FOUR

Eva lay on the floor with David collapsed on top of her, sweating, panting, listening to their heartbeats slow.

For a moment as they'd come, she'd seen them running together in some kind of rain forest straight out of *Avatar*, surrounded by plants in colors she'd never even imagined. He was a huge cat, a streak of black with silver stripes along his haunches and massive forelegs, his eyes pale as sapphires. And she was in wolf form—a real wolf, not a were, running full out. And she'd felt him in her mind, intelligent and powerful and somehow incredibly *old*. Had it been real? Gathering her courage, she asked, "Did you feel that?"

Bracing himself on his elbows, David looked down at her with a sound midway between a laugh and a snort. "I felt a great many things." He grinned and kissed her on the tip of her nose. "All delightful."

Eva blinked, oddly flustered. Though why she'd find a kiss on the nose more intimate than everything else they'd done, she had no idea.

Maybe it was because the gesture was so sweet and silly—something shared between true lovers, not a pair of strangers scratching a seductive itch. Eva found she liked that about him—that he'd do something that gently goofy. The gesture gave her courage.

Taking a deep breath, she told him about the—vision? dream?—whatever it was. Running through that hyper-real forest together, linked mind to mind. "For a minute there, it felt like we touched." Her courage almost deserted her, but she managed to get the rest out anyway. "Mentally, I mean. Like in some kind of psychic connection."

God, that sounded lame.

But David nodded. "Yes, I experienced the same thing." Absently, he smoothed a lock of hair back from her face, his gaze thoughtful. "We were running in a jungle together, and we were . . . happy. You were a wolf, while I was some kind of huge cat. What do you think it means?"

She stared at him. "You're asking *me*?"

"You're the one with a memory longer than three hours ago."

"Ah. Good point. I have no idea what it means. I don't even know if I can really turn into a wolf—the four-legged kind, anyway. Maybe it was just a dream."

"We could experiment. See if we really can transform into animals." David yawned hugely and gave her a lazy grin. "Tomorrow. I'm afraid I won't be good for much more tonight. You've exhausted me." His smile took on a wicked quirk. "Fabulous sex does that."

Eva's cheeks flamed. "How do you know it was fabulous if your memory only goes back three hours?"

"Trust me, darling. A man knows." David leaned down and kissed her, but this was no affectionate peck on the nose. He took his time with it, conducting a deliciously lazy exploration, with tongue and teeth and male sensuality so intense her head spun.

Amnesia victim or not, the man knew how to use his mouth. And his tongue. And his hands.

And his truly incredible dick, added Fluffy, sounding sated and smug.

For once, Eva agreed with her.

* * *

Tristan trailed Belle to her house on the outskirts of Avalon, bitching all the way. It was a modest place by the standards of the magical city: three stories of gray fieldstone
with a slate roof, arched windows and doorways, and a
courtyard planted with orchids.

The master bedroom sprawled across most of the second
floor. The furniture was dark cherry, intricately carved in a
whimsical tangle of ivy and honeysuckle. Fairies, dragons,
and unicorns lurked among the leaves—here a sinuous tail,
there a tiny face framed by gossamer wings, over there a
proudly lifted horned head. She'd spent more raw magic on
the canopied bed alone than most social-climbing witches
blew on entire mansions.

Tristan stopped complaining for ten whole minutes
while he contemplated the furniture. His brows flew up.
"Creating all this must have knocked you on your ass for
a week."

"Pretty much," she admitted cheerfully.

"You magic these, too?" He toed one of the colorful rag
rugs scattered on the gleaming pine floor.

"Nope. Made 'em by hand." Unable to resist displaying
her handiwork, Belle pointed at the thickly embroidered
bedspread with its dragons and fairies in countless shades
of silken thread. "The quilt, too. Took me four months."
And she'd relished every stitch.

Some tasks are too important to the soul for shortcuts.

Tristan grunted as Belle started for her dresser to begin
packing.

"It's not going to work." With narrow green eyes he
watched her pull out a drawer. His seductive mouth drew
into a tight frown. "You don't like me."

"I'm a professional. I don't have to like you." She found
the huge .45 pistol, pulled it out of its holster, and checked
to make sure it was unloaded. Satisfied, she slid it back into
the holster and tucked it into her Louis Vuitton pilot case.
Then under Tristan's glower she added a box of bullets and
a couple of spare clips.

"You're a witch. What do you need a gun for?" He braced his hands on his hips. His shoulders looked ridiculously wide beneath the blue knit shirt he wore.

She gave him the look that comment deserved. "Magic doesn't work on Dire Wolves. As you damned well know."

"Which is why *I'll* have a gun."

Belle stopped in the act of picking out a selection of shirts to take. "So, what? I'm supposed to stand there with my thumb up my butt while you fight giant vampire-eating werewolves?"

"Why not? You spend most of your time with something stuffed in some part of your anatomy. I'm told you do your best work that way."

Belle imagined how he'd look after she hit him with a fireball: singed and blinking. It was such a satisfying fantasy she mentally added a curl of smoke from his nose. "You're deliberately being a jackass."

"I do that. It's why nobody wants to work with me." He glowered and folded his arms. His biceps appeared as round and firm as cantaloupes beneath his tanned skin. If he would only shut up, he'd make good scenery.

She considered conjuring a ball gag and stuffing it into that tempting mouth. "You do realize that if I bow out, no witch will work with you. Which will seriously crimp your werewolf hunt."

"I'll manage."

She smiled at him sweetly. "Then go to Morgana and ask her to rescind my assignment."

A muscle flexed in his angular jaw. "Morgana doesn't change her mind. She's worse than Arthur."

"Then it would appear you're stuck with me." Belle strolled into the walk-in closet and considered the selection of pants. She didn't find anything that looked suitable, so she conjured a few pairs in various shades and walked back into the bedroom with them.

"Leather?" Tristan looked like a man sucking on a lemon. "You're packing *leather pants*?"

"They hold up better in a fight." She bared her teeth at him. "And they make my ass look fabulous." Just to piss him off, she conjured a pair of black boots with stiletto heels. No way could she fight in them, but he didn't need to know that.

When his nostrils flared, she added tight leather tops to match, each with a neckline plunging halfway to the navel. Then she threw in a corset, just to watch him turn purple.

"Look, I'm going to be going up against *Dire Wolves.*" He stalked over to her, the better to loom. "We're talking at least seven feet tall, with fangs, claws, and a tendency to disembowel people. And they shrug off magical lightning bolts like snowballs. You won't stand a chance."

"I'm touched by your concern for my well-being." She gave him a smile sweet enough to give cavities to an entire dentists' convention. "I had no idea you cared."

"I don't. I just don't want to get killed trying to keep your hapless ass alive."

The hapless thing stung. "You won't. I can take care of myself."

"With what? That ridiculous cap gun?" He pointed a contemptuous finger at her pilot case and its pistol. "All bullets do to werewolves is piss them off."

Belle marched over to the corner, picked up the long bag lying there, and tossed it on the bed with a leaden thump. Unzipping it, she drew out a five-foot great sword, admiring the way the massive weapon gleamed in the firelight with lethal grace. If it hadn't been enchanted, she wouldn't have been able to lift it. "Actually, I figured this would do a pretty good job of discouraging anybody the gun didn't."

Narrow-eyed, he considered the weapon. "Do you even know how to use that thing?"

That qualified as "asking for it." She swung the sword in a flat, hard arc, stopping it a fraction of an inch from his throat.

Tristan raised an eyebrow over the gleaming length of the blade. "I repeat, do you know how to use that thing?"

"I've used it rather effectively before." She glared at him. "And I'm strongly considering using it now."

"I've got a better idea. Why don't you go find some pretty Latent boy and fuck him into the Gift? It would be so much more pleasant for all concerned."

"Tristan, I'm not really interested in making *anything* pleasant for you."

"Yes," he gritted, "I noticed."

Eva had no idea how long she lay on the floor with David, a heap of dazed, exhausted flesh. At last she managed speech. "We really need to get up."

"Yes." He blinked at the ceiling. "The floor is very hard."

"And I've got this bed. It'd be a hell of a lot more comfortable."

"It would have to be." He sighed and rolled to his feet, lithe as the cat she'd dreamed about. Reaching down to take her hand, he helped her to her feet.

For about two seconds, she considered showing him to the guest room, but that would be like closing the barn door after the horse won the Kentucky Derby. Instead, she led the way to her own bedroom, flipped back the covers, and crawled between them as he joined her.

He pulled her into his arms and curled his big body around her like a boy with a teddy bear.

Lying on her side, her head pillowed on his brawny biceps, Eva felt surrounded by him—not just the muscular power of his body, but the in-and-out puff of his breath on her cheek. A thick lock of his long hair lay across her face, mixing with her own chocolate strands. It felt . . . good. She hadn't slept with a man since she'd broken up with Joel. Being what she was, her nightmares could have ugly consequences for the man in her bed. Luckily, tonight had proved that David could take care of himself. It was safe to cuddle into him and drift off to sleep.

Dreams would do no harm tonight.

He ran with her through the rain forest, his big paws thudding over the ground as she raced at his side. He'd never felt such pure joy.

Shooting through a tangle of brush, David plunged into a tendril of mist on the other side. The mist instantly

*thickened, going as impenetrably dark as a burning house.
He skidded to a stop, afraid of colliding head-on with a tree.*

*He listened to his breathing rasp in the blackness until
it suddenly melted away. He was human again.*

Carnage surrounded him.

*Corpses lay sprawled among blazing huts, bodies
twisted, horribly burned. Men, women, children, orbited
by clouds of flies. Crows hopped among the bodies, peck-
ing at flesh, cawing and squabbling and plucking out eyes.*

*He turned in a slow, horrified circle. Grief tore at him,
sharp as a vulture's beak. He knew these people. They
weren't random victims of a horrible disaster. They were
friends, relatives, brothers, sisters, nieces, and nephews.*

*Yet he didn't remember them. How could he have for-
gotten his people?*

*"This is on your head." The woman's voice was as chill
and acid as iced poison.*

*He turned to find a Sidhe female standing naked among
the bodies. Blood smeared her body and hair, as if she'd
bathed in it. Her blue eyes stared out of the gory mask of
her face, pale and insane.*

*"How could you do this?" he whispered, disbelief and
betrayal a ball of cold lead in his chest. "How could you
murder our people?"*

*"Our people?" She curled her lips—the lips he'd once
kissed with such delicious greed. "Your people. They
loved you, not me. Yet you would be nothing without me!
They would be nothing without me." She smiled viciously,
spreading her arms to indicate the carnage. "And now
that's exactly what they are. Nothing."*

*Fury replaced the grief and shock with a blinding red
haze. He threw up a hand and sent a roiling blast of magic
right at her murderous face.*

"David!" Eva's alarmed shout snapped him out of the
dream.

He was kneeling on the bed, hand still lifted just as it

had been in the nightmare. Across the room, one of Eva's figurines lay in smoking fragments.

"You blew up Batman." Eva stared at the remains of the statuette. "How the hell did you blow up Batman?"

"I have no idea." He fell back against the pillow, his mind still reverberating with grief and rage from the remains of the dream.

"That must have been one nasty dream."

He stared blindly at the ceiling. "It was. Gods, it was."

Warlock jolted up on the thick pile of cushions and silk. His heart pounded in his furry chest as he bounded out of his sleeping pit to stand there panting, fighting his fear, his clawed hands shaking.

For a moment, the Demigod had taken some of his power and memories back. Warlock had felt them being dragged away, had felt the ruthless strength of the immortal's mind.

He'd felt himself weaken.

His shaking morphed from fear to rage. Weakness was unacceptable. Merlin had chosen him to become the wizard werewolf because he was the strongest, the most worthy of his Saxon race. And Merlin had needed someone like him to make sure Arthur's knights didn't turn on humanity.

For centuries, the Direkind had followed him in his quest. Even those who had no idea of his existence—which was most of them—had followed the Chosen he led. The Chosen, who were the aristocratic descendents of those Merlin had personally selected to become Direkind. Most of the rest were Bitten—transformed by the magic of a werewolf's bite.

The Direkind, unlike the Magekind—or him, for that matter—were not immortal. Another thing that gave him power.

He'd taken the strength Merlin had given him and built it. Now, with Smoke's added magic, he had become stronger yet. Strong enough to meet the hated Celt king's power, even with all the witches Arthur could command.

Always, always he'd feared failing his people—going against Arthur only to be defeated by the overwhelming magic of the Magekind. That fear had become an obsession, eating at him for centuries, until he'd known he could let nothing stop him in his quest for power. Even if it meant doing the necessary but distasteful. Even if Merlin would not have approved.

Merlin, after all, was gone. Warlock was the one left to clean up the Celt's mess—unnecessary wars that could have been prevented, starving children, racial and religious hate boiling over into violence. If the Celt had only had the balls to use the power at his disposal, so many lives could have been saved. But Arthur didn't have the stomach for the job.

Warlock did.

He just had to get Arthur out of the way so he could do it.

So he'd fathered sons, attempting to create magic-using partners, but one by one they'd become a threat, and he'd had to eliminate them all. More recently, he'd gotten a daughter on a woman of the Chosen, reasoning that since she was a female, she could be no real threat.

The grandsons she'd give him would not have the talent to be true competition, while still providing the magical assistance he'd need to go up against Arthur's witches. It would take decades to put such a plan in motion, but since he was immortal, he had all the time he needed.

Now he'd suddenly acquired the power he'd craved for so many centuries. And it was everything he'd ever dreamed of, as intoxicating as any drug.

It was delicious being a god.

As for the alien memories that came with that power, he'd realized he needed them. Otherwise he wouldn't have the experience to shape all that wild magic.

I'm not going to give this up. Not any of it.

The Demigod had to die before he could take his powers back. Because he would. Eventually Smoke's spirit would call the magic back to him, and it would answer that call. Only the cat's death would allow Warlock to keep his stolen abilities.

Should I do it myself? It would be easy. Stripped of his magic, Smoke would be unable to defend himself.

But what if proximity allowed Smoke to draw on his powers? What if they jumped back to him when Warlock got within killing range? Now that he'd tasted the cat's magic, he knew he definitely didn't want to be on the receiving end of it.

So, no.

Fortunately, he had plenty of killers at his disposal. Handpicked murderers he'd bitten to create Dire Wolves. Those men feared him so much they would do anything for him.

Even kill a god.

Miranda Drake sprawled on her belly on her pink lace canopied bed, reading *Guilty Pleasures* for something like the fifteenth time. Whenever she got particularly depressed, she liked to read about Anita Blake kicking monster ass. Especially since kicking any kind of ass was something Miranda was never allowed to do.

Thus the whole depression thing.

She supposed it could have been worse. The house she lived in was a thirty-room Gilded Age mansion with high walls of cream stone and a low-pitched roofline. It had been home to Drake werewolves since 1898, and it was drafty and pretentious as hell. Miranda's very pink bedroom was better suited to a tween than the twenty-four-year-old she was.

But at least she had books.

Anita was locking horns with Jean Claude when her mother tapped on the door. "Miranda?" Without waiting for permission, Joelle walked in. She paused with one nervous hand on the doorknob, a too-thin, perpetually wary woman in a Vera Wang tank dress. Its flowing emerald silk contrasted with the flaming red tumble of her hair. All that color only emphasized her pale skin and the dark hollows under her green eyes.

Miranda looked up, frowning in surprise. Her mother normally had more respect for her privacy. Unlike her step-father, who usually barged in like a man hoping to catch her at something.

Her surprise became unease when Harold Worthington sauntered in at her mother's heels, an expression of ugly anticipation on his handsome face. Worthington was a big man, tall and powerfully built, with silver threading his black hair. Dressed in a tailored pin-striped gray suit with a red power tie, he looked like a bank CEO. Which was exactly what he was.

He was also a very big, very nasty werewolf.

None of which explained what the hell he was doing in here. Her parents had never let any male in her bedroom before.

Miranda rolled off her bed and faced the two warily. "What's this about, Mom?"

Joelle licked her lips and pasted a too-bright smile on her face. "Randy, you remember Mr. Worthington—uh, Harold. He's been a friend of the family for years."

"Yes, but he generally doesn't make a habit of coming into my bedroom." She met her mother's gaze. "Especially not during my Burning Moon."

Worthington grinned at her. "Then I'd think you'd be glad to see me. Leave us alone, Joelle." He gave the order without even looking at her mother.

Joelle hesitated, her expression torn. "This is what your father wants, Miranda."

Oh, fuck. "What about what *I* want, Mother?"

"That's not even relevant, Miranda. Get out, Joelle."

"This isn't your house, *Harry*," Randy spat. "You don't tell my mother what to do in her own home."

"Miranda, please don't make this harder than it has to be. Please!" Joelle turned and fled. The door banged closed behind her.

So much for mother love.

Randy stared at the older man coldly. Her heart was hammering, and she wanted to throw up, but she kept the fear and dread from her face. She'd perfected an expressionless mask before she could read. "If you think I'm going to sleep with you, you're out of your mind."

"Do you really think you have any say in this?" He tossed his jacket on her bed and went to work on the gold cuff links fastening his French cuffs. "Warlock wants you pregnant, and I'm going to make sure he gets what he wants."

Yeah, that's what she'd figured. "I'm not going to let you rape me, Harry."

He looked up from tucking his cuff links into his pants pocket. "You're in your Burning Moon, my dear. It won't be rape for long."

Some part of her growled in agreement—her wolf had been denied a lover for far too many years. She snarled denial at both the beast and Worthington. "Burning Moon or no Burning Moon, *I* choose who I sleep with. You're twenty years older than I am, for God's sake. You could be my father!"

"But I'm not." He coolly unbuttoned his shirt, revealing a powerful chest covered in a thick mat of black hair. "If I were, I assure you, you'd be a lot better behaved."

She curled her hands into claws and glared at him. "I'll fight you."

"And I'll win." He folded the shirt and put it aside, then began to unbuckle his belt.

"Maybe." Reckless rage curled her lips into a snarl. "And maybe I'll make you hurt me too bad to give Warlock his grandson."

He gave her a supercilious smile that gradually faded as he realized she meant it. Then he snorted and tossed his belt aside. "You're just a woman. You don't have the guts."

"Try me." Being Dire Wolf, she could heal virtually anything he did to her. It wouldn't be pleasant, but she would survive.

"You'd let an innocent baby die?"

"That's almost funny, coming from you. Anyway, it's not a baby until you get me pregnant. And you're not going to get me pregnant." She started to reach for her magic . . .

"If you change, your mother pays."

Miranda froze, horror slicing through her fury. "What?"

Worthington stared at her through eyes like icy slits. "If you fight me, I will beat your mother bloody."

She was going to be sick. Swallowing hard, Miranda forced a laugh. "You wouldn't dare. My stepfather . . ."

". . . Will entirely approve, if you have defied Warlock's wishes."

Ice rolled over her from heels to hairline. He was right. Gerald Drake had been holding Joelle hostage for Miranda's behavior since she'd hit puberty. He'd never cared about her mother; he'd married the already-pregnant Joelle only because Warlock ordered him to. Joelle had never meant anything to anyone except Miranda.

A faint, chilly smile quirked Worthington's lips. "Strip. I won't tell you again."

"I've never . . ." No. Damned if she'd beg the bastard for mercy.

". . . Had sex?" The smile widened, took on a sadistic edge. "I know."

Sickened, Miranda stared into his eyes. The moment she'd dreamed of as something born of love would be an act of violence at the hands of a man who would enjoy her debasement.

She'd always let her father hold her love for Joelle over her head. Joelle, her sweet and adoring mother, who insisted Gerald knew best. Even when he carried through on his threats and beat her to force Miranda's cooperation.

"Goddamn you." Hands shaking, she reached for her T-shirt and jerked if off over her head. "Damn you to hell."

His smile broadened as he reached out grabbing one breast in a rough hand. "Bra, too. I want to see these tits."

When she obeyed, he closed a thumb and forefinger over her nipple and gave it a vicious twist. Pain brought tears to her eyes, and Miranda blinked hard, fighting the need to slap him. It would only make matters worse.

His grin broadened.

He was so busy enjoying his sadistic pleasure, he didn't see the conjured knife appear in her hand.

She drove it through the underside of his chin, ramming it right into his brain. Worthington's cold eyes widened with astonishment, then turned glassy as blood poured from his mouth. His body swayed and fell as she released the knife. He hit the floor with a meaty thud.

Werewolves could heal damn near any injury, but not if they died so fast there wasn't time to transform. And though they were immune to magic, her weapon hadn't been magical. She'd only used magic to conjure it.

Dead. Miranda stared at Harold's twisted body, taking a deep, relieved breath. *The bastard's dead.* He wouldn't rape her now. He'd inflict no more pain on her or anybody else. Someone should give her a medal. She'd be lucky if they didn't gut her instead.

The last of her rage collapsed inward, a psychic black hole of weariness. Even this would change nothing. Nothing that mattered, anyway. The Chosen were as set in their collective path as a glacier grinding across a valley.

The bedroom door banged open, and Joelle rushed in. "What was that crash?" She broke off, staring in horror at Worthington's corpse. "Merlin's Cup, what have you done?"

"Nothing he didn't have coming." With a flick of her fingers, she sent a blazing ball of magic at Worthington's corpse, which burst into flame and vanished.

Mechanically, Miranda turned toward her walk-in closet and threw the door open, searching for her suitcase. She finally located it behind a box of clothing.

"Randy, you can't." Joelle stepped into her path and tried to take the case from her hand. "This will only make things worse."

Miranda pulled away, ignoring her mother's pleading eyes. Now that the flare of murderous rage was spent, she felt numb. Empty of everything, even the bitter anger of so many years. "At this point, I don't have a choice."

"They won't kill you, Miranda. You're too essential to Warlock's plans. Yes, you'll have to be punished, but . . ."

"I've already been punished." She flung the suitcase on the bed, then walked over to her dresser and dug out an armload of clothing. "They've been making me pay since the day I was born. All I did today was balance the scales."

FIVE

There were twelve Dire Wolves, with fur that ranged from coal black to cinnamon red to honey blond, in textures from horsehair to silk. Most were tall and massively built, though a few were as deceptively lean as fencers. Their intelligence varied from brutish to gifted. There was, in fact, only one thing they all had in common.

Every last one of them was a sociopath.

For centuries, Warlock had maintained a corps of killers, men who had none of the idealism Merlin had ingrained in the rest of the Direkind, even the most cynical of the Chosen aristocracy. These twelve were Warlock's shock troops, the ones who did his bidding without question.

The group's small numbers limited what he could do with them, but it couldn't be helped. More than one emperor of Rome had been assassinated by his own Praetorian Guard, and Warlock had no intention of suffering the same fate.

No, twelve was the perfect number.

Besides, Arthur had his twelve Knights of the Round Table.

Warlock had his twelve Bastards.

He'd opened magical gates to transport them—easy

enough to do, since he'd dictated that members of the three teams live together. Now they stood in the central cavern of the network of caves he used as a headquarters.

The thick stone helped shield him from magical detection by Arthur's witches, and the glowing ward runes carved into the rock looked impressive as hell. So did the massive throne that supported Warlock's eight-foot-frame. Carved of ebony wood and studded with gemstones, it was damned uncomfortable under his ass. But it did create the right effect, so he put up with it.

Though all the Bastards looked expressionless, even bored as they faced his throne, every one of them smelled of fear. They had reason. The last time he'd brought them together, he'd killed the one whose job performance had dissatisfied him.

Then he'd produced the man's replacement, whom he'd Bitten the day before.

The others got the point.

"I have a mission for you," he said slowly, looking from muzzle to wolfish muzzle. "There is a man I would be rid of."

"Just a man?" Tommy Danvers was one of the more intelligent of his team leaders, a cunning wolf who led his three subordinates with ruthless skill and brutal discipline. "Or a Dire Wolf?"

"At the moment, he's nothing more than human, but that may change. And he has a female Dire Wolf with him, which complicates matters a bit."

Danvers curled his lip. "A female? Shouldn't be much trouble."

Warlock made a dismissive gesture. "She won't be, not for you. But at the moment, she's an inconvenience, because I can't use my magic to pinpoint the male's location as long as he's near her. And so far, judging from my lack of contact, she's stayed pretty damn close."

"I'll bet," said Steve Miller, Danvers's second-in-command. The chorus of laughter that followed held a nasty note, with more than a little anticipation.

Warlock shot him an impatient look, and the laughter

cut off as though he'd flashed a knife. "Sooner or later, they'll separate, and at that time I should be able to get a location on him. I'll need you all to maintain readiness, because you'll have to move within minutes."

The men exchanged looks. "Move how?" asked Kevin Wheeler, the Fenir team leader, who had a surprising intelligence for all his brawny size.

Warlock made an impatient gesture. "I will transport you."

"We'll be ready whenever you give the signal." Scott Brown headed the Geri team with a cool, murderous efficiency. Warlock considered him the best of the team leaders.

"As usual, you'll work in your established teams." Warlock nodded at Brown. "If Skoll fails, I want Geri ready to go in, then Fenir." He'd named the teams for wolves from Norse mythology. "You will stop him at all costs."

"We won't fail you, sir," Danvers said with easy confidence.

"See that you don't." Warlock pinned him with a cold glare. He gestured, conjuring a set of photographs in the hands of each man. "This is your target. I want him dead as quickly as possible."

"What about collateral damage?" Danvers asked.

"Eliminating him is the priority. If bystanders get in the way, you have my permission to eliminate them as necessary, so long as you can do so without witnesses. However, avoid police involvement. Police mean media, and media mean Arthur may get wind of this. That is not acceptable."

Warlock watched in satisfaction as all twelve nodded their understanding. They wouldn't fail him.

They didn't dare.

Miranda clattered down the sweeping stairs with her suitcase, ignoring her mother, who fluttered in her wake. "Randy, please! You can't just leave!"

"Watch me, Mom." *Got to get to the car before Dad comes back,* she thought, her mind flashing through the possibilities. The blue Volvo belonged to her mother, and Miranda knew Gerald would call the police and report it stolen. Fortunately, Miranda had been making contingency plans for years, and she'd already prepared spells to take care of that problem. She could take the car and go anywhere.

As long as it was away from here.

New York. Even she could vanish among eight million people. She'd set up wards to hide her magical signature, making it tougher for Warlock to pinpoint her location. If she was careful not to use magic, she could stay hidden indefinitely.

As for their usual threat—beating Joelle—they'd have no reason to harm her mother if she wasn't around to watch.

Maybe. Miranda frowned, worrying. They were petty bastards, Warlock and the Dire Wolf who called himself her father. What if they took out their anger on Joelle?

Did Miranda have the right to save herself if her mother paid the price?

But if she didn't leave, she was setting herself up for rape and brutalization. She wasn't that big a martyr. "Get the hell out of here, Mom," Miranda said over her shoulder. "It's the only chance you've got after I'm gone. Or come with me. Either way, I'm not staying."

But before she could reach the front door, it banged open. Gerald Drake strode in and slammed it behind him. He was Changing before the door was even closed. "What the fuck have you done?" His voice deepened as he transformed, growing into a shattering roar.

She whirled on her mother. "You *called* him?"

"I had to! I . . ."

Miranda didn't hear the rest. Gerald's fist hit the side of her head like a ball-peen hammer. Hurtling through the air, she curled into a protective ball the instant before crashing through the stair handrail. Pain detonated in her back as she hit the hardwood floor in a rolling tumble. Her right arm took the brunt of the impact, and it snapped with a wet crack that blinded her with agony. She started changing before her body had even rolled to a stop, the pain triggering an instinctive transformation that healed her injuries.

Miranda could survive damn near anything her father did to her. Sometimes that wasn't a blessing.

Enough. The word blasted through her mind in a roar of Burning Moon rage. A sword materialized in her hand as if forged from her fury. Miranda bounded to her feet, healed and whole and seven feet tall, a rippling growl vibrating her red-furred chest. She lifted the blade . . .

Only to lower it as the strength drained from her arm.

Gerald Drake held her mother in a tight, vicious hold. Joelle hung there, limp, one shaking hand resting on his thick forearm. She was obviously afraid to move. And she had reason. Gerald's huge hand was wrapped around her head, the claw of his index finger a fraction of an inch from one terrified eye. "Get rid of the sword or I'll break her neck."

Miranda hesitated.

"Now!" His roar seemed to shake the house.

Defeat tasted acrid, and she could smell her own fear stink. But she could smell her mother's, too.

The sword fell from her hand.

Eva watched David stalk around her shop, examining its contents intently. Her father had acquired an extensive collection of film and comic book memorabilia over the years, and most of it was proudly displayed at the Comix Cave. There were all kinds of colorful superhero figurines in freestanding display cases, but the object that interested David most was the replica sword that hung point-down on one wall.

"May I examine this?" he asked, the third time he'd gravitated over to the big weapon.

"Sure. Just don't break anything with it." The thing was solid steel; it had been used in a sword and sorcery epic a few years back, so it was a fairly hefty prop.

David lifted it from its brackets with great care, then sighted along its length before testing its edge with a thumb. "Dull." He hefted it and swung the weapon in a circle with a twist of his wrist. "The balance is not bad. A bit gaudy, but it would make a decent practice weapon."

"It's more for looks than anything else. Dad paid a pretty penny for it several years ago. He loves stuff like that."

David grunted and fell into a crouch. His blue eyes narrowing, he surged forward into a lunge, thrusting the weapon through an imaginary opponent. Pivoting on the balls of his feet, he slashed the sword in a shining arc.

Luckily there were no customers in the store; they might have been a little alarmed. That, or awed. Eva propped her elbows on the counter and rested her chin on her hands, settling down to watch.

David went after his imaginary enemies like a professional swordsman, flipping and spinning the heavy weapon as if it weighed no more than a yardstick.

When he started sweating, he paused just long enough to tug off his knit shirt and toss it onto the counter. Before Eva could frame an objection, he was hard at work again, half-naked, sweat painting gleaming trails down his broad chest.

Fluffy started purring.

Eva had to agree. Watching the muscle work in his broad chest made her remember the way he'd felt stretched along her body, thrusting slowly, using his mouth and hands to drive her straight out of her mind.

He wheeled, revealing a set of parallel scratches down his broad back. Eva winced, remembered digging her claws in at a particularly intense moment. "Ouch. Does that hurt?"

David gave her a blank look. "What?"

"Your back. I scratched you up pretty bad."

"Ah." He grinned, broad and slow and more than a little wicked. "Feel free to wound me whenever you want."

She snorted. "That's a dangerous offer, stud."

"Sometimes danger makes a delicious spice." The grin broadened. "Even on the tastiest dishes."

Eva laughed. "Flatterer."

The bell jangled a bright note as the shop door swung open and closed. The customer stopped in his tracks, eyes going wide at the sight of the muscular, half-naked man with a sword in his hands.

"Hi, Joel," Eva said, thinking frantically. "This is David. We brought him in for a swordsmanship demonstration."

"Oh." Joel Harmon edged past David, watching in fascination as he hunted imaginary werewolves. Circling display cases or lunging down the aisles, the big man moved with a predator's silence and a bullfighter's cruel grace. His brilliant eyes were narrow, intent, and his sensualist's mouth flattened into a grim, cold line.

Beautiful killer.

Joel seemed as helplessly fascinated as she was. "He's uh . . . really good."

"Yep." Remembering last night, Eva grinned. *That's putting it mildly.* "Want your bag?"

"Yeah." Joel leaned against the counter, still watching David. The prop sword flashed as he wove thrusts and parries in response to phantom attacks, every move fast and fluid, yet utterly controlled.

Eva dragged her gaze away with an effort and pulled open a file drawer. She started flipping through bags, searching for Joel's. Most of the shop's customers maintained a "pull list" of the comics they collected, which were put aside for them every week. Once a month, they were supposed to come in and pick up those books. Being a more dedicated fanboy, Joel came in as soon as he got paid every other Thursday.

Eva slipped the comics from his bag and started scanning them, the cash register beeping as it totaled the purchases. "Is he a stuntman?" Joel asked.

"Something like that." She gave Joel a brooding glance. Even when they'd been dating, he'd given her no more than a pleasant tingle.

David damn near set her on fire.

Objectively, Joel was almost as handsome; tall, blond, and athletic, he was an assistant football coach at Ditko High. Eva had dated him until she almost bit him one night in an excess of passion. Since she'd become a werewolf from a bite, she figured that wouldn't have ended well for Joel. She'd broken off their romance the next day, much to his pained bewilderment; he'd fallen for her pretty hard. Eva regretted the situation, but she'd have regretted turning him into a werewolf even more.

David spun in the center of the shop, sweeping his blade in a figure eight that drew Eva's helpless gaze. Last night, he'd made love to her with sensuous generosity, so intent on pleasuring her, he'd seemed to read her mind. Today that kind lover had been replaced by a cool assassin, skilled, quick and merciless.

And God, he turned her on. Eva wasn't sure she liked what that said about her.

"Oh." She blinked and looked around to find Joel watching her with knowing eyes. "It's like that." There was a note of pain in his voice. "I'd hoped . . . but I guess not." His shoulders slumped.

Eva sighed and reached out to rest her hand on his. His curled possessively around her fingers. "Joel . . ."

"Who *is* this?" David appeared at Joel's elbow, his gaze narrow on the young man's face.

"Ah . . ." Oh, hell, his pupils were doing the slit thing again. And Joel, dammit, had noticed, judging by his widening eyes. "Joel Harmon, this is David . . ." Oh, damn, she hadn't invented a last name for him. ". . . Feral." Because he sure looked feral at the moment, with those cold cat-blue eyes.

"She is *my* lover, boy." A muscle ticked in his jaw. "Remove that hand before I break it."

"David!" Outraged, Eva glared at him even as Joel pulled hastily away.

"I'll . . . get my books later, Eva." Thoroughly spooked, the young man hustled out.

The minute the door jangled closed behind him, Eva exploded. "That was a customer, David! Not to mention a good friend of mine . . ."

"Yes," he said icily, "I noticed."

"You had no right! Okay, yeah, I used to sleep with him." She dropped her voice to a low hiss, in case Joel came back in. "I stopped because I'm a freaking werewolf, and I didn't want to turn *him* into a werewolf. So we're not lovers anymore, but even if we were, one night does not give you the right to threaten the poor man!"

David drew himself up to his full height, looming impressively. She was seriously tempted to turn into Fluffy so she could loom back. "If you think I will be content with one night . . ."

"You'll be content with whatever I give you! *I* decide who I sleep with!"

"Of course you do, but . . ."

She was in no mood to be placated. "I already hurt him once. Now I've hurt him again, and he doesn't deserve it!"

"He's not worthy of you." David's strong jaw jutted stubbornly. "He's a coward."

"He is not!" She gestured at his slit pupils. "You just intimidated him with the freaky eye-thing you do when you're pissed."

"Had it been me, I would not have backed down. I would have fought for you." His lids veiled a hot stare. "A woman like you is worth the risk."

Eva felt her anger deflate. *Well, hell.* What was she supposed to say to that?

His head lowered toward hers. She watched his lips as her heartbeat leaped into a gallop.

Joel Harmon started to get into his candy apple red Pontiac, only to discover his hands were shaking so hard, the keys jangled. Okay, obviously he needed time to calm down. Maybe he should grab a bite from the coffee shop and chill.

Jesus, Eva's new boyfriend had the weirdest eyes he'd ever seen. Must have been wearing some kind of contacts.

Still shaking a little, Joel walked down to Sandwiched In, three doors down the strip mall from the Comix Cave. He and Eva used to go there for lunch all the time while they were dating. The menu included a decent ham and cheese panini, but it was the caramel frappe that was his favorite guilty indulgence.

After his encounter with Eva's new boyfriend, Joel figured he owed himself a splurge. He'd run an extra couple of miles in the morning to make up for the calories.

He was waiting in line when Eva's dad walked in. Joel mentally cringed. He'd known Bill Roman since he'd started reading comics when he was nine years old. The man loved to talk, but just now, Joel wasn't in the mood.

Sure enough, Bill stepped in line behind him. "Hey, kid. How's it goin'?"

Joel pasted a smile on his face and turned. "Great. Met Eva's new boyfriend at the shop. He's really good with that sword. You definitely got your money's worth."

Bill blinked, looking honestly astonished. "Boyfriend? Since when? And . . . money?" His graying brows drew down.

Wait, he didn't know? *Way to go, Joel. Eva's gonna kill me.* "Ah . . . Well. Apparently she's dating that stuntman you hired."

"*Stuntman?*"

Oh, shit. Eva's really gonna kill me—if her new stud doesn't do it for her.

Eva had no idea how she'd ended up in David's arms. One minute she'd been screaming at him in a howling That Time of the Year rage. The next, they were playing tonsil hockey.

God, he could kiss.

One massive arm was wrapped around her, and she was plastered against every hard ridge of his powerful chest. He filled her senses with potent masculinity—his scent, his taste, his hands. He simply overwhelmed her, and she went under with a sigh.

Lost in him.

His big hands stroked away the last of her anger with tender skill. The last of her rage wafted away like a curl of smoke from a bonfire. He smelled of clean sweat and steel and a fizzing whiff of magic.

Eva had never wanted any man so much.

So of course, cue Daddy.

SIX

The door jingled a manic note before banging shut loud enough to make Eva jump. "What the hell is going on?" her father roared.

Eva tore out of David's arms as though he'd scalded her. She met Bill Roman's hot gaze and felt a furious blush roll to her hairline. "Uh . . . Hi, Dad."

He stalked toward them, his muscular shoulders tense with under the black fabric of his Batman T-shirt. "This is the stuntman 'we' hired?"

"I guess you ran into Joel." Eva smiled weakly.

"Who *are* you?" One scalding look took in David's long black hair and bare, sweating chest. "And what the hell are you doing kissing my daughter?"

"I am David." He straightened, stepping a bit in front of her as if to protect her from her father's anger.

"You got a last name, *David*?"

For a moment, Eva's mind went completely blank as she struggled to remember what she'd told Joel. "Feral! His name is David Feral."

Bill shot her a cold look. "What, he can't speak for himself?"

"I can speak." David studied her father, eyes narrowed.

"How long have you known my daughter?"

"Since yesterday."

Bill rocked back on his heels in surprise. "And you're already kissing her like *that*?"

Fluffy promptly started snarling. "Wait a minute, Dad. How is that any of your business? In case you haven't noticed, I'm not sixteen anymore."

Bill ignored her, staring hard into David's face. "Are you wearing some kind of contacts, or what?"

Oh, hell, this situation was skidding right off the cliff. "Look, David, would you mind taking a walk and letting me discuss this with my father?"

He gave her a little dip of his head. "Of course." Still carrying the sword, he walked out, shirtless.

"What the hell is going on?" her father exploded. "Who is that guy? Where'd he come from?"

Eva rubbed the ache throbbing between her eyebrows and wondered how she was going to talk her way out of this one.

It went against the grain to leave Eva to confront her father alone, but David knew anything he said would only inflame the situation. Apparently Bill Roman did not know his daughter was a werewolf, so she would have to lie to explain how they'd met. Any lies of his could inadvertently contradict hers.

He strode down the sidewalk away from the shop, just walking, taking in the surrounding neighborhood—shops, a few houses, a car or two cruising past in a cloud of fumes that made his nose wrinkle. The sun was just disappearing behind the trees, edging the purpling clouds in blood red. David absently played with the dull sword, rotating his wrist to spin it as he walked and brooded.

It galled him, having to lean so heavily on a woman for his very survival. He should be the one supporting her. Instead, he was only making her life more difficult.

Perhaps he should leave. Get out of her life and find some way to support himself until his memory returned.

Assuming it did. If it didn't . . .

Well, even if he had no past, he did have a present—and a future he would have to deal with. He . . .

David froze as a terrible awareness suddenly rolled over him.

His enemy. Suddenly he could feel the other like an intense pressure crushing down on his skull, all black power and malevolence.

And if he could sense his enemy . . .

David whirled and ran back toward the shop. He had to get Eva and her father to safety—whether they liked it or not.

The squirrel raced up the tree trunk in a panic, its furry little legs a blur of effort.

For all the good it did.

The laser-thin bolt of magic hit the tiny creature right in one beady eye. It tumbled off the tree and hit the ground, a charred corpse.

Warlock pivoted, drew a bead on a robin sitting in frozen terror, and blasted it, too. The tiny blackened body hit the leafy forest floor with a papery rustle.

The Dire Wolf grunted, dissatisfied. He was making progress, but not fast enough to suit him. He scented a rabbit, and turned. The animal broke from cover, moving in desperate bounds.

He drilled it through the skull in mid-leap. It went down, its fur still soft and gray, no visible injury to explain its death.

Better. Much better.

A familiar presence burst into his consciousness, and he froze in blind instinct and an instant's fear.

Smoke. Gods and devils!

Then realization kicked in, and he knew he had only seconds. He cast the location spell with a flick of his clawed fingers. An instant later, he had pinpointed the Demigod's location.

A slight, cold smile curved his thin black lips, and he reached out to Skoll team.

He had the bastard now.

We met through one of those online dating sites," Eva told her father, her mind working frantically. "David's a movie stuntman specializing in swordplay. Flew in yesterday to meet me. I didn't want to leave him alone all day, so I brought him in to work. He was just showing me his latest choreography . . ."

"With his mouth?" Her father folded his beefy arms and glowered.

"And like I said, that really isn't any of your business." A bead of sweat rolled down her back, itching furiously. She ground her teeth and ignored it.

"This guy could be some kind of psycho for all you know. People have ended up murdered by men they met online."

"The site makes everybody pass a background check." Eva hated lying to her father. He knew her too well. They'd always been close, even during her rebellious teenage years when she and her mother had fought like two cats in a very small sack.

"I just don't understand why you never mentioned this guy. Not even to your mother. I called her, and she didn't know a damn thing about him either." Was that a hint of hurt in his hazel eyes?

She winced. "Well, at first, I wasn't sure it was going to work. But now I am. I was planning to introduce you today, but Joel came in and . . ."

"Another thing—isn't this guy awfully damned possessive for somebody you met online?" Bill leaned one brawny forearm on the shop counter, worry in his eyes. "And he's a big guy. What if he turns out to be some kind of nutball? You could find yourself in real trouble."

"He's not like that." She put a hand on her father's shoulder and gave him her best earnest look. "Dad, trust me. It's going to be fine."

Bill glowered at her for another long moment before he sighed, his expression turning resigned. "You're a grown woman, Eva, so I can't tell you how to run your love life." His gaze sharpened. "But if he gives you any trouble, let me know and I'll kick his ass."

And he would, too. Or he'd try, anyway. Smiling, Eva stood on her toes to kiss his bearded cheek. "I won't have to. He's a good guy, Dad."

Bill grunted. "Tell him to put on a shirt, would you? He's scaring the customers."

Eva was just about to ease her father out the door when it banged open with a furious jangle. She and Bill took a step back as David barged through, the prop sword in one hand, his expression grim. "My enemy has sensed me. We must go."

Dad gave him the kind of wary look reserved for people in tinfoil hats. Eva wanted to smack David upside his oblivious head. All her hard work, undone with one loony-tunes sentence. "Enemy? What the hell are you talking about?" Bill snapped.

"There is no time for explanations." He clamped his left hand over her father's shoulder, pivoted, and started pushing the smaller man out the door, still carrying the prop sword in his right. The bell jangled a discordant note as the door hit the back wall. "We must go *now*."

"Dammit, I'm not going anywhere. This is *my shop*." Bill tried to set his feet, but David switched his grip to his upper arm and hoisted, forcing him to walk on his toes or be carried. "Cut it out! That hurts. Are you nuts?"

"Where is his vehicle?" David demanded.

Eva stared at him, alarm streaking through her irritation. If the white werewolf really was on the way, David was right. They had to get the hell away from the area as fast as possible.

She pointed over Bill's thick shoulder toward the line of cars parked nose to the curb. "That red Tahoe. Dad, it would probably be best if we left."

"Screw that." He glared at them both. "You and your pet nutjob can leave if you want. I'm not going anywhere."

* * *

In the living room of a seedy little house on the outskirts of Chicago, two Dire Wolves circled, lips peeled back from teeth, growls rumbling. They were in full wolf form, big as ponies, one charcoal gray with white markings, the other red as a fox's fur. As if obeying some inner signal, they exploded toward each other in a chorus of snarls and snaps. The gray's fangs sank into the red-furred one's flank, and the big beast yelped.

Blood flew, splashing across the sketch Tom Danvers was studying. "Goddammit! Cut that shit out! I'm trying to work here."

The two wolves froze, wide eyes flying guiltily to Danvers as he glared at them. They immediately separated, the gray tearing his fangs from the flank of the other as they slunk in opposite directions, heads down, tails low. The two headed up the stairs to the den, claws clicking on the wooden steps. One beast nosed the door open, and they slipped out. It closed behind them again with a quiet click, leaving the basement in silence.

Danvers watched them go with grim satisfaction. Three months ago, he'd have had to Change and rip into them, but he'd successfully established who was in charge.

"Fuckin' idiots," Steve Miller muttered from the other side of the battered Ping-Pong table. A sixty-watt bulb hung over his head, casting his craggy face in deep shadows. The smoke from his cigarette floated in a lazy blue haze over the cinder-block room.

"Yeah." Danvers returned his attention to the sketch he'd drawn after casing FBW Savings and Loan that afternoon. He tapped the door he'd drawn in rough, slashing lines. "You, me, and Frank will go in here. Jim'll be in the Hummer outside. The tellers will cave right in when they see the shotguns . . ."

Miller's eyes gleamed, yellow and cold. "'Specially if we shoot one of 'em first."

"Right. We'll . . ." He jerked up from the schematic as his Direkind senses detected a burst of magic. "Oh, fuck."

Warlock stepped through the dimensional gate, eight feet of white fur and gleaming black claws. They had never seen him in human form. Tom wasn't sure he had one. "Go to your vehicles and prepare to gate out. I've found the cat."

Hiding his irritation—Warlock's idea of discipline was even bloodier than his own—Danvers tossed the pencil on the table and reached for his keys.

Eva looked into her father's irritated hazel eyes, knowing she'd better talk fast. Preferably with at least a kernel of truth. "David and I had a little run-in with Ronnie Gordon last night. He'd beaten the heck out of Shelly and hit Terry a couple of times. Terry came banging on the door in hysterics, so David and I went over there. Ronnie pulled a gun on us, but David backed him down."

"And he's on the way now," David said, right on cue. "He is armed. He seeks revenge."

Bill gave him a long, cool look before transferring it to Eva. "Who writes your boyfriend's dialog? I used to play Dungeons and Dragons with a guy who talked just like that."

"He's getting in character for a movie role. *Please*, Dad. Mom would kill me if I got you shot."

Bill lowered his head like a bull. "I am not running from Ronnie Gordon. He needs his ass kicked."

"Dad, you are *not* faster than a speeding bullet." Eva hauled the Tahoe's door open. The dome light came on, spilling light over the darkening parking lot. "Look, you can pound Ronnie when he's not armed to the teeth. Right now, go home."

David lifted his head and looked across the street. With a mutter that sounded like some exotic curse, he literally lifted her father off his feet and stuffed him into the Jeep.

"Dammit, *get off*!" Going red, Bill plowed a fist right into David's face with a crack of bone on bone.

Eva's heart catapulted into her throat. *Oh, holy God, that tears it . . .*

David's head didn't even rock. He lowered his head, the

better to subject Bill to a long, cool stare from his six-five height. "Do you really want your daughter in the line of fire? Because we both know she will not leave you."

Bill's rage-narrowed eyes widened as the shot struck home. He glowered at David as Eva held her breath. Finally he threw up his hands. "Fine. I'm gone. Take her and get out of here. I'll deal with that bastard later." He threw the Jeep into gear as Eva slammed the driver's door with a grunt of relief. The Tahoe's big tires screeched as he backed up and tore out of the parking lot, almost hitting a pair of motorcycles and a Hummer.

"Oh, man." Eva shook her head as she watched the Tahoe's taillights disappear up the street. "I hope that doesn't blow up in our faces. I think Ronnie's still in the county jail."

"Your father is the least of our worries." He jerked his chin toward the Harley-Davidson motorcycles and the Hummer. All three vehicles had pulled over onto the side of the road. A street lamp illuminated the motorcyclists as they dismounted. Two others piled out of the Hummer. "Those men smell like were."

He was right. The scent of werewolf rode the cool night breeze: fur and magic and a trace of old blood. *Claws, ripping into her guts, fanged jaws opening over her face, dripping hot saliva, the flash of yellow eyes . . .*

"In the car!" Big hands closed over her shoulders. She cried out in terror, swinging wildly, but a fierce shake snapped her out of the flashback. "We don't have time for that. Get in the car!" David snarled, jerking the driver's door open and bundling her inside. "Drive!"

He vaulted over the hood in one astonishing leap, jerked the passenger door open, tossed the blunt sword inside, and dove after it even as Eva started the car and threw it into reverse. She stomped the accelerator and sent the Focus shooting backward, tires squealing, forcing the two big men directly behind it to scatter. As she put the car in drive, she saw all four race across the parking lot after them. She floored it.

Brakes squealed and a horn blared as the little Focus

shot into traffic. Eva spun the wheel, narrowly avoiding a head-on collision with a Toyota. Somehow she got the car into the proper lane and floored it again. "Fasten your seat belt, David!" With one hand, she hauled her own belt out and fumbled until it snapped home.

Darting a glance into the rearview mirror, Eva saw the four werewolves racing for the Hummer and their Harleys. They were still in human form, but she knew that wouldn't last. And once they changed . . .

"You're panicking," David growled. "Calm down and drive."

Eva jolted, hearing herself chanting, "Fuck fuck fuck fuck fuck," in a mindless stream of profanity. She clamped her teeth shut and concentrated on dragging every possible ounce of speed out of the laboring Ford. Spotting a side street, she whipped down it, then took another left, then a right, glancing in the rearview mirror every few minutes as she drove, in the blind hope she'd shake the wolves.

The two Harleys stayed stubbornly on her tail, their headlights bright in her mirror, the Hummer roaring after, its lights riding higher. If she couldn't lose them . . .

Fangs ripped into her belly. Blood sprayed. Hot, bright agony. Oh, Christ, Oh, Jesus, he's eating me . . . !

"Eva!" David's roar snapped her back to full awareness just as the car's right tires left the road, bumping over the thick grass of the shoulder. She jerked the wheel, overcorrected, and almost ran off the road on the left. Somehow she got the car back under control and tromped the accelerator again.

Fighting terror, she blindly took turn after turn along the narrow county roads, trying to lose their pursuers. Yet the two bikes stayed stubbornly on her tail, hanging back just far enough not to lose sight of the Focus, sometimes whipping into oncoming traffic despite blaring horns and swerving cars.

Dammit, where the hell were the cops? She'd be happy to get a ticket, if only a set of blue lights would show up to force those furry bastards to back off.

Swallowing bile, she jerked the wheel for another

tire-shrieking turn, ran a stop sign, and ignored the furious blare of a horn. "Call the fucking cops!" she spat at her rearview mirror.

Which wasn't a bad idea, if only her cell phone wasn't buried somewhere in her purse. Which was God knew where. Had she even put it in the car, or had she driven off without it? She'd be lucky if some jerk didn't make off with her bank cards . . .

I'll be lucky if one of those damned werewolves doesn't eat me.

"They're getting closer." David sat sideways in his seat as he calmly watched their pursuit.

"I know that!" The steering wheel creaked in her frantic grip, and she loosened her hold, afraid she'd break it in a burst of terror-fueled werewolf strength. Her mouth tasted brassy, and her heart felt as if it were trying to pound its way out of her chest. She swallowed hard. *You're going to get David killed if you don't get it together.*

The thought hit her like a slap, stiffening her spine, narrowing her widened eyes. *I am not going to get David killed.*

An image flashed through her mind: David, braced over her on sweating, muscled arms, his gorgeous eyes lost and blue as he filled her so impossibly full with those long, delicious strokes.

Her beautiful lover. She set her teeth. *He's not going to die today. Not because I lost it and turned into a werewolf in the fucking car.*

She whipped the Ford into another turn. This time her hands were controlled and sure on the wheel. Spotting another turn, she took it.

Eva cursed. The road stretched before her, a straight shot, moonlit fields and woods to either side. And not another turnoff to be seen.

David lifted his blunt sword. "They're going to catch us."

She flicked a glance toward the rearview mirror—and saw the Hummer's headlights filling it. "Shit!" Eva stomped harder on the gas, but the accelerator was already floored, the engine whining as it labored for more speed.

The Hummer hit the Focus's bumper on one side in a precisely controlled bump. Eva felt the wheel jerk out of her hands. Heart in her throat, she grabbed for it and fought it with all her strength as the car spun out.

The Focus rammed the ditch in a crunching crash of metal and a furious pop of deploying air bags. The back end of the car lifted as the hood crumpled. Eva yelped in pain as her body hit the unyielding seat belt and the air bag smacked her nose.

"Out!" David roared, shouldering the passenger door open before the car had even jolted to a complete stop. "Get out and run!"

Eva clawed at the belt, managed to unlock it. The driver's door jerked open, startling her into a scream, but it was David. One big tanned hand grabbed hers and pulled her out of the car. "Run!" he gritted, giving her a shove toward the woods that lay across an expanse of kudzu-covered field.

"'Fraid it's a bit late for that." The voice sounded unnaturally deep, rasping, more growl than anything else. Eva spun.

Four werewolves moved toward them, muscular and obviously male. They'd already transformed, and they were all well over eight feet tall. Which made them considerably bigger than she was.

The biggest of the four rumbled speech again. "If you surrender quietly, Cat, we'll let the girl live."

But the others grinned at her, eyes glowing yellow, reflecting the wrecked car's taillights. One of them had a hard-on that jutted from his furry groin.

Magic rolled over Eva before she was consciously aware she'd called it, a hot, tingling wave that sheered rapidly into agony. Her clothing simply vanished as it always did, bone and muscle twisting, jerking, fur rushing across her skin in an itching tide. It was all she could do not to scream.

David opened his mouth to snarl what he thought of the werewolf's offer of quarter. An offer he might have accepted for Eva's sake, had it not been so obviously a lie.

He was going to kill the one with the erection first.

But before he could step forward with his useless, blunted sword, Eva seemed to explode in a magical detonation. One minute she was lovely and a little dazed and very, very terrified. When the light faded an instant later, she towered next to him, seven feet of glossy sable fur, fangs, and curving claws. Her hair had become a lovely mane that fell to her shoulders, while a sleek pelt covered the rest of her body. Her face had lengthened and contorted into a wolflike muzzle, and she stood on two legs that curved backward, more like those of a wolf than a human's. She snarled at the werewolves and spoke, her voice startlingly deep and savage. "Fuck. You!"

Yet despite the intimidating length of her fangs, he could feel her terror, scent it flooding the air, bitter and acrid.

And the werewolves laughed.

It was an ugly sound, edged in a whipping chain-saw snarl. Studying them, David realized they were much bigger than Eva, even after her magical transformation. Muscle bulked beneath thick fur, and three-inch claws tipped their big hands. Judging from the grins on their fanged faces, they smelled Eva's terror as clearly as he did.

And it amused them.

"What a pussy," a hulking ginger wolf said to their evident leader. "She's about to piss herself."

The leader shrugged powerful shoulders covered in a honey brown ruff. "She's female." To David, he added, "Looks like she won't be much protection, Cat. Might as well surrender now. I may not be in the mood to be so nice later."

Eva's snarl broke off, and she seemed to shrink from their mocking laughter.

Protective rage screamed over David's mind, so hot and intense his consciousness went white. He heard a sound in his mind, a furious roar, coming closer, growing louder, until it plowed into him like a physical thing that rocked him on his feet.

Power blazed down his arm and into the blunt sword, igniting a blaze of golden light that raced along the blade from hilt to point, sharpening the weapon to a razor edge. The roar exploded from his lips as he swung the weapon up and leaped, an impossible bound that surprised even him as he cleared the ten feet to the dark-furred werewolf with the erection.

His sword arced downward. The werewolf threw up a hand to knock away the blade.

The sword cleaved the clawed fingers off the werewolf's hand and buried itself in a thick, furred shoulder. He howled, more in horrified astonishment than agony.

David hit the ground like the cat they'd called him, ripping the blade out of the werewolf's body as the monster staggered backward. The werewolf grabbed his maimed, bleeding hand with his whole one. "You son of a—!"

David spun, whipping his sword around in a furious stroke that cleaved through the werewolf's neck. The creature's head went flying, body keeling over to land in a heap of slack, furry limbs.

"Shit!" yelled one of the surviving werewolves, a cry as much of astonishment as of rage.

The leader's lips peeled back from long yellow fangs, and his eyes flashed red in the darkness. "You're going to die for that, fucker."

And they charged.

SEVEN

Eva watched in frozen disbelief as David roared a battle cry and slammed into the werewolves, his sword carving flesh, sending one wolf reeling back with a howl of pain. But another lunged for his throat, jaws snapping in vicious, toothy clicks.

David ducked, dropping to one knee to shove his sword right through his attacker's black-furred belly. The monster reeled back as David jerked the blade out and attacked the leader, forcing the big werewolf into an incredible upward leap to avoid the lethal stroke.

The one David had gutted transformed in a flash of light, becoming a four-legged wolf the size of a black bear. The gut wound disappeared with the change. Eva blinked in astonishment. Despite the dream she'd shared with David, she hadn't known becoming a *wolf*-wolf was really possible. She stored the idea away to try later.

Assuming there was a later.

Right now, she had to get her paralyzed body moving before those bastards turned David into Puppy Chow. The shame of their laughter stung, but even that wasn't enough to break the paralysis.

Then the four-legged wolf lunged at David, jaws wide, obviously intending to hamstring him.

Eva's paralysis snapped like a guitar string, and she charged.

David leaped away from the snapping teeth as Eva reached down, grabbed the wolf by the scruff, jerked him up, and flung him twenty feet through the air as he yipped like a puppy.

I probably should have eaten him, she thought, watching him sail into the moonlit kudzu. *Nah. I'd just get hair balls.*

"You should have stayed out of it, bitch."

She turned to see the leader swinging three-inch claws at her face.

Warlock had been pacing his lab when it hit—a wave of weakness that cut his legs out from under him and knocked him to all fours.

He blinked at a line of gleaming silver cutting across the gray stone of the floor. It took his dazed mind far too long to realize it was part of the silver spell circle inlaid on the tiles.

Something's wrong with me. The thought felt fuzzy, as weak as the arms and legs that shook under him in wracking shudders. Finally dazed realization slid through his crippled mind. *Smoke's done it again. The bastard's draining me.*

Warlock shook his head hard, fighting the effect, trying to clear his thoughts enough to cast a spell to drag the power back. Yet his mind remained clouded, and he felt a stab of fear.

The fear instantly triggered a flash of rage that cleared the fog from his mind. He didn't *do* fear. Other people feared him.

Big hands curled until his claws cut his palms. *I'm going to kill that God-cursed Cat.*

Eva jerked back, but she wasn't quite fast enough. The leader's claws raked her muzzle, and she yelped at the blinding pain. She jumped backward, hooked a heel on a jutting stick, and fell flat on her ass. He laughed, a sound more bark than humor, and leaped, claws lifted to disembowel. Her mind gibbered in panic as she remembered the ripping scarlet agony of her rapist's attack. *Oh, God, not again!*

The werewolf was still in midair when David slammed into his side like an NFL lineman sacking a quarterback. The force of the tackle drove the huge werewolf sideways so that he slammed into the ground beside Eva instead of on top of her. The leader yowled, half rage, half pain.

David bounded to his feet, jerking up something bright red that flung drops of blood into the air. He chopped downward with it over and over like a berserk Iron Chef. Eva realized the red thing was the prop sword.

That damned sword didn't even have an edge. How the hell was he killing werewolves with it?

Eva rolled to her feet, staring with sick horror as he minced the leader of the assassins into hamburger. A line from *The Wizard of Oz* shot through her mind, paraphrased in a flash of lunatic humor: *"He's really most sincerely dead."* The werewolf's head was no longer even attached, but David kept right on hacking, bared teeth and wide eyes shining white from the twisted mask of red that was his blood-covered face.

She'd read *Wolverine* often enough to know a berserker rage when she saw one.

A sound snapped her head around. The last of the werewolves bounded for David's unprotected back in a streak of ginger fur, stiletto fangs gleaming in the moonlight, claws reaching.

Eva didn't even think. She stepped into the werewolf's path and swung both fists into the right side of his head like A-Rod going for a homer. Something cracked, and the werewolf flew backward. She hissed as pain radiated from her abused hands all the way to her shoulders.

The assassin landed in the kudzu with a crackling crash. He didn't get up. Eva blinked at the clump of broken vegetation. *Did I do that?*

"Wow," she whispered in astonishment. "I hit him."

Not only had she hit him, she'd knocked him fifteen feet. And since he had to weigh a good four or five hundred pounds—most of it claws—that was saying something.

I didn't even know I was that strong.

Warily, she crept closer, afraid he was faking it. She really didn't want him to explode out of the kudzu and carve her into sushi.

There was no sound except a steady *drip drip drip* coming from God only knew where.

One step. Two.

Heart in her throat, Eva rose on her clawed toes and craned her neck until she could look down into the big green leaves, at the fallen monster.

Well, he definitely ain't faking that.

The werewolf lay in a boneless heap, head flopped over at a thoroughly unnatural angle. She'd snapped his neck like a breadstick.

Eva swallowed hard and dragged her eyes away before her lunch could hit escape velocity.

Plop. Plop. Rustle.

"AHHHH!" She jerked around, her heart catapulting into her throat. She sighed in relief as she recognized the source of the noise.

It was only David, walking toward her with the bloody sword, his eyes fixed on her, glowing blue, catlike and intent in the dark.

He slipped silently closer. Suddenly Eva thought of Snowball, the neighbor's cat, who often crept up on unsuspecting birds wearing an identical murderous gleam.

Which was when she realized David had just killed three werewolves in a berserker rage.

And she was a werewolf.

Oh, shit. He doesn't know who I am.

"David, it's me!" Holding up both hands in a warding gesture, she shrank backward. "It's Eva!" But even as she spoke, she noticed her werewolf voice rumbled a full octave lower than her human voice. No wonder he didn't know who the hell she was.

David lifted the sword and took another step closer. He was six inches shorter than she was in werewolf form, but he was also covered in blood and wearing an expression that reminded her of Mel Gibson killing people in way too many movies.

Eva knew she could hit him upside the head—which had worked once today, but was likely to end really badly no matter what—or she could grow a pair of ovaries and take a really big chance.

Blue eyes glittered. The sword lifted, ready to swing.

Eva grabbed for the magic and *changed*.

When the blue glow faded, her jeans and T-shirt had returned from wherever they went when she shifted. And she was looking up at David, who loomed over her with that big blade dripping blood. She tried to square her shoulders and meet his gaze with the fearless courage of Lois Lane staring down Lex Luthor.

Unfortunately, a cowardly squeak emerged from her lips and blew the whole effect.

He blinked. Took a step back and lowered the sword, looking confused.

She gave him a broad, totally unnatural smile. "It's me, David. It's Eva." Voice dropping, she added on a mutter, "*Please* don't chop me into teeny tiny bits."

He blinked again and frowned, as if coming back to himself from a very long way away. "They were going to kill you." His voice growled around the consonants in a way that didn't sound like him at all.

"But you stopped them, didn't you?" *Boy, did you. The coroner won't even know what species they are. Good thing, too. Werewolves on the front page would be bad.*

David's gaze turned catlike and intent again, but this time his mood was visibly more horny than homicidal. He reached for her.

"If you kiss me covered in blood," she informed him with brutal honesty, "I'm going to yark on your shoes."

David froze. His face worked, expressions flashing over it too fast for her to be entirely sure what they were.

And he . . . *changed*. His shoulders drew back, his head

came up, and something shifted in his eyes. He blinked, a long, slow drop and rise of his lids, and when he met her gaze, something new looked out of his eyes. Something ancient and intelligent she didn't recognize.

"Well. We can't have that, can we?" He made an intricate, graceful gesture with the hand that wasn't holding the sword. Sparks shimmered above his head, spiraling down his body in a glittering double helix. When the glow vanished, so did the blood. His clothes were wrinkle-free, as if freshly laundered, and his hair lay smooth and dark over his broad shoulders, clean enough to gleam in the moonlight. Even his formerly gory sword was bright and shining again.

Eva blinked in astonishment. "David, how the hell did you do that?"

He shrugged. "Magic. But my name isn't David. I'm Smoke."

"You've regained your memory?" Eva frowned, surprised at her sinking heart. This should be good news. Why did it feel like a disaster?

"For the moment." He cocked his dark head, studying her with that alien intelligence that made her skin creep. It was as if he'd been possessed by something very, very old.

And not human at all.

"What do you mean, 'For the moment'? You think you'll forget again?"

"If Warlock has anything to say about it. Which unfortunately, he does." Turning, he moved away to crouch over one of the butchered bodies. The feral bloodlust was gone from his face, replaced by a clinical interest. Definitely not the man she knew.

But whoever he was, he was scary as hell.

He rose and circled the bodies, studying them, head cocked. "Warlock isn't here."

"Uh—Warlock?" She watched as he sank onto his haunches to examine a particularly mangled corpse, breathing deep as if seeking the man's scent. He didn't even move like David. There was something animal about the way he held his head and placed his feet, something more tiger than man. "Who's Warlock?"

"The Dire Wolf who tried to steal my magic and memories."

"Dire Wolf?"

"That's what they're called. That's what you are. Except unlike the rest of you, Warlock is a sorcerer. He attempted to strip me of my powers." He glanced up at her, teeth flashing in a snarling smile. "So I rammed it all down his throat and tried to choke him with it." Broad shoulders rose and fell in a shrug. "I did not quite succeed, but at least I escaped. Or rather, most of me did."

Realization dawned. "You're talking about when I found you—when you fought that big white werewolf—Warlock?"

David—Smoke—nodded. "He wishes to become a god to his people. Fool. There is more weight than worship in being a god. And I would know."

She swallowed. "You're a god?" *Oh, great. Time to fit Dave for a tinfoil hat.*

"Not anymore."

What the hell does that mean? "Ummm. Not *anymore*?"

The blue gaze went distant. "Once I was. Many, many years ago. I do not remember how many centuries gone. After a thousand years or so, even such dark memories dim." Rising to his feet, he started across the field in the direction of their wrecked car. "We must leave. Warlock will try to steal my powers again, and I don't have the strength to stop him. He's kept just enough of what he has taken to bar me from taking my power back." A muscle flexed in his angular jaw as if he ground his teeth. "But he won't keep it long. And he will regret the theft."

Centuries? Did he say centuries? Eva hurried after the stranger in her lover's body. "Look, what exactly are you? And what happened to David?"

He looked around at her in surprise. "I am David."

"No. No, you're really not."

Smoke started to speak, then closed his mouth and shook his head. "No, I suppose as far as you're concerned, I'm not."

"Then what the hell are you?"

He hesitated a moment even as he lengthened his stride until she had to run to keep up. "That would take entirely too long to explain, and we must get out of here *now*."

Eva jolted to a halt in the knee-high kudzu, eyeing her poor Ford Focus in dismay. "We're not going anywhere in *that* car."

Her baby had gone into the ditch at an angle, hard enough to crumple its front end like a crushed beer can. The right front wheel was bent completely under the body, and the vehicle tilted as it sat nose-down so the left rear wheel was completely off the ground. Looking through the shattered windshield, Eva saw the limp white shapes of both deployed air bags. "It's totaled." She felt sick, thinking of her thousand-dollar deductible. Managing that and the rent this month was going to be a bitch. "I'll have to call a wrecker and have it towed."

"Warlock will be here before the wrecker arrives." Smoke handed her the sword and stepped into the ditch.

Biting her lip, Eva eyed the werewolves' vehicles. None of them were damaged at all, though she couldn't imagine herself playing Hell's Angels on one of those big hogs. As for Smoke/David—who the hell knew what he could do? "We could take the Hummer. Bet Wolfie left the keys in the ignition."

Smoke shot her an impatient look. "Do you really want the police to find you driving a vehicle whose owner has been chopped into very bloody pieces?" He shook his head. "The cat outdid himself. He's quite protective of you."

Puzzled, Eva frowned. "What cat?"

"Our third spirit brother." He bent, hooked his hands under the car, and heaved upward, jerking the Ford's front end out of the ditch with a grunt of effort.

Damn, Eva thought in stunned astonishment, *I'm sleeping with Superman.*

Smoke dropped the crumpled front end of the wrecked car on the shoulder with a grinding crash.

"Wow." Eva took a step back as he scrambled out of the ditch. "That was damned impressive, but the car's still not going anywhere. Not in the shape it's in."

"Patience, child. I'm not finished." Smoke grimaced as he put a hand to the small of his back, arching his spine and rolling his shoulders. "Gods and devils, I think I pulled something. Feh. Well, I'll heal it later. If there's time."

He set his feet apart and closed his eyes, bowing his head. His dark hair tumbled forward.

"What are you doing? And who are you calling a child?"

"Shush." When he raised his head again, his eyes glowed a blue so bright, they lit his face like torches. His hands lifted. Blazing power poured from his palms. The magic made Eva's skin tingle and warm, as if she was standing too close to a roaring fire. Instinctively, she took a step back as the glow engulfed her battered Ford, winding around it in a blinding double helix that grew brighter and brighter. She smelled ozone and heating metal, heard a grinding pop and the tinkle of glass.

Smoke let his hands fall in an abrupt gesture, and the blinding glare faded.

"Hot damn," Eva muttered when she could see again.

The car sat on all four wheels, looking as if it had just rolled off the showroom floor, its chrome glittering in the moonlight. Not so much as a ding marred its paint job.

Awed, she walked the length of it, running her fingers along its cool metal skin. Not only had Smoke repaired the Hummer damage, he'd fixed the dent in the front door inflicted by an errant shopping cart. Even the scrapes from her run-in with a concrete pylon a year ago had disappeared. The car hadn't looked this good when she'd bought it. "Damn." Eva turned to grin at him. "It looks . . ."

Smoke's face was white as paper and streaming sweat. He swayed like a man fighting a gale, his hands shaking as he lowered them to his side.

"Oh, hell." She dropped the sword and dove for him. She barely managed to catch his shoulders before his knees buckled.

"No, you bastard." Warlock's lips curled back from his teeth. "The power's *mine* now. You don't get it back."

He knelt in the center of the silver spell circle, both hands fisted on the grip of a massive battle-axe planted butt-down on the stone floor. Lips curling back from his fangs, he stared into the great red gem that tipped the shaft between massive double blades. The stone, responding to his will, blazed a sullen crimson, the glow burning its way along the deep runes engraved in the alien steel.

Arthur had Excalibur. Warlock had Kingslayer.

Kingslayer's gem could act as a focus for his power, amplifying it as a ruby intensifies light into a laser. Kingslayer was Warlock's most powerful weapon, and he guarded it jealously. No one living even knew of its existence, not even the core leaders of the Chosen. He had not used it in decades. Hadn't needed to.

Panting with effort, Warlock stared into the heart of the gem, seeking the bright cord of magic that stretched tight between him and the godling. He could feel Smoke fighting him, trying to drag the power away, to steal it back into himself, reassemble his fractured mind.

Too bad, Cat, he thought, gritting his teeth and tightening his psychic grip. *It's mine now.*

Gathering all his power, Warlock blasted mind and magic through the stone, sending it ripping into Smoke's wounded consciousness. He heard a short, psychic howl that suddenly cut off.

And he smiled.

The new magical cage Warlock had conjured with his axe was much stronger. Strong enough to separate Smoke's power from his memories and the fragments of his godling's soul.

He wouldn't escape again. And once his body was dead, the elemental's rebellion would be over.

Forever.

"Arrrrrrrghhhhh!" Smoke's powerful back arched as he screamed, his arms flinging wide, hands clawing at empty air.

"David!" Eva fought to support his writhing body. If

not for her supernatural strength, she'd have gone down with him in a heap. As it was, she barely managed to hang on to him as she dropped to her knees, cradling his head and shoulders in her arms. His eyes squeezed shut, his lips pulled back from gritted teeth as he twisted in her grip like a man tortured. His face gleamed with sweat, and she could feel his heart slamming in his chest. "David, what's happening? David!"

As suddenly as he'd begun to convulse, he collapsed, his body going boneless in her arms.

A dead weight.

Her heart jammed her throat until she saw the rise and fall of his chest. She put her ear to his sternum and listened with desperate attention.

Yes, his heart still beat. It was slowing down, which was probably a good thing, considering it had sounded as if it was about to burst from his rib cage a moment ago.

She sat up again, licking dry lips. "David?"

A long tense moment passed. Finally he stirred, a frown line forming between his thick dark brows.

"David, we need to get out of here. That Warlock guy you were talking about . . ."

His eyes flared wide at the name, rage hot white in their depths, pupils tightening into ovals in the moonlight. His lips peeled back, revealing fangs, and he growled, a low, savage sound. His alien gaze met hers, burning blue.

Who the hell is he now? Eva thought, staring at him in sick despair. *That's not Smoke, and it's sure not David.*

Wait. Smoke had said something about a cat—*"The cat outdid himself. He's quite protective of you."*

So he had multiple personalities now? David, Smoke, and this "cat."

And where in the name of God and little fishes did Warlock fit into this mess?

Reminded that they needed to get the hell away, she braced her hands under David/Smoke/Cat's shoulders and pushed him into a sitting position. Thank God for werewolf strength. "Listen, Fang, we've got to get the hell out of Dodge. Smoke said Warlock's coming." And how weird was it, to tell him something he'd just told her as if he was somebody completely different? But he was, so she was just going to have to deal.

Shouldn't be too hard. She'd been breaking the laws of common sense for years now.

"Warlock?" His voice rumbled, even deeper than normal.

"You can talk? Good. Yeah, Warlock. In the car, Fang."

And he was out of her arms and on his feet, fluid and fast. He put down a hand, caught hers, and pulled her up. By the time Eva found the sword she'd dropped when his convulsions began, he was in the passenger seat.

Well, at least he's obedient. Now if we can only get out of here before Warlock shows up. She tossed the sword on the backseat, then slid into the driver's side and buckled her seat belt out of pure habit. "Buckle up, Fang. The sooner we're away from here, the better. There's way too many dead people here."

Fang obeyed without fumbling and settled back in the seat as Eva started the car. The Ford ran more smoothly than it had in years.

"I killed our enemies." His growling voice barely sounded like the same man at all.

"I got one, too, but yeah." Looking back over her shoulder, Eva pulled into the empty road. Now if only she could figure out where the hell she was and how to get home. It was really time to spring for a GPS.

"What happened when I left you?" Fang asked.

"This guy, god, whatever . . ."

"His name is Smoke."

"Right. Smoke . . . umm, came out"—*just in time to keep you from dicing me into a Bloomin' Onion*—"and fixed the car. He said Warlock was coming, and then he fell over and went into convulsions. Do you know what happened?"

"Warlock happened." Fang flexed his big hands on his jeans-clad knees like a cat kneading a cushion. "Warlock stole our powers. And a good portion of the god. All that is left is the Sidhe and me, and we are in pieces. Too many pieces. Too scattered. We cannot"—he drew spread fingers into a fist—"connect."

"She? She who?" God, was there another one? A girl? *Shit.* Because the lesbian thing was *so* not happening.

"Sidhe," Fang corrected. "Fae. The one you call David."

"Oh, *Sidhe.*" She'd read enough high fantasy to recognize the word. Reaching an intersection, she stopped as the light went red. "Were you together before?"

"We have been Smoke for many centuries." With brooding eyes Fang watched a Toyota pickup roll past. "The god arrived in our world with others of his kind. His people are elementals, and alien—no more than magic and will. He would not have survived without a living host. He called, and I answered."

As the light turned green, Eva frowned, tossed a mental coin, and turned left. She still had no freaking idea where she was, but she'd lived in Greendale for twenty-five years. Eventually she'd hit a street she recognized. "So this Smoke is some kind of *alien*?" As if her life wasn't weird enough.

"Well, yes. But by your standards, so am I."

EIGHT

Eva blinked at him before jerking her eyes back on the road. "What?"

"We are not from this Earth. We're from another . . . dimension, I suppose you would say, an Earth where there is magic."

Christ, weirder and weirder. I'd think he was nuts if I hadn't seen him voodoo the car. "But how did you get here?"

Fang shrugged. "A magical portal."

"Oh, Lord, I'm trapped in an episode of *Stargate*."

He frowned at her. "What?"

"Never mind. So a noncorporeal alien whatsit arrived on magic Earth. Then what?"

"I was a *ciardha* then . . ."

"A what?"

"A *ciardha*. Something like a tiger, but a little bigger, black, with silver stripes on the haunches." He smiled at some memory. "All the *ciardha* females thought I was very beautiful."

"Yeah, I'll bet." Eva spotted a strip mall she thought she recognized and turned down the street.

"I had only an animal's mind until Smoke merged with me. He changed my brain, increased my intelligence, made me more than an animal. Later we found David's people, and became their god. The one you call David was the greatest warrior of his tribe then, and Smoke selected him to be our new host. When he moved into David's body, I went with him."

Another red light brought her to a halt. "But . . . *why*?"

He shrugged. "His people were suffering at the hands of the Dark Ones, who were predatory invading aliens who lived on the energy of human suffering. We needed hands, and all we had were paws. Good body for killing, less so for leading a tribe. And there was a priestess who wanted us." Fang stopped, and his features suddenly contorted in feral rage as if at some horrible memory. "We should have killed her instead of loving her. Bitch. Oh, foul, foul bitch. We killed her too late."

Which sounded like her cue for a subject change. "Ah, yeah. So, about this Warlock character. How did you end up locking horns with him?"

"He was trying to kill the son of Arthur Pendragon—"

Eva damn near ran off the road. "*King* Arthur?"

Fang nodded. "So he was, once. Now he leads the vampires of Avalon."

Eva rubbed her aching head. "Of course. What else would he do? Jesus."

Power surged and sang in Warlock again, and he shuddered at the drugging pleasure. Gods and devils, but it was sweet having such magic burning wild and alien in his soul, ready to leap to his will.

And I'm not giving it back. He snapped his jaws together, crunching imaginary bone. Soon he'd have Smoke dead and the power safe, beyond anyone's ability to strip away.

But first he'd have to find out what had gone wrong.

The dimensional gateway formed at a flick of his clawed fingers, and he stepped through, every sense wary and alert.

An empty field lay around him, silent except for the sigh of the wind through rustling kudzu. But when he inhaled, the smell of blood and death coated the inside of his nose. Frowning, he followed the scent.

He found what was left of the Skoll team lying in crushed green leaves sticky and splattered with drying blood. Striding around the corpses, he mentally reconstructed the combat with eyes that had seen fifteen centuries of war.

At first Warlock wondered if Smoke had changed to his great cat form in order to kill his warriors. The godling had done it before. But no—these wounds had been inflicted with a blade, swung with great force and equal skill.

And tremendous rage.

Smoke hadn't just killed the Dire Wolves, he'd butchered them. Warlock was reluctantly impressed, considering that each of his wolves outweighed Smoke's human form by two hundred pounds and topped him by more than a foot. Yet he'd overwhelmed them.

Warlock would just have to make sure the next team didn't underestimate the cat. Nothing less than Smoke's death was acceptable.

It was just as unacceptable for the mortal police to stick their noses into this business. And they would, if they found all these werewolf corpses. That would draw the attention of their media, which would alert the Celt and his knights. *I don't want to confront Arthur until I have gained control of my power. Then I'll kill him.*

With a sweeping gesture, Warlock sent a wave of magic rippling across the field. Everywhere it touched, sparks devoured the corpses of his men and eliminated every bloodstain, every crushed leaf, every broken stem. Even the Hummer and the two motorcycles disappeared, their component energy stored for later use as thundering blasts of magic. When it was done, there was no sign anyone had ever fought and died here.

Warlock summoned another gate and stalked through it, back to his lair deep in the mountains of North Carolina.

It was a damn good thing Danvers had called during the

chase to report the tag number of the girl's car. Otherwise Warlock would have no idea how to find her. As it was, the Fenir team's computer hacker would be able to track her.

And where she was, they'd find Smoke.

Fluffy did not, as a rule, like cats. But she sure liked Fang.

Actually, Eva didn't blame her. Now that she'd figured out where the hell they were, and Fang had finished his mind-blowing story—witches, vampires, and god cats, may Jesus have mercy—she was feeling a little better about life.

Besides, Fang looked way too much like David, flavored with just a hint of *Animal Planet.* There was heat in his burning blue eyes, and his pupils were fat black ovals he kept fixed on her.

His shoulders looked very broad in that short-sleeve knit shirt.

She had a thing for shoulders. Also biceps that looked thick and round and bite-able. Add a narrow waist and a truly world-class ass . . . Come to think of it, she liked the whole damned package.

Especially the *package.*

Oh, yum, Fluffy purred. *I want.*

She smelled like sex.

Cat breathed deeply, drinking her scent, the femininity brushed with traces of fur and wind and deep forests. He'd finished telling her what he knew of their situation, and she'd begun to make her peace with it.

Which was a good thing, since his cock lay long and hungry behind the zipper of his jeans, eager for a taste of her.

Her gaze flicked sideways at him as she drove, and his keen night vision detected the blush that darkened her high, pretty cheeks.

Eva was as aware of his scent as he was of hers. And she liked it. Maybe more than she was comfortable with.

Shifting in the car's leather seat, she focused on the road with obvious determination. Cat let his gaze drift down her body, lingering on the rise of her breasts, her delicate hands gripping the wheel, her thighs encased in well-worn denim.

"You're purring," she said, without looking at him.

"*Ciardhas* mate for life."

As he'd known it would, the statement brought her wide eyes darting to meet his. She immediately jerked them back to the road, swallowing. "And your point would be?" Her obvious attempt to sound cool failed when her voice cracked.

"We dreamed of you. Before we were broken, when we were still one. We dreamed of you for weeks. We knew we would meet you, but we did not know when."

"David never said anything about that." She frowned at the rear of the SUV just ahead and accelerated as the light changed. "Then again, David doesn't remember a damned thing." Her gaze flicked to him, then as quickly away. "But you do."

"I kept parts of us he did not." Cat shrugged. "Smoke believed shoving our magic down Warlock's throat was the only way we would survive. But he did not realize how devastating it would be for us, or how difficult it would be to regain what we lost." He took a deep breath, deciding the time had come to explain. "When they attacked us—hurt you—my rage drove me to the surface and I pushed David aside. At the end . . . I did not know who you were in your werewolf form."

She turned to look at him, eyes wide. "So it was you who . . ."

"Butchered them? Yes." He bared his teeth. "They *hurt* you. But when I saw how you feared me, I called Smoke. He tore away from Warlock and answered. At least, until Warlock dragged him back."

"Wait—Warlock has Smoke's *mind*?"

"Most of it. Warlock has walled it away to keep from being overwhelmed. The elemental is very powerful, and he would wipe Warlock's mind if given the chance. But with his power turned against him, Smoke is trapped behind that spell. Reaching him is difficult, even with our bond. Luckily, your fear so infuriated me, I was able to free him." He sighed, the sound brooding. "Unfortunately, it didn't last."

She said nothing for a long moment, her gaze fixed on the road. "Yeah, well, I'm afraid of a lot of things. I was useless in that fight." Her lips peeled off her teeth. "Sucks being a coward."

Studying her profile, Cat recognized shame. He found himself bitterly missing his spirit brothers. Either of them would know what to say to comfort her, but he had no idea.

"You are *not* a coward." His snarl made her look over in surprise—and, he saw to his shame, a little fear. He fought to gentle his tone. "A coward would not have stood beside me when you could have run away."

"Key word there is 'stood.' I didn't fight."

"Yes, you did. You killed one of them."

She brightened a little. "He was charging you from behind, and I just . . . hit him. Didn't even have time to think about it."

"That doesn't sound like cowardice to me. You saved my life, Eva. You need to stop selling yourself short."

Eva looked startled. He decided to let her think about that.

She'd saved his life.

Well, maybe he'd have heard the guy coming and defended himself—he'd sure made short work of those other jerks. But maybe he wouldn't have. Maybe she *had* saved him.

True, it wasn't the first time; Eva had helped David escape Warlock last night. But this was different. She'd actually *fought a werewolf*, and she'd won. Her fear had not paralyzed her. Which meant it didn't have to. She could gain control.

Still, she needed to learn how to fight. Eva didn't delude herself; she'd gotten in a lucky shot she'd seen in a Spider-Man comic book. That was not the kind of thing that she could pull off twice.

Still, whether he was Cat or David, her lover knew his way around a fight. He'd probably be willing to teach her what she needed to know.

She stole a glance at him as she pulled into the Drayton Apartments complex. He was watching her, his gaze steady and intent in a way that just radiated sex.

Fluffy woke up with a happy little bounce. *Yeah, baby, yeah!*

Down, girl.

Oh, come on! Look at him. Yum.

That's not David, that's Fang.

So let me have him.

Come to think of it, Fang and Fluffy would probably be very happy together. One big ball of furry fornication.

Eva, however, had no intention of cooperating. She wanted David.

She parked the car in her assigned spot and set the hand break with a savage jerk.

Fang saved your life, Fluffy pointed out.

Hard to argue with that. If Fang hadn't turned those guys into minced asshole, she'd be dead right now. And it wouldn't have been a fun death, either.

But, still.

Carefully not looking at Fang, Eva got out of the car, recovered the sword from the back, and started up the stairs. She could almost feel Fang's hungry gaze on her ass.

Fluffy started singing "I Want Your Sex" in the key of R. Fluffy wasn't going to be on *American Idol* anytime soon.

Cut it out!

Fluffy just snickered.

Eva's cell phone rang as they were walking in the door. She pulled it out of her pocket to check caller ID, and winced. "Oh, hell." Flipping the phone open, she reached for a cheery tone. "Hi, Mom!"

"Eva Naomi Roman, I have been going out of my mind!" Charlotte Roman's normally pleasant voice sounded just a little shrill. "Why didn't you call?"

Eva winced, dropped the sword on the table, and started lying. Fortunately, five years as a werewolf had made her good at it. "I'm sorry, Mom. David and I were a little busy talking to the police."

"What happened? Your father told me that creep Ronnie and some friends showed up at the shop. He was scared to death for you—" Her father's voice interrupted with a rumble of protest. "Oh, shut up, Bill. We've been married thirty years. You think I don't know when you're scared? Eva, what happened?"

"We got lucky." She turned to find David/Fang listening with acute interest. "We saw a police car, so I turned on my flashers and blew my horn. The cop pulled over, and I pulled in behind him. Ronnie and his friends roared off."

"But you made a police report, right?" her mother asked anxiously. "Is he going to be charged?"

"Probably not." This was turning into a very complicated lie. Which sucked, but there wasn't much she could do about it. "The cop said if Ronnie tries anything else, we can file charges."

Bill came on the line. "That's not going to stop the bastard. I'm coming over there to kick his ass."

Oh, hell. "No! No, Dad, David's already dealt with Ronnie. He promised he won't try anything else again."

"You mean that long-haired pussy—"

"Bill Roman!" her mother snapped. "Watch your mouth!"

"—Actually *did* something?"

"He's not a pussy, Dad." *A cat, maybe, but definitely not a pussy.* She grinned. "And yes, he gave Ronnie a punch in the teeth. Made him promise he'd never try anything like that again. So everything's fine."

"Are you sure?" Suspicion darkened Charlotte's pleasant voice. Something had definitely set off her momdar, God help them all.

"I'm sure. We won't have any more trouble with Ronnie."

Which was the utter truth, unlike the rest of the conversation.

"Well, let me know if you do," Bill growled. "Ronnie's a shit. Do him a world of good to be on the receiving end of my fist."

"I'm sure it would, but David's got it covered. Listen, I need to fix dinner. I'll see you tomorrow."

"Nope, it's Thursday. You've got Friday off, remember?"

"Oh, yeah." Good thing, too. There were a number of things she needed to work through.

After saying good-bye and plugging her phone into its charging stand, Eva headed for the kitchen. Changing into a werewolf always made her hungry enough to eat a yak—violating the laws of physics will do that to you. Which was why she kept a stack of T-bones in the freezer.

She got out a couple and stuck them on a pan under the oven's broiler, uncorked a Cabernet Sauvignon and poured two glasses full of fruity red goodness, then went to work on a salad.

Eva chopped vegetables until it was time to turn the meat. That done, she went back to work at the cutting board, all the while acutely aware of Fang standing far too close. Eva stopped slicing bell peppers to look at him. "I tawt I taw a puddy tat."

He blinked. "I do not understand."

"You're staring at me like a cartoon cat watching something in a cage. Cut it out."

He contemplated her, frustration replacing hunger. "Sometimes you make no sense at all."

Eva snorted. "You're not the first man to tell me that, Fang."

"My name is Cat." He took a step closer, forcing her to look up at him. She was acutely aware of his hands, his heat, his strong, hard body. And his eyes, so very, very blue. "Fang is a joke. I am not a joke." His hand caught her behind the back of her neck and drew her against him. And his mouth swept down to cover hers.

He was right. There was nothing at all funny about his

kiss. His mouth moved over hers, slow and hot and tempting. He caught her lower lip between his teeth in a gentle bite until she opened her mouth to gasp. His tongue swept inside in a bold, licking stroke.

By the time he took a lazy step back, she was left staring at him with her heart pounding in deep lunges that vibrated her sternum.

Cat picked up a pot holder, opened the oven, and pulled out the broiler pan. The steaks sizzled loudly as he put the pan on the stove.

"Oh," Eva muttered. "I thought that sound was me."

One corner of his mouth quirking upward, he took the flatware and wineglasses and sauntered to the kitchen table. He had really broad shoulders.

Told you, Fluffy said.

Shut up. Eva started plating the food. *Maybe if I stuff him full of meat, he won't be able to molest me.*

Fluffy hooted. *You want something stuffed full of meat, but it's not him.*

You've got a trashy streak, furball.

Yeah, and you talk to yourself.

Eva was uncomfortably conscious of Cat the whole time they ate. The slide of muscle in his strong forearms when he cut his steak with neat efficiency, the crow-wing gleam of his long hair, tucked back to reveal the elegant curve of one pointed ear. The way his sensual lips closed over a bite of steak and drew it off his fork. His hungry gaze watched her over the rim of his wineglass whenever he took a sip. As aware of her as she was of him.

Her nipples hardened. Eva crossed her legs under the table and looked away from the precise angles of his face.

Feeling the need for a little more distance, she got up and started clearing the table as soon as they were finished eating. The tactic backfired when Cat rose to help her, his big hands brushing hers as he collected knives, forks, and salad bowls.

They loaded the dishwasher, Eva showing him where

the different items went. By the time they finished, her senses were thrumming with awareness of his size, his masculinity, his sheer heat.

Collecting the wine bottle and her glass, Eva retreated to the living room couch. Which was a tactical mistake. Cat sauntered after her lazily, his own glass cupped in long fingers.

She looked up at him as he sank down next to her. "Cat, I really . . ."

Before she could finish her sentence, his mouth covered hers again, hot and demanding, his fingers brushing her jaw, trailing fire along her skin. She made a little sound, a tiny, helpless moan.

God, he tasted good. Wine and masculinity and a trace of something wild. His hand slipped down the line of her throat, a teasing dance that made her shiver in anticipation.

Fluffy started purring.

Heat raced over Eva's skin as fierce desire ignited, the feral need blazing high. His fingers closed over her breast, squeezing and stroking as he kissed her, his tongue swirling inside her mouth in hot demand.

Bending her back against the arm of the couch, he reached down, grabbed the hem of her Comix Cave T-shirt, and pulled it high to reveal the pale curves of her breasts cupped in rose lace. He lowered his head, took the lace between his teeth, and dragged it down until he could reach her nipple. Then he began raking it with his teeth and swirling his tongue over the peak until she twisted in need.

Drowning in a rising tide of heat, it took her a few minutes to realize something was missing. He looked like David, but he didn't make love like her lover. His hands were just the slightest bit rougher in the way they handled her, the rake of his teeth a fraction harder. Not enough to hurt, but more ruthless, more demanding. The tenderness David had shown her just wasn't there. Cat made love as if he was demanding her surrender.

And she wanted to surrender. She really did. But she couldn't.

Don't you dare bail, hissed Fluffy. *I want him!*

"Cat," Eva gasped.

He kept licking, kept raking those sharp teeth across her nipple.

"Cat!" But he kept right on. "Cat, dammit, stop!"

He looked up to meet her gaze, his pupils hairline slits across irises of ice blue. "What?"

She tried to jerk out his arms, only to wince when his urgent hands didn't release her. "Ouch! Let me go!"

Instantly, he opened his hands. She scooted back. "I am sorry! Did I hurt you?"

"No, I'm fine." She closed her eyes to shut out the panic in his eyes as he started to reach for her, only to pull back. "I'm really sorry."

"What's wrong?" He looked her over anxiously. "Are you sure I did not hurt you?"

"I said I'm fine, okay?" Between frustrated hunger and her own confusion, the words came out more sharply than she'd intended, and he flinched slightly. Eva rose from the couch and began to pace restlessly, not sure how to put her sudden conviction into words. "Look, this just isn't going to work."

"What do you mean? Talk to me, Eva." It was a command, half-growled in his deep voice.

"This doesn't feel right—making love to you. You're not David."

He blinked and drew back, a flash of pain darting across his eyes. "No. I am Cat."

"It's not that I'm not attracted to you . . ."

"But I'm not human."

"No, I mean—" She raked her hair out of her eyes with a growl of frustration. "Fuck, I don't know what I mean."

"Yes, you do." His mouth twisted. "As you said, I am not David. And David is who you want."

She winced, but she had to be honest with him. "Yeah."

Cat shook his head. "Eva, if our enemy does not kill us, sooner or later we'll be one again. Will you think we are not David enough then?"

Eva stared at him, feeling a little sick. "I don't . . ."

"Very well," Cat said, lifting his chin. "If you want David, you will have him."

"Look, I only meant . . ." Before she could say anything more, his body arched in a bow of pain. His eyes rolled back, hands curling into helpless claws.

"Cat!" She jumped forward, managing to grab him just before he convulsed his way right off the couch. For a moment, it was all she could do to contain the furious lash of his big body, even with her were strength.

Abruptly he went limp in her arms with a weak groan.

Fear chilled her. "Cat? Cat, are you . . ."

His eyes opened to look at her in dazed confusion. "Eva?"

As she gazed into his handsome face, she realized David was back.

Cat had indeed brought him back to the surface for her.

NINE

By the time Eva finished telling David everything that had happened, her mouth was dry, though they'd worked their way through the bottle of wine. She'd carefully left out Cat's attempts to seduce her, as well as his parting shot about what would happen when the three personalities were reunited.

David saw the implications anyway.

"What you're saying is that I am a fragment." He took a long, deliberate sip of his wine. "If I survive Warlock's attempts to kill me, eventually the others will return. And since one of them is a god, I may cease to exist as myself at all."

"David, I . . ." She trailed off, staring at his expressionless profile, feeling helpless. Until, on sheer impulse, she leaned forward and caught his chin, turning his face to hers.

The kiss started out slow and flavored with pain, until David's arms closed hard around her. He dragged her close, his mouth going fierce against hers, kisses almost like bites, his tongue thrusting and swirling. She felt her senses spin.

Her body ignited in a blaze of heat that made her throw her head back to gasp. He promptly trailed kisses down the line of her throat, pausing to use his teeth and tongue against her banging pulse. Impatient hands caught the hem of her shirt and jerked it upward. She drew back eagerly, raising her arms to let him drag it off over her head. The tee went sailing across the room as David hooked two fingers in the top of her bra and pulled the cup down. Her nipple jutted into the cool air an instant before he engulfed it in the wet, eager heat of his mouth. His tongue swirled over and around the tip. He sucked hard, and she groaned, threading her hands into his hair, tracing the delicate points of his ears.

Hands closed around her waist, pulling her over into his lap. She caught her breath at the feel of his erection, thick and hot under her ass.

David reached behind her to unfasten her bra, sent it flying after the tee and bent her backward, arching her breasts so her nipples jutted at the ceiling. His teeth and tongue and hot, wet mouth played loving court to them as she curled her nails into the silk of his hair, eyes closed in delight. Almost lazily, she rolled her butt downward, teasing his cock through two layers of denim.

With a growl of impatience, David picked her up and stood, in a display of strength that had her eyes popping wide. He turned and put her down on the couch, then reached for her zipper. It hissed downward in his impatient fingers, and they both went to work dragging off her clothes. It didn't take them long to get her naked.

He took even less time.

Eva caught her breath, dazzled as always by the stark, carved beauty of his body, muscle sliding under tanned skin, shoulders mantled in the gleaming length of his black hair. His eyes blazed down at her. She reached up for him . . .

He grabbed her by the hips and flipped her over, dropping her belly-down across the arm of the couch. Her palms thumped into the carpeted floor as she started to push back up. "Hey—"

Before she could get the rest of the protest out of her

mouth, he pulled her legs apart and buried his face between them. She yowled in delighted shock as his tongue stroked the length of her sex. "David!"

"What?" He gripped her hips and parted her labia with his thumbs.

Hanging head-down, hands braced on the floor, she made a sound midway between a giggle and a growl. "I was planning to participate."

"Unless I'm very much mistaken"—lick—"you are participating."

She squirmed as he zeroed in on her clit and started swirling figure eights of heat around it. "I mean I was planning to do fun things to *you*, too."

"I have other plans." He slipped two fingers into her pussy and gave her a couple of slow pumps.

"I—*ah!*—gathered that."

"You're quick, you are." Slipping a hand between her legs, he found her wet clit and began strumming it as he licked her up and down like a particularly juicy peach.

Her eyes rolled back. "I'm going to come if you keep that up!"

"I was hoping you would." He licked again, very slowly, before stopping suddenly. "Unless you'd rather not . . ."

She dug her nails into the carpet. "You want to die?"

"Not particularly." He slid a finger into her sex again, pumped. "Though I can certainly think of worse ways to go."

David contemplated the round perfection of Eva's bottom with lusty appreciation. Her sex was slick and hot and deliciously tight around his index finger, and he licked his lips, imagining how she'd feel gripping his cock.

Impatience sizzled through him, but he controlled it. He wanted to make this good for her.

No, he wanted to drive her insane.

He wanted to make sure she never forgot him. No matter what happened. No matter who—or what—he became.

Dipping his head again, he parted her and went back to

pleasuring her with long, teasing strokes that circled and flicked her clit. She tasted musky and slightly astringent, yet so delightfully sweet with eager arousal. He loved the smell of her, the feel of her satin ass under his fingers, the long, strong legs tensing under the weight of his body. She wiggled against him, and he grinned, thoroughly enjoying himself.

He found he liked her helplessness. He liked being in charge.

For once.

David's lips peeled off his teeth at the reminder of just how little he otherwise controlled. He reared off her, grabbed his cock, and aimed it at her deliciously creamy opening. And shoved all the way home in one ruthless stroke.

Eva threw her head up with a cry.

He froze, his heart in his mouth. "Did I hurt you?"

"No! No, God, please—more!"

Well, that certainly sounded sincere. He forgot his qualms and pulled out, loving the silken heat of her grip clamped around his cock. Gods, it was sweet.

He leaned into her ass, holding her pinned as he began to grind, slow and hard, in and out. Watching her toss her beautiful dark curls, gasping and moaning in helpless delight.

Oh, yes. He *liked* this.

Eva braced her hands on the floor and arched back to meet his pounding thrusts. She felt dizzy from the searing pleasure of his width and length reaching so deep inside her. Her climax boiled like a storm ready to break.

David shoved all the way in, right to the root, almost too deep, and stiffened with a roar.

That last thrust was all it took. Fire roared up from her belly and tore through her blood, making her writhe and scream with its sheer violent glory.

Finally she collapsed to lie limp as a rag over the arm of the chair. The room spun around her as David picked her up, sat down on the couch, and draped her across his lap, boneless as a sock puppet. She wrapped her arms around his waist and lay her head against his chest. Content, they cuddled as their sweat cooled and their pounding heartbeats slowed.

Some hours later, David lay staring up at the bedroom ceiling, brooding over Eva's revelations. She curled next to him, her breathing deep and slow in sleep.

He had no real memory of what had happened during the fight with the werewolves, but according to Eva, two other beings normally occupied his body, one a god, the other some kind of big cat. Which explained how his decorative practice sword had acquired an edge sharp enough to massacre werewolves.

What would happen to him when those beings returned? Would he cease to be himself? He wished he could ask this Cat, but his attempts to communicate had garnered no response at all. He . . .

"Arhhhhhhhhhh! Get off me! Get off! Get! Off!" Eva shrieked right in his ear, a shattering cry of panic and agony. He shot upright, but she was already moving, rolling out of bed to land on the floor in a crouch. Her eyes were wild, glowing red in the darkness. She screamed again, the sound dropping, going guttural as it grew in volume, becoming a roar. "Stay away!"

Even as he hit the floor, he saw magic spill over her, lengthening her head into a wolf muzzle. Her hair became a wild, dark mane as a wave of fur rushed across her bare skin. Her delicate hands grew huge, tipped in talons, and her teeth sharpened into tearing daggers. Her snarl rumbled, low and menacing as she stared at him through the darkness, no recognition at all in her crimson gaze.

David had bounded out of bed with every intention of catching her in his arms. Now he realized that was exactly the wrong thing to do. "Eva?" He kept his voice low and soothing.

She ignored him, gathering herself to attack. And with

that wolf body, she could hurt him badly before she woke up enough to realize what she was doing. She'd never forgive herself.

And he wouldn't exactly have a great time either.

"Eva, you're dreaming." He said the words firmly as he kept out of reach. "You're safe. Wake up. Wake up, love."

She hesitated, cocking her head as if trying to remember him.

He lowered his voice to a soothing croon. "Eva, love, wake up. It was just a nightmare. You're safe."

Awareness suddenly filled those dark chocolate eyes. "David?"

He blew out a relieved breath. "Yes, it's me."

"I had the most god-awful nightmare . . ." She lifted her hands—and froze, staring at them in horror. "Oh, shit. I turned, didn't I?"

"Yes."

She took a step toward him, her gaze going frantic. "I didn't hurt you, did I? Shit, shit, shit. This is why I never sleep with anybody!"

"I'm fine." To prove it, he stepped in close and slid his arms around her waist. "And so are you." As he embraced her, his head came to rest under her chin. Her breasts were as large as the rest of her. Unable to resist, he cupped one, enjoying the silken caress of fur as soft as a kitten's. "Mmmm." He grinned up at her, teasing. "This has possibilities."

Her hands came tentatively to rest on his shoulders, almost painfully careful of her claws. "Uh. Yeah. It feels weird, you being this—" She broke off.

"Short?" Despite the alien shape of her head, the eyes were still Eva's, big and brown and human.

"Something like that." She sighed and stepped away from him. "I'd better turn back."

With acute fascination, David watched the magic spill. Fur disappeared as her body shrank from big and powerful to delicate and feminine. When it was over, Eva sank back on the edge of the bed, panting. "Jesus, that hurts. I've lost count of the times I've shifted, but I never get used to it."

He moved to the other side of the bed, sat down, and propped his back against the headboard, opening his arms to her. "Do you want to tell me about it?"

"It's the same damned nightmare I've been having for years now." Eva crawled across the mattress and settled into his arms, resting her head against his shoulder. "Anytime things get tense, I dream about the werewolf attack. The one that changed me."

He rested his head on the top of hers. "It must have been horrific."

"Yeah." She wrapped her arms around him and snuggled so close, she was practically lying on top of him. "The thing is, if I hadn't been such an idiot, it wouldn't have happened at all." She brooded for a moment. "The problem is, I'm tall—tall enough to look most men in the eye. I never really thought of myself as vulnerable. Not that way."

David abruptly realized he really didn't want to hear this story. Which was just too bad, since she obviously needed to tell it. "What happened?"

Eva took a deep breath and blew it out. "I used to go running every evening that I didn't have to close up the store. There's this park in town, and it was spring like it is now, so everything was in full bloom. The path loops between water features and flowering bushes, and it's really pretty and peaceful, especially at sunset. Usually there are a lot of people walking through the park, but the sun had set and the usual crowd had gone home. I was finishing up my run when I saw this guy walking toward me in the illumination of a trail light."

David's heart thudded with uncomfortable speed in his chest. A kind of sick anger rose. He definitely didn't want to hear this. "He was the one?"

"Yeah. Thing is, he didn't look like Mr. Stranger Danger. I remember thinking he was good-looking, big and blond, the kind of guy I'd normally flirt with. I nodded at him, gave him a smile, and he grinned back. That's when I knew he was off."

"Because of his smile?"

"No. It was his eyes. There wasn't anything human in

there, you know? It was like looking into a shark's eyes. Just as I was thinking that, he turned into something out of a horror movie."

David swallowed, glad she couldn't see his face. *She's probably never told anybody about this before. She needs to talk it out.* "You must have been terrified."

"I completely froze. I couldn't believe what was happening. I kept thinking he couldn't be real. I figured I must have fallen and hit my head, or maybe somebody had slipped LSD into my Diet Coke. And then he grinned at me with all those god-awful teeth, and he said, 'Run.' So I did."

"He wanted to chase you." David realized his fingers were digging into her shoulders. He carefully relaxed his grip.

Eva was too lost in her nightmare to notice. "I ran. I ran until I had a stitch in my side, until every muscle I had screamed, until I couldn't breathe. And then I kept running, because he was right behind me. He could have grabbed me anytime he wanted. That finally pissed me off. I knew he was going to catch me and I was going to die, and the bastard was *playing* with me. So I whirled around and aimed my fist for his balls."

David's chest ached. "Good for you."

"Yeah, except it pissed him off. He caught my fist, and backhanded me so hard I saw stars. Next thing I knew, I was on the ground, and he was on top of me. It was like being crushed by a boulder. He snarled, 'Bitch, you're gonna pay for that.' Then he just dove for my belly and started . . . ripping. I screamed with everything I had because it was the only thing I could do. That seemed to annoy him, but I refused to quit. So he got up and dragged me into the woods." Eva broke off. She was pale, and her expression was lost. He could smell her terror.

I will find that thing and kill him.

"I don't know how long it took, but somebody must have heard me screaming, because some eternity later I heard sirens. He jerked up and looked off toward the sound, cursed, and then he was just . . . gone."

"They found you?"

"No. By then I wasn't capable of screaming anymore. I kept floating in and out of consciousness as I lay there under the trees. I heard people, I guess cops, calling and walking around, but the only sound I could make was this kind of gasping whimper. I kept hoping they'd find me, but they never did. So then I started hoping I'd die, but that didn't happen either."

David's eyes stung, and he blinked savagely. He wanted to hit something.

"I really should have died from what he did. I guess I didn't because he infected me. After a long time lying there in a bloody heap, I shifted, no waiting for the full moon. God, it hurt. When you change, it feels like you're being ripped apart and burned alive. But after it was finally over, all my injuries had completely healed. All those god-awful wounds, gone. Like it never even happened." She shook her head. "Magic."

David rested his chin on the top of hers and hugged her close, relieved the horrific story was over. "Thank the gods."

"Except for my head." Her voice sounded bleak. "What's in my head never healed."

After a long, aching pause, David asked, "Once you realized you'd survived, what did you do?"

"Hid out in the woods until I changed back. I guess I wanted to be human again so bad, I just called the magic without knowing what I was doing." Eva paused. "You know what I've never figured out?"

He stroked one hand through her hair. "What?"

"Where do my clothes go when I change? You'd think they'd rip like they do in the movies, but no—they just vanish. Then they come back when I become human again. Along with my car keys, cell phone, and anything I have in my pockets. Makes no sense."

David laughed. The sound cracked in the middle, and he cleared his throat. "Never expect logic from magic." Her body was slowly relaxing against his now that the worst of the story was over.

He still wanted to throw up.

To distract his heaving stomach, he asked, "What did you do after you became a werewolf?"

"Freaked the fuck out. I thought I was a monster, and I was terrified I was going to start killing people. I told my dad I had a stomach bug and couldn't go to work."

David frowned down at her. "You didn't tell him what happened?"

"What was I going to say? 'Hey, Daddy—some werewolf ate me, and now I turn fuzzy'? My folks would have lost their minds. I finally realized I couldn't hide out forever, so I went back to work. I'd run home after closing every night, until I finally figured out I wasn't going to start eating people. Guess the creep who attacked me was just a serial killer."

"And you never told anyone?"

"God, no. I wanted to come out to Mom and Dad, but I was afraid. They'd think I was nuts unless I changed in front of them, and then they'd think I was a monster. I couldn't face that. So I never told anybody. Until you."

They fell silent together, Eva lost in her memories, David struggling to deal with his sick rage. Finally she said, "David?"

"Yes?"

"I want you to teach me how to fight." The words spilled in a rush. "I froze out there. When those werewolves jumped us, I just froze. All I could think of was when Cujo . . . hurt me."

David took a deep breath and blew it out. "I'll teach you everything I can."

"Thanks. I think if I knew how to defend myself, maybe I wouldn't be such a fucking coward."

"You're not a coward!" He spat the words with more force than he'd intended, and she jerked against him. David winced and moderated his tone. "An experience like that would give anyone mental scars. But they can be overcome."

"God, I hope so."

They subsided into silence again as he cuddled her. At last, exhausted by her story, she fell asleep again.

Battling images of Eva being attacked by the werewolf, David held her as she slept. She felt so delicate, so fragile. The idea of some psychotic monster ripping into her made him feel as if he'd been gutted himself.

Somehow, some way, he was going to find that prick and kill him.

Another thought pierced his rage, sharp as Eva's claws. So sharp he felt his rage drain into cold depression.

I am in deep, deep trouble, and sinking deeper.

In only a few short hours, Eva had become the center of his fractured universe. The pain he felt at what she'd suffered made that all too clear.

It was more than sex, more than his delight in her admittedly beautiful body. Hell, he even found her lovely in her werewolf form. Her Fluffy self.

He snorted amusement at the name. It was a prime example of her skewed sense of humor, especially considering he could sense how deeply uncomfortable she was with being a werewolf.

If Eva feared it, she made a joke about it.

Oh, he was definitely in deep, deep trouble. Here he was, one fragment of some other man, waiting for the rest of his mind to return. Would he even exist once *they* came back?

Would he still love Eva?

David winced. And there it was: the trouble. What kind of idiot let himself become obsessed with a woman in a situation like this? All he was doing was setting himself up for more pain.

If he had any wit at all, he'd keep away from her. Or at least, he'd stay just close enough to protect her from whatever hell Warlock rained down on them.

He definitely shouldn't make love to her at every opportunity, ensuring that his obsession with her only deepened.

Because the deeper he got, the more likely it was to blow up in his face. True, the sheer lush pleasure of loving her might be worth whatever pain he suffered at the end.

But what if Eva ended up hurt?

No, that wasn't acceptable.

Unfortunately, he strongly suspected he wasn't going to be able to keep his hands off her. His arms unconsciously tightened around her, and she sighed in her sleep. Her breath puffed against his mouth, and he looked down at her. God, he wanted to kiss her.

Idiot.

David ended up watching the sun rise through the bedroom window, red light spilling across the sky like blood. An omen that was just a little too damned apt.

Joelle Drake's delicate hand closed hard around the orange half, squeezing a stream of juice from it with easy Dire Wolf strength. The air smelled of the eggs, bacon, and pancakes she'd just prepared, but she wasn't hungry. Still, it felt good to be busy, especially since she was making Miranda's favorite breakfast. The smell of it would hopefully lure the girl off the couch, where she'd been sulking her way through a *Bones* marathon. Probably looking for grisly inspiration while she plotted matricide.

Sticking her head around the door frame, Joelle checked on her daughter. She still lay sprawled under an Afghan, looking like a glum ghost. Even the sight of a shirtless David Boreanaz failed to cheer her up.

Joelle's lips tightened, and she retreated back into the kitchen to slice another orange in half with a single angry pass of her knife. She'd barely slept the night before, haunted by guilt and worry. She knew her daughter viewed her call to Gerald as the worst kind of betrayal.

And maybe she was right. Unfortunately, Miranda didn't realize what Gerald was capable of. Joelle knew from hard, bloody experience. It wasn't just what he did to Joelle; those injuries would heal.

It was what he might do to Miranda that had driven Joelle to pick up the phone.

Grabbing another orange half, Joelle gave it a vicious squeeze, watching it bleed juice into the pitcher. She wished she could get Miranda to accept there was no escape for either of them. Even if Joelle had run away with the girl—and she'd considered it more than once over the years—there was no evading Warlock for very long.

They'd have to work to support themselves, which meant there was no practical way they could remain together at all times.

True, as long as Joelle remained with her daughter, the sorcerer would be unable to track them because her resistance to magic would shield the girl. Unfortunately, Randy was a magic user, so she wasn't immune to spells. The minute the two separated, Warlock would have her. And he'd be pissed, so he'd go after Miranda like a wolf on a lamb. Joelle shuddered, imagining what he'd do to her then.

Miranda thought she'd seen abuse in Gerald's slaps and scratches. She had no bloody idea what a werewolf was really capable of. And Warlock—mad, vicious, *powerful* Warlock—was inclined to do much worse.

Joelle had tried to explain all that, but Miranda insisted she could find a way to shield herself from Warlock's magic. Joelle knew better. No spell was that good.

Judging the pitcher full enough, she put it on the table with the rest of the food and walked to the doorway again. "Miranda, breakfast is ready."

Randy didn't even glance away from the TV. "I told you I'm not hungry."

"And I told you you're going to eat. Get in here."

With a sigh, Miranda rose and trudged into the kitchen. She'd always been an obedient child, and the habit had fortunately persisted into adulthood.

Joelle watched her drop into a chair and mechanically fill her plate. She sat down and followed suit.

The silence that followed was a sullen thing, but Joelle knew how to break it. "The Chosen ladies are holding a Grieving for Joan Devon. Her husband and daughter were killed a few days ago, and she lost her son at Christmas." She sighed and forked up a bite of pancake, chewed, swallowed. "That poor woman. So much tragedy."

Miranda snorted. "Her son was a serial killer who was killed by the sister of one of his victims, who just happened to be a Maja. As for Joan's husband and daughter,

those two murdered a dozen innocent Latents in a quest
for revenge against the Magekind. They would have assassinated Arthur's son if Logan and his lover hadn't killed
them first. So I'm really not interested in expressing sympathy, when they fucking *deserved* to die."

"Language!" Joelle snapped. The girl had a point, but still.

Miranda dropped her fork on her plate with a clatter
and stared at her with defiant eyes. "Mom, they strapped
suicide vests on two human children. Those kids would
have died if Logan hadn't disabled the bombs. That is not
exactly the kind of behavior Merlin expects of us."

"Regardless of what they did, Joan did nothing—"

"But she knew what was going on." Her jaw flexing,
Miranda picked up her butter knife and started sawing
through her pancakes. "That makes her an accessory."

Do you consider me an accessory, too? Joelle didn't
dare ask the question. "But she's one of *us*, Miranda.
She's a lady of the Chosen, and ladies of the Chosen stick
together." *We have to, because we're the only defense we
have against our men.* But that wasn't something she could
say to Miranda. Her daughter was rebellious enough as it
was. "So we are going to visit her and express our sympathies, just like all the other women. And you, my girl, are
not going to be rude enough to say one word about who
deserved what."

Miranda sighed. "Fine. Whatever."

Joelle took another bite of her pancakes. They tasted
like ashes.

TEN

The next morning, Eva and David shared a long, hot shower. Much to Fluffy's delight, it ended with Eva's back pressed against the tile wall as David held her in his arms, pounding them both into a delicious orgasm.

As Eva blew her hair dry, Fluffy hummed "Do That to Me One More Time." Oh, God, she'd degenerated from George Michael to Captain and Tennille. Daddy sung that song to Mom when he wanted to embarrass her.

That was just *wrong.*

From the corner of one eye, Eva watched David shave with surprising skill. Where had a Sidhe warrior learned to use a disposable razor?

As she watched him, she realized he wore a troubled frown. *Huh. After the way we just made love, you'd think he'd be in a better mood.*

And when he looked at her, was that . . . guilt?

Eva frowned, wondering what the hell was going on in his head. Before she could ask, he said, "I want you to change."

She lifted a brow at him in the mirror. "Well, I wasn't planning to go out buck naked. Might scandalize the neighbors."

David shook his head, sending black silken hair sliding around his broad shoulders. "I mean change into your werewolf form."

She stared at him before throwing a nervous glance at the mirror. "Now? Inside?"

He nodded and leaned back against the wall, folding his muscular arms. "Now."

"Well, okay. But I really don't see the point." She started for the bathroom door. "I'll be too tall to . . ."

He caught her by the arm and drew her back. "No, Eva. I mean in here. In front of the mirror."

Dammit, she'd been afraid of that. "I can't."

David frowned and tipped his head to one side, studying here. "Why?"

Eva felt her cheeks going hot. *Great. Blushing like a sixteen-year-old.* "Because my reflection freaks me out, okay?"

Angry more at herself than him, she stalked out of the bathroom and headed through her bedroom for the kitchen.

He trailed her. "But why?"

Opening a kitchen cabinet, she took out a frying pan and banged it down on the stove. "Because when I change and look at myself in the mirror, I don't see me. I see a freaking *werewolf*, and werewolves scare the crap out of me. And yes, being scared of your own reflection is the stupidest phobia ever."

"But it can't hurt you."

"You think I don't know that? You think I don't feel like a fucking fool?" Eva stalked to the refrigerator, jerked the door open, and reached inside for the carton of eggs. Banging a cabinet door open, she got out a bowl. "I've tried to make myself look in the damned mirror. My heart starts pounding until it feels like I'm having a heart attack. I want to throw up. And since being scared pisses me off, the werewolf in the mirror starts snarling, and then I run out of the room. Last time I hit my head on the door frame and fell flat on my ass. I think I gave myself a concussion."

David caught her wrist before she could smash an egg on the rim of the bowl. Gently, he took the egg from her and put it back in the carton. "That's actually a very good thing."

She stared at him, her sense of humor surfacing through her angry embarrassment. "What, giving myself a concussion?"

"No, the fact that you react to your reflection the way you do to any other werewolf. We can use it to teach you not to freeze."

Her stomach laced into a sick knot. "David, it won't work."

"I think it will." He put the carton back in the refrigerator. "At the very least, we'll overcome your fear of mirrors."

Oh, hell. This is not *going to be any fun.*

Eva braced her clawed hands on the sink and forced herself to meet the eyes of the huge werewolf in the mirror. Her heart bounded like a terrified rabbit. She fought the need to run for the door. *I'd just give myself another concussion.*

"Shhh." David slid an arm across her furry back. "You're panting. Breathe with me." He inhaled deeply. "In." When she didn't obey, he gave her shoulder a squeeze to get her attention. "Eva, breathe in."

"This isn't going to work." Her hands tightened on the vanity edge as she fought to keep herself from bolting.

"*It will.* If you keep going into combat like this, eventually one of those wolves will kill you. And since they will have to go through me to do it, I'll die, too."

Dammit, he knew just which buttons to push. He was also right. *I've got to do this. Got to. I will not be responsible for getting him killed.*

And I will not *throw up.*

Eva was trembling, a fine vibration David could feel as he pressed against her side. Her muscles jerked under the arm he'd wrapped around her back. "Breathe with me, Eva."

She finally obeyed, dragging in a deep, shuddering breath,

blowing it out, head down, not looking at herself. He didn't push it, knowing she had to get her breathing under control before she could confront her reflection.

"I wish I could spare you this," he told her in a deliberately soft voice. "Your fear tears at me. But you can overcome it if you just hang on."

She turned her muzzle toward him. "What's this 'we,' Kemo Sabe?"

He smiled at her, encouraged that she was able to joke, though he had no idea what she meant. He rarely did. "You are *not* alone, Eva."

At that, she lifted her head and looked into the mirror. He could feel the effort it took in her shivering body. "Yeah. I noticed."

Eva licked her lips—and jerked, probably at the sight of her own fangs. She started talking, the words hurried, as if in a desperate attempt to distract herself from her fear. "One of my earliest memories is sitting in Dad's lap listening to him read a comic book. Don't remember what it was. Probably *Spider-Man*. My dad loves Spider-Man."

"Does he?" David caressed her back in long, soothing strokes. Her fur felt surprisingly soft under his hands, not coarse at all. Like a kitten's coat, it tempted him to stroke and touch.

"Yeah. Most kids learn to read with Dr. Seuss or something. With me, it was Batman and Spider-Man. I used to run around the house leaping off furniture, pretending I was Wonder Woman."

A high-pitched screech drew David's attention downward. Her claws flexed on the edge of the sink, raking furrows in the porcelain. He covered her hand with his to still those restless fingers. "Wonder Woman?"

"She's kind of like a female Superman, except she's got this cool golden lasso." She closed her eyes a moment before forcing them open again. A muscle ticked in her jaw. "My mom made my Barbie a Wonder Woman costume, even though she said it was a really sexist outfit. She's right—it's a strapless bathing suit kind of thing. Who the hell would wear something like that in combat? I'd be afraid the top would slip and I'd flash my tits at the bad guys. Not a good career move."

He turned into her side until he could stroke her forearm with his free hand while he rubbed her back in slow circles. Her trembling had almost stopped. "Why did they give her such revealing clothing?"

Eva snorted. "Because their target audience is fourteen-year-old boys." She looked up at her reflection and flinched, but didn't drop her eyes. "There's this saying Spider-Man has: 'With great power comes great responsibility.' That's kind of the whole philosophy behind comic books. And I guess I grew up believing it."

"You should, since it's true. The powerful have a duty to protect the vulnerable."

She gave him a smile rendered disconcerting by the length of her teeth. "Yeah, of course *you'd* think so. Other people, not so much. My ex-boyfriend, Joel—he's a bigger geek than I am. But when I said that to him, he told me that works only in comics. He said reality is more complicated."

David snorted. "Yes, he's the type who would think so."

"Which brings me to my point." Eva looked her reflection in the eyes. "I'm powerful. I've got all these teeth. I'm big. I'm strong. I've got claws. Being like this . . . I hate this. I can't stand this . . . fear." Her lips drew back, and a snarl rumbled from her chest. She jerked at the sound. "God, I despise being a coward."

He kept his voice controlled and even. "I'm growing really tired of repeating myself, Eva. *You are not a coward.*"

She curled her lip, frustration hot in her eyes. "David, I'm afraid of my own reflection!"

"But you're not running from it. You stand here with me, facing yourself. Fighting your fear. That's real courage."

"No, that is me not wanting to look like a seven-foot chicken in front of the man I—" She broke off.

His breath caught, but she didn't complete the sentence. "You make a mistake in thinking fear is a weakness," he said finally. "Fear can be turned to rage, to power, to something you can use. Look at yourself."

She snorted. "I've been looking. So far, not so good."

"You may be looking, but you don't really see."" He pointed at her reflection. "Is that a victim, or is that a predator?"

"It's a predator on the outside," Eva said dryly. "Inside, it's a seven-foot chicken."

Deeply frustrated, David glowered. It was time to quit coddling her. "So you're just going to let him win, then."

She blinked at his harsh tone. "Who, Warlock?"

"No, that bastard that tried to eat you five years ago. You survived what he did . . ."

Eva snorted. "Because of magic. Otherwise I'd be dead."

"It doesn't matter why you survived," David said sharply. "It doesn't matter that you were afraid when you faced those wolves yesterday. It doesn't matter if you're afraid when you face the next set of wolves. It only matters what you *do*. You can go on being a victim, or you can cram their laughter down their throats. You can show them you're not a victim. You can show them your rage."

"But when I face them, I don't feel rage." She raked both hands through her mane in frustration. "I feel scared shit-less."

"Of course you do. You're not stupid. But you don't have to let that fear be a weakness." He grabbed her hand, dragged it up in front of her face, and spread her fingers to display the white curve of her talons. "Look at those claws. Do you have any idea how much damage you can do with them?"

"Yeah, but the other werewolves have claws, too."

"And they may use them on you, but that doesn't matter, because you'll heal. Just as you healed when that bastard ate a chunk of your belly. So you don't let the pain stop you. You hit them, and you go on hitting them until they go down. If you can't kill them then, I will. Either way, they'll die and you'll live. *That's all that counts*."

He released her hand and turned toward the door. "Change back and come on."

She padded after him into the bedroom. "What now?"

"Now I teach you how to make those furry bastards bleed."

* * *

Warlock sat at his desk in one of the deeper chambers of his mountain lair, his head bent over a conjured book. His gold fountain pen scratched feverishly over the fine linen paper as he tried to record every detail he could recall from the Demigod's memory. He'd been at it so long he was getting writer's cramp.

As much as he hated to admit it, Warlock knew there was a possibility Smoke would reclaim his memories and powers. If he lost those abilities, he could always find an alternative, but the cat knew a great many very valuable things Warlock didn't want to forget. Which meant he needed to write them down.

He was particularly interested in other elementals like Smoke. Not many had survived, but there was at least one. And that one might be the key to turning the tables—if his plan to kill Smoke failed.

He grinned viciously. *There truly is more than one way to skin a cat.*

Because Eva's living room wasn't a good place for the kind of training he had in mind, David told her to drive them to somewhere more private.

She chose a spot in a nearby state park she remembered from childhood rambles. It lay deep in the woods beside a shallow, snaking creek where she'd caught frogs as a kid. Best of all, it was far enough away from any homes that they shouldn't have to worry about interruptions.

Eva felt a strange combination of excitement and worry—excitement that he would teach her what she wanted so badly to learn, worry that she would somehow screw it all up. "I've been thinking. Wouldn't it be better to get me a gun and just shoot them? I think Dad's got a pistol. I could probably persuade him to give it to me."

"Shooting a Dire Wolf is a waste of time," David told her, walking around the clearing examining the thick layer of fallen leaves that covered the ground. "They can heal the injury too quickly. It takes massive damage to put them down for any length of time, and for that you need a bladed weapon."

She frowned at him. "What did you just call them?"

"Dire Wolves. That's what they call themselves."

"Yeah, I know—Cat told me. But how do *you* know that? For that matter, how do you know the gun thing?"

David looked at her, opened his mouth, then shut it again. "I have no idea. But it's true." He shrugged. "It just feels right."

"Okay. So we know swords work. Why don't we get one for me? We probably don't have time to order something like that online, but I bet we could find a machete at a garden supply store."

"Using a blade effectively takes a lot more training than we have time for. As it is, an attacker would probably take it away from you and behead you with it."

Eva eyed him. "Thanks for the vote of confidence, Dr. Phil."

He met her gaze with a cool lift of an eyebrow. "Would you rather I told some flattering lie that got you killed?"

"Not really."

"Good, because I'm not going to do it." He gave her a come-on gesture. "Change now. I want to show you something."

When she'd recovered from the grinding pain of transformation, he extended a powerful arm, bent at the elbow. "Take my hand." Eva obeyed, instantly conscious of the warm roughness of his callused palm beneath her furry one. "Now see if you can force my arm down."

Eva eyed him dubiously. "So we're arm wrestling now?"

"Yes." His cool gaze did not invite argument.

"Okay." She started to push.

He lifted a dark, faintly amused brow. "Is that the best you can do? Because I don't believe our enemies will be impressed."

Anger zipping through her, Eva bore down hard against

his arm. Thick muscle rippled as he fought her strength, but he still looked faintly contemptuous. Anger growing into rage, she applied more force.

And wrenched his arm down. He released her and jumped back, shaking his hand and flexing his fingers.

"Did I hurt you?" Alarmed, she caught his hand and examined it anxiously.

"No." He watched her check him over. "You know, you're considerably stronger than I am."

Eva blinked, eyeing the width of his shoulders and the curve of the powerful muscles in his arm. "Who, me?"

"Yes. Which implies that the werewolves we fought yesterday were even stronger. Yet who won?"

"You did, but you had a sword."

"Was that the only reason?"

"No." She remembered his savagery as he'd chopped his blade into the fallen werewolf, his face contorted with ferocity. "You hit them so hard, you caught them by surprise."

He nodded. "A bigger fighter expects to win against a smaller one. And usually, he's right. He's got the leverage, he's got the reach and the strength, and nine times out of ten he's going to wipe the floor with the smaller man. So how does someone like me win against an eight-foot werewolf?"

She considered the question thoughtfully. "You didn't hold back at all. You hurt them so bad, so fast they don't have time to counterattack."

"And you can do the same thing. More easily, in fact, because you're bigger and stronger in this form, but you're also female, which means they're not going to expect you to give them a fight at all. They think women are weak and cowardly, and when they smell your fear, they'll assume they can rape and kill you and get away with it."

He sounded so calm about it, she started to get a little pissed off—until she looked in those blue eyes and saw his cold anger.

So she decided on honesty. "David, I just don't see how I can take on four werewolves and win."

"That's because you can't. Luckily, they won't send four wolves against you. I'm Warlock's primary target, which will make me the main threat in their minds. So they'll send most of their number against me, with one wolf to get you under control so they can play with you later. But you're going to turn the tables."

"Ummm. Turn the tables. Right."

"Grab my wrists and try to keep me from pulling free."

She obeyed cautiously. He started jerking back and forth, so she tightened her grip until he finally stopped. "You see how pointless this is," David told her. "You can hold on all day while I tire myself out. Attacking into your strength is not only a waste of time, it would eventually get me killed. I need to attack your weaknesses." His sneakered heel abruptly rammed her shin with bruising force. She lost her grip in surprise at the shooting pain.

Twisting, he hooked a foot behind her knee and shot his elbow into the underside of her jaw, snapping her head around. She fell flat on her ass, and he kicked right between her legs, pulling it at the last moment so the blow did not land with full force. Even so, it stung.

"That's always a good target," David told her cheerfully, "especially since your pants vanish when you change."

"Kick 'em in the 'nads," Eva said dryly, staring up at the leafy canopy over her head while she waited for the pain to fade. "Why didn't I think of that?"

"Do whatever wins, darling. Now grab me from behind."

Thirty seconds later, she was on her ass again.

He had her attack him from the front, from behind, and from the side, then from lying on top of him, then from lying on his back. Each time, she thought she had him pinned beyond his ability to escape, yet he'd throw her off, sometimes with a simple thrust of his hip. Then he'd slam an elbow into her jaw, throat, or ribs, curl his fingers into her cheek in lieu of clawing her eyes, or kick her in the shin, thigh, belly, or ribs.

Once she was sore and thoroughly pissed off, if not

particularly hurt, he had her change to human form and started teaching her how to use the same techniques against him.

"The difference in height and strength is about the same between me and you in human form as between you and the wolves when you change," David explained.

The kicks, strikes and throws he demonstrated weren't complicated, but they were surprisingly effective. Eva and David practiced them all day and well into the evening, hour after hour.

By the time they got home, her muscles felt like over-cooked pasta. Sore, overcooked pasta.

Eva lay stretched out across the width of the bed, naked and clean. She'd had a shower and an impressive supper, but she still felt as drained as a teenager's cell phone the day of the senior prom. "I used to think you were a nice man. I was wrong. I was so, sooo wrong."

Equally naked, David rattled around in a bedside bureau, pulled out a bottle, and considered the label. "Perhaps this will help." His grin was distinctly wicked.

She whimpered as he climbed onto the bed to straddle her ass. "David, like I told you in the shower, I'm too tired and full for sex."

Speak for yourself, Fluffy told her.

Hey, you ate all those Whoppers. She'd been too exhausted to cook.

I'm not taking the rap for that. You were the one stuffing your face.

Because you threatened to eat the neighbor's dog if I didn't stop at Burger King.

"This is not sex." David poured a handful of something from the bottle. "This is a massage."

Too wrung out to move, Eva rolled her eyes to watch him warily. "How do you know how to do a massage?"

"The same way I know how to do everything else."

"Good point." Big hands landed on her shoulders, and long, slick fingers dug into knotted muscle in a burst of instant heat. He'd found the warming oil. "Oh, holy God."

The man was right—he was as good at giving a massage as he was at everything else. Really, really good.

He coaxed the kinks from her back with a precise pressure calibrated just short of pain. And that oil—God knew when or why she'd bought it—left a trail of heat everywhere his kneading fingers touched, filling the air with the smell of cinnamon. He found knotted muscles she hadn't even known she had and worked them like bread dough until they released.

She started purring. He purred back, a throaty rumble that made her wonder if Cat was surfacing again.

Hot fingers found her ass, caressed and stroked. Her libido woke up with a growl.

Ha, said Fluffy. *Told you.*

Then those wicked hands slid right off her butt and proceeded down her thighs. "Hey," she told the pillow. "You're headed the wrong way."

David chuckled, the sound warm and teasing.

He kept going the wrong way right down to her feet, where he found and demolished knots the size of seed pearls between her toes. Who knew you could get knots between your toes?

Marry him, Fluffy demanded. *We can fly to Vegas and find a preacher dressed like Elvis.*

Would you shut up? You're interrupting my toe-gasm.

"Turn over," he said in a baritone rumble when her toes were limp.

I'll get oil on the sheets.

Fuck off, Martha Stewart, Fluffy said. *This is the good part.*

Eva turned over, and he straddled her.

Glancing down, she went cross-eyed. His cock rested on her belly, thick and massively erect, a bead of arousal glistening on the tip.

I think I hear the dinner bell, Fluffy said. *Let me at it.*

He did not, much to her disappointment, start with her tits. Instead he went to work on her shoulders and biceps and hands, until Fluffy started growling with impatience.

Apparently he heard the impatient psychic rumble,

because his next stop was her breasts. Oily fingers stroked aching nipples in tender figure eights, then squeezed and pinched slippery flesh until she squirmed. The warming oil tingled deliciously, burning just short of pain.

If he hadn't turned her arms into overcooked noodles, she'd have grabbed his cock to speed things along. As it was, she just didn't have the strength.

He massaged his way down her torso, moving to straddle her thighs as he went. His cock lay along her belly, a solid weight. She eyed it like a bird fascinated by a snake. A really big snake. "I have an idea for a new comic book movie."

"Mmm?"

She sang it. "Ana-CONDA Man!"

He grinned. "You're good for my ego."

"I'd come up with a theme song, but all the blood has left my brain."

"Too bad."

"Not really." The words spiraled into a yip as slippery fingers found her sex, skating back and forth over her outer lips. He lifted his weight off her legs and spread them until he could settle in between. "It'd have to be a porno."

Then he parted her and traced her clit with a slick fingertip, and she almost swallowed her tongue. Heat jolted from her groin straight to her brain stem. "Oh, God!"

Slowly, deliberately, he traced lazy patterns over and around her button, stopping periodically to pump his fingers deep in her slick core.

Then he'd lean close and blow a stream of cool air over her hot clit, and she'd damn near levitate off the bed.

"David!" Eva yelped finally. "Anytime now!"

He gave her a slow, far too innocent blink. "Anytime what?"

Unable to take any more, she wailed, "Fuck me!"

"Not yet." A finger skated another set of designs around her clit. Hearts, moons—Was that a clover? *Oh, God, he's channeling Lucky Charms.*

She grabbed his shoulders. "Now!"

"Not yet."

"Now!" Her voice deepened into a Fluffy growl, and her nails dug into his skin.

He grinned. "Well, if you insist."

God, he moved fast. One minute he was doodling marshmallow shapes between her legs. The next he was on top of her, his cock in his hand, and then he was *in* her, deep and hard and thick and pumping, and she realized he was just as turned on as she was, and oh, Jesus, it was so good . . .

ELEVEN

Eva gripped him in swollen heat, incredibly tight, hooking her feet over his butt so she could meet his rolling thrusts. A spike of raw pleasure stabbed into David's skull, and he threw back his head, riding the surge.

She cried out, sweet and high, and he had to watch her come. Her beautiful dark eyes looked drowned in delight as her lips parted on helpless moans, full and tempting. Her hair spilled over the bed in a tangle of gleaming curls, and her breasts bounced in time to his thrusts, lovely handfuls tipped in candy pink.

So lovely. So brave and vulnerable.

God, I love her. The thought hit him like a bolt to the brain. *I just wish I could stay the hell away from her before I hurt her worse than Warlock.* Yet even though he knew he should stay away, every time they touched, he went up in flames.

The flash of guilt vanished in a blaze of orgasm. She screamed even as he went over, and he watched those beautiful eyes go blind in climax.

* * *

David collapsed onto the mattress and hauled her over on top of him. Struggling to get his breath, he savored the way she felt lying across him like a sweet-smelling scarf, silken hair tumbled across his skin, tangled with his own.

"I've come up with a sidekick for Anaconda Man," she murmured sleepily.

"Oh?"

"Her name is Noodle Woman. She's not much of a side-kick. Just kinda lies there with her eyes rolled back in her head and a sated smile on her face. But she drives all the female super-villains crazy."

He laughed, savoring the sound of her giggle.

Then a thought wiped the grin off his face. *How can I keep them from killing her? How can I keep from hurting her?*

"The car is registered to Eva Naomi Roman," the were-wolf said. "She lives at 605 Millview Road, Building Five, Apartment E-8, Greendale, South Carolina. I checked the Dire Wolf rolls, but she's not registered."

Warlock grunted in satisfaction. Joe Byrnes was the Bastards' computer hacker. Five minutes after Warlock gave him the car tag number Danvers had called in, Byrnes had the desired information.

"She must be a Bitten rogue," Warlock said thought-fully. It was, of course, strictly forbidden to give a human the Bite without informing the local clan. It was too easy to create a rogue who had no knowledge of what it meant to be a Dire Wolf—and who was therefore a danger to every-one else. "She was probably one of Trey Devon's victims. He always was an idiot. I'm not surprised he couldn't con-trol his Bite." Trey had murdered women for years, until a Maja who was the sister of one of his victims tracked him down and killed him.

That Trey had slaughtered all those women meant

nothing to Warlock, but he was deeply irritated that the case had attracted Arthur's attention. The Magekind always slew their own mad rogues; the Direkind's inability to do the same pricked his ego. Adding insult to injury, one of the Magekind had cleaned up his mess.

To make matters worse, Trey's father had set out to avenge his son's death, only to fail miserably despite Warlock's assistance. Arthur's son, Logan MacRoy, had survived all his assassination attempts. The only positive thing that had come out of the incident was Warlock's acquisition of Smoke's power.

Warlock considered the members of Geri team as they lined up in his throne room. They'd all transformed to face him—four big, capable wolves. Unfortunately, Skoll had been just as tough, just as capable, but they'd still fallen to Smoke's merciless skill.

"We're going to try something a little different this time," Warlock told them.

The wolves moved closer to listen.

This, Tristan thought, as he pulled up to Joan Devon's sprawling brick McMansion, *is going to be one of those missions.* The kind where you rammed your head repeatedly against a brick wall with nothing to show for it except a bloody skull.

They'd been hunting Smoke and/or Warlock for the past few days with zero success. Tristan figured the cat was dead and buried in an unmarked grave somewhere. Which sucked, because he'd liked the fuzzy little bastard. Warlock—well, nobody knew nothing, which was a sure sign everybody was lying.

He was starting to hate werewolves. What the fuck had Merlin been thinking?

"She's got company," Belle observed, as he parked the canary yellow Porsche 911 behind a charcoal gray BMW, one of a number of very expensive cars parked along the tree-lined street. "Should we come back later?"

"Nope. Prime opportunity to meet new werewolves and listen to them lie through their pointy white teeth."

Belle eyed him with disfavor as they got out of the car. Moonlight skated along her high cheekbones and the pure line of her nose, then explored the hint of cleavage revealed by her cream lace blouse. He was beginning to give serious thought to seducing her. "You're a cynic, Tristan."

He shrugged. "People lie. Some are hiding something, some don't want to get involved, and some just for shits and giggles. The trick is to figure out who's lying for a reason, and then dig at them until you can pry out a truth or two." Luckily, he'd been listening to lies for so long, he'd gotten good at classifying them. He now considered himself a gourmet of prevarication.

"But Arthur said Joan Devon told them the truth. If we question her in front of other wolves, we're not going to get anything out of her."

"No, but we can always come back to her later. And we might be able to shake something loose from one of the others." They walked up the gracefully curving brick steps to the colonnaded porch. The mahogany door had a beveled glass insert depicting the family's coat of arms: a wolf rampant over a pair of crossed swords.

Tristan glanced at Belle, to find her rolling her eyes. They shared a snort at pretentious werewolves before he rang the doorbell.

A blond woman answered the door dressed in what was obviously a uniform of black slacks and a white blouse. She carried that particular magical buzz Tristan associated with werewolves. "Yes?"

"We're here to see Joan Devon," Tristan said, and used their true names rather than the identities he gave mortals. "Sir Tristan and La Belle Coeur."

"Oh!" The maid's eyes widened, and she looked flustered as she realized he was a Knight of the Round Table. "Please come in." She ushered them to a sitting room off the foyer, then hustled off.

Maybe this wasn't going to be as bad as he'd assumed.

Nah. Anytime he even thought things might not be an utter disaster, a clusterfuck was a virtual certainty.

"I thought she was going to ask for your autograph," Belle murmured.

"Hey, at least all that hero worship got us in the door," Tristan pointed out. "Though—a Dire Wolf maid?"

"Even werewolves need jobs."

They'd barely found seats in a pair of comfortable armchairs when a slim, middle-aged woman ghosted in. And ghost was definitely the word. She was so pale, even her skillful makeup couldn't hide the circles under her big brown eyes. Tristan thought she might actually be pretty, if not for the emotional stake in her heart. *It's a bitch being collateral damage.* She wore a stark black dress with a single string of pearls, and her dark hair was styled in a chignon.

The woman offered her hand as Tristan and Belle stood to greet her. Her fingers felt brittle as sticks of ice in his hand. "I'm Joan Devon." Her smile looked strained. "It's a pleasure to meet you, Sir Tristan. And you, of course, La Belle Coeur."

"We regret disturbing you at such a painful time," Belle told her, sympathy lighting her lovely eyes. "And we're deeply sorry for your loss. Is there anything we can do?"

"No, but thank you for offering." She lifted one dark, elegant brow. "But I assume there's something I can do for you."

"We're searching for one of our people, a Sidhe shapeshifter," Tristan explained. "He disappeared while he was trying to protect some mortal children. The kids told us he was fighting a huge white werewolf we believe was Warlock."

"Are you sure?" She frowned. "I've never heard of Warlock going into combat. He usually sends his Bastards when he wants someone killed."

"Bastards?" Belle asked with a quirk of the lip. A lip Tris was finding far too tempting these days . . .

Joan shrugged. "That's what he calls his version of the Round Table. Twelve assassins."

"We," Tristan said coolly, "are not assassins."

"No, but the Bastards definitely are. They're greatly feared."

"Do you have any idea where to find Warlock or any of these Bastards?" The assassins would probably be a great source of information. Though getting them to talk would no doubt be a challenge.

But then, Tristan enjoyed a challenge.

She shook her head. "As I told Arthur, all I know about Warlock is what I overheard when my husband was discussing him with other members of the inner circle. Warlock considers women inferior, so I've never met him."

Though sexism had been the rule everywhere on mortal Earth until recently, it amazed Tristan that the Chosen practiced it. They had to know that Merlin and Nimue would hardly have approved.

"We noticed there were other cars here," Belle observed with that charming smile she did so well. The woman made an art form out of seduction. Even her own gender wasn't immune: Joan smiled back. As for Tristan—well, he was only human. More or less. "Would it be all right if we talked to your other visitors?"

Joan lost the smile. "They're all women, so they know very little about Warlock. And they probably won't tell you whatever they do know. The Chosen still regard the Mage-kind with suspicion."

"You're probably right," Belle said easily. "But we'd like to talk to them anyway."

She shrugged. "Come, then. But don't be surprised if they're hostile."

Tristan and Belle followed Joan into the elegant living room as the knight gave their surroundings his professional paranoid's glower. Belle could almost hear him ticking off the findings: A sprawling fireplace had brass andirons that could be used as weapons. The coffee table and end tables were slabs of gleaming white marble veined in gold. A werewolf could probably lift the table and swing it like a battering ram, or break off the curving brass legs for sinister purposes. Art Deco bronzes of women danced here and there, long skirts swirling around them; Tris was probably imagining them used as blunt objects.

Belle's attention was diverted by the huge painting that hung, flanked by the bronzes, over the fireplace. It depicted George Devon Jr. sitting in a massive chair, more throne than anything else. His wife stood behind him with one hand on his shoulder as his two children leaned on either arm, the boy blond, the girl a redhead. Somehow Joan looked very alone surrounded by her family, her large, dark eyes filled with secrets and sadness.

By contrast, her children and husband looked as if they knew themselves to be the center of the universe. Yet she was the only one of the four still alive.

The real Joan spoke with a sweeping gesture at them that snapped Belle out of her preoccupation. "I'm pleased to introduce Lord Tristan, Knight of the Round Table, and Lady La Belle Coeur."

"We've come to convey the sympathies of the Magekind Court to Mrs. Devon," Tristan said with a courtly bow. He did have pretty manners when it suited him.

"Very kind," said a round-faced lady in frosty tones, narrowing green eyes surrounded by too much makeup. "Considering you killed them."

"No, actually, they did not," Joan said in a clear, cold voice. "And they are guests in my home. I would beg you to respect the hospitality I extend to all." Without giving any-one a chance to respond, she began a complicated round of introductions Belle carefully committed to memory.

Two of the other women looked sour at the introduc-tions, while three stared as coldly as the plump woman. One looked nervous, and the young woman next to her showed no emotion at all. Judging by the particular shade of red hair they shared, they were mother and daughter.

It was the girl who brought Belle's instincts to quiv-ering attention. She was pretty in a long-boned, angular way, tall and slim, yet with a certain wiry strength in the line of her shoulders. Her eyes were a clear, bright amber that verged on gold, markedly different from her mother's

emerald green. Definitely not a combination you saw in
humans without benefit of hair dye and contacts. Belle was
willing to bet the odd coloring was genuine in this girl. But
what really riveted her attention was the power that swirled
around the girl in a cloud that was almost visible.

Magic surrounded all the women, of course, but it was
Dire Wolf magic, deep and blue and cool, not the busy
dancing gold of the Magekind. Any spell cast on one of the
Direkind seemed to roll right off like water on a raincoat.

This girl's magic sizzled and popped like oil on a hot
griddle. Its sheer steaming heat made Belle instantly wary.
If she proved as hostile as the glares they were getting from
everyone else, Belle and Tristan were in serious trouble.

On the other hand, this girl was a werewolf who obviously used magic. Warlock was a werewolf who used magic.
Maybe she knew something about Warlock. Finding out
was definitely worth the risk of a magical brawl in the middle of a werewolf tea party.

Merlin help them all.

Introductions complete, Joan ushered Tristan and Belle
to a love seat, a piece of irony that was not lost on Belle.

As their hostess rang for more tea, Belle put a hand on
Tristan's brawny knee. He started and shot her a what-the-
hell-are-you-doing look. She gave him a get-over-yourself
eyebrow lift and silently cast a communication spell. *"Do
you see that girl?"*

*"Little hard to miss her. She's lit up like the Eiffel Tower
on New Year's Day."*

*"It strikes me she might know something about War-
lock. Do what you do best, Tristan."*

One corner of his firm lips quirked upward as if he
imagined she meant something a hell of a lot more com-
plimentary than what she had in mind. *"And what would
that be?"*

*"Annoy the hell out of everybody while I see if I can
establish communication."*

"As my lady commands." The thought sounded distinctly dry.

He didn't waste any time. Joan was still preparing their

tea when Tristan announced, "We're here investigating the disappearance of one of our people, a shapeshifter named Smoke."

"And why do you imagine we would know anything about this . . . person?" Calista Norman was a gray-haired woman who was thin to the point of desiccation, with a horsey face and an expression that suggested she'd been sucking on the lemon in her tea. A diamond broach the size of a saucer adorned the lapel of her steel gray Donna Karan suit, suggesting more money than taste, and her shoes were Prada.

"Because he was fighting a werewolf the last time he was seen."

"There are many werewolves." This from the plump matron who'd spoken first, whom Joan had introduced as Theresa Carington. Her blue eyes were hard and narrow in her soft, dimpled face. "We certainly do not know them all."

"This one is distinctive. He's a sorcerer."

Calista Norman sniffed. "Dire Wolves can't use magic. Not beyond transforming." She lifted her teacup to her lips.

"This one does. His name is Warlock."

The teacup froze.

Theresa Carington didn't even blink. "Warlock is a myth."

"So is Arthur Pendragon," Tristan shot back. "So am I. Ask any human."

Calista had recovered enough to snort. "Humans are ignorant. We are not. And we tell you Warlock exists only in legends told to gullible children."

Belle tuned out the rest of the argument in favor of watching the girl Joan had identified as Miranda Drake. She sat quietly next to her mother, who watched Tristan as if she was waiting for him to detonate a suicide vest.

Yet the girl seemed indifferent to it all. Defeated, for all her power, staring hopelessly into her teacup.

Belle decided to risk a communication spell. *"Miranda?"*

Amber eyes flicked to hers, widening in surprise. *"Umm. Yes?"* Despite her evident hesitation, her magical reply rang like a great gong in Belle's mind. *Merlin's Cup, the child has power.*

"How is it that you can use magic when other Dire Wolves can't?"

The girl regarded Belle warily, before flicking a glance at her mother. Joelle Drake was still fixated on Tristan. *"I'm not your typical Dire Wolf."*

"Neither is Warlock. What can you tell me about him?"

"These women are lying," Miranda said promptly. *"Warlock exists, he's extremely powerful, and he's insane. He probably murdered your friend. Warlock doesn't tolerate any opposition, and he's extremely paranoid."* Naked hate burned in her amber eyes.

"I gather you know him personally?"

The girl snorted. *"You might say that. He's definitely got plans for me."*

Belle frowned. *"Are you in danger?"*

"As I said, he doesn't tolerate opposition. And I don't intend to cooperate."

Belle sat forward. *"We can get you away from him, Miranda. We can help you escape to Avalon. The Mage-kind would protect you."*

The girl's hollow eyes widened. *"You would do that?"*

"Yes."

Miranda's gaze flicked sideways to her mother's tense face, then to the surrounding Dire Wolves. *"This isn't the place to discuss it. Is there a way for me to contact you?"*

Cell phones did not reach into the Mageverse, of course, but there were ways around that. *"I can give you a spelled gemstone."*

Eagerness flashed across her face. *"Yes! That would be perfect."*

Belle had a number of such stones prepared in case she needed to give one to a lover. She carried several in her bag, along with various other magical odds and ends. Slipping a hand into her purse, she found one of the gems and willed it into Belle's grasp. The girl's fingers tightened convulsively as a smile of sheer relief broke across her face.

"What are you doing?" Her mother stiffened as if

goosed with a cattle prod, staring from Miranda to Belle. Her eyes narrowed on her daughter's face. "Are you *communicating* with them?"

"Mom, what are you talking about?" In contrast to her mother's fury, Miranda looked no more than mildly annoyed. You'd never know she was lying through her teeth. "I've been sitting here not saying a word."

"Don't lie to me!" Joelle sprang to her feet, glaring at Belle, fear and rage in her eyes. "You've cast some kind of spell on my child. Stop it!"

"I'm not a child. I haven't been a child in years." Miranda rose to glower at her mother. "For God's sake, I'm twenty-four years old!"

The woman's attention fell on the fingers of Miranda's left hand, closed protectively around the spelled gemstone. "What's that? Did they give you something?" She extended an imperious palm, her lips tight with fear and anger. "Hand it over, Miranda. Now!!"

"Joelle, calm down." Joan stepped around the coffee table as the other women rose and fled from their respective couches like flushed quail. The five ladies huddled at the other end of the room, eyeing the furious werewolf with nervous disapproval. "Remember, these people are my guests. They serve Merlin, the same as we do."

"They're fools, and so are you if you think they can protect you." growled Joelle, her voice dropping with every syllable as magic swirled furiously around her.

"Joelle," Joan began, alarmed, but the protest came too late. Miranda's mother was already transforming.

Fur spilled over Joelle Drake's contorting body as she grew in a magical rush until she towered over her daughter. Almost seven feet tall, she had a long, wolflike muzzle and sharply pointed ears. Her thighs curved, densely muscled, as if she stood on a dog's hind legs, and her hands were tipped with sharp, two-inch claws. Her short, fine coat and shoulder-length mane were the same shining copper red as Miranda's hair. "Do you want him to kill you? Give me that!" She grabbed Miranda's wrist and pried her fingers open.

"Dammit, Mother, that hurts!" Miranda yelped as her mother's talons sliced her skin. Joelle ingored her, plucking the stone away to toss it across the room. It hit the ground and bounced with a rattling *click click click*.

"That's enough!" Tristan roared, bounding to his feet to push between the two. He glared fearlessly up at the towering Dire Wolf. "What the hell is wrong with you?"

Belle shot to her feet, magic glittering around her hands as she prepared to conjure armor around them both. A flick of her fingers summoned the fallen gemstone into her palm.

"You have no idea what you're interfering with," the werewolf spat at him. "You'll get us all killed."

"This is no affair of yours," Calista added, glaring from Tristan to Belle as if they were the ones menacing Miranda. "That girl is Chosen. Tend to your own."

"I am. I'm a Knight of the Round Table," Tristan snapped. "It's my duty to ensure no one is abused while I'm around." He turned toward Miranda. "What do you want to do, kid? Say the word, and Belle will gate us to Avalon."

Under cover of the argument, Belle spelled the gem back into the girl's hand. She looked startled and gripped it tight again.

"No!" Lips peeled back from her teeth as Joelle lifted her clawed hands and curled them in a blatantly menacing gesture. She took a step toward the knight. "You have no right to interfere in family business. She's my daughter, and you are not taking her anywhere!"

Without taking his eyes off the Dire Wolf, Tristan extended his right hand toward Belle. She promptly conjured his sword into his palm, then spun his armor around him with a swirl of power. Tristan gave her a nod of thanks without looking away from the Dire Wolf. "Your daughter is an adult. She has a right to make her own choices."

"She's Chosen." Theresa Carrington drew herself to her full height and tilted her round chin. "Her duty is to her father, and her mother has a responsibility to enforce his will. You're interfering where you're not wanted."

"Mrs. Carrington, I hate to break it to you, but this isn't

the nineteenth century anymore," Belle growled, sending the massive coffee table skidding out of the way with a flick of power. She strode over to stand at Tristan's side. "Say the word, Miranda, and we'll get you out of here."

"You can't!" The werewolf's ears flattened as she turned a pleading look on her daughter. "You know what he'll do!"

Miranda stared up at her towering mother, and the defiance bled away from the set of her shoulders. "Yes, I know exactly what he'd do." She turned to Belle and pressed the communication gem into the witch's hand. "I appreciate the offer, but I can't leave my mother. Her husband would kill her. And that's not a figure of speech."

"Miranda!" Calista sounded scandalized. "We don't share our business with outsiders!"

"Her husband? Not your father?" Suddenly two plus two clicked together in Belle's mind. "Warlock *is* your father, isn't he?"

Joelle grabbed her daughter's shoulder and pushed her toward the door. "We have to go, Miranda."

"We can protect you." Tristan started after them in that fluid swordsman's stride. "Both of you, even against Warlock."

"There is no Warlock!" Calista's voice rose, going shrill and insistent. "He's just a legend! Tell them, Miranda!"

They all ignored her. "Let's go," Joelle insisted. "This isn't safe for either of us. If Gerald gets wind of it . . ."

"Mrs. Drake, let us transport you both to Avalon," Tristan interrupted. "No one will be able to attack you through the city's wards."

"And trigger a war?" Joelle snapped. "Do you really want a war with the Direkind? Personally, I don't need that much blood on my conscience, so no, I'm not going anywhere with you." She turned a demanding gaze on her daughter. "Warlock would declare war on Avalon to get you back. You can't go with them either."

"You're right." The girl's mouth twisted as her shoulders slumped. "I can't leave her. Thanks, but—I just can't." And as Belle and Tristan watched helplessly, she let her mother hustle her out the door.

TWELVE

In the dream, three dragons surrounded the human child: a brawny gold and a pair of blues, one sleek and well fed, the other wiry as a snakedog with small, cruel eyes. They weren't particularly big dragons, being not long out of the egg themselves, but they towered over the little boy as they surrounded him. Smoke thought him no more than ten or so, his build slim, with enormous brown eyes that dominated his elfin face under a disordered thatch of dark hair. He smelled of terror, but he held himself erect, chin up and defiant as he faced his tormentors.

"Let's eat him," hissed the snakedog, creeping closer and staring at the boy as if he were a fat stag. "He trespasses."

The gold frowned. "We are not to eat these creatures. Cachamwri himself commanded it." The god of the dragons had befriended the Sidhe millennia before, and he insisted his people observe the peace he'd declared.

"He said we are not to eat the Sidhe," the well-fed blue corrected. "This one is not Sidhe. He is a mortal with no magic at all."

"Interloper!" snarled the snakedog, examining the child with greedy interest, his tail lashing. *"I want a bite of him. He will crunch. And then we will throw his bones into the human city as a warning, and they will leave our world."*

Rage drew Smoke's lips off his great fangs as he gathered himself and leaped, landing between the child and the snakedog. He'd learned the dragon tongue long before the death of his people, and the words spilled from his mouth on a river of fury. *"Touch him and die, egg sucker."*

The snakedog drew back from his bared fangs, confused, his thin tail whipping in agitation. *"It speaks? But it looks like a ciardha."*

This fight could go badly. The dragons might be young, but they towered over Smoke. Still, the gold took a cautious step away. *"'Tis no ordinary ciardha. Look at its aura—it's inhabited by an elemental. And something else . . ."* The creature lowered his head for a closer look, then jerked back as Smoke slashed a warning paw at his nose. Iridescent eyes widened in puzzled surprise. *"Sidhe. Its soul is Sidhe."*

"Aye, and I claim this boy as one of mine." Smoke crouched, tail lashing. *"You will not touch him."*

"We saw him first!" the snakedog objected.

Smoke roared even as he sent power thrusting at the cloudy sky. Thunder rolled in deafening reply, and lightning forked the ground, so close the dragons ducked. The boy screamed and dropped to his knees, curling into a tight ball with his thin arms over his head. He was evidently unaware that Smoke had surrounded him with a shield to protect him from the charge.

"The next bolt lands between your beady eyes, lizard!" Smoke snarled.

"Keep him, then!" Thoroughly spooked, the snakedog leaped into the air and flapped away, his fat brother blue following with an awkward hop.

"We did not realize he was yours, Great One," the gold said, dipping his muzzle in a shallow bow.

"It should not have mattered if he was or not," Smoke snapped, thoroughly incensed. *"You do not eat sentient*

creatures, hatchling. I know Cachamwri, and he would not approve, whether the boy is Sidhe or not. Don't allow those fools to lead you into sin."

"I will not, Great One," the gold promised. With another dip of his scaled head, he took to the air, his wings blowing a storm of leaves and dust around Smoke and the boy.

When the dragons were no more than black specks among fat gray clouds, Smoke turned his attention to the child. He still lay huddled on the ground, eyes squeezed shut, shivering in waves as tears wet his dirty cheeks.

Smoke tried a few words in all the Sidhe tongues he knew, but the child did not respond. With a sigh, the cat reached into the boy's thoughts, spinning a delicate magical connection between them so that he could absorb the child's language. Smoke went slowly, for if he wasn't careful, he would burn out the boy's mind with the ancient power of his own. So the cat was exquisitely careful as he plucked grammar and vocabulary and syntax like a village maiden gathering fat sweet berries that would bruise with a harsh touch.

With them came other knowledge: the boy's name was Logan, and his parents were Arthur and Guinevere Pendragon, a vampire and a witch respectively, both warriors sworn to protect the humans of an Earth that was twin to this one.

Unfortunately, the child was also thoroughly terrified of Smoke's huge cat self. With a mental sigh, the cat searched the child's thoughts for a form he would find more reassuring.

It didn't take long to find it. He reached for his magic and shifted.

"Logan?" Smoke said in his newfound English. "You're safe now."

The child only shuddered, squeezing his eyes tighter with a sob that made the cat's chest ache. Moving closer, Smoke extended his head, and rasped his small pink tongue over the dirt-smeared little face.

Brown eyes sprang open, and the child jerked back, sitting up to frown down at him. "Hey, kitty." Peering around *in confusion, he scooped Smoke into his arms and scrambled hastily to his feet. "What are you doing here? Something's gonna eat you. They've sure been trying to eat me."*

"Yes, well, I put a stop to that," Smoke said, settling comfortably into child's arms.

The boy stiffened and stared down at him in astonishment. "You talk?"

"Among many other skills, such as tossing lightning bolts at homicidal young dragons." He angled his head to the side in invitation. "Would you mind? I seem to have an itch just behind my right ear ... Ah, yes, that's it. What are you doing here, child?" He knew perfectly well, of course, but it would be better if the boy told him.

"I went exploring and got lost." Logan sighed, still scratching gently behind Smoke's pointed housecat ear. "Mama's gonna kill me for sneaking off."

"Better your mother than other candidates for the job." Flicking the end of his tail, he opened a gate to the magical city he'd seen in the child's mind. "Let's get you home, shall we?"

David, dreaming, had no idea that he'd just called his magic.

"That girl's going to die," Belle growled, and sucked down another swallow of her rum and Coke.

"She's mortal," Tristan pointed out. "Dying goes with the territory." He tipped up his bottle of Corona and drained half of it.

"Yes, but being murdered by a werewolf doesn't!" Across the polished surface of the bar, the bartender looked over at her, eyes going wide. Belle curled a disgusted lip and cast a quick spell. He blinked and shook his head, deciding he must have misheard. Collecting her drink, Belle headed for a booth on the other side of the Peach Pit, Tristan striding in her wake.

They'd both switched their magical armor for jeans and cotton shirts, though the fabric wasn't anywhere near as comfortable.

"What is it with those people?" Belle slipped across the cracked red vinyl seat. Sweeping a pile of peanut shells out of the way, she plunked down her glass. "Merlin chose them for the Great Mission just as he did us. He and Nimue would never have tolerated the abuse of women, especially not by the same warriors who should be protecting them. And yet those bimbo Chosen seem to regard submitting to those bastards as their duty."

"Makes no sense to me, either." His expression brooding, Tristan began absently peeling the label off his bottle. "I spoke to Diana . . ."

"King Llyr's wife?" The lord of the Sidhe had met and married the pretty werewolf a couple of years before.

"Yeah, that's the one. Anyway, she said the Chosen were the Direkind's version of an aristocracy. Apparently, these guys can trace their lineage back to the original Saxon warriors Merlin chose to make Direkind."

Belle nipped a cherry off the end of a cocktail skewer. "What about the rest of them?"

"They're descendents of the Bitten, people those original warriors bit in order to give them Merlin's Curse . . ."

She lifted her brows. "Merlin's Curse?"

"Don't look at me—that's what *they* call it. Anyway, the Chosen seem to have gotten a little inbred and squirrelly over the past fifteen hundred years. Some of them are members of what Diana described as a religious cult, but she didn't know much about the cult leader."

"Warlock?"

"That's my guess. Evidently there are a whole lot of legends and not much fact about him. The story is that Merlin gave Warlock the ability to work magic in case the Direkind should ever need to go into battle against us."

Belle frowned. "Why just one werewolf? Why not all of them?"

Tristan shrugged powerful shoulders inside the blue oxford cloth shirt that brought out the color of his eyes. "Apparently Merlin wanted them to be immune to magic, and you can't be immune to magic and work it at the same time."

"What I don't understand is why he thought he needed somebody to fight us to begin with," Belle took another sip, enjoying the pleasant buzz that was beginning to erode her furious tension.

"Evidently, his chosen warriors on another planet went a little power-mad and destroyed the very people they were supposed to protect." His expression brooding, Tristan started feeding pieces of his Corona label to the jar candle on the table. "So he created the Direkind just in case."

"Yeah, but who keeps *them* in line?"

"We do, I suppose."

Belle frowned. "And what if we can't?"

"Then we're screwed."

"Along with the rest of humanity. I . . ." Magic bloomed in her awareness, a cool dancing wind she instantly recognized.

Smoke.

Belle sucked in a breath and grabbed for that spurt of power, sending a spell after it as she tried to track it back to its source. Unfortunately, she lost the trail as it disappeared like a Roman candle shooting into the night. "Merlin curse it!"

"What? What do you see?"

She blinked and became aware of Tristan's intent green gaze. She felt her nipples peak. *Oh, cut that out,* she told them, sitting back in the booth with a disgusted flounce. "For a minute there, I sensed a burst of magic that felt like Smoke. Unfortunately, it vanished before I could home in on it."

Tristan grinned in genuine delight. "At least we know the fuzzy little bastard's alive. I always liked him."

"And he's a damned good man to have on our side. Or kitty cat, or god, or whatever the hell he is this week." Belle raked a hand through her curls. "But where *is* he?"

Eva woke to the sound of David purring in that feline in-and-out rumble she'd come to associate with great sex. She smiled a little, blinked sleepily, and rolled over. "Hi, love . . . What the fuck are *you* doing here?"

There was a house cat lying next to her. David was nowhere to be seen.

Fluffy hated cats, and cats hated her right back. This left Eva caught in the middle, trying to keep Fluffy from eating the cats and the cats from clawing any part of her they could reach.

Eva lifted her voice, eyeing the furry interloper in irritation. "David, why did you let a cat in here?"

The cat opened familiar crystalline blue eyes and said, "What cat?"

"Ahhhhhh!" Springing off the bed, she slapped the wall with her back. Horrified, Eva stared wide-eyed at the seven-pound black housecat occupying the center of the mattress. "David?"

"Why are you looking at me like . . ." He broke off, his eyes widening as they fell on the paws stretched out in front of him. He leaped to all four feet in astonishment. "Oh, gods, what now?"

Eva did what she always did when she was upset: she cooked.

Her knife thunked against the wooden cutting board as she sliced a bell pepper into fragrant emerald slices. She'd already diced tomatoes, ham, pepper jack cheese, and mushrooms for the huge omelet she had in mind. Not that she was particularly hungry. She'd feed it to David, but it probably weighed more than his entire body—including fur.

Make him turn back, Fluffy growled. *We can't fuck him like this.*

He's been trying to turn back. For the past hour, in fact, in between telling her about that weird dream he'd had. *It didn't work.*

He needs to try harder. He's a cat. *That's just wrong on too many levels to count.*

Eva glanced up to watch David pace along the countertop, his tail lashing in agitation. He was a beautiful little beast, his fur so black its highlights looked blue. Silver striped his haunches and shoulders in a pattern she'd never seen in a house cat's fur. He did, however, look exactly like the tiger-creature she'd seen in her dream, except smaller.

Much, much smaller.

And how the fuck is he supposed to fight werewolves like this? She felt sick.

Abruptly he stopped pacing and sat down in front of the cutting board, coiling his tail neatly over his feet. Lifting his elegant little head, he looked her in the eye. "I must leave."

She considered the idea. "Under the circumstances, that might be smart. Where are we going?" Eva lifted an egg and prepared to crack it into a mixing bowl.

"You're not coming." He said it in a flat tone, his blue eyes narrowing.

Eva's fingers tightened convulsively, crushing the egg and raining yolk and shell fragments into the bowl. *"What?"*

"As I am now, I can't protect you. If I left, you'd be safe from Warlock's assassins."

"Forget it." Eva started plucking bits of shell out of the yolk with short, agitated gestures. "I might as well roll you into a burrito and serve you to the bastard. He'd snack the minute he found you. No way in hell is that going to happen if *I* have anything to say about it."

David peeled his lips off dainty fangs. Those crystalline eyes were the only part of him that looked familiar. But wrong, so wrong, in that tiny triangular head. "Do you seriously think you can stop him? You can barely face down your own reflection!"

Eva stared at him in astonished hurt. "Thanks a fuckin' hell of a lot, David!" She picked the bowl up and dumped its contents down the garbage disposal. No way would she be eating anything now.

"I do not want to die knowing I have doomed you!"

"Yeah, well, I don't want to live knowing I let you die!" She leaned down until she was nose to tiny black nose with him. "I repeat: *not happening!"*

He lifted his chin with regal pride. "I may be small, but

I'm fast. I can hide from Warlock until I can shift back to my proper form and defend myself."

"And you can hide just as well right here, so drop the melodramatic bullshit."

"What if he sends another team of assassins? They will butcher us both. At least alone, I may be able to elude them."

"You couldn't elude the neighbor's poodle right now, and you know it."

"I may be in cat form, but I still have my intelligence. And you have no right to keep me here."

"There's the door." She pointed a shaking finger at it. "Go!"

"I can't turn the doorknob!" he roared, his voice startlingly loud coming from such a small body.

"Then how the hell do you think you're going to fight off fucking *werewolves*?"

With a snarl of rage, he leaped off the counter and headed for the door, crouched, and began to stare at it as if he could will it to open.

Blinking burning eyes, Eva picked up her cutting board and began raking the makings for the omelet into the trash.

Dogs lazed in the shade of the woods behind the Drayton Apartments. There was a huge red Great Dane, a black Doberman, a German shepherd, and a muscular pit bull with curly steel gray fur. They scratched at fleas, panted, chased squirrels, and terrorized a fat Persian cat who was lucky to get away with her life.

But they never strayed far from Building Five. Periodically one or the other of the dogs would get up and stroll around the building, stopping only long enough to lift a leg at the shrubbery.

If anyone had bothered to look more closely, they might have noticed that the animals seemed fascinated by the second floor. Yet they kept a careful distance, as if wary of drawing attention.

And all four came to quivering attention whenever anyone

went up or down the stairs, only to subside when they got a good look at whoever it was.

But they were, after all, only dogs, so nobody paid much attention to them.

Tension rode like a nauseating weight in Gerald Drake's belly as he stood at attention in Warlock's inner sanctum.

What kind of lunatic has an inner sanctum?

He stifled the thought as soon as it flitted through his brain. The last thing he needed was for Warlock to detect any hint of disloyalty in his mind. The sorcerer was already furious with him as it was.

Gerald had reported Miranda's slaying of Worthington right away, knowing Warlock would want to know of it. He'd expected to be summoned immediately for discipline—which would be highly unpleasant, judging from past experience.

Instead, Warlock had seemed oddly distracted during the call, as if he was far more concerned with something else. He hadn't even been able to make time for Gerald's full report until just now, hours after the initial incident.

Odd. Warlock had been obsessed with Miranda's every move for years. Now she'd killed the man the sorcerer has designated to breed her, and he scarcely seemed to care.

Not that his distraction would save Gerald. He'd always known the little bitch would be the death of him. Warlock would lose his temper over something she'd done, and Gerald would end up a dead werewolf. He'd never expected to survive her rebellious teenage years, much less into her twenties. Luckily, she loved her mother, though Merlin alone knew why. Joelle was good for very little else, but she made an excellent hostage.

At first, the task of raising the werewolf witch had seemed simple enough. Marry Joelle, control her little brat, and reap the considerable rewards Warlock rained down on him in the form of magical advantages for his construction business. Gerald had grown rich thanks to the sorcerer's spells, as government contracts fell into his hands like ripe peaches, while competitors suffered disasters natural and otherwise.

Now his corporation was the largest in three states, with multimillion-dollar contracts to build everything from schools to bridges.

But the price—Merlin's balls, the price was high.

Warlock had left him waiting in his throne room for the better part of an hour now, uneasily considering the glowing magical runes carved into the stone walls. A circle of inlaid silver lay set in the floor at the center of the space, surrounding a low dais and Warlock's massive ebony throne. Stone statues of Merlin's original Direkind Chosen stood in niches around the room, and the scent of exotic spices filled the air, making Gerald's nose itch.

He stifled a sneeze as his sensitive ears picked up the click of claws on stone. He straightened to his full height as Warlock padded in. To Gerald's uneasy surprise, four strangers followed him, all in Dire Wolf form. They were huge even by Direkind standards, tall and massively built—one with thick black fur, two in shades of brown, a fourth who was as blond as a movie starlet.

Must be the Bastards. At least some of them; weren't there supposed to be twelve? Where were the others?

Not that it mattered. *This isn't good. This isn't good at all.*

Warlock flung himself down on his throne, his white fur seeming to glow against the dark wood. Black lips peeled off white fangs as his eyes glowed amber with a sullen, feral rage. "Now, Gerald. Tell me again how you failed to control my daughter."

Terror tied his belly into a sick knot. *Miranda, you're going to pay for this.*

The silence steamed with rage for the first half of the trip home. Miranda knew it wouldn't last, and it didn't.

"You've destroyed us." Joelle's grip made the steering wheel creak in protest.

"What the hell do you want from me, Mom?" Miranda

exploded, a knot of frustrated rage coiled in her belly. "Am I supposed to just submit to being raped with a smile? Fuck that! I'm not a doormat like—"

"Me?" Her mother's voice had gone deep again, growling with fury and an incipient transformation. "Did it ever occur to you to wonder *why*, Miranda? Why I put up with everything Gerald does—the cheating, the violence, the casual contempt? Do you honestly think this is the life I wanted?"

Miranda threw up her hands. "Oh, yeah, that's right— book me another flight on Guilt Air. I'm not responsible for your choices, Mom."

"What choices? When did I have a choice?"

"Half an hour ago! Tristan and La Belle Coeur would have taken both of us to the Mageverse if we'd said the word. But no—you had to fucking *attack* them!"

"Because it really would have triggered a war, you little twit! Don't you understand, Warlock is not going to let you go." Her mother's eyes flashed red in the blue glow of the Volvo's dashboard lights. "You're the key to the dynasty he's determined to create, and he'd declare war on the Magekind to get you back. Merlin created us to fight them—odds are, we'd kill them all!"

A chill stole across her skin, but Miranda shook it off. "Oh, come on! Ninety percent of the Direkind don't even believe he exists. They're not going to go to war with Arthur just because some loony tune werewolf wizard says the word."

"Warlock's not crazy. And you have no idea what he's capable of, so don't underestimate him. He's got charisma, and our legends have turned him into a hero. The Direkind wouldn't realize what he's really like until it was too late. By then who knows how many people would have died on both sides? Is it worth all that just to keep you from a little—"

"Rape?" Miranda gritted her teeth. "I'm not going to just lie down for whatever they've got in mind. I don't care what kind of rationales you throw in my face or what kind of guilt trips you put on me. You don't have the right to ask that of me."

Joelle thumped the steering wheel with a frustrated palm. "Miranda, it doesn't have to be rape. You're in your Burning Moon—if you don't fight, it won't be that bad."

"Yeah, Worthington said the same thing—which is when I stuck the knife in his brain. Listen to me, Mother: I am *not* going to submit. If I can find a way to escape, I'm going to take it. Now, you can go with me, or you can stay and keep being a victim. It's your call."

"Don't you understand—I've already tried that! Warlock found me, and it cost me . . ." Tears glittered in her eyes. "God, what it cost me."

Miranda frowned at her. "When did you try to escape?"

"When I was pregnant the first time." As Miranda gaped in surprise, Joelle pulled the Volvo over onto the shoulder and parked there. Opening the door, the older woman got out and stood looking toward the moon as it rode over the trees like a white ship sailing through the clouds. Finally she started into the woods, her steps slow and weary.

Miranda followed her. "You never mentioned you'd been pregnant before. What happened?"

"It wasn't rape that first time." Joelle pushed a tree limb out of the way and continued into the thick brush. "I thought I was in love with him." She laughed in a bitter bark. "He really had me fooled."

Gaping, Miranda stared at her mother's back. "You were in *love* with Warlock?"

"I was young, and he was handsome and powerful and immortal." Joelle stopped, turning her face up. A shaft of moonlight lit her skin and painted silver reflections in her eyes. "I was so flattered that he wanted me. Of all the women of the Chosen, he picked me as the mother of his child. He said I had the perfect bloodline."

"What happened?"

She shrugged. "I made him angry. I don't remember what I did now—it could have been anything. It's easy to make Warlock angry. Anyway, he beat me. Very, very carefully, mostly in the face, since I was seven months pregnant at the time, and he didn't want to hurt the baby. So I ran away."

Miranda swallowed. "He found you."

"Oh, yes. He has extensive resources even aside from magic. It took him less than forty-eight hours to track me down. That time when he beat me, he wasn't so careful. I lost Mary Catherine."

Miranda winced. "I'm sorry, Mom."

"The next time he took me, it was rape." She pushed her hair out of her face, and Miranda saw a tear paint a glittering trail down her face. "After that, he told my parents he'd found a husband for me. Of course, they made no protest. They were as frightened of him as I was."

"You never tried to escape again?"

"And watch you die as Mary Catherine had?" She shook her head. "Miranda, you can't fight men like Warlock and Gerald. They're ruthless, and they know what your vulnerabilities are. The only hope you have is submission, because that's the only way nobody dies."

"But, Mom—why didn't you tell me this before?"

Joelle gave her another weary glance. "Because I knew it wouldn't do any good. And I was—" She blew out a breath. "I was ashamed Warlock had played me for a fool. He never loved me any more than Gerald does. Besides, telling you this story changes nothing. Does it?"

Miranda bit her lip, but she couldn't lie. "No. In the end . . . no."

Joelle smiled sadly. "I didn't think so. Come, I need to get you home. Gerald is probably impatient for his dinner."

THIRTEEN

Blade rang on blade in the furious music of combat as the vampires and witches fought.

Not very well.

They swung their weapons clumsily, the vampires with more power than skill, the witches hesitantly. Here and there someone fought a bit better as natural athleticism overcame a lack of experience. But they weren't an impressive bunch.

Tristan and Belle stood on the sidelines of the combat grounds, watching the new recruits practice, neither particularly impressed. "I swear to Merlin, they get worse every year," the knight grumbled.

"Everyone has to learn, Tristan," Belle told him. "You probably did, too. You've just forgotten because it's been fifteen centuries. Give them a few more weeks, and Reece and Erin will have them whipped into shape."

The tall Champion of the United States and his Maja wife passed among the ranks of their pupils, stopping here to correct a grip, there to demonstrate the proper technique of a parry. Belle saw Reece pause beside Davon Fredericks and take the surgeon by the wrist, correcting the way he held his sword.

"Poor Davon," Belle murmured. "He's used to being the best at everything he does. This must be hard for him."

Tristan curled his lip. "After his . . . association with you, he should be used to having things hard."

She shot him a poisonous smile. "Why, Tris—that almost sounded like a compliment."

"It wasn't."

"Better luck next time." Before he could fire off the retort he was no doubt brewing, she nodded across the field. "There's Logan."

Not surprisingly, the ex-cop seemed to be instructing his opponent rather than fighting him. When Arthur Pendragon is your father, you know how to use a sword before they take the training wheels off your bike. Logan could probably have taught the class almost as well as Reece, though the other vampire was a good two centuries older.

Tristan waved to attract his attention, but with everything going on, Logan didn't appear to notice. "Hey, kid!"

"Even a vampire couldn't hear you in all this." Belle stuck two fingers in her mouth and blew a piercing note that made everyone look toward them in surprise. She gestured Logan over. "And Tris—if you say one word about me and blow jobs, I swear I'm turning you into a frog."

He gave her a smirk. "Sensitive, darling?"

She returned the smirk with interest. "Wouldn't you like to know."

Watching Logan jog toward them, Belle thought again how incredibly glad she was that Arthur's son had fallen for Giada Shepherd.

When he was just twelve years old, Logan had had a violent crush on Belle. He'd even said he wanted her to give him the Gift when he grew up. She'd rather have been waterboarded than tell him how that prospect horrified her. It was one thing to seduce young studs she didn't know, but she'd changed Logan's diapers. He might have grown into a handsome, brilliant man, but she had no desire whatsoever to sleep with him.

Unlike, say, Tristan.

Shut up, she told that treacherously honest inner voice.

"What's up?" Logan asked after he and Tristan exchanged backslapping greetings.

"I think I've found Smoke," Belle told him. "Or at least, I've found the general area he's in. Anyway, I'm pretty sure he's still alive."

Logan's dark eyes, so like his father's, lit with joy. "Thank God! Where is he?"

Belle described the burst of magic she'd sensed. "I think he's still somewhere in Greendale County." Which was where he'd disappeared the week before. "Unfortunately, I haven't been able to sense him since that burst. It's as if something's blocking me."

Logan nodded. "Yeah, Mom and Giada said the same thing. Even Morgana had no luck."

Belle frowned. That didn't sound good; Morgana was one of the Magekind's most powerful witches. But still . . . "I thought if you had some object of his, I could use it to create a tracking spell."

Logan frowned as he considered the question. "Well, there's the little pewter cat he gave me when I was a kid. It's got a communication spell on it so I could call him, but when I tried it last week, it didn't work. If you think you can use it, it's yours."

"Worth a try, especially if it already has a spell of his on it. If he pops up again, maybe I could establish a connection with it." Belle frowned. "Sounds like I'll need to build a pretty powerful spell, though."

"Probably." Logan turned his gaze across the field to meet that of his lovely blond lover. The woman nodded and summoned a gate, then disappeared through it. "Giada's gone to pick it up."

"Enjoying your Truebond?" Tristan asked, referring to the psychic link the couple had obviously formed.

"Oh, yeah." Logan's handsome face lit with a grin. "Giada's amazing. She's so fucking brilliant . . ."

"And you love her for her mind." Tristan's smile was gently mocking.

Logan laughed. "Among other things."

A moment later, another swirling dimensional gate

opened, and Giada stepped through. The tall, stunningly beautiful witch extended a tiny cat statue between tapered fingers. "One pewter kitty, as ordered."

"Thanks, Giada," Belle said, accepting the cat. Its moonstone eyes glinted in the field's lighting, and she could feel power humming through it. She smiled, encouraged. "This should work nicely."

"I hope so." Giada linked an arm with her fiancé. "We've both been so worried about Smoke. He's a good friend."

"And he practically raised me," Logan said. "I was going nuts thinking that bastard Warlock killed him." A muscle flexed in her jaw. "We really need to end that fucker."

"If we can figure out a way to do it without triggering a war with the Direkind." Tristan shrugged.

"I'd better get to work on that spell," Belle told them, opening a gate back to her home, where she kept the magical tools she'd need. "I want to have it ready if he surfaces again."

"Not without me," Tristan growled, grabbing her wrist before she could step through it. "You'll go off on your own and get yourself killed."

She gave him a narrow-eyed glare. "Tristan, I'm perfectly capable of taking care of myself."

He sneered. "Yeah. Sure."

But she let him follow her through the gate anyway.

David hunkered down on the coffee table, his eyes shuttered as he attempted to contact the godling hidden somewhere inside himself.

He had to escape this form before he ended up costing Eva her life. Unfortunately, so far all he had for his pains was a savage headache.

"David?" Eva crouched in front of the coffee table, putting herself at his eye level. She looked impossibly huge, as if she'd transformed into a giant. But then, everything else looked wrong, too, blown completely out of scale. For a moment he had the horrifying sense he was about to disappear, that he'd shrink until he vanished. He gritted his small jaws and fought rising panic.

Eva's lovely brown eyes pleaded with his. "David, talk to me, dammit. Please."

He ignored her, focused on his ferocious need to transform into something that could defend her. Even if it wasn't human. Even if it was the tiger form he'd seen in his dream, that would be better than this utterly *useless* creature.

Eva rose and began to pace the living room, frustration in her voice. "Look, I know you're pissed, but dammit, what would you do if our positions were reversed? If I'd been turned into a toy poodle, you wouldn't let me go out and get eaten either."

"That's different," he growled, unable to resist the topic. *"Why?"*

"Because I'm the male." David knew the argument was irrational, but he really didn't give a damn. "I'm supposed to be the protector. It's what I do. It's who I am."

He opened his eyes to find that Eva had stopped in her tracks to stare at him. "That is such *total* bullshit. I . . ."

Someone rapped knuckles against the front door. "Eva? Are you in there?"

"Oh, hell, it's Mom!" Before he had time to twitch an ear, she pounced, snatching him into her arms.

"Let me go!" When he tried to struggle, she grabbed the scruff of his neck, holding him helplessly immobile while she wrapped one arm securely around him.

"Forget it," she hissed. "I'm damned if I'm going to let you race outside."

"Eva?" her mother asked again.

She got the door open before he could decide whether to sink his fangs into her wrist. Stepping back to let her mother in, Eva forced a smile, hoping it didn't look too frantic, as she tried to maintain her grip on David. "Hi, Mom!"

Charlotte Roman strolled in, a slim and youthful figure in a cream pantsuit and peach blouse. Atypically, she wore a frown as she glanced around the room. "Who were you talking to? I thought I heard a man's voice."

"It was the TV, Mom." Eva kicked the door closed and prayed David would keep his muzzle shut. All she needed was to be outted by a talking cat. "What brings you over? And where's Dad?"

"It's Saturday—he's running his Magic tournament."

"Oh yeah, that's right." Magic the Gathering was a collectable card game; Dad had been holding weekly tournaments at the Comix Cave for years. He also sold the wide variety of Magic card decks, so it was good for business all around. "So you decided to stop by and kill some time."

"It's not killing time, it's spending quality time with my baby girl." But Charlotte's attention was focused on David, her brows raised. "I didn't know you had a cat. I didn't even think you liked cats anymore."

"This one kind of followed me home." The door safely shut, she put David down. He gave her a dirty look, the tip of his tail flicking in offended rage. She winced.

Her mother crouched, extending a hand to him. To Eva's surprise, he sniffed delicately at her fingers, and permitted himself to be picked up. "You're a beauty, you are. What unusual coloring! I've never seen a cat with markings like this. Usually, if a cat is striped, it's over his entire body."

"He's not your typical cat." Boy, that was an understatement.

Charlotte walked over to the couch and settled down on it, then proceeded to give David's ears a good scratch. Judging by the way his eyes shuttered in pleasure, he liked it. "What's his name?"

"Uh. . . ." Fang would *not* do. He'd probably shred her curtains in revenge. Or her ankles, in his current rotten mood. "T'Challa." Which was the secret identity of an obscure Marvel superhero named Black Panther.

Charlotte shot her a look. "I should have known. You're such a geek, darling."

"Hey, you knew who it was. What does that make you?"

"I've been married to your father for three decades. Of course I'm a geek."

Eva laughed as she headed for the kitchen and the bottle of white Zin stashed in the refrigerator. After spending the day trying to convince David not to commit suicide by werewolf, she was in desperate need of alcohol. "Would you like a glass of wine, Mom?"

"That would be wonderful. I've been grading papers all day, and I've got a horrible headache." She taught English at Steve Ditko High, a thankless job if ever there was one. "My students think if you can text it to somebody, it's perfectly acceptable use in a term paper. If I see 'yo' spelled as the letter 'u' one more time, I'm going to start foaming at the mouth."

Still stroking David absently, Charlotte rose and followed her daughter into the kitchen. Eva got a pair of glasses from the cabinet and put them on the counter, then went to work on the wine bottle and its cork. It yielded easily; there were some advantages to being a werewolf.

"Eva, is something wrong?" Her mother's gaze was a bit too acute.

More than I've got time to list. She concentrated on pouring the wine. "No, why do you ask?"

Intelligent brown eyes studied her with obvious concern. "Maybe because I've known you all your life, and I can tell when you're hurting."

Eva handed her mother one of the glasses and summoned her best everything's-cool smile. She'd gotten good at it after five years as a lying werewolf. "Everything's fine, Ma. I just had an argument with David, that's all." Which at least was the truth.

"Where is he, anyway?" Charlotte sipped her wine, still cuddling David's small furry body in the other arm.

Eva managed a shrug. "Like I said, we had a fight. He stalked out in a huff." *Or at least, he would if I let him.*

"Your father said he's very handsome," Charlotte said, scratching him under his furry jaw. "Not to mention partially naked, at least when Bill met him. He works in movies?"

"No—" Eva remembered she'd said he was a stuntman. Keeping her lies straight was becoming a problem. She really needed to make them less complicated. She took another sip of her wine to give herself time to think. "Oh.

Yeah. He specializes in sword work. He was in *Kor the King*." So much for simplifying the lies.

Shut up now, Eva.

Charlotte took another contemplative sip as she cuddled David/T'Challa. "Do you really think it's a good idea to look for a boyfriend on one of those Internet dating sites?"

"Well, all I'm meeting at the Comix Cave are geeks."

"I know, darling, but you *are* a geek, so that shouldn't be a problem. Besides, I married a geek, and that turned out rather well."

"Ah. Yes. Good point." Without thinking, Eva picked up her own glass and drained it in one long swallow.

Charlotte put down her glass and dropped David, who landed like a—well, cat—then promptly streaked across the living room and under the couch.

Eva, watching him in worry, was startled when Charlotte cupped her face in both cool, slender hands. "Something *is* wrong."

Pulling away, Eva picked up the wine bottle to pour herself another glass. "Everything's fine, Mom."

"Which must be why you're guzzling the Zin." Charlotte brushed a lock of Eva's hair back and studied her, dark eyes narrow. "Baby, this is your mother you're talking to. I can always tell when you lie. And you're lying now."

Eva pulled out of Charlotte's light hold to give herself time to think. She had to come up with something her mother would believe. Preferably because it was true. "Like I said, I'm just a little upset about David."

"Are you afraid of him?" Charlotte's eyes flashed with sudden anger. "Has he hurt you?"

Eva blinked, startled. "David? God, no."

Charlotte nodded slowly. "Okay, that was honest. But you are afraid of something. Really afraid." Brown eyes narrowed. "Is it that asshole neighbor of yours?"

"Ronnie? No, David took care of him."

"Then what is it? I know there's something. There's been something for at least five years now."

Which was when the werewolf attacked her. Eva froze,

the glass halfway to her lips. *Mom's getting entirely too close to the truth. I need to distract her.*

"We did notice, you know," Charlotte continued, eyeing her. "One day you were fine, the next you started hiding from everybody, including us. You lost weight, and there was a look in your eyes no mother ever wants to see on her child's face. You scared the hell out of us. And just like now, you insisted nothing was wrong when we knew damned well something was. What are you hiding?"

Shit. "Nothing, Mom."

"Don't give me that." Charlotte's honey brows lowered. *"Who are you afraid of?"*

Should she come clean? Tell Charlotte she was a werewolf and transform to prove it? Tell her about David, the hunk currently hiding under the couch? "Mom . . ."

Before she could say anything more, the tinny notes of the sixties *Batman* theme started playing from the depths of Charlotte's purse. "Dammit, Bill, your timing stinks." Grumbling, her mother picked up the handbag and started digging through it in search of her cell phone.

A reprieve. Thank God. Eva sagged against the counter, her mind working frantically. She really hadn't wanted her parents to know what she'd become. It would only scare them, especially considering this Warlock character had drawn a bead on David—and Eva along with him.

"Talking to Eva," her mother said into the cell. "Bill, it's really not a good . . . Can't you—? All right, dammit, I'll go pick the damn things up. But next time, pack them in the car the night before, would you?"

Grumbling under her breath, Charlotte folded the flip phone and stuffed it back in her purse, then looped the bag over her shoulder and headed for the door. "Your father left the prizes for the Magic tourney at the house, so he wants me to go pick them up. I swear to God, that man would forget his head if it wasn't bolted on his shoulders." She opened the front door.

Alarmed, Eva straightened. "Ma, don't . . ."

David streaked right past her ankles, out the door and into the night.

* * *

When Miranda opened the front door, her stepfather stood on the other side—seven and a half feet of enraged, fully transformed werewolf. He stepped inside in one long stride, slamming the door behind him. She backed away, heart in her throat.

"You utter fool!" Baring the knife length of his fangs, Gerald backhanded her before she could get her arms up to block the blow. She slammed into the foyer wall with a crash that rattled the portrait of her grandfather, then fell flat on her ass. "You betrayed your people." His voice rose to a roar. "You betrayed your *god!*"

Miranda shook her ringing head as she fought to scramble to her feet, desperate to get away before he hit her again.

"Gerald, wait!" Joelle darted in front of her husband, raising her hands in supplication. "Miranda has done nothing to betray anyone, much less Warlock!"

He seemed to swell in his rage, towering over the fragile figure of his wife. "Don't you dare lie to me, you stupid cunt! Calista Norman called—she told me all about what you did. How could you let Miranda anywhere near a Knight of the Round Table? You knew she'd talk!"

Calista, you bitch, Miranda thought, steadying herself against the wall as the room rotated slowly around her. Stars flashed in her vision, and she strongly suspected he'd given her a concussion.

"We had no idea the knight would be there," Joelle said, talking fast, as if trying to get through to him before he killed them both. "The ladies were holding a Grieving for Joan Devon, and . . ."

"Joan Devon!" Gerald mocked in a high, singsong voice. "Why do you think Joan's husband is dead, you idiot? She gave him up to the knights! Just like *she*"—he pointed a curving talon at Miranda—"gave up Warlock!"

"No, no you're wrong!" Joelle wrung her hands and darted a frantic glance at Miranda. "She told them nothing. Did you, darling?"

"Not a damn thing." Miranda forced herself to meet her

stepfather's furious yellow gaze without flinching. "The woman tried to give me a communication spell, but Mother knocked it out of my hand and told her to stay away from me. So we left."

Her father's long muzzle twitched, drawing in her scent.

Oh, shit, Miranda thought. *I should have talked around it. He's going to smell the . . .*

"You lie!" He sprang at her, knocking Joelle aside with a sweep of one furry arm. Miranda skittered back, calling her magic as she retreated from his snapping jaws. Her transformation raced over her body in a wave of fur, muscle, and bone contorting like soft clay in the grip of her power.

"You dare change?" As she met his frenzied gaze, she realized he'd lost control completely. And he intended to kill her. "You dare fight me? *You dare?*"

Fear iced her veins, but she made herself sneer. She was tired of cowering from these bastards. "Oh, I dare. And if I get the chance to talk to Belle again, I'm going to tell her *everything.*"

"Then I'll have to see you don't get the chance, you traitorous bitch!" He drew back a clawed hand as if to rip out her throat.

Joelle threw herself between her daughter and the blow. "Ger—"

His claws ripped into her face before she could get the rest of the word out of her mouth. She flew sideways, her body slamming into the base of the stairs with a crash. Something snapped.

The sound seemed to echo in Miranda's skull. "Mother!" Forgetting her father, she leaped to her mother's side, landing beside her in a coiling crouch.

Her mother's head lay at an impossible angle, the life draining from her eyes.

Oh, God. I finally got my mother killed, Miranda thought in dazed horror.

FOURTEEN

Numb with horror, Miranda started to snatch her mother into her arms, only to freeze, afraid to touch her and hurt her even more. "Call 911!" she yelled at her father.

"It's too late." He sounded indifferent. "She broke her neck. She's dead." He bared his teeth, stalking toward her on clawed feet. Grabbing her by a fistful of mane, he hauled her up away from Joelle's body, drawing back for another open-handed swipe of his claws. "And I'm not done with you."

He didn't notice the short sword shimmering into her hand, but he did when she rammed it into his chest. Miranda's lips peeled off her teeth. "Well, I'm done with *you!*"

She jerked the blade out of his chest, and he fell onto his knees, gagging at the sudden pain. Miranda felt nothing at all when she swung the weapon up and took his head in one swing.

He won't be healing that, she thought, feeling a wave of ice roll across her mind.

Tossing the sword aside, she knelt by her mother and let the tears fall in a hot tide of guilt and grief. In her pain, she was barely aware of changing back to human form.

Miranda cried until her eyes were swollen, cried until there were no tears left. Until there was nothing left, in fact, but an aching emptiness and a small voice that asked, *What's the point?*

She was done.

Warlock would find her even if she ran, and when he did, she would die. Either he would kill her himself, or he'd send so many assassins even her magic would not be enough to protect her. She might as well dig a hole and wait to be pushed into it.

But even as she considered surrender, her mother's empty eyes seemed to catch hers. *Mama didn't die so I could give up.*

Miranda stared at Joelle's broken corpse. Determination begin to grow from an icy little seed buried somewhere in her numb heart.

What if she could find a way to get to the Magekind and tell them everything they needed to know to destroy Warlock?

Unfortunately, she had no idea how to reach La Belle Coeur. "Dammit, Mama, why couldn't you let me keep that communication gem?"

Well, she'd just have to find another way to reach the Magekind, preferably before Warlock found *her*.

So the race was on.

She'd need to run, which meant she'd have to have money and a car. Gerald could provide her with both—albeit posthumously.

The thought tore a bitter, rasping laugh from her lips.

The library safe was hidden behind a massive nineteenth-century painting of fox hunters riding to the hounds. Luckily, Gerald had never been a very creative man; it took Miranda about two minutes to deduce that the combination was his birthday.

Well, it wasn't as if it would have been her own.

The safe's thick door swung open to reveal piles of cash in thick, banded stacks. "Hell, Gerry, what were you doing—dealing cocaine?"

She packed the money into one of her two suitcases,

then filled the other with her clothes and loaded the lot into her stepfather's dark gray Lexus. Then she unbolted the car's license plate and carried it upstairs.

Miranda had been strictly forbidden from studying magic. Which, naturally, hadn't stopped her. She'd read every book she could get her hands on, trawled forbidden Internet sites, and experimented endlessly.

It hadn't taken her long to determine that damn near everything she read was utter horseshit. Yet sometimes the spells she attempted did work, largely because they helped focus her own innate magic on her goals.

So it was that she flipped the license plate over, got out a bottle of black enamel paint and a fine brush, and began to paint a spell across the back of the plate.

It wasn't a particularly powerful spell—if it had been, any werewolf who saw the plate might notice it. All it would do was keep cops from taking an interest in Gerald's car.

Satisfied, Miranda reattached the plate to the Lexus and slipped back inside the house.

Now she needed something to keep Warlock from sensing her if he decided to conduct a magical search. And sooner or later, he would.

She found what she was looking for in her mother's jewelry box: Joelle's favorite cameo on its black velvet choker. The Victorian piece had come down from her great-great-grandmother. Generations of werewolf females had worn it, which gave it a certain power all its own. Power that would provide Miranda with a matrix to support the spell she planned.

The cameo in her hand, she crouched in her bedroom closet, flipped back a section of carpeting, and lifted up the floorboards she'd unscrewed years before. In the space beneath them, she found her spell book, chalk, several beeswax candles, a few bottles of dried herbs, and an athame—a ritual knife.

The spell Miranda had in mind was both powerful and complex, and to cast it she needed more space than there was in her bedroom. So she carried everything down to the basement, to begin the painstaking process of drawing the necessary chalk designs on the cement floor.

Hours passed while she drew and chanted, candlelight throwing dancing shadows on the basement's contents— dusty old toys, boxes of clothing her mother had planned to take to Goodwill, even a Christmas tree that stood in one corner, wrapped in a shroud of green plastic. All the bits and pieces of Miranda's old life.

At last it was time for the spell's finishing touch. Still chanting softly, Miranda used the athame to slice her left hand. Tilting her palm carefully, she let a few drops of blood drip onto the back of the cameo.

The spell snapped to life. With a sigh of relief, Miranda tied the necklace around her throat.

Now she could make her escape.

By the time Miranda left the house half an hour later, her mother lay in the big bed upstairs, hands folded neatly on her chest, sightless eyes closed.

She'd left Gerald's corpse where it fell.

Miranda clicked the key fob on Gerald Drake's Lexus and tossed her suitcases in the trunk. Just before she got in, she looked back at the mansion that had housed generations of Drakes. She sketched a design in the air and murmured a spell. Sparks of blue magic trailed her fingers.

And the house burst into flame.

"That's all the warning you're going to get from me, Warlock." She slid into the driver's seat and started the car.

Belle sat six inches above the floor, her golden hair whipping back from her face on a magical wind, her eyes glowing the same milky moonstone as the pewter cat she held in one hand. Her long legs were folded in a lotus position that made Tristan's thighs hurt just looking at them. All while wearing a black lace teddy that made her breasts look like mounds of fresh cream.

Sadist.

When he'd commented on her choice of magic wear, she'd told him he could always leave. Damned if he would, though, with her working some kind of potentially dangerous spell.

So Tristan made a point of leering at her until she was so far gone in the magic that she didn't even see him anymore. Then, and only then, did he pull up a chair and sit down to keep watch.

The floor beneath her floating backside was covered with an intricate pattern drawn in golden light on the blue hotel room carpet. Apparently, the pattern was designed to act like a lens, gathering and focusing whatever magic Belle could pick up from the cat statue she cupped in both hands.

She looked like she was having really good sex. Her glowing eyes were wide, her full mouth parted and glistening under a coat of that gloss stuff she wore. Tristan was getting a hard-on just looking at her.

But then, he'd basically kept a hard-on the entire time he'd been working with her. When he didn't want to strangle her, anyway.

Tris hated to admit it, but he was actually enjoying himself. The Majae he'd worked with before had tended to fall into two camps: the hard-core professionals who acted like they had Excalibur up their butts, and the party girls who wanted to do him solely because he was a Knight of the Round Table. Maybe while lying on it.

No thanks, he'd had that with Isolde.

Unlike all the other witches, Belle took his crap and dished it right back with a sarcastic twinkle that made him want to laugh. Or smack her. She . . .

Belle screamed, the sound deafening and shrill. Her slim body flew out of the pattern as if hit by a cannonball. She slammed into the wall behind her, and the wallboard cracked with the impact, the floor shaking under Tristan's chair.

"Shit!" He leaped to his feet as Belle fell on her face, plaster dust and bits of Sheetrock raining around her.

"Belle!" Tristan dropped to one knee beside her. His

first instinct was to jerk her into his arms, but he'd been in enough fights to be wary of internal injuries. Instead he bent to look into her face and cautiously touch her slender back. Her skin felt like fine Chinese silk. "Belle?" His heart was hammering, and his mouth tasted metallic with fear. "Belle! Wake up, dammit!"

She groaned. "Jesu, stop yelling." The words came out as a rasp. Bracing her hands on the floor, she tried to push herself upright.

"Stay down! I'll call a healer . . ." He reached for his belt, where a cell phone rode a clip. It was spelled to reach Arthur or Morgana at a word.

"No, that's . . ." Belle swallowed and rolled onto her back. "Not necessary. Bastard just took me by surprise, that's all. Threw me for a loop, but I'm not hurt. Much. I'll have some nice bruises, though."

Sitting back on his heels, Tristan studied her. She looked too damn pale for his peace of mind, and he decided if she didn't start looking better in a minute, he was calling Morgana anyway. "I gather whoever the hell it was you contacted, it wasn't Smoke."

"No. I think . . ." She swallowed and closed her eyes. "I think it was Warlock. And he was not happy to be pinged."

Tristan frowned. "What's he doing responding to Smoke's communication spell?"

Belle started to sit up. He slid an arm around her back and steadied her. She gave him a what-the-hell-are-you-doing look, but he stubbornly refused to back off. He didn't want her eating carpet again.

Bracing herself back on her arms, Belle sighed. The deep line between her blond brows suggested a ferocious headache. "He must have usurped Smoke's powers. God knows how."

Tristan frowned. That didn't sound good. At all. "So was it Warlock you sensed when you thought you felt Smoke?"

"No, it was definitely Smoke. I've touched his mind before."

She had? When the hell had she . . . *Shut up, Tristan.*

Unaware of his flash of jealousy, she continued, "Or at least, it wasn't the same person whose mind I just touched. Warlock felt . . . well, evil. And paranoid."

"Really? I never would have guessed," Tristan drawled.

She ignored him. "There was such chaos in his thoughts. I only touched him for a moment before he blasted me out of his mind like a feather in a leaf blower." Raking her blond hair out of her eyes, Belle frowned. "Where did that pewter cat go?"

Tristan glanced around before spotting it under a straight chair sitting at the opposite end of the room. "There it is."

He got it for her, and dropped it into her palms. She was sitting up again, her legs bent and crossed at the ankles, tailor fashion. She no longer looked quite so pale, much to his relief.

"Thanks." Belle eyed the cat thoughtfully. "I wonder if I could use it to break Warlock's grip on those stolen abilities."

Tristan stiffened. "Only if you can avoid getting your skinny little butt blown across the room again. And somehow I doubt it."

"Skinny?" She snorted. "Hardly." Scrambling to her feet, Belle erased the designs on the carpet with a sweeping gesture and a wave of magic, then started redrawing them again.

Since her attention was now safely diverted, Tristan leaned a shoulder against the wall and closed his eyes in relief.

That had been too damned close.

David had disappeared.

Her heart in her throat, Eva galloped down the stairs of the apartment complex, frantically scanning for him. Still nothing.

Her mother spoke from the landing. "Oh, damn. I'm sorry I let out your cat. You want me to help you look for him?"

Eva ground her teeth to keep from screaming, *Just go!*
Instead she managed a relatively sane "Don't worry about
it, Mom. I'll find him. You just go take Dad his prizes."

Charlotte sighed. "Yes, he's probably going to be paw-
ing at the ground by the time I arrive. I'll see you later,
darling." Her heels clipped down the stairs.

Eva gave her mother a wave, eyeing the shrubbery as
Charlotte got in the car and drove off.

"David!" she hissed when the coast was finally clear.
"David, where the fuck did you go? Don't do this to me!
Somebody's going to *eat* you!"

Which was when she heard a sound that sent terror sliding down her spine on a river of ice: a growl. Low, rumbling, and savage.

It was definitely not a house cat, and it was coming from
the other side of the building.

"Shit!" Eyes widening, Eva raced through the breezeway toward the sound. There was a strip of grass, a few
spindly trees, and still more bushes between her building
and the back of the next one.

Right in the middle of all that stood a dog the size of a
pony. It looked like a Great Dane with thick red fur, but the
wind blowing past told a different story.

It was a werewolf.

Another snarl brought her head whipping around.

A black Doberman eyed her with drooling malice, next
to a German shepherd larger than any dog she'd ever seen.
They were flanked by a muscular pit bull with a curly steel
gray coat. All three were downwind, but Eva didn't have
to smell them to know they were werewolves. The vicious
intelligence in their eyes told the story.

Eva was changing before she was even consciously
aware of calling her magic, pain exploding in her awareness as her body transformed. *Damn you, David,* she
thought. *I'm screwed now.*

David stared in horror from the shadow of one of the
shrubs that stood against the building. Sable fur gleaming

in the moonlight, Eva stepped back, her head swiveling frantically as she watched the four werewolves move closer.

They transformed in a fur-ruffling rush of magic, each dog shooting upward and outward as it grew to full, powerful Dire Wolf form. If anything, they were even bigger than the werewolves he'd faced the last time.

And David was much, much smaller.

Magic, he thought desperately. *I have to change. I have to defend her, or she's dead.*

Panic soured his stomach, but he pushed it down. He couldn't afford fear now. He had to be calm. He had to open a psychic path to Smoke, or at the very least to Cat.

"Where's your friend, bitch?" demanded a tall, red-furred werewolf who stepped out in front of the others. "We know he's around here somewhere." He made a show of sniffing the air. "I can smell the little fucker."

"I don't know what you're talking about," Eva said, lifting her chin in a gesture of defiance. Unfortunately, the scent of her fear came to David's nose as sharply as a scream.

She was terrified, and he was hiding under this bush like a coward. Yet until he could transform, emerging would only put Eva in more danger, because she would try to defend him. It just wasn't in her to do anything else, despite the odds, despite her fear. And her courage could get her killed.

Sick with fear, he watched the werewolves move toward Eva in a slow stalk. "Smell that, boys?" the leader purred, making a show of inhaling. "She's scared shitless."

"I like 'em scared." This from a wolf whose muscles lay in thick slabs under his black fur. "Makes me horny."

The leader raised his voice. "Don't you think you'd better come out, Cat? Otherwise, we're gonna fuck up your scared little girlfriend. And then we'll just track you down and tear you apart anyway. But if you grow a pair, we'll let the girl go."

Eva spoke up in a surprisingly deep growl, glaring at the werewolves in contempt. "Bet you feel like real men, huh?" Her voice shook, but now there was as much rage as fear in her scent. "Four of you against one woman. You sure you don't want to go find a few more friends to back you up? I might hurt you."

The leader glanced at her, anger sparking in his hot red eyes. "We can handle you just fine, bitch."

For God's sake, Eva, shut up! David thought in despair.

She curled her lip. "You want me, asshole? Come get me." It was the same doomed defiance that had led her to try a a groin punch on the werewolf who'd transformed her. She thought she was finished, and she wanted to spit in her enemies' faces.

But he couldn't let her die. Wouldn't. There had to be something he could do. Yet he'd fought all day to reach out to both Cat and Smoke with every ounce of his will. Nothing had worked.

"You need to learn a little respect, bitch." The werewolves' leader lunged at Eva, swinging out with one clawed hand. She ducked, but not fast enough. Blood sprayed from the raking blow across her lovely breasts. Striking out in rage, Eva caught the leader across his muzzle with a hard, clawed swat.

"Oh, that's it! You're done now, cunt!"

They all jumped her at once, grabbing for her wrists as they dodged her snapping jaws. A fist hit her head with a meaty thump, and their combined weight forced her to the ground. She cried out.

Anguish knifed through David's chest, a searing psychic pain. Unable to suppress the sound, he snarled. At that, the leader's gray-furred head came up. Yellow eyes speared through the sheltering leaves of the bush. And found his.

FIFTEEN

A universe away, a creature of pure energy swirled like smoke within the spell that caged it. For endless hours Smoke had battered at the cage, fighting to escape fighting to reach the powers Warlock had stolen.

Nothing worked.

Smoke had called for his spirit brothers out beyond the spell cage, begging them for help. He could feel himself eroding without the body and wills of his spirit brothers to give him form.

Warlock was trying to transform the elemental into nothing more than a power source for his own magic, and Smoke knew he wouldn't last much longer.

So of course that was when the pain hit—a sheering agony that tore at his soul.

The girl. They were killing the girl.

Both Smoke's spirit brothers cried out in ringing rage. In that instant, the elemental realized he could use their pain as both conduit and power source. With a cry of mingled victory and fury, the creature began to craft a spell to shunt his stolen magic back to his brothers. Perhaps he couldn't escape Warlock's cage, but once they had the power, the brothers could rescue themselves—and him.

It was the only chance any of them had.

At last the spell was complete. He could feel how weak it would leave him, how helpless, but he didn't care. All that mattered was saving his brothers. And Eva, their precious Eva.

So with the last of his strength, he cast his spell, ripping the energy from Warlock and sending it flying back to his brothers. The sorcerer's psychic scream of fury made him smirk.

There, you bastard. Reap what you've sown.

The werewolf leader smirked through the leaves of the bush as he spotted the cat. "Well, what have we here? Is that you, Cat? No wonder you hid."

"Leave him alone, you bastard!" Eva shouted. A hand cracked hard against her head, and she yelped.

The werewolf pulled away from her, rising to his full seven and a half feet. Turning, he stalked toward the bush. Eva screamed and threw herself against the hands that gripped her arms and legs, but the wolves held her down easily.

The leader bent down over the bush, grabbed David by the scruff, and hauled him out. Fanged jaws gaped in a grin. "So much for—"

The magic hit David in a breath-stealing electric surge that convulsed his black-furred body. The wave was so powerful, its nimbus slapped the werewolf like a fist. He dropped the cat and staggered back to fall in a heap of stunned fur.

David grew. Grew past man size, grew past the size of the big-cat form he'd so often assumed.

Grew to nine feet of muscle and claws and fangs, his body given the shape of his rage by the power surge from Smoke.

He leaped over the unconscious leader to grab Eva's nearest captor by the mane, jerking him up and around. Claws flashed, and the werewolf howled, gutted. David grabbed the monster's long muzzle in one hand and clamped the other over a brawny shoulder. He jerked in opposite directions. *Crunch.*

The werewolf fell dead.

With a howl of fury, the sable wolf flung himself off Eva and barreled into David's powerful cat thighs. The two went down in a chorus of chain-saw snarls.

Which was why David didn't see the remaining were jump to his feet, fist buried in Eva's dark mane as he hauled her up to use as a shield.

David had turned into a furry Incredible Hulk—more than a head taller than any of the werewolves and half again as broad, his shoulders massive, his fangs like blades, big hands tipped in claws the length of a man's fingers.

And he was really, really pissed off.

"Get him, David!" Eva screamed as he buried his fangs in the werewolf's throat with a savage snarl.

"Shut up, bitch!" the gray werewolf yelled in her ear as he dragged her backward. "You're coming with me. And you're gonna keep your fuckin' boyfriend off my ass."

Oh, screw that, Eva thought, and used the move David had taught her for just this situation.

Her clawed hand shot backward to grab the werewolf's dick and balls, curling into a vicious fist. Testicles squirted like an overripe tomato.

The werewolf howled, agony loosening his grip on her hair. She snapped around in the second part of the move, slamming her elbow into the creature's sternum. He bent double with a wheeze, unable to breathe, much less scream.

Eva promptly grabbed his muzzle in the third move of the sequence, and jerked his head up with all her considerable werewolf strength.

There was that *crunch* again. When she let go, he fell, dead before he hit the ground.

Her stomach twisted in nauseated triumph as Eva looked around just in time to see David rising from the body of the werewolf he'd just slain. Nearby lay another one who was just as dead.

Which left the leader, still out cold from the blast that had transformed her lover.

David grinned at her, distinctly smug. She flinched only a little at the sight of his bloody jaws. Then a sudden motion out of the corner of her eye made her whip her head around.

The werewolf leader reeled to his feet, shaking his head, obviously still half-stunned.

David snarled.

"Oh, fuck," the werewolf said, his eyes going wide as he realized every one of his men were dead. He whirled to run.

Eva looked away, wincing as David shot after him. The two disappeared around the corner. She heard a yip, cut off by a rolling feline roar.

From somewhere overhead came the sound of a glass door sliding open. "What the fuck is going on down there? Do I have to call the cops?"

Shit. Eva dove into the concealment of the Building Five breezeway. "Sorry! My dogs just killed a coyote."

"Well, hold it the hell down!" The door slid closed again.

"Eva?" A voice came out of the dark, a full octave deeper than normal, but unmistakable.

"David?" she whispered.

"Here." He came around the corner of the building, an immense dark silhouette.

She went into his arms hard enough to thump, her hands closing tightly around his waist. His body felt huge—and wet, but she wasn't in the mood to quibble over a little blood. "Oh, God, oh, God, I thought we were dead! I thought they had us for sure."

"Yes, well, they didn't." He sounded grimly satisfied.

"I did just what you told me to do," she said, dimly aware she was babbling and not giving a damn.

He pushed her back a pace. "No, you didn't, because what I actually told you to do was run like hell if we were ever in this situation."

"And let them *eat* you? Not fuckin' likely." Pulling out of his arms, she looked around. Dead werewolves sprawled in the dim light of the moon, blood-splatted, heads and limbs at unnatural angles. It made for a sickening sight—until she remembered that if the creatures had had their way, she and David would be the dead ones.

"Well," she told him, "we made one hell of a mess."

When Belle and Tristan stepped through the dimensional gate after she'd finally gotten the cat spell to work, the first thing they saw was a dead werewolf. The creature's throat had been torn out, and his neck was broken.

"Looks like Smoke's here," Tristan said dryly. "And he's pissed."

"Definitely." Belle gripped the pewter cat. Its eyes glowed so brightly, they illuminated the scene like tiny flashlights.

They'd been back at the hotel when she'd sensed the roaring force of Smoke's magic suddenly activating. It had taken fifteen precious minutes to trace the pulse and cast a gate that led to its source. Which had evidently been more than enough time for Smoke to express his extreme displeasure to whatever werewolf had pissed him off.

Tristan's helmeted head lifted suddenly, and he silently pointed toward the corner of the building. That was when Belle heard the soft murmur of voices.

Despite his armor, Tristan could move with surprising silence when he wanted to. Belle followed him, her own armor creaking and scraping, plate against plate. She was considering a spell to silence it when they rounded the corner.

And saw Smoke. Or actually, they saw a nine-foot werebeast that shared the cat's dramatic coloring of blue-black fur and silver stripes. Behind him stood a female Dire Wolf who looked delicate next to the cat's menacing brawn.

"Oh, God," the female said, "what now?"

With a rolling, vicious snarl, the werecat leaped at Tristan. The knight went down with a shout and a clatter of armor under the massive beast's weight. The cat dove for his throat, only to be frustrated by his enchanted gorget.

"Smoke!" Belle shouted, "we're friends! Don't hurt him!"

But before she could get anything more out of her

mouth, something hit her like a four-hundred-pound running back. She slammed into the ground so hard she saw stars and tasted blood. Claws raked her armor with a metallic screech.

It was the female werewolf, snarling and savage.

Though the wolves were immune to magic, that only meant energy attacks did nothing against them. They still couldn't tear their way through armor spelled to resist physical attacks. The Dire Wolf growled in frustration as she tried to get her claws in Belle's neck.

"Get off, dammit!" Belle slammed a backward kick into the werewolf's thigh she didn't even seem to notice. "We're Smoke's friends!"

"Yeah, right. That's why you showed up with the rest of the assassins." The werewolf paused, as if to consider a better place to rake. Belle twisted for an elbow slam. The armored joint hit the werewolf right on the end of her sensitive nose, and she yowled in pain.

Belle had spent a thousand years learning how to fight dirty. As the werewolf jolted up in pain, Belle twisted onto her back and slammed a fist into her furry groin.

A groin punch hurts regardless of gender, and the female tumbled backward, yelping as she cupped her abused sex. Belle rolled, grabbed her fallen sword, pounced on the wolf, and slammed the pommel into the girl's temple. Dark eyes rolled up. It was a blow that would have killed a human, especially delivered with a Maja's supernatural strength, but Belle knew it had only bought her a moment to think.

She bounced to her feet and looked around for Tristan and Smoke. Unsurprisingly, the knight was having a far harder time with his opponent than Belle had had with hers. The huge cat raked his claws across Tristan's armor, fighting without success to get through to flesh. Tristan was giving as good as he got, but since he didn't really want to hurt Smoke, he was handicapped. All he could do was punch and kick, while battering the beast with the flat of his sword.

Smoke should have recognized Tristan; the two had been buddies since he'd rescued Logan more than twenty years ago. That the cat was attacking his friend now suggested that Warlock had done something to his mind, just as Belle had suspected.

She reached into the pouch on her weapon's belt and grabbed the pewter cat. Being a creation of Smoke's, the cat was a direct link to his mind and magic. She pulled off one gauntlet and tucked it in her belt before curling her bare hand around the cat and reaching for her magic. The spell took hold with a snap, and she sent a message rolling along it. *"Stop, attacking us, Smoke. We're your friends. We're trying to help you."*

The cat froze with his jaws wrapped around Tristan's gauntlet. He released his fanged grip, though he still held the knight down with massive clawed hands. Crystalline blue eyes flicked from Belle's face to the fallen werewolf girl. Rage curled his lips into a savage snarl. *"You* hurt *her. Get out of my mind."*

He rose off Tristan with a rumble of rage. And sprang.

Five hundred pounds of pissed-off werecat shot toward Belle like the space shuttle. She had only a fraction of a second to cast her power toward the great beast in a net of energy. Chains of force materialized around huge paws even as she spun aside like a bullfighter.

The cat hit the ground hard, tumbling in a tangle of magical energy. It was such a near miss that the tip of his tail brushed Belle's arm as he passed. Smoke roared, a deafening bellow of rage.

Tristan raised his sword and raced toward them in a desperate sprint. "Belle!"

She blinked at the note of fear in his voice. Fear for *her*? "It's all under control, Tris."

He slammed to a stop, sucking in hard breaths as he watched the cat fighting the chains in a spitting, clawing fury. "I can tell. Offer him a blow job or something and get him to calm down."

Typical Tristan. Just when she thought he might have some glint of basic humanity, he turned back into a jackass. Belle flipped him off and moved cautiously closer to her prisoner.

A glass door rolled open somewhere overhead. "What the fuck is going on!" someone roared. Other voices lifted in alarm.

Damn. Bystanders. Belle inhaled and called her power from the Mageverse, breathing it out in a sleep spell that rolled over the complex in a wave of sedation. Silence fell as various innocents decided they'd dreamed the roaring tiger and wandered off to bed.

"Somebody probably called 911," Tristan pointed out, moving over beside her. He sheathed his sword with a scrape of steel on leather.

"Let me know if you hear sirens." Belle told him absently, fighting to keep the cat in his magical chains. He hissed and growled as he struggled just as hard to break them. "I'll cast a nothing's-wrong-here spell to send the cops away."

"Let. Me. Go!" the cat snarled. He stopped fighting the spell chains; either he'd decided he couldn't break them or he was gathering strength for another attempt.

Belle dropped to her knees, the better to meet his infuriated blue stare. "Look, Smoke, we have no intention of hurting you. I'll be happy to release you as soon as you promise not to eat us."

"Because quite frankly," Tristan muttered, crossing his muscular arms, "you're not my type."

"Ignore him, he's an asshole," Belle told the cat.

"Whereas you are the soul of charm." The cat gave her a smile that showed far too many teeth. "I promise not to eat you. Now get the magic chains off."

"Somehow I'm not reassured." Belle eyed him and sighed. "Look, I have no idea why you don't seem to know this—but we've known each other for twenty years, ever since you rescued Arthur Pendragon's son."

The cat went still, the rage draining from his eyes, leaving only bewilderment behind. "The boy. The one the dragons were trying to eat."

"That's right." Belle smiled at him, encouraged. "His name is Logan, and he's a grown man now. He's very worried about you. We were all afraid Warlock had killed you."

Smoke studied her for a long moment before he spoke.

She could feel the cat deciding whether to trust her. "He almost did. He cast some kind of spell that stripped me of my powers and memories. It's fragmented me. I have managed to get some of it back for short periods, but then he rips it all away again. If he holds true to form, he's going to attack again very soon. And I won't be able to resist."

"Can you help him?" Belle started as the voice spoke behind her. She whipped around to find the female werewolf towering over her, her eyes glowing with reflected moonlight.

They didn't smell like liars or crazy people. There was none of the acid reek Eva had come to associate with people who were just pulling her chain, nor was there the frightening stench she'd smelled from the schizophrenic who'd wandered into the shop last year.

These people believed what they said—and it sounded an awful lot like what Cat had told her, right down to the stuff about King Arthur. Besides, when they looked at David, there was genuine affection in their eyes, despite the overlay of fear in their scents. Given how big and furious he was, she really couldn't blame them for being alarmed.

"They're telling the truth, David." Eva turned to examine the glowing golden chains that bound him. The fetters looked like really good film special effects, but David couldn't seem to break them. What's more, she could feel the magic radiating from them like a current of electricity tingling across her skin. "Weird as that sounds. You really did rescue the son of King Arthur? It wasn't just a dream?"

"Apparently." He studied the witch warily, his pointed ears gradually rolling forward as he sniffed delicately, sampling the strangers' scents.

The blond woman started to reach for him, then stopped as his eyes narrowed. "May I touch you?"

He considered her a moment, then nodded. "If you free me."

The big armored man took a half step closer. "I don't think that's a very good idea, Belle."

"That's because you're a professional paranoid, Tristan," the woman said lightly.

"Wait, *Tristan*? As in Tristan and Isolde?" Blinking, Eva gave the woman a closer look. "You're Isolde?"

"God, no," the woman and Tristan said in a chorus so fervent, Eva was surprised into a grin.

"I'm La Belle Coeur," the woman explained. "Everyone calls me Belle."

Eva still remembered a little high school French. "The beautiful heart?" She frowned. "But what happened to Isolde?"

"She's dead." Tristan's harsh tone did not invite further questions. He turned toward his partner and flipped up his visor, apparently so he could glower at her. "So are you going to help the kitty cat recover his memory, or what?"

"Is that what you want?" Belle met David's gaze.

For some reason, his blue eyes flicked over to Eva's face, and he hesitated.

Eva remembered something Cat had said. *"If our enemy does not kill us, sooner or later we will be one again. Will you think we're not David enough then?"* A chill crept over her, but she shook it off. "David, as long as you can't remember who you are—as long as you can't control your powers—you're at Warlock's mercy. What if you turn into a house cat again? What the hell would we do?"

"He likes being a house cat." Tristan folded his arms and leaned a thick shoulder against the vinyl siding of the apartment building. "It makes people underestimate him."

"Except this time I could not turn back." David's tail lashed in agitation.

"And Team Fido tried to gang rape me and eat him," Eva added. "Which they'd have done, if he hadn't managed to turn into the Incredible Hulk with fur."

The knight winced. "Yes, I can see how that would suck."

Eva snickered, amused at the thoroughly American phrase spoken in Tristan's precise English accent.

"You're right—I need my memory," David said, his eyes meeting hers. "I have to control my magic." He looked at Belle. "If you can help me, do it."

* * *

Belle murmured a chant, dissolving the spell that held Smoke chained. She reached out and touched the cat's big head with one hand while she fished out the pewter cat with the other. Smoke's fur felt thick and surprisingly soft under her fingertips. She closed her eyes and called her magic, wrapping it firmly around the pewter cat. Because Smoke had created the spell when his mind and powers were whole, she should be able to use it as an anchor for the spell to reintegrate him.

Then she dove into his consciousness like a cliff diver plunging into the ocean.

Belle had contacted Smoke's mind before, in a particularly rough patch during Logan's teenage years, and she vividly remembered the Demigod's thrumming power and the great depths of his consciousness.

The mind she touched now was nothing like that. Belle frowned. It felt as if holes had been ripped in his psyche, as if he'd been savaged by some kind of magical shark that had devoured hunks of his soul. And the pieces that were left were scattered, disconnected. Confused and bleeding.

She plunged deeper, sensing that some vital part of him had been severed. Something responded to her psychic touch with a rumbling, wordless question. The Cat, Belle realized, the most primal part of him, all animal instinct and elemental power. Her hand curled tightly around the pewter figure as she drew hard on her magic, then sent it pouring into him, drawing Cat up out of the darkness, so that she could bind him and the Sidhe warrior together again.

"No," Cat's voice rumbled. He began to fight her, pulling away, resisting her attempt to reweave the connections between them. *"Our mate will reject us."* To the Sidhe he added, *"I would not cost you her love."*

"She swore she wouldn't turn from us," the warrior said. *"She knows we need each other to defeat Warlock. Otherwise he'll kill us all, including Eva."*

"That is logic," Cat warned. *"There is no logic in the*

heart." Belle could sense his sadness. *"But I suppose we have no choice. And I have missed you, my brother."*

She felt them reach for each other. Acting on pure instinct, she poured magic into them to make up for the elemental's missing energies. Something clicked, snapping home as if some magnetic force had kicked in, unifying them into one.

David sucked in a hard breath as Cat's mind brushed his consciousness with feral energy that felt as if it had always been part of him.

Not always, Cat said, *but close enough.*

The alien beast extended a great paw and touched him, and he gasped. Memories streaked through his consciousness, striking like lightning bolts, illuminating his mind with sensations, thoughts, with parts of his consciousness that had been lost. *You're back,* he thought in incandescent joy.

Yes, but we've more of us to find. Warlock has the elemental, and we've got to get him back.

Cat was right. He could feel his spirit brother out there in the hands of his enemy, aching and cold and lost.

We can't let Warlock use us as a battery to power his insanity, Cat said.

"*I can anchor you,*" Belle said, her voice a smooth, silken whisper. *"But I'll have to remain with our bodies or Warlock could send someone to kill us all."*

That would be wise. David couldn't tell who'd thought the words, and it really didn't matter anyway.

It would matter to Eva, Cat thought grimly.

It might, David replied. *But I want her alive, whether she loves me or not.*

So he and Cat dove deep, swimming along the Mageverse's most hidden trails, leaving the witch standing guard over their empty flesh.

Searching for the elemental.

SIXTEEN

"Oh, Jesus," Eva said, stiffening in alarm as she stared at David's limp, furry form.

When Belle had first touched him, a web of energy had sprung up around his body, the pattern following the jagged silver stripes cutting across his shoulders and haunches. He'd stared into Belle's eyes, his own wide, absorbed. And then his gaze went fixed, the expression draining away from his face.

"What's happening?" Eva demanded, her gaze flying to Tristan, who at least seemed aware of her. Unlike the witch, whose eyes were as blank as David's. "Is he dying?" She heard the panic sharpening her voice and clenched her fists, trying to contain the frantic need to hit something.

Tristan's mailed hand fell on her arm, restraining her. "It's all right. They're just working some kind of magic. He'll be back." His voice dropped to a murmur. "*She'll* be back."

Unfortunately, he didn't sound all that convinced.

They found the elemental swimming slowly in a cage of light. David/Cat remembered Smoke as sleek and powerful, a blazing thing of energy and joy, not at all physical.

Pure magic.

Now the poor creature looked tattered, so dim as to barely burn at all. Starving and desperate.

Oh, gods. David felt sickened. *What has that bastard done to you?*

It's you, it's you! At last . . . oh, free me, Smoke begged in a voice so faint, they could barely hear him through the containment spell's buzz of magic. *I grow so weeaaak. I sent our power to you, but I used too much of my own to do it. I die . . .*

Damn Warlock. Shared rage burned through David and Cat, a blazing anger that Warlock would dare so abuse the elemental. But with the fury came fear. If the sorcerer could do something like this to Smoke, near god that he was, how could the two of them stand a chance?

Screw that, David growled, rejecting the fear. *Once we get Smoke out of there, we'll kick Warlock's ass.*

Cat rumbled a feral growl of assent.

Do you know if the cell has a weakness? David asked the elemental, slipping closer to the bars to examine them.

Stay clear! Smoke's faint voice went high with alarm. *If you get too close, it will suck you in. It's very powerful.*

Yes, it is, rumbled a deep voice. *And so am I.*

Warlock had discovered them.

A vision flashed through David's mind: a huge white werewolf crouched in the center of an intricate pattern inlaid in silver in the center of a stone floor. A focus spell. He held an enormous double-bladed battle-axe in massive clawed hands. Magic swirled around the great gemstone set in the axe handle, glowing an intense crimson. Somehow David knew the axe was called Kingslayer, presented to the Saxon sorcerer by Merlin himself fifteen hundred years ago.

And I'll use it to kill you, you little bastard, the werewolf snarled. *Leaving your body was a serious miscalculation. You're mine now. You're dead, you and your cat. And once you're gone, the godling's power will be mine. As it should be—because I deserve it.*

He pointed the axe at David/Cat, and magic exploded from it in a rolling burst of red fire.

* * *

The silence was nerve-racking. The only sound Eva could hear was the steady pant of David's breathing. It was too fast, and that, along with the glazed emptiness of his eyes, was beginning to seriously freak her out.

This isn't good, Fluffy said, a totally out-of-character remark for a career smart-ass. *Why'd you let him go? God knows what he'll come back as, assuming he comes back at all.*

How was I supposed to stop him?

And what's with Sir Asshat of the Round Table? He looks like the last reel of Old Yeller.

Eva dragged her gaze away from David—it took real work—and saw Tristan sitting with Belle's head in his lap. He looked up and caught Eva staring at him. He glowered back. "What?"

"Uh, nothing."

"She shouldn't be doing this." He said it through his teeth. "She's not a field witch. She does seductions. Combat's not her thing. Especially not combat with giant magic-slinging eight-foot werewolves."

Eva blinked. "Seductions? That's a job?"

"How do you think you get vampires? The three-bites-and-you're-a-vamp thing is bullshit. You become a vampire from having sex with a witch. Or drinking from Merlin's Grail, which is what I did."

"Wait, you're a vampire?" She frowned in confusion. "I thought you were a Knight of the Round Table."

"I am. I'm also a vampire."

"Is that why there's no Isolde?"

"Would you shut up about Isolde? And no, we don't drain people. You watch too much trashy TV."

"Hey, Joss Whedon is god, Sir Fangsalot."

Tristan opened his mouth, but before he could speak, David roared in pain, his big body convulsing.

"David!" Eva grabbed for him, but had to duck as one clawed hand swung wildly. "Oh, shit!"

* * *

Another magical blow hit David and Cat like a hammer.

We've got to attack him before he rips us apart! David thought desperately. *What do I do?*

Cat snarled, an incoherent blast of animal rage and desperation. *I don't remember! Ask Smoke.*

David growled and threw himself at the image of Warlock as the werewolf lifted Kingslayer again. The figure sent another torrent of magic slamming into him, then vanished like morning mist. David shook off the blow just as the sorcerer reappeared to hit him again.

Snarling, David chased Warlock as he appeared and vanished, swinging claws and snapping teeth the sorcerer always managed to avoid.

It's an illusion, Cat told him. *Warlock's using it to distract us.*

David swore, knowing he was right. *How can we hit something we can't even see?*

"Oh, hell," Belle spat, her eyes flying open. She blinked, registering Tristan's face above hers. "What am I doing in your lap?" She rolled onto hands and knees and scrambled toward Smoke and the werewolf woman. Smoke roared again, unmistakably a cry of agony. "Dammit, Warlock's frying them. I'm going to have to go in."

"Go in where?" Tristan demanded, lunging after her. "And why?"

"David—Smoke—oh, hell, whoever it is, he has the power, but he doesn't remember how to use it," Belle said tightly. "Warlock's got those memories locked up in some kind of magic cage in his mind, along with the rest of Smoke."

"Whose mind? Smoke's?"

"No, Warlock's. Help me control him before he hurts himself." Smoke convulsed again as if someone was hitting him with a Taser powered by a high-tension line.

"I'll take care of him. You keep your distance before

he turns you into pate." Tristan pounced on the werecat and straddled his chest, grabbing for the creature's thick wrists. He damned near got dumped on his head when David arched like a bow.

"Get his left arm. I'll get his right," the werewolf girl snapped, pinning the cat's right hand to the ground.

"That's right," Belle said. "Now hold him still while I go in after them."

A furry thigh snapped up, hitting Tristan's armored back so hard he almost bit his tongue. He wrestled the cat back down again and gritted, "What do you mean, you're going after them?"

Belle trapped Smoke's thrashing head between her palms. "They can't break the spell that's bound Smoke's memories, but I think I can."

"You'll get yourself fried," Tristan snarled. "Call Morgana. This kind of shit is her job."

Belle had thrown her visor up, and now her gaze met his over Smoke's head, fierce and determined. "There's no time, Tristan! And I've already got a spell connection to him, so it's me or he's dead."

"But . . ."

"Let me go with you," interrupted the werewolf girl. "I can help you reach him."

"How the hell do you think you can do that?" Tristan demanded, heartily fed up with both the suicidal little bitches.

"He loves me." Eva reached for Belle's hand, engulfing it in her clawed paw.

"But magic doesn't work on werewolves!" Tristan protested.

"A communication spell is very low energy compared to an attack," Belle told him tightly. "Besides, Queen Diana says the Direkind have something similar to a Truebond, so we should be able to make a psychic link work."

"What if it doesn't?"

"Then we're probably fucked." She and the werewolf stared at each other with a desperate intensity.

And nothing happened.

"I can't . . ." the girl began.

"Shhh!" Belle snapped. "I've almost got it." She whispered something in French Tristan didn't catch. The werewolf toppled over.

David's clawed hand, suddenly freed, slapped Tristan hard in the helm. Before the knight could do more than swear, Belle fell backward, her body arching over her bent knees.

"Dammit, Belle, you're not a combat witch!" Tristan spat at her unconscious form. "That damned werewolf is going to kill you."

Belle and Eva floated along the mental trail David and Cat had left on their way to the captive elemental. The connection between the two women was more fragile than the Maja would have liked, but there wasn't a hell of a lot she could do about it, except hold on.

Until they arrived in a flash of magic deep in Warlock's mind.

The first thing they heard was Cat's howl of pain as the sorcerer launched a flaming psychic attack against him and David. Luckily, Warlock was so totally focused on his victims, he didn't even notice the women's arrival.

"David," Eva whispered.

"Shush!" Belle snapped. "We've got to free Smoke. Without him to draw on, Warlock will have a lot less power to use."

Concentrating hard, she slid like a ghost toward the spell cage. The elemental reminded her of a gaunt sea lion, its glow dim as it swam in frantic circles, watching Warlock rip into David and Cat. He'd pounded the two so hard, they'd fractured into psychic chunks.

Fight him, the elemental groaned. *You have the power!*

"But they don't know how to use it," Belle said in a mental whisper.

Smoke jerked toward her as she drifted carefully to his cage. *"Belle!"* Then joy flashed in his eyes as he spotted the werewolf girl. *"Eva, you came! I never thought you'd come for me . . ."*

She frowned. *"Why wouldn't I? You're part of him, and you're in pain."*

"Do you know how I can get this thing open?" Belle interrupted.

Smoke blinked great, luminous eyes. *"Yes, there's a weakness. I've been working on it for days now. Here."* The creature nosed downward toward the corner of the psychic lattice, where some of the glow had dimmed fractionally. Examining the spot, Belle realized he had indeed managed to weaken the glowing bars. *"I just don't have the strength to finish it."*

"Luckily, Warlock's concentrating so hard on the rest of you, he's diverting power from the spell." Belle closed her eyes and drew hard on the Mageverse's power, preparing the blast she'd need to launch. *"As soon as you're out of there, merge with the others."*

Smoke stared at her, worry in his great, soft eyes. *"Warlock will attack you. He's going to try to rip you apart."*

"Not if I distract him," Eva said. Before either of them could protest, she flung herself toward the sorcerer.

"Oh, hell!" Belle launched the spell at the cage with all her magical strength. Light burst around it with the impact, great fractures appearing. Smoke pressed hard against the crumbling bars, trying to force his way clear.

Gritting her teeth, Belle gave the cage another rolling blast.

With a cry of triumph, Smoke shot to freedom in a burst of golden light.

This is suicide, Eva thought, shooting toward Warlock's back as he pounded her lover. She had no idea how to work any spell that didn't involve turning into something furry. Yet here she was, attacking Darth Fang.

"You don't have to work spells," Belle said in her mind. *"Here, it's all about will. Just concentrate on how much*

you want to pay Warlock back for everything he's done. You'll be surprised at how much damage you can do."

A slow, cold smile curved Eva's mouth. She imagined sinking her fangs into Warlock's neck and shaking him like a rat.

Suddenly she was on top of the wizard, her insubstantial jaws clamping into the sorcerer's flesh. He roared in shocked rage. She ripped away a psychic mouthful, then went to work with her claws.

"Eva, no!" David watched in horror as his lover ripped at the wizard, ignoring how he could hurt her.

"Bitch!" Warlock roared, twisting around to rake his claws across her face. *"You're going to pay for that!"* Blood flew, both his and hers.

He's going to kill her, David said through gritted teeth.

No, he won't, Smoke said. *Because we're going to get him first.* He darted toward them, a dim blur of energy that rocked them as he hit.

They remembered.

Thousands of years of knowledge, of magic, of power, exploded in David's consciousness like a nuclear bomb, stunning in its sheer savage magnificence. In a flash, the fractured parts of his spirit brothers slotted together, becoming one again. He roared in triumph, knowing what to do now. He could feel the magic waiting for his call deep in the Mageverse. And he knew how to hurt Warlock, even as the Dire Wolf prepared to direct a blast of magic at Eva.

"Get her out of here, Belle!" David shouted.

"Right." The witch captured Eva in a net of will and whirled to dive back along the psychic path they'd used. Utterly focused on killing them, Warlock roared in pursuit.

David hit him with a blast of magic that tumbled him ass over ears. On the physical plane, the sorcerer's huge body convulsed in his cave.

A savage pleasure surged through David. Now, after all these days of frustration and pain and fear, after seeing Eva hurt trying to protect him, he could finally kill Warlock. There would be no mercy. There would be no hesitation.

He would *end* the fucker.

David sent another blast into the sorcerer, fire surging from his melded spirit. Again and again he fired in searing concussions of magic that boiled into his enemy's skull.

Warlock writhed in the center of the focus circle, screaming in pain as his four remaining Bastards hovered helplessly.

The cat was killing him from the inside out. And there was nothing he could do about it. But he was damned if he'd just give up and die. He couldn't leave his people unprotected.

Warlock knew what he had to do. It was forbidden, but he didn't care. His people would have turned from him in horror, but that didn't matter either. He had to stop the pain.

He had to live.

Warlock rolled over, fumbling blindly for Kingslayer. His fingers closed around the thickly engraved haft, and he felt its power sing a deep, low note in his mind.

Another blast ripped at him, and his body convulsed again, but he clung to his blade and gritted, "Wheeler! Wheeler, get over here!"

The leader of Fenir spoke from somewhere over his head. "Warlock? What would you have of me?"

Warlock reached up blindly with his left hand and grabbed Kevin Wheeler by the muzzle. "Your life." Swinging Kingslayer, he beheaded the Dire Wolf with one stroke. He heard the other wolves gasp in horror.

Arterial blood splashed into his face, as Warlock began chanting the forbidden spell, collecting Wheeler's spilling life force, dragging it deep even as another blast of Cat's magic blinded him.

He wrapped both hands around Kingslayer's blood-slick haft and focused all his will, all his strength, all the magic of his warrior's stolen life force on a single thought, a single spell.

"Get OUT!"

* * *

David gathered his power for the final stroke. He could feel Warlock weakening. The werewolf's life force guttered like a candle in a draft. One more good blast, and the bastard was done.

And then . . .

Dark magic surged, black and thick as tar, and *evil*, so evil he recoiled.

Warlock hit him.

The blast slammed him right out of the Dire Wolf's skull, tumbling him like a leaf in a storm, so viciously strong there was no fighting it. He opened his eyes to see a starry sky overhead.

Dammit, no! he howled in rage. *I almost had him!*

There will be other chances, boy, Smoke said in his thoughts. *As it is, we all live. That is no small thing.*

Furious, frustrated, David focused his attention on Eva, who looked down at him in worry. She'd changed back to human form, and he had to smile at her delicate, dark beauty. You'd never know she'd just tried to rip Warlock's mental guts to sushi. David himself was Sidhe again, lying on the grass with his head in Eva's lap. The last of his lingering rage drained away. "Gods and devils, I'm tired," he said.

Darkness fell over him like a black velvet curtain, so heavy it smothered all thought.

Eva jerked in alarm as brilliant blue eyes slid closed. "David!"

Belle, kneeling next to her in the grass, reached out and laid one hand across his forehead. She blew out a breath in relief. "It's all right. He just blacked out. A little too much magic and effort, plus the strain of having all his assorted pieces shoved back together."

"Good," Tristan said. "Let's clean up this mess and get the fuck back to the Mageverse before Warlock shows up for round two."

The witch looked up at him and made a face. "Slave driver." She frowned as she looked around at the gory scene.

Werewolves sprawled in blood-splattered grass that gleamed black as oil in the moonlight. "I'm not going to be able to take care of this mess alone. I'm drained. I'll have to get Morgana to send a cleanup team."

"Great. So open up a gate and let's go." Tristan bent over David, picked him up as if he weighed no more than his house cat form, and draped him over one armored shoulder.

Eva rose anxiously to her feet. "What about me?"

"You're coming with us." Tristan grimaced and repositioned David's weight on his shoulder with a little bounce. "Unless you want to hang around here and wait for Warlock to turn you into a werewolf-skin rug."

Belle rolled her eyes. "You are such a charmer." She gestured, and a tiny spark flashed in the air, quickly expanding into a rippling oval more than seven feet tall and five across.

"Dimensional gate," she explained, noticing Eva's wary frown. "It leads to the Mageverse, the source of all magic. You and I and our armored friend here all draw our power from the Mageverse."

"Oh," Eva's eyes widened in sudden realization. "So that's what I sense when I change." Ever since the werewolf attack, she'd sensed a presence that was stronger at night and much weaker during the day, but which never disappeared. From the beginning, she'd instinctively reached out to it whenever she wanted to transform.

Apparently she was about to get the answers to a great many mysteries. She really should feel better about that.

Eva's gaze slipped to David, lying unconscious across the vampire's shoulder, his dark hair spilling down to brush the ground. *God, I hope he'll be okay.*

Belle stepped through the rippling dimensional gate as casually as a woman strolling through a door. Tristan followed, carrying David as easily as if he were a shawl. Eva took a deep breath, braced herself, and stepped through after them. Magic danced over her skin in a cool, tingling wave, and she shivered.

Then she was on the other side, and her mouth fell open on a shameless gape.

SEVENTEEN

They'd stepped into a grove of cherry trees. White blooms glowed in the moonlight like cloud banks, and Eva looked skyward, her gaze following the puffy shapes—until she saw the sky.

For a long moment, she just stood gazing in dazzled fascination. More stars than she'd ever seen spilled across the velvety darkness in alien constellations, and the moon rode three perfect little clouds edged in silver and blue.

There was a feeling in the air, an intoxicating buzz that seemed to call the magic in her. Eva could feel it reverberating in her bones and her muscles like a deep, thrumming chime. It made her want to transform, to spill into her wolf and race the moon across the night.

A smile spread helplessly across her face.

"Don't just stand there grinning," Tristan said over his shoulder as he strode after Belle. "Come on. Arthur's waiting for us."

That woke her up. "Ummm—Arthur? King Arthur?"

"Don't call him that," Tristan told her impatiently. "He's not a king anymore, and he hates it when people use that title. He's Liege of the Magi."

"Okay." She hustled after them, emerging from the little orchard that was apparently some kind of park.

"Holy God, it's Disney World," Eva muttered, barely resisting the urge to stop and gape again. Tristan would probably smack her, and then Fluffy would have to eat him.

I'll leave that to Belle, Fluffy said. *She likes him one hell of a lot better than I do.*

Scottish castles, grim gothic towers, French châteaus, Italian villas—you name an architectural style, and somebody had built it along the cobblestone streets. Yet somehow it all fit together, gleaming under the moon, surrounded by rolling green lawns and flowering trees and topiary shaped like knights and dragons.

"Some of the younger witches get a little carried away," Belle explained with an indulgent little smile. She'd dropped back to watch Eva gape like a tourist. "Everything here was built from magic. The more elaborate the structure, the more powerful the witch who created it."

"It's ostentatious," Tristan growled. "Not to mention a waste of power."

"But good practice," Belle pointed out. "Once you learn to manipulate and stabilize magic on such a scale, you can put it to good use in combat."

"Either way . . . Wow." Eva blinked as a tiny glowing figure zipped by, gossamer wings a blur. "Was that a—?"

"Fairy? Yep. Probably a courier carrying documents to the Sidhe kingdom." Belle nodded toward a three-story stone house surrounded by great mounds of blooming white rose-bushes. A single massive oak tree presided over the house, its great branches spread wide. "And there's Pendragon House. Come, child. It's not every day you meet a legend."

Eva's brows shot up as she followed her new allies up the stone walk. "Arthur lives *here*?"

"Expecting Camelot?" Tristan sent her a sneer. "Castles are drafty as hell, miserably cold in the winter, and you need a staff of a hundred to run one. Those of us with nothing to prove go for comfort over ostentation every time." He paused. "Except for Morgana and that palace of hers. She always did have to outdo everybody."

"Or maybe she just loves beauty." Belle stepped up on the stone porch to knock on the polished oak door.

It promptly swung wide to reveal a soccer mom, the kind of slim, delicate blonde that always made Eva feel like a moose. She wore a peach polo shirt and dark blue skinny jeans, with white Nikes on her dainty feet. Actual Nikes, like she shopped at Target. "Arthur, they're here!" She grabbed Belle's hands and kissed her on both cheeks. "Gods, I'm glad to see you." Soccer Mom turned a dazzling smile on Eva. "All of you."

Belle walked into the blonde's arms for a quick hug before stepping back and beginning the introductions. "Gwen, this is Eva Roman, who sheltered Smoke when he lost his memory." She turned to Eva, one arm still around the woman's narrow waist. "Eva, this is Guinevere Pendragon."

Eva had deduced as much, so she managed to shake Gwen's hand and greet her without swallowing her tongue. "It's an honor, Your Majesty."

"Oh, please." The blonde swept her into a warm hug. "I haven't been a queen since before the Norman Conquest. Call me Gwen like everyone else."

"I hate to interrupt the love fest, but can you point me somewhere I can put Smoke?" Tristan curled a lip. "He could stand to lose a few pounds."

"Hey!" Eva turned on him, indignant. There wasn't an ounce of fat anywhere on David's solid muscle, and she should know. *Jerk,* said Fluffy. *Let me bite him.*

"She's in love." Tristan rolled his eyes.

Hell, Eva thought, as her cheeks heated, *I'm going to bite him myself.*

Gwen sighed. "Tris, must you be so bloody rude?"

"Apparently," Belle growled. "I've been working with him for days, and he seems to treat being a jackass as performance art."

"Critique my manners later," Tristan retorted. "I need to either put Smoke down or turn him back into a cat."

"Come on then," Gwen said, and turned to lead the way down a short foyer and up the stairs. "Though I would suggest that if you'd hit the gym more often, you might not have that problem."

Tristan shot her a glare. "You want to carry him?" He shrugged as if to transfer David's solid weight to the blonde's delicate shoulders.

"Fine." Gwen made a swift, sharp gesture, and David levitated off Tristan's shoulder. A flood of sparks spiraled around him as if forming a cradle for his big body, and he floated upward in the witch's serene wake.

"Show-off," Tristan grumbled.

Belle laughed at him. "She certainly showed *you*."

"'People come and go so quickly here . . .'" Eva muttered, quoting *The Wizard of Oz* as she followed Tristan and Belle up the winding stairway.

The woman really didn't look anything like Queen Guinevere ought to look. Blond and pretty, yes, but not the kind of Helen-of-Troy-gorgeous Eva would have expected. Her delicate oval face was more wholesome than femme fatale, as if she spent her time driving the kids back and forth between Little League games and piano recitals. She sure as hell didn't look like a fifteen-hundred-year-old witch.

"This should do." Gwen floated David through a door at the top of the stairs into what proved to be a guest room. It was homey and well appointed, with tapestries on the walls and gleaming mahogany furniture.

She sailed David to the huge bed that dominated the room, its thick hunter green comforter flipping aside without anyone's touching it. The witch gestured, and the flood of sparks settled David's sleeping form on the fine cream sheets.

Automatically, Eva stepped forward to cover him with the comforter. She looked up from smoothing the fabric over his broad chest to find all three Magekind studying her with lifted brows.

It felt as if her cheeks burst into flame.

"See what I mean?" Tristan said to Gwen, his tone a trifle smug.

"Good for you," Gwen told Eva.

Before Eva could think of anything to say, a dark-haired man wandered in. He wasn't particularly tall, but he was as broad and powerfully built as a professional athlete. He wore his hair down to his brawny shoulders, and a beard framed his handsome mouth and square chin in a dark goatee. "I see you found the cat. Good work." He slapped Tristan's back, which clanked as he gave them all a broad smile. "I imagine you'd like dinner. Come on down and eat."

This, Eva realized numbly, had to be Arthur Pendragon, a suspicion that was confirmed when Gwen introduced them as they walked back down the hall.

"Thanks for taking care of Smoke," Arthur said, shaking Eva's hand. "He means a lot to us."

"He means a lot to her, too."

"Shut up, Tris," Belle told him.

The Pendragons escorted their guests to the family dining room, where Arthur and Tristan drank a goblet or two of witch-donated blood—*eeew*—while Eva, Belle, and Gwen ate thick rib eye steaks, baked potatoes, and tender green asparagus with hollandaise sauce.

Meanwhile Belle and Tristan briefed the couple on the fight with Warlock.

"We're going to have to do something about that bastard," Arthur said grimly.

"Yeah, but it won't be easy." Tristan shook his head. "And it'll probably be bloody. The rest of the wolves are going to be pissed."

"Too damned bad," Arthur said, with such a cold, ruthless gleam in his eyes that Eva could suddenly believe he'd once been High King of England.

After dinner, Eva excused herself to slip upstairs and check on David.

It didn't look as if he'd twitched so much as a muscle since they'd gone downstairs. His broad shoulders seemed to take up half the bed, and his tanned skin looked dark against the pale sheets. Eva sat down next to him with an exhausted sigh. "Well," she said softly, "it's been one hell of a day."

"Apparently."

Eva looked up to see Guinevere leaning on the door frame watching her. The ex-queen's gaze was so interested, it quickly drove Fluffy a little nuts. "Do I have spinach on my teeth, Your Majesty?"

"Gwen," Guinevere corrected patiently.

"Sorry." Eva scrubbed both hands over her face. "I'm a little frazzled."

"You have reason to be." Gwen crossed the room to stand next to her. For a moment, both women looked down at David. "I can't get used to seeing him as a human. Or a Sidhe, anyway. He's always been a cat of one kind or another."

"He's been human—Sidhe—with me. Except for a little while earlier today, when he became a house cat and scared hell out of both of us." Eva frowned. "Why would he choose to be a cat most of the time?"

"I have no idea." Gwen eyed her with that calm, compassionate gaze that made Eva want to jump out of her skin for reasons she didn't really care to examine. "You love him a great deal, don't you?"

The words lodged a hot little needle of pain inside her heart. "I don't know."

Gwen lifted a blond brow. "A woman doesn't watch a sleeping man with such intensity unless she's in love."

Busted. Eva sighed. "I'm in love with David, but I don't know if that's who he is now."

The witch frowned. "David?"

"The Sidhe part of him didn't know his own name, so that's what I call him. There's David, Cat, and Smoke, but I've never known them as one united person." Sudden frustration made her growl. "Why the hell won't he wake up?"

"Probably because he needs to sleep."

Eva scrubbed a hand over her face. "So do I. Changing back and forth from werewolf form always wipes me out."

"Then I'd better let you get some rest." Gwen gave her a smile and headed for the door.

Boy, that hadn't come out right at all. "I'm sorry, I didn't mean to be rude."

"You weren't rude." Gwen paused to look back at her. "But you do need sleep. That and a good breakfast in the morning will do you a world of good."

"As if I didn't eat like a pig at dinner." Eva was a trifle embarrassed at the way she'd literally wolfed that steak. But then, it had been so thick and tender, she hadn't been able to resist. Especially given all the shapeshifting.

"Magical transformations burn a lot of calories. Good night, Eva. Sleep well." Gwen stepped out and shut the door behind her with a soft click.

Tired to the bone, Eva wasted no time turning out the bedside lamp, slipping out of her clothes, and easing naked into bed. David still wore his jeans and shirt, but she was afraid stripping him might wake him up. Instead she curled against his side, closed her eyes, and was asleep two minutes later.

Eva woke to magic dancing over her skin like the brush of feathers and fur, a warm electric tingle that swirled over her erect nipples and stiffening clit. She inhaled sharply. David's scent filled the air, masculine, warm, with a trace of animal musk. Licking her lips, she arched her breasts into the flickering heat, savoring the lush pleasure, the eager need. Her hand slipped between her legs and found her flesh swollen and slick. She moaned helplessly and opened her eyes, then sucked in a startled breath.

David floated above her in a cloud of golden sparks. When she looked down the length of their bodies, she saw his erect cock pointed at the apex of her spread thighs. A stream of sparks spilled from the rosy plum head, feeding the swirl of magic that glided over her hungry body.

"David," she whispered. "God, what are you doing?"

"Making you come." He gave her a wicked little smile, his eyes white hot with magic, his hair a dark nimbus around his head. His hands glided over her body, fingers a hair's breadth from her flesh, trailed by the glittering dance.

His eyes glowed brighter, and the heat intensified until she writhed, craving the penetration of his cock. "Fuck me." The words emerged in Fluffy's feral growl.

He only grinned. "Not yet."

But his cock was right *there*, a fraction of an inch from her desperate sex, and she was not in the mood to wait. Not with heat running through her in pursuit of his magic, not with her cunt heating, tightening in juicy anticipation.

Finally Eva could take no more. She reached up and grabbed his warm, muscular shoulders, hooked her legs over his ass, and *pulled*.

She'd intended to drag him down to her, but instead the magic swept her upward, supporting her as if she were as weightless as a dream.

Unable to resist his taunting smile, Eva slipped a hand up and fisted it in David's hair, pulling his head down for her kiss. She moaned against his lips.

He tasted of mint and magic, and he smelled of a cool spring breeze sweeping through a forest of pines. His tongue slipped into her mouth, and magic seemed to burst between them. Her vision went white.

In that instant, David drove that thick cock into her with one ruthlessly delicious thrust. His arms closed tight around her, one hand slipping down to support her ass as the other threaded through her hair to cup her head.

Then he began the rolling thrusts that always drove her right out of her mind. His cock slid deep, pulled out, pushed deep again through swollen, slick lips, until she could feel his balls brush her ass. Her climax danced like a mirage just beyond her reach.

"God, David, you feel incredible." She whispered the words against his mouth as she rolled her hips, surging up at him, craving that last hot push that would send her over the edge.

"Good." A triumphant grin flashed across his mouth before he claimed her lips again, kissing her as magic swirled around them and their bodies ground together, rolling, pushing, striving, the swirl of sparks triggering lust everywhere they touched.

The climax stormed over Eva, and she threw back her head, gasping, her hair tangling with his, her sex gripping him hard, thighs clamping over his ass.

David roared out his climax. Magic poured into her with every hot jet, tingling waves of it that made her entire body tighten and jerk and writhe in helpless delight. Sending her orgasm higher, higher, as she gripped him with nails digging into his ass.

The deep jerking pulses finally quieted as the pleasure receded like a passing storm. Eva was barely conscious when her back touched the sheets again and David's warm weight settled over her. He braced on elbows and knees to keep from crushing her and buried his face between her head and neck.

Drawing him close, Eva let her eyelids drift closed as the thunder of their heartbeats began to slow in her ears.

"Damn, that was amazing," she said when she was capable of speech again.

His teasing grin flashed. "You're welcome." Pushing off her, he rolled onto his back and looped an arm over her shoulders, pulling her into a full-body hug.

Eva nestled into the warm, smooth curve where shoulder met chest. "Where the hell did that come from?"

He turned his head on the silken sprawl of his hair. "I wanted you."

"And you got me." She smiled lazily and turned on her side to drift her fingertips down the hard muscle of his chest, over the warm ripple of abdominals to the slack, sated curl of his cock. She cupped his balls, rolling the soft skin between her fingers. To her vast satisfaction, David shivered.

Her stomach picked that moment to growl. Loudly.

David's laughter rumbled softly. "I think that's my cue to feed you." He sat up and gestured. Magic spilled from his hands, swirled over the edge of the bed, and pooled on the floor. A moment later, the golden sparkles congealed into a red checkered tablecloth spread over the floor. A selection of dishes were arrayed across it, emitting the delicious odor of ham, eggs, bacon, and pancakes. "Breakfast," he announced with a wicked little smile, "is served."

Eva eyed the spread hungrily. "It looks delicious, but I think Gwen was planning to feed us."

"Gwen's immortal—she can wait. I want to spend a little time alone with you." There was something in his eyes. Insecurity? Where the hell did that come from?

"Oh. Okay. It does smell good." She let him tug her out of bed and followed him over to his impromptu picnic.

It proved to taste every bit as good as it smelled, which was why fifteen minutes went by before Eva managed to stop eating long enough to talk. "You're really good at the magic thing," she observed, licking maple syrup off her fingers.

"I've had a lot of practice." David picked up a piece of bacon and crunched.

Eva cocked her head, ogling him shamelessly.

He tucked a lock of hair behind one pointed ear and grinned. "What?"

"So you really are a fairy?"

David smirked. "Have you been paying attention? I'm definitely straight."

"Smart-ass. I mean Sidhe."

He lifted one shoulder in a half shrug, picked up a strawberry, and popped it in her mouth. "Yep."

Eva had to chew the berry before she could go on. Like the rest of the meal, it was delicious, squirting juice over her tongue. "So now that you can remember who the hell you are, tell me about yourself."

David looked a little wary, and she wondered why. "What do you want to know?"

"The usual." Before he could grab it, she snatched the last piece of bacon and bit down, enjoying the smoky crunch. "How did you end up a trio?"

"I already . . . I mean, Cat already explained that." His

gaze shifted away from hers. "The Dark Ones had invaded and were killing people. My tribe needed to fight them off, so he and Smoke needed a body with hands."

"Yeah, but what did you think about having them move in?"

"What did I think? Sweetheart, I fought like hell for the privilege." He snorted and flicked his fingers. Another plate of bacon appeared, and he picked up a piece. "All the men of my village competed. It's not every day you get a chance to become one with your god."

"Smoke said something about that. Your tribe really thought he was a god?"

"We'd been worshipping that cat for generations." He lay back on the floor, bracing on one brawny elbow. "This was a long, *long* time ago, before the Sidhe became immortal or gained much in the way of magical abilities. My people were essentially a Stone Age tribe then, and Smoke impressed the hell out of us with his powers."

"What was it like?" Fascinated, Eva sat up tailor fashion. She couldn't imagine any life further removed from her own middle-class childhood of comic books and school. "I mean, growing up like that?"

"Up until the Dark Ones showed up, it was pretty idyllic. Thanks to Smoke. We had plenty of food, and we rarely encountered other tribes, so we didn't go to war very often." He shrugged. "Before I was twelve or so, I gathered food with my mother and the other women. I learned which berries and roots you could eat, and which ones would give you one hell of a bellyache. I also learned how to make an arrow that would fly straight, and how to flake a pretty decent axe head out of this green rock we called *ca'ita*." David smiled. "Basically, they taught me everything a man needed to know in the equivalent of, oh, 10,000 B.C. or so."

"What about after you were twelve?"

"I started hunting with the men. Smoke always led the hunting parties, so we were generally pretty damned successful. We certainly never went hungry." He paused, one hand rubbing his thigh, a frown on his face.

His expression made her sit up. "What's the matter?"

"Damn. I suddenly remembered the day I almost died. I haven't thought of that in years."

"What happened?"

"I'd gone fishing alone—I guess I was fourteen or so. My people didn't have all that good a grasp of the passage of time, so it's hard to tell. Anyway, I was in the shallows of the river, tying to spearfish, when this snakedog burst out of the brush and hit me like a compact car."

"Snakedog?"

"It looked something like a furry crocodile. Mean little bastards. Had a set of teeth like you wouldn't believe. Anyway, it ripped the hell out of my thigh. I managed to ram my spear through its left eye, which killed it, but it still did a hell of a lot of damage."

"Oww." Eva felt sick, remembering the sensation of teeth ripping through her own flesh.

"Yeah. I was bleeding to death, when all the sudden, Smoke was there, my parents wild-eyed on his heels. He started licking my leg . . ."

She wrinkled her nose. "Eeew."

"Hey, don't knock it. Smoke could do a hell of a lot of magic with a lick."

"I'll buy that," Eva said, grinning. "So can you."

"Smart-ass. Anyway, he saved my life." His grin faded. "It wasn't long after that when the Dark One found us. Those creatures were big, horned bipeds, looked like a medieval woodcut of a devil. Mostly because they inspired the woodcuts. Smoke damn near died fighting off this particular devil. Ri'ae said she'd had a vision that he needed to merge with one of us warriors." He fell silent.

Eva studied him. The expression on his face was a little chilling. Finally she prompted, "Who was Ri'ae?"

"His priestess. Smoke had enhanced her magical abilities a century before so that she could assist him in running the tribe."

Eva sat up with a jerk. "That's the one Cat said was a bitch!"

"Exactly. She and Smoke held a contest among the warriors. I won and merged with him, which is when she became my lover."

"Big surprise there," Eva grumbled.

He gave her a smile. "Jealous?"

She bared her teeth. "Who, me?"

David snorted. "Don't be. She was a psychotic little bitch who eventually decided she didn't like sharing power with me. Or sharing me with Smoke, which made no damned sense whatsoever. Anyway, she killed the whole damned village one day. Murdered everyone, including my parents, brothers, sisters, and nephews."

The pain on his face made Eva lean forward and cup his cheek in her hand. "I'm so sorry."

His bleak gaze met hers. "I killed her."

And it had devastated him, she realized suddenly. *My God, he loved her.* She searched for something to say, managed nothing more than a lame "I'm sorry."

"Yeah, well." David rose to his feet and flicked his fingers. The picnic vanished. Eva looked around, blinking in surprise.

"Come on, I'm still hungry." He reached down for her hand.

She let him draw her to her feet. "After eating all that?"

"Not for food." His grin flashed. "For magic."

EIGHTEEN

Eva watched as David drew an elaborate pattern in the air with his free hand, conjuring a dimensional gate like the one Belle had created the night before. "Shouldn't we tell Arthur and Gwen we're leaving?"

"It's already taken care of." He tugged her toward the shimmering opening. "I'm not completely rude."

"Do you people ever *walk* anywhere?"

"All the time. But the spot I have in mind is too far." He flashed that grin at her again, all promise and temptation.

"Wait," Eva protested, resisting the pull of his hand. "Where the hell are my clothes?"

There was that grin again. "Where we're going, you don't need clothes."

"But what if somebody's there?" Before she could get another protest out of her mouth, he'd tugged her through the gate. Magic rolled across her skin, and she was on the other side.

They stood in a clearing in what looked like an honest-to-Tarzan jungle. Mounds of blossoms covered trees and bushes and stood in brilliant clumps of flowers—deep crimson, shimmering yellow, a dozen shades of blue shading into purple, white petals edged in pink. Leaves in every shade of green—emerald, olive, Kelly, hunter, fern, moss—blazed so vibrant they made her eyes ache.

In the center of the clearing lay a rock-edged pool of water that foamed around the foot of a waterfall. The falls danced and tumbled down the face of a cliff, trees jutting here and there from the wet black stone. Eva tilted her head back, tracing the splashing path of the water until it passed inches beneath a rippling oval high overhead. "Is that a dimensional gate?"

David paused and surveyed the pool, a smile curving his sensual mouth. "Oh, yes."

She frowned up at the oval. There seemed to be clouds on the other side, boiling and misty. "Who cast the spell to open it?"

He tilted his head back and closed his eyes, as if enjoying the warmth of the sun on his face. "Nobody. Or possibly the gods. It's been there as long as I can remember. And I can remember a very, very long time." Opening his eyes again, he stared up into the rippling oval, his gaze going distant. "It leads to another universe, one where magic is even more potent than it is here, where the rules of physics are so alien, they'd rip you or me apart. Smoke's home universe."

"He's from another *universe*?"

"Yep. If Cat hadn't been drinking at this pool, Smoke would have lasted no longer here than we would have there."

"Then why come here?"

A frown gathered between his dark brows. "Now, that's a little tough to explain. I guess you could say they were having a war on his world, and his people were losing. The winners meant to exterminate Smoke and his kind, so the survivors came here. A lot of them died anyway if they weren't able to find the right kind of hosts." Sadness darkened his eyes. "Many of those that did survive fell prey to the Dark Ones."

"Okay, that sounds sinister."

"It was. The Dark Ones fed on life force, so they just

loved the elementals, who were basically nothing *but* life force. There are only a few of us—of them—left anymore."

Eva studied him, fascinated. "What happened to the evil aliens?"

"Merlin and the Sidhe ran them off. They didn't care for the ugly bunch either." David padded out onto a finger of smooth black stone that thrust into the water. He stood there a moment, morning sunlight gilding his shoulders, before leaping upward, ass and thighs flexing. Light painted a golden glow across his shoulders and the hard curves of his arms as he cut into the water with barely a splash.

He surfaced a moment later and rolled over onto his back, an almost sexual pleasure on his face. "As that waterfall rolls past the gate, it picks up ambient magic," he called. "Which makes this pool the most magically potent spot on the planet. Since that bastard Warlock used me to power his magic like a flashlight battery, I need to soak some of that energy up. Being in the Mageverse has helped, but to fully recharge, I need quality time in here."

Eva frowned, remembering the orgasmic surge of magic when they'd made love. "Did what we did this morning drain you?"

He shot her a grin as brilliant as a boy's on Christmas morning. "It was worth it. Besides, I drew in as much magic as I gave you." David began to backstroke across the water with smooth kicks and powerful sweeps of his strong arms. His cock rolled over his wet, gleaming thighs.

Yum, purred Fluffy, *I have an urge to go bobbing for dick.*

Grinning, Eva strolled onto the stone and dove in a long, flat leap that carried her well out over the pool. She plunged deep, arrowing toward the bottom, savoring the cool rush of bubbling current around her. It should have been darker so far underwater, but the liquid seemed to glow. Did glow, in fact, the air bubbles around her glittering with a magical sheen. Arching upward, she broke the sunlit surface with a splash. Her flesh buzzed and tingled, reacting to the intoxicating energy of the pool's magic.

Eva shivered in pleasure, gasping. And gasped again as

strong arms closed around her waist from behind, turning her into David's hot kiss. Moaning softly, she hooked her arms around his strong neck. Their legs brushed together as they kicked lazily, keeping themselves afloat.

He swirled his tongue around hers, stroked softly over her lower lip as he cupped one breast in his hand, his thumb flicking back and forth over the hard little nubbin. She felt his cock grow as it pressed against her belly, stretching upward between them. "You're so beautiful."

A sudden realization struck her. "You don't sound like you did before. Not as formal." Pinpointing the difference, she felt her eyes widen. "You're using more contractions."

Unease flashed through his eyes. *Will we be David enough for you?* His smile looked forced. "Want me to start talking like the cast of *Lord of the Rings* again?"

She frowned. "No. I . . ."

Before she could say anything else, his mouth took hers, so fierce and hot it snatched her breath. His thumb went back to teasing her nipple, until she gasped at the heat that rolled through her in shivering waves of delight. His free hand scooped under her ass, lifted her in the water as he went on kissing her, tongue stroking, thrusting, licking. She wrapped her legs around his waist, hooking her ankles together, holding his big body close and tight.

The smooth head of his cock found her sex and drove to her depths in one hot thrust. She gasped, and he ate the sound out of her mouth, hunching, driving, a breathtaking surge of hot flesh and male power. Bending her backward across his arm, he lowered his head and covered one pebbled nipple with his mouth. Growling in satisfaction like a cat, he began suckling, fierce and strong. Pleasure shot through her like burning arrows that lanced deep in time to every delicious thrust. She came with a high, helpless yowl, dimly aware of his bellow of triumph.

They were floating lazily in the pool, their breathing beginning to slow, when a mental voice rang out like the peal of a great bell. *"Smoke?"*

Eva lifted her head from David's shoulder and caught her breath in a combination of surprise and awe.

There on the water's edge stood a huge white stag with the most magnificent rack of antlers she'd ever seen. He had to be six feet at the shoulder. Sparks of magic danced around the thick, sharp points like fireflies. The creature's eyes were the same crystalline blue as David's. He took another step into the water on shining cloven hooves.

"Smoke?" he asked again.

"Zephyr!" David pulled away and gave her a smile. *"Eva, that's one of my—Smoke's—fellow elementals. Come on, I'll introduce you."* He started stroking toward the shore, strong legs kicking. Curious, Eva followed.

"It has been some time since we last spoke," the stag said, cocking his magnificent head. *"And you have found a mate. Congratulations. I know you had grown lonely, even among your humans."*

"Actually, she's trying to decide if she'll have me." He pulled himself out of the pool and grinned as he swept his soaked and streaming hair out of his eyes. *"How goes it with you?"*

"Well enough. The dragons have grown no more fleet of wing and claw, thank the gods. The hellhounds, too, chase me still, just enough to keep my horns sharp." The stag eyed Eva as she cautiously climbed from the pool to stand just behind David. *"And you, girl."* He extended his elegant head to give her a sniff. He smelled of forest shadows and magic so strong, she found herself taking a wary step back. From the glint in his intelligent gaze, she suspected she had amused him. *"You are wolf."*

"Umm, yeah. I guess," Eva said out loud, having no idea how to project her thoughts as they were doing. "It's nice to meet you."

"And you. He needs such a one as you to run with."

"And you do not?" David retorted. *"You should seek some Sidhe warrior to bond with, that you may take a bride of your own among them."* He'd fallen back into more formal speech again.

The stag looked away, off into the distance. Sadness

darkened his great blue eyes. "*It is too late for that, my friend.*"

David stiffened. "*What do you mean? What have you seen?*" He took a step closer and caught his friend by the horns, pulling the great head around to face him. "*If you need help, you know I'll fight for you. I always have. I drove that Dark One away, remember?*"

"*I could not forget such courage, my friend. The demon would have devoured me had you not killed it first, at great cost to yourself.*" Gently, the stag twisted his head, pulling his antlers from David's light grip. "*But everything has an end time. Even immortals. And I fear I have come to mine.*"

Before David could say anything more, the stag whirled away and leaped across the pool in one long, soaring bound. With the rapid thump of hooves on the loam, he vanished into the trees, leaving a trail of sparks in his wake.

"Wow." Eva scraped her dripping hair back and stared, but there was no sign of the stag. "He's really . . ." She searched for a word and had to settle for "Powerful."

"In many ways, yes." David frowned after his friend as if troubled. "But remaining a deer has limited him. Even with Zephyr's magic, that stag doesn't have the brain power he needs."

"What do you mean?"

"The host form contributes a great deal of will and intelligence to shape the elemental's magic. Deer are not particularly bright to begin with, and they are prey animals. He needs a large predator at the very least." He sighed heavily. "The warriors of my tribe would have fought for the honor of hosting him, but he's always preferred to be as he is. I don't think he wanted to share his mind the way I do."

"Why?" Eva wrapped her arms around herself and shivered. Something about the conversation chilled her.

"He saw what happened to me when I lost my people. He said he did not want the grief." David noticed her quiver and stepped closer, running one big hand down her back. Instantly a thick towel appeared around her shoulders. He picked it up and began to dry her off. "Unfortunately, I know him well enough to know he's too damn stubborn to let me help him. Short of chasing him through the woods for the next year—assuming he'd even let me—there's nothing I can do."

Warlock woke sprawled across the center of the spell circle, Kevin Wheeler's cold body lying beside him. He was covered in the Dire Wolf's dried blood, his white fur matted with great sticky brown smears and sprays of it. He felt sick and weak, scarcely able to think at all.

Worst of all, he felt powerless. The cat had taken his stolen abilities back. True, Warlock had driven Smoke out before the creature could kill him, but that was all he'd accomplished.

Still, he lived. One does not survive as long as Warlock had without tasting the occasional defeat, and he knew living meant he still had the opportunity to regain the power to avenge himself.

Rolling onto his back, Warlock considered the ceiling through narrowed orange eyes. His first thought was to attack Smoke yet again, but that sounded far too much like the definition of madness: attempting the same thing over and over, expecting a different result.

So no. He would not let that creature back into his mind again. He'd come far too close to being destroyed. He wouldn't court death that way again.

What he needed was a power source that did not have so many teeth. One unprotected by ruthless will and feral intelligence. Unfortunately, he knew of no such power source.

But Smoke might.

When he'd first realized that maintaining control of the cat's memory and powers might not be as simple as it seemed, Warlock had set to work creating a backup of sorts, in case the beast stole his memories back.

Now he rose from the spell circle and padded over to the workshop table where he'd spent so many nights of late. In the center of that table sat a book flipped open to reveal pages of notes. He no longer remembered exactly what he'd written, but he intended to find out.

Warlock smiled in grim satisfaction, then grimaced as he scented himself.

First, however, he was in desperate need of a bath.

The bell over the Comix Cave door gave its habitual merry jingle as Eva walked in. "Hi, Dad, I'm . . ."

The shop was splashed in red paint. Great swaths of it cut across the new arrivals racks, splashed the walls and the expensive hero statues. Oh, shit, *she thought.* The stock is ruined. Dad's gonna have a stroke. Who the hell did . . .

She saw them.

They lay in a tangle on the floor, Bill Roman huddled over Charlotte as if trying to protect her from the claws that had ripped into them both. Her father's throat was gone, his empty eyes staring in horror. Her mother had no face at all.

"Mom! Dad!" *Eva* woke changing, her voice spiraling from a scream of horror to a roar of agony. She rolled to her feet on the blanket where they'd made love yet again before drifting off into sated sleep. "Daddy!" It was a shriek that made the bushes sway.

"Gods and demons!" David sprang upward and came down with a sword materializing in his hand, hard eyes scanning the clearing for whatever had torn that sound out of her. "What the seven hells was that?" As he caught sight of her face, his voice dropped to a more soothing register. "Did you have another nightmare?"

"I hope that was all it was." She started to push her tangled mane out of her eyes and winced as her talons sliced her forehead. "Dammit!"

"You cut yourself." He stepped over to her and caught the side of her head to draw her muzzle down and examine the wound. "It's not deep. You need to watch those claws, Eva. What did you dream?"

"I walked into the shop. Mom and Dad were dead. Warlock had . . ." She couldn't say it. As it was, she had to swallow hard as her stomach heaved at the gory memory. "David, we've got to check on them. What if it was some kind of prophetic dream?" An equally unsettling thought pierced her fear. "Warlock's first set of flunkies found us at the shop, so he must know where it is. And if he tracked us down, he could find my folks just as easily."

David frowned up at her. "It's possible. And Warlock likes to strike at family. I'll open a gate and we'll go check."

She nodded, feeling sick with anxiety. "I'd better change back. If they're all right, I don't want to scare the hell out of them."

"We'll need to take them somewhere safe." He rubbed his hand over his jaw in thought. "Arthur has safe houses on Mortal Earth that are heavily warded against magic. We built them during the Vampire Wars a couple of years ago. I'm sure he'd let us use one."

"The problem will be convincing Dad to go. He's not going to want to leave the shop." Still, she could burn that bridge when she came to it. She needed to make sure her parents were all right.

David opened his gate in the alley behind the shop. It was Sunday, which meant the Comix Cave would be closed so Charlotte could drag Bill to church. Afterward there'd be televised golf—not his beloved football, not this time of year, but Dad loved sports. Or at least, he loved drinking beer and eating buffalo wings while somebody knocked a ball around on his giant high-def screen.

But Eva couldn't get that dream out of her mind. She had to check the shop.

David at her back, she strode around the building to the Comix Cave's front door. Pausing, Eva gathered her courage, before she unlocked the door and opened it. The bell jingled cheerily as she flicked on the light.

The store was empty. The hard knot in her stomach loosened just a bit. Blowing out a breath, Eva turned to

David. "Can you open a gate to their house if I give you the address?"

"Of course." He shot a glance over his shoulder. "But let's get inside first. We'll gate from there."

Charlotte and Bill Roman owned a two-story home with beige vinyl siding and white trim in a comfortably middle-class development. The lawn was green and well tended, the better to showcase her mother's lovingly tended azaleas, which surrounded the house in a brilliant profusion of white and pink blooms.

David and Eva stepped through his gate into the thick spring woods that lay behind the house. She managed not to break into a run as they crossed the lawn and climbed the brick steps to the porch, but it took all the self-control she had. Stomach knotted, Eva threw David an agonized look and knocked. Heart in her throat, she listened with every bit of werewolf acuity she had.

Footsteps. Thank God. Unless it was a werewolf . . .

Charlotte opened the door, her smile of welcome turning to a frown of concern as she took in Eva's pale face. "Baby, what's wrong?"

"Hi, Mom. Mind if we come in?" It was all she could do not to leap on her mother in relief.

"Sure. This is still your home, Eva. You know that." Charlotte opened the door wider and called, "Bill, Eva and David are here." She looked past them as they walked in. "Dear, where's your car?"

"Car trouble," David said smoothly. "We had a friend drop us over."

"Oh. Do you need to call a tow truck?"

Dammit, she should have thought to bring the car, but she'd been in such a tearing hurry . . .

"No need." David gave her mother a smile so charming, Charlotte blinked and looked just slightly dazzled. "I'll take a look at it in the morning. I'm pretty good with engines."

Finally realizing the two hadn't actually met, Eva

performed the introductions as they walked into the living room, where Bill—surprise—was indeed watching a golf game. Her father shot David a narrow-eyed look that was just shy of hostile, before reluctantly rising to offer his hand.

"What brings you two by?" Bill asked as Eva and David settled on the gold-striped love seat that stood at an angle to the couch.

Charlotte shot him a quelling look at his cool tone. "May I get you two anything to drink?"

"Got any wine?" At least it would give her something to do with her hands.

"There's a Riesling in the fridge."

Eva managed another smile. She had to get them out of here. Somehow. "Sounds great."

David looked at the bottle of Coors on the coffee table. "I'd like a beer." He probably suspected that asking for wine would cost him masculinity points with Bill. And he was right.

An uncomfortable silence fell as Charlotte bustled out.

"Have you read the new *Scarlet Reaper*?" her father asked.

Eva usually made a point of reading damn near everything that came into the store so she could discuss comics with her customers. "I haven't had a chance." *I've been too busy trying not to get killed.*

"That new writer's an idiot. If he retcons one more character out of existence, I'm dropping the book." Retroactive continuity—declaring that something which had happened in a previous issue had never happened at all—irritated Bill no end.

Silence fell again. Bill glowered at David. David gave him a polite smile in return. Eva dropped a hand on David's knee by way of silently telling her father to dial back his disapproving daddy act.

How the hell were they going to persuade her parents to go to Arthur's safe house?

"Eva and I have been talking," David began after Charlotte had served the drinks and curled up next to her husband. "Mr. Roman, I realize I got off on the wrong foot with you the other day, and I'd like a chance to get to know you both better. A friend of mine has a beach house on the coast. It's a private beach. Eva and I were planning an impromptu week's vacation, and we thought we'd ask you to join us while Mrs. Roman is on spring break."

Bill frowned, his puzzled gaze flicking to Eva's face. "We can't close the shop, Eva, particularly not for a week. Not with the economy in the tank. We need every sale we can get. You know that."

"But it's a nice thought," Charlotte added hastily.

Oh, hell, she'd known that was going to be his reaction. Maybe she could tell them just enough of the truth to get them to agree. "Thing is, we've got a problem. Those guys—the guys that followed us the other day. We're afraid they're going to come after you, too. I'm worried about you."

"Dammit, I told you," Bill said to Charlotte. "I told you there was something wrong." He shifted his glower to Eva. "Why in the hell haven't you called the cops?"

"What are they going to do, Dad?" Eva burst out in frustration. "These guys haven't done anything yet. The cops will come out if they show up again, but by the time they get here, you could be hurt." *You could be eaten.* The memory of her nightmare made her fists clench. She stuffed the emotion down, afraid it would make her shift in front of her parents.

"Ronnie frickin' Gordon isn't going to run *me* out of town, Eva!" His hazel eyes blazed in offended rage.

"It isn't Ronnie, Dad. It's somebody a hell of a lot more dangerous. Somebody who'll kill you." She rose and began to pace, restless and urgent as she tried to find the words to persuade them. "They'll kill *Mom*."

A muscle flexed in Bill's bearded jaw, and Eva winced, recognizing a very bad sign from years of daughterly experience. His narrow gaze flicked to David. "You're some kind of criminal, aren't you? A drug dealer, most likely. And now my daughter is in danger from the assholes you run with."

David's wince was microscopic—he probably thought there was far too much truth to the accusation.

Bill rose to his feet, the movement slow and deliberate. He didn't shout. It would have been better if he had. "Get out of my house and stay away from my family."

"Dad, no! He's not a criminal—it's not that." Eva stepped between them, frantic to defuse the situation. "It's not drugs, or anything else illegal."

David rose, too, but there was no anger in his face. He just looked tired. "It's too late for that. Even if I go, he'll still come after you. He knows how much she means to me, and he wants revenge. And he'll use you to get it."

"Then the last place my family needs to be is anywhere around you. I won't tell you again." Bill lowered his head with a growl that would have done a werewolf proud. "Get. Out."

David didn't move. "I can protect your family, Mr. Roman. I'll see to it that nothing happens to any of you. Just come with me. Please."

Bill stepped up to him until barely an inch separated them and glared up into his face, despite the fact that David was easily nine inches taller. "Get out or I'm putting you out."

Oh, God, he's going to take a swing at David, Eva thought.

"Bill," Charlotte said, her voice shaking ever so slightly, "I think we should call the police."

Shit. Eva's stomach coiled into a sick knot. "Daddy, I swear to you, he's not a criminal. I wouldn't bring a criminal into your house. You *know* that."

Bill looked at her, his lips tight with rage. She'd never seen her father look so furious. Or so betrayed. "You've been lying to us since this bastard walked into your life." Registering her flinch, he ground his teeth. "You think we haven't noticed?"

There was only one thing she could do. "I've been lying to you for a lot longer than that."

David's blue eyes widened. "Eva, don't. I can . . ."

She ignored him and let her magic spill, fueled by fear,

guilt, and raw, shaking dread. Fur flowed across her skin in an itching, tingling wave, and muscle and bone twisted, expanded, reshaped her body in painful jerks and pops.

When it was over an eyeblink later, she was a werewolf.

"What the fuck!" Bill leaped back and pushed Charlotte behind him with an automatic sweep of one arm. Eva's mother sucked in a shocked breath, covering her mouth with one shaking hand. David rubbed one hand over his eyes, his broad shoulders slumping.

"I'm not going to hurt you." Eva burst into speech, frantic to fill the astonished, frightened silence. "I would *never* hurt you. I've been a werewolf for five years. I know I should have told you, but I was afraid of what you'd think. All that stuff about werewolves killing people is bull. Well, not everything, there are some werewolves who are nasty bastards, but *I'm* not a killer. Except for two guys, but they were werewolves and they were trying to kill us, and I didn't have a—"

"Eva, you're babbling," David interrupted with a sigh. "Let your parents process this."

Bill turned a stunned gaze on him. "Did you do this to her?"

"*No*, Dad. David's not even a werewolf. He's . . . well, he's something else. There was this guy, he attacked me. I went jogging one night and . . ." Eva cut herself off, realizing she was babbling again. And God, she was tired. Without thinking, she sank down on the love seat. It produced an alarming creak of protest. She jumped up and almost tripped, but David grabbed her elbow and steadied her with automatic, offhand strength.

"I keep thinking it's got to be a costume," Charlotte said in a distant voice, "but it's not, is it?" She reached out and stroked a trembling hand over Eva's furry arm. "It's warm. It's really you." She looked up into her daughter's face. "Your eyes are the same. They're just the same." Her fingers lifted to trace the length of Eva's muzzle, feeling flesh and muscle move beneath the thinner fur there. "That's definitely not a costume." Suddenly her eyes went fierce with a mother's anger. "Somebody *attacked* you? He hurt you? Eva, is this the same man who's after you now?"

"No, Mom." Her father had taken her hand to examine her claws, one thumb brushing absently over her palm in a soothing gesture. At her mother's words, his grip tightened.

"If it was the man I suspect it was, he's dead," David said. Eva shot him an astonished look—*when did he find that out?* He lifted one shoulder in a half shrug. "Trey Devon was a serial killer. He murdered the sister of one of our people, and she and her fiancé hunted him down. There was a fight, and they killed him."

Bill's jaw dropped and he stared at David. "A serial killer?" He transferred his horrified gaze to his daughter as if he was only just now starting to process what he'd heard. "You were attacked by a *werewolf serial killer*? Why didn't you tell us, Eva!"

"Because she was afraid we'd freak, Bill," Charlotte said tartly. "Which is exactly what we're doing." She looked up at Eva again. "For the record, you're still our daughter, furry or not. We love you, and nothing will ever change that." She turned toward the kitchen. "Now I need something a hell of a lot stronger than white wine. In fact, I'll get some for everybody."

"I'll help you," Bill said, and strode after her.

"Which sounds like my cue to change back," Eva muttered, and summoned her magic.

NINETEEN

When her transformation was complete, Eva sank down on the couch again. This time it didn't creak. She leaned forward and buried her head in her hands. "Oh, God." A short, semi-hysterical laugh burst out. "Believe it or not, that actually went better than I expected."

David sat next to her and looped an arm around her shoulder to pull her close. "You know, you didn't have to do that. I could have cast a spell to make them go with us."

She shot him a horrified glance. "Oh, God no. It's bad enough that I lied to them for all these years."

He sighed. "I thought that would be your reaction. I think we might as well bite the bullet and take them to the Mageverse. They'd be safer there than they'd be in the safe house. We strengthened the city's wards a couple of years ago so nothing can get through without a spell key. And besides, even Warlock isn't going to want to take on the Knights of the Round Table."

"What?" Bill stopped short in the doorway, a glass of something amber in his hand. "Did you say Knights of the Round Table? *They're real? And alive?*"

Eva rubbed a hand over her aching forehead. "Yeah,

they're real. And they're definitely alive. You'd like . . . well, Arthur. Tristan's an asshole."

Bill's eyes got even wider. "Arthur?"

David stood, dropping a hand to her shoulder. "Why don't you three talk. I need to make a call." He turned toward the front door.

"You can use our phone," Charlotte called, but he'd already stepped outside.

Eva sat back on the couch. "That would be one hell of a long distance bill." She noticed her father staring at her in puzzlement. "What?" Her voice sounded a trifle defensive.

"Your clothes are back. Where did they go?"

She shrugged. "Got me. It's magic, Dad. I have no idea how it works."

Charlotte handed her a glass. Eva accepted it and discovered it was a Coke with enough rum in it to burn all the way down. "Yeah," she sighed, sitting back and taking another sip. "That's about right."

"Is your boyfriend a werewolf, too?" Charlotte asked, sipping from her own glass as she sat down next to her daughter.

"Actually, he's kind of a werecat. And he works spells."

"I knew there was something weird about him. And did you just say you know King Arthur?" Bill demanded. There was a familiar gleam in his eyes.

Charlotte choked on her drink and sputtered, "Oh, God, he's starting to geek out!"

"We are not running a halfway house for mortals, Smoke." On the screen of the enchanted iPhone, Arthur glowered.

"I'm aware of that, but these particular mortals are in danger because their daughter helped me when I needed it most."

"Good point." The vampire rubbed his temple, grimacing as if he had a headache. With his duties, it was probably perpetual. "And I'm aware of how much I owe you. My son's life, for one thing—a dozen times over."

David's lips twitched. "The boy did have an interesting childhood."

"Yeah, in the sense of the old Chinese curse: 'May you live in interesting times.' But your friends can't stay here forever, Smoke. And there's no way of knowing how long it's going to take to wrap up this mess with Warlock."

"Oh, I fully intend to take care of Warlock as soon as possible." David curled a lip in a snarl. "I owe him. And I'm going to pay him back."

The white stag raced through the forest in huge bounds, barely one leap ahead of the enormous wolf that snapped at his flanks. Zephyr could feel waves of magic and rage and sheer madness radiating from the creature. They sent blind panic careening through the stag part of him.

Perhaps remaining in the body of a prey animal hadn't been the best choice after all.

He thought about calling for Smoke. His friend would have fought for him, but the future he'd seen along that path had ended with the death of both Smoke and his mate. And Zephyr's fate had not been changed.

The only hope he'd seen had lain on this path—and it was not one that would save him. He was fated for the destruction of all he was, his power drained to feed the wolf's madness, ambition, and hate.

Helpless fury surged through him at that thought. He spotted a tree up ahead, and he shot around it. The wolf didn't turn in time, allowing Zephyr to circle behind it. He drove his antlers into the beast's white haunches, impaling the creature and sending a death spell blasting into it.

With a heave of his head, he picked the wolf up and sent it flying. It yelped in agony as it landed, tumbling through the leaves to slam into a tree trunk. He felt its magic rise, fighting his spell.

"*I am no easy prey, you foul bastard!*" Zephyr bugled in fury and charged, head lowered, another death spell sizzling on the points of his antlers. The wolf whirled and fled around the tree with a single startled yip. Vast satisfaction surged through Zephyr, and he pursued his foe, head still lowered. The wolf ran from him, weaving through the

trees, forcing the stag to slow his furious pursuit as he followed. The creature disappeared through a pair of enormous bushes standing side by side. Zephyr had to stop to
force his greater bulk through them.

A blast of magic exploded just beyond the thick brush.
It was too late to stop.

The creature had transformed into an enormous werewolf. He held a double-bladed battle-axe in one hand,
sparks spilling from the great gem implanted in the spiked
tip. Zephyr planted his cloven hooves and tried to twist
away, but the axe was already swinging.

The blade bit into the stag's muscled neck, and the spell
blasted after it. Zephyr felt it rip into him, dragging his
power and essence from the stag and sending it funneling
into the werewolf's greedy brain. He fought the pull with
all his strength, tried to shield, but the stag was dying, its
blood running red as its legs buckled under it. Without the
animal to anchor his magic, Zephyr couldn't hold on.

The werewolf dragged him under like a riptide, slashed
at him with the power the stag's death had given him. Used
it to rip him into pieces and keep what he wanted.

And then he hurled the core of Zephyr's spirit into the dark.

Much better, Warlock thought, as the elemental ceased
to fight his will. The notes he'd taken based on the cat's
memories had suggested the stag was vulnerable. And just
as Smoke had suspected, without a human host's intelligence, Zephyr didn't have the resources to fight him off.
The psychic core been comparably easy to discard, leaving
Warlock with power and memories he could control much
easier than he had Smoke's.

Unfortunately, the cat was still a threat. There was no
way to know what the elemental had learned while impris-
oned in Warlock's mind. He had to die.

And this time, Warlock was going to take care of the
job himself.

Rising from the stag's body, the Dire Wolf flicked the
blood from his axe and opened a gate back to Mortal Earth.

* * *

Eva thoroughly enjoyed watching her parents' gape as, suitcases in hand, they stepped through David's dimensional gate onto the cobblestoned streets of Avalon.

"Jeez, it's like somebody made Disney World into a bedroom community." Bill Roman turned in a slow, delighted circle.

Eva laughed. "You know, I said the same thing. This place is really amazing, isn't it?"

Charlotte elbowed Bill and gestured with her overnight bag. "Look at that castle, Bill. It's gorgeous." She turned to Eva. "They built all this with magic?"

Eva nodded, having repeated the spiel that Belle had given her the day before. "Belle said it takes a lot of power to conjure such enormous buildings. I gather it's a sort of rite of passage. Build one of those, and you're considered a real witch."

"That's amazing. Which one of them is yours?" Bill turned to David, whose stock had gone up considerably with her father.

He frowned, his gaze sliding to Eva. "I haven't built a house here. When I'm in Avalon, I usually stay with the Pendragons, generally in house cat form."

Charlotte's dark eyes widened with sudden realization. "You're Eva's cat, T'Challa! Your hair is the same color, right down to the stripes."

David laughed, a low, pleasant rumble that made Eva smile. "Yes, I had changed form during a dream, but because of my memory loss, I didn't know how to turn back."

Charlotte frowned. "Why'd you run out the door? Eva was really upset about that."

His expression turned grim. "That was a miscalculation. I felt I was putting her in danger from the other werewolves, especially given that I couldn't defend her in cat form. I thought if I left, the werewolves would come after me and leave her alone. What I didn't realize was that they were watching the house."

"And they damned near ate both of us," Eva said,

grimacing. "Luckily, he turned into a furry Hulk and saved my fanny."

Her father blinked and stared at David, his graying brows on the rise. "How the hell did you do that?"

David shrugged. "Magic."

Bill snorted. "Yeah, I figured that part out."

"Actually, I have never assumed that form before, but Eva was in danger, so . . ." He spread his big hands.

Bill gave him a long, considering look, then nodded in satisfaction. He opened his mouth to say something else, but a huge shadow glided across the ground. Automatically, they all looked up.

"Shit!" Bill half ducked, and dragged Charlotte behind him. "It's a freaking dragon!"

"It's only Kel," David told him, watching the great beast spiral lazily overhead. "He's one of the Knights of the Round Table."

Charlotte frowned. "There was no Arthurian knight named Kel."

"He's a recent addition. Besides, the Arthurian legends are largely wrong."

"Just like the stuff about vampires and werewolves." Eva watched the dragon spread his wings and come in for a landing in a tower over the trees.

"If the dragon's a knight, he must be able to turn into a human," Bill said thoughtfully.

David nodded approval of his deduction. "Exactly. But unlike the rest of us, being human isn't his natural state. He really is a dragon. He uses magic to assume human form."

Bill exchanged a look with his wife. "Like I said, Disney World."

While they'd been sightseeing, David had led them to the Pendragon house. Now they climbed the brick stairs as Charlotte and Bill gazed around with interest.

Arthur answered the door before they even had time to knock, a smile of welcome on his bearded face. "Gwen said you were coming up the walk. Come on in." Today he was dressed in blue jeans, running shoes, and a T-shirt with a sketch of the Black Knight from *Monty Python and the Holy Grail.* The lettering over the armless, legless knight read, "It's only a flesh wound!"

Bill grinned at the shirt and affected an English accent. " 'Listen, strange women lyin' in ponds distributin' swords is no basis for a system of government. Supreme executive power derives from a mandate from the masses, not from some farcical aquatic ceremony.' "

Arthur threw his head back and roared with laughter. "I always loved that line. You memorized that?"

Bill chuckled. "Hell, I memorized the whole *movie.*"

"Oh, God," Charlotte whispered to Eva as he waved them all inside. "Your father has found a kindred geek."

Sure enough, the two started swapping lines from the "Dead Parrot Sketch" on the way down the hall.

Charlotte was, as usual, right. Two hours later they'd stashed their suitcases in the Pendragons' guest rooms, had dinner, and settled in to get to know their hosts. The three women ate slices of tart lemon meringue pie in the dining room while the men bonded over Monty Python's cockeyed version of the Grail legend. Deep laughter boomed through the house, along with chorused snatches of dialogue.

"What's with all the pop culture?" Eva asked. "I noticed you folks seem to have DVDs of damn near every television show, movie, and music video ever made."

Gwen snorted. "And you haven't seen the Magekind's main library yet. It takes up four buildings in the middle of town, full to the rafters. It's like a magical Library of Congress."

"You're trying to stay caught up," Charlotte said suddenly. Correctly interpreting Eva's lifted brows, she shrugged. "I don't get some of the references on TV either, and I'm just fifty-five. If *I* lose track . . ."

Gwen nodded. "You can't understand a people until you understand their culture. You have to know why they believe the things they do if you're going to change behavior." She grimaced. "Which is why we've been watching a whole hell of a lot of Middle Eastern television these days.

Not to mention hanging out in mosques in very heavy disguises."

"Gee," Eva said wryly, "why didn't the CIA think of that?"

Charlotte frowned. "Why not just cast a spell on the bad guys? Tell them not to blow people up anymore?"

"Wouldn't work. Well, it might have when the problem was only a couple of nutcases, but we didn't know about them at the time. Once you get a big movement going, it's like an aircraft carrier. Changing its direction is a bitch."

Before a political discussion could get going, David sauntered in. "I thought you should know Arthur's trying to talk Bill into following him around with a pair of coconuts."

Gwen rolled her eyes and explained to Charlotte, "To make clopping noises for his imaginary horse."

Charlotte's eyes widened in horror. "I know. And Bill'd do it."

"Oh, Lord." Both women bolted out of the dining room to save their husbands from themselves.

The minute they were out of sight, David grabbed Eva's hand and pulled her from her seat. "Quick, while they're distracted, let's go neck."

Eva laughed as he hauled her toward the stairs. "Neck?"

"Snog? Do the horizontal mambo? Fuck like forest creatures?"

She dropped her voice to a horrified whisper. "I am *not* having sex with you in King Arthur's house with my mother right downstairs!"

"Then we'll gate somewhere else. I haven't made love to you since yesterday. My favorite bits are turning blue."

Eva snickered. She lost the smile as it occurred to her that her David—the David before he regained his memory—would never have told that particular joke. What other differences were there? And was this still the man she'd fallen in love with?

He shot her a sharp look, and she realized he'd picked up on her flash of doubt. His eyes narrowed before he regained his easy grin and kept right on pulling her up the stairs. His big hands moved in an elegant gesture, and a gate appeared at the top of the stairs. Eva, who was getting used to dimensional travel, followed him through it with hesitation.

Into sunlight.

The contrast between indoors and the brilliant streaming light blinded her for a moment, and Eva stumbled, blinking, to a stop. As she waited for her eyes to adjust, she became aware of the roar of ocean waves and the feeling of fine sand underfoot. Magic bloomed in a warm and tingling tide across her skin, and she realized she was naked.

Her vision returned at last, revealing a sweep of deserted beach with sand as fine and white as powdered sugar. A high granite cliff stood off to the left, spilling huge black boulders here and there across the beach and into the water. The sea flung foaming waves against the cliff and rolled up onto the beach, booming and hissing to itself.

"This is beautiful." Eva released his hand and ran down to the water's edge. A wave ran up over her feet, foaming and warm as bathwater. "Where the heck are we?" She cast a puzzled glance at the sun, which hovered somewhere well above the horizon. "*When* are we? I thought it was the middle of the night."

"It is, back home in Avalon. We're halfway around the planet. Little island out in the middle of nowhere Arthur and Gwen like to use as a vacation spot." David joined her, slipping a muscular arm around her bare waist.

He was just as naked as she was, and she turned to enjoy the view. Golden sunlight spilled over his brawny shoulders and sculpted chest with its thatch of silky blue-black hair. His cock rose as she gazed at him, thick and rosy over fat, round balls veiled in thick curls.

He gazed at her with the same hunger she felt, his eyes flicking from her eyes to her nipples, down to her sex, then back up to her mouth. His eyes, so pale and bright in the sun, darkened with his need.

With a sigh of delight, she stepped into his kiss.

David's mouth tasted of lemons and meringue with a tingling fizz of magic. She savored the lush warmth of his mouth as he lingered, his tongue sweeping inside, tracing her lower lip, teeth closing over it to gently tug.

He held her hands as he made slow love in slow kisses, fingers threaded through hers, warm and just slightly rough with sword calluses. They stood close enough that his cock rested against her belly, a length of urgent warmth. The erotic promise in the sensation teased a hungry growl from Fluffy. Eva ignored the bright burst of lust, too busy savoring the subtle pleasures David offered her like a gift.

At last he drew his hands from hers and began to touch her, a drift of fingertips along the line of her jaw, the sensitive lobe of her ear, the delicate cord of her throat, the hollow of her collarbone.

And then he went lower.

David traced a gentle swooping path along the rise of Eva's breast, all the way down to the tip that jutted, so deliciously eager for his attention. His fingers circled the sensitive areola, teasing out delicious sensations. His eyes never left her face, watching her with catlike intensity as he drew out her heat.

His other hand slipped downward, tracing the muscles that quivered under the skin of her torso, lower and still lower until he found the soft nest of hair at the top of her thighs. Eva gasped as his fingers slid over the hot, juicy button of her clit, paused, then slid back again, seductive and slow.

The cock brushing her belly was now hard and hot as hammered steel, ripe with wicked promise. Eva captured it in her fingers and began to stroke, taking her time as she thought of how he'd feel buried inside her.

His eyes widened, blue as a gas flame, and a muscle jerked in his jaw as he fought to control his reaction to her.

Eva remembered how he'd used his mouth on her with such maddening skill. She wanted to do the same, wanted to make him crazy with need.

And then she wanted to make him scream her name as he came.

Dropping to her knees, she crouched at his feet and eyed the cock she held captive in her hand. She leaned forward and took him into her mouth, forcing herself to go slowly. Suckled hard in long draws, as if she was trying to suck a thick milkshake through a paper straw. He gasped and shuddered against her. "Gods and demons, Eva!" His eyes drifted closed, and he swallowed as if his mouth had gone suddenly dry.

Eva smiled around his cock and took him deeper.

He was weak. David shivered, feeling the wet heat of her mouth, the careful scrape of her teeth, the way her hand reached up to cup his balls. He'd had plans for this night, careful plans, and they did not include letting Eva suck him off. If anything, he intended to suck *her* off.

But her mouth felt so incredibly good. Her tongue rolled back and forth over the underside of his shaft before she withdrew just a little so she could lick and nibble the sensitive head of his cock. And the sensation was so exquisite, so erotic, like the sight of her as she knelt there, her hand cuddling his balls as she licked him, her tongue dancing and lapping over the round, rosy head. She pushed his cock up until she could lick down the underside, following the big vein there.

Gods and devils, it was sweet.

But she doubted him. Doubted he was the same as the man she'd fallen in love with just because he'd remembered who he was, what he was capable of. Remembered the life that had so often been a bitter, lonely thing.

Remembered what it had been like to stand in the center of his village with everyone he'd ever loved lying dead around him. Remembered what it had been like to kill the lover who had so thoroughly destroyed him.

That was why he'd spent so much time as Cat. Cat lived only in the present. Cat forgot the pain. Only the man remembered and suffered.

Until he'd forgotten it all and found the woman who'd offered him everything he'd lost, all unknowing. The woman whose lush, eager body and kind eyes had taught him love again.

So, tempting as it was, he knew he couldn't just stand there and let her pleasure him. He had to make her see that he was still her David.

So he waited, and the moment she drew him out of her mouth for another teasing lick, he bent over and swept her into his arms. She yelped in surprise and laughing protest. David sent the magic rolling ahead of him as he strode across the fine white sand. Guided by his will, the swirl of power became a big brass bed, canopied in thin lace that blew and danced in the salty sea wind. He lowered her to the mattress covered in fresh linen sheets and red rose petals. The scent of the flowers rolled up around them, mixing with the smell of salt and sea.

He spread her legs wide with impatient greed and buried his face between them.

"David!" she yelped, looking down along her body as he spread her pretty labia and began to lap in long strokes. "Isn't it my turn to do that to you?"

"No." He lifted his head and looked up her torso only long enough to capture her pretty breasts in both big hands. "It's definitely my turn." He gave the pink tips of her nipples a gentle tug and licked again, savoring the salty cream. His index finger found her sex and glided inside for a slow, driving pump.

She fell back against the pillows and arched her spine. "Okay," she gasped. "If you're sure."

Her skin felt so deliciously warm and smooth under his exploring fingers, fine as silk. She smelled like pure, distilled femininity, musk and salt, and her delicate body twisted beneath his with erotic greed.

She threaded her hands through his hair, grabbing double fistfuls of it. "Please, David! Let me have your cock while you . . . Oh, God!" Eva shuddered, a hard, racking quiver that ran from her head to her feet. He could feel her vibrate against him.

It was a demand David couldn't quite refuse. He moved away just long enough to roll onto the bed with his head at her feet, then picked her up and draped her on top of him, her long legs bent to either side of his head.

Hungrily, he spread her delicate lips with his fingers and gave her a long, smooth lap, beginning at her clit and circling her opening. Then he thrust his tongue deep, listened to her helpless moan, and smiled as he licked.

Until her mouth closed over him with ferocious hunger, and he damn near levitated off the bed. Gasping, he wrestled his unruly body back under control and went to work with his tongue again.

He thought she growled.

TWENTY

Eva shivered as David sucked and tongued her sex, his fingers pumping hard inside her, on the verge of blasting her into a blaze of orgasm like a rocket climbing into orbit.

She fought to ignore the twitching build of climax as she concentrated on the taste of his cock, on its nubby width and silken length and raw male heat. Closing her lips over the plum head, Eva sucked hard, swirling her tongue over the delicate flesh. His hips rolled upward, but not as if he'd intended it. She rumbled in satisfaction and worked another inch of cock into her mouth. He was deep now, but she wanted him deeper, wanted to make him feel the maddening delight she felt. Wanted to make him come.

He palmed a breast in one long-fingered hand, squeezing gently, thumbing her nipple back and forth. Pleasure zinged her with every teasing stroke, and she felt the muscles in her thighs begin to twitch. David caught her clit in his mouth and suckled in steady, gentle pulls that made her roll her hips against his face. Maddened, craving the heated steel of him, she pulled away, turned to face him, and swung a leg astride his hips.

"Eva . . ." he began, and grabbed for her. "I wanted . . ."

"I don't care," she growled, and aimed his length at her cunt. She came down hard, so hard he seemed to spear to her ribs. Gasping, Eva went still, letting her body adjust to being so very, very full.

His eyes were wide and intensely blue. Apparently she wasn't the only one who felt a little stunned.

Slowly, carefully, she lifted off him until only the broad head remained inside her, then slid down again, bracing her hands on his shoulders as she rode.

The sun was sinking into the ocean, flinging veils of scarlet across the darkening sky. Its light painted his handsome face and powerful body in reddening gold. His hair spilled across his pillow like a black silk. She reached down and pushed an inky strand out of his face so she could look into those amazing eyes of his. They burned with a blue light of their own, glowing softly with magic and masculinity. "Beautiful man," she whispered. "You are such a beautiful man."

"Not as beautiful as you." David watched her riding him in those slow, careful strokes, loving the way she felt gripping him, loving the way her eyes had gone so dark and dazed. Her sex felt slick, tight as wet silk knotted around his shaft. Her thighs stroked his ribs as her breasts bounced gently in his palms, impossibly soft as he squeezed her hard little nipples.

But her mouth was too damned far away.

He sat up so he could reach her lips. She tasted of his body tinged with that sweet, feral femininity that was solely hers. Eva stopped thrusting as if to concentrate on the kiss, and he lifted one hand to rake a fistful of her silken mane. Her delicate fingertips found the line of his jaw, slid up to trace the points of his ears, then the thick arch of his brows. Her tongue circled his, slipped into his mouth only to retreat again with his in pursuit. Licking and suckling, they nibbled each other and began a slow, hypnotized rolling of hip against hip. Pleasure heated and flowed like a warm, creamy spring.

Sweet, sweet. Gods, so sweet.

He felt her fine inner muscles begin to clench and release.

He opened his eyes—he hadn't even known he'd closed them—because he wanted to watch her come.

Eva cried out, her head rolling back, the last light of the sun pouring red gold across her face, gilding delicate bones and the long black fans of her lashes. She opened her dark eyes, and the intoxicated joy in them tripped him right into orgasm.

The first hot pulse hit him like a spur digging into a stallion's ribs, and he arched, driving his cock deep, grinding in a hard, rolling circle that made her gasp.

He watched her tumble into another climax—or maybe the first one hadn't ended—and she threw back her head and screamed, a raw cry of passion as the sun drowned itself in the sea. His hoarse shout rose like an echo, and his arms wrapped hard around her back and pulled her down with him.

Eva floated in the honeyed aftermath, listening to the surf and the wind, feeling his chest rise and fall in deep gasps under her cheek. The sea tugged at the lace curtains, and they belled from the wind as the tide crept up to swirl around the bed's brass legs. A chill rose over her, and she cuddled deeper into David's warmth.

"It feels so good to be here with you," she told him sleepily. "It feels so . . . right. So perfect." In fact, it had never been this perfect with any man, ever. It was almost frightening, but she felt too damn good to worry about it.

He kissed her forehead. "Good. It feels wonderful to me, too."

She shivered as the wind blew over her bare back. "Maybe it's time to go in. It's getting a little late." Which probably made it dawn at the Pendragon house. "Mom and Dad are going to wonder where we are."

He gave her an amused look. "Can't have that."

She glowered. "Don't smirk. No, I don't have a curfew. Daddy just worries."

"I don't blame him." She felt his magic rise, and a moment later they were both dressed in jeans and long-sleeved shirts. The fabric felt warm, as though fresh from the dryer. More of David's thoughtful magic.

"Need a coat, too?" he asked her, giving her an appraising look.

"Nope, this is good." Eva rolled off the bed, splashing into the seawater that swirled around it. As her running shoes were instantly soaked, she grimaced and bounded up onto the beach. David loped after her, and she looked back to watch him just as the bed faded away like a dream.

A very sweet dream.

He caught her hand as they started up the beach. Her shoes squelched, and she wrinkled her nose. "I hate wet sneakers."

He looked down at her and smiled, and just like that her shoes were dry again.

Eva laughed. "Damn, I could get used to that."

"That's the idea. I want you addicted to me." He twined his warm fingers with hers. "Because I'm definitely addicted to you."

"Silver-tongued devil." The sand seemed to glow in the moonlight as whitecaps rolled toward the shore. "That was really beautiful," she told him softly. "Thank you."

He shot her a glance and a wry smile. "There can be advantages to having a lover with certain magical abilities."

"Yeah, you definitely have magical abilities."

"But I'm still your David." There was a trace of a question in the words. "Aren't I?"

Eva stopped in her tracks to stare up at him.

That's when it hit her just how much she'd been hurting him. Her refusal to accept Cat, her unconscious tendency to call him "David" even after his three personalities recombined—all of it had communicated a very ugly message.

"What have I done to you?" She asked the question in a low, shaking voice.

He frowned. "What do you mean? You haven't done anything."

"Except hurt you worse than Warlock. At least that bastard valued your magic. I've rejected you over and over."

His brows drew down. "No, you haven't. You just . . ."

"Told Cat I didn't want to make love to him. Refused to

call you anything but David. Acted like I only loved one third of you. Which is utter bullshit."

"No, that's not the way I took it." But his blue eyes flickered ever so slightly.

"Now you're lying to me, love." She stepped up against him and took both his hands. "I love you. All of you. Period. The Cat part of you, who made diced asshole for me and then gave me David again because he realized that was what I wanted. The elemental with his beautiful eyes and ancient power, who greeted me with such joyful surprise because he didn't think I cared enough to rescue him. And the Sidhe warrior who turned himself into a giant werecat to save my life." Her lower lip trembled as her eyes stung. "How could I not love all that?"

A muscle ticked in his jaw. "But I'm not human."

"Which is a damned good thing," Eva said tartly, "because a human would have died a dozen times over this past week. A human couldn't have helped me save my parents. And in case it's escaped your notice, I'm not human either."

He shook his head. "You're trying to be logical about this. As Cat says, there's no logic in the heart. If you don't love the other parts of me, there's nothing either of us can do about it."

"Then answer one question." She called her magic, let it spill over her in a breathtaking explosion of pain. The hands that held his acquired claws as she grew until she towered over him with sable fur covering her body. "Can you love me like this?"

He looked up at her, and his lips quirked. "Of course. You're beautiful."

Eva snorted. "Baby, every other man I know—with the possible exception of my dad and a couple of vampires— would be running like hell right now. Even Daddy freaked the first time I showed him what I am. Yet you never even batted an eye. You just hugged me and implied something kinky about my furry breasts. Do you have any idea how much that meant to me?"

He shrugged. "Your werewolf form is as beautiful in its own way as your human body."

"And when you look at me like that, I believe you." She lifted his hand. "Let me ask you something I should have asked a hell of a long time ago. What's your Sidhe name?"

He blinked. "What do you mean?"

"What's the real name of that part of you that's a Sidhe warrior? Because it's sure as hell not David. David is a statue in Italy."

He frowned at her, his expression uneasy. "I like David."

"But it's not your name. What's your Sidhe name?"

"Urúvion. It means 'fiery.'" He shook his head. "I doubt you can pronounce it."

She concentrated fiercely, working to reproduce his pronunciation. "Oo-roo-vee-on. How do you spell that? O-r-v . . ."

He laughed. "I have no idea. My people didn't have a written language. Even if we had, I haven't gone by that name in millennia. Not since I began hosting Smoke and Cat. Everyone else simply calls me Smoke."

"So." Eva blew out a breath. "Smoke." She met his bright blue gaze, her own steady, level with perfect honesty. "I love you, Smoke."

He blew out a breath. For a moment she wondered if he was going to insist on being called David. Instead he said, "And I love you, Eva."

The joy she felt surprised even her with its leaping incandescence.

Eva changed back to her human form, and took his hand again as they started up a winding sand path. The surrounding hillside was covered in long stalks of rustling beach grass and the tiny violet-blue flowers. She swung their joined hands like a child. "You know, I can't think of the last time I felt this good."

Smoke laughed. "You made me feel pretty damned good, too."

"I'm not talking about that." When he threw her a look of mock hurt, she grinned. "Well, not *just* about that."

"Ah." He sent her a small, warm smile. "So what's the other reason?"

"Coming clean with my parents after five years of lies. Knowing they're safe from Warlock."

His smile faded, and worry darkened his eyes as he looked off into the distance. "Unfortunately, they can't stay in the Mageverse indefinitely. We're going to have to find out where he is."

"You don't know?" She studied his face, frowning at the unease there. "But Smoke—you—were in his head for days."

"Yes, but he had me walled up so I wouldn't overwhelm him. As I tried very hard to do. I got flashes of things, but nothing useable."

"What was it like?" She asked the question softly, sensing whatever memories he had troubled him. "What's *he* like?"

"He's insane," Smoke said bluntly. "He sees himself as some kind of infallible messiah for his people solely because Merlin chose him."

"Which begs the question—what the hell was Merlin *thinking*?"

"He wasn't like that in the beginning. The problem is that Merlin ordered him to keep an eye on the Magekind in case they ever began abusing humanity. He's been at that job for a very, very long time, and he eventually grew paranoid. He has a pathological jealousy of Arthur, who has been saving humanity for a millennium and a half, while Merlin ordered Warlock to hide and do nothing. But he wanted to be a hero, too."

"So instead he decided to become a villain?"

Smoke shook his head. "He doesn't see himself as a villain. He wants to destroy the Magekind so his people can become humanity's guardians—and the heroes he thinks they should be."

"Why do I have the distinct feeling that wouldn't be a good thing?"

"Because you're perceptive. Given the chance, Warlock would become exactly the kind of tyrant Merlin feared."

"Irony sucks."

Smoke laughed. "With enthusiasm."

They crested the hill to see the moon rising in pale splendor above a landscape of enormous stone blocks that stretched for miles in the dark. Eva stopped in her tracks and stared.

Some were square, some tall rectangles, a few looked like squashed donuts, and still others had been piled together as if by a giant child. The blocks looked too big and new to be ruins, yet their arrangement seemed utterly random. "What the hell is that?"

"One of the Magekind's practice sites," Smoke explained. "The new recruits can run around those blocks shooting magic at one another to their heart's content. If they tried that in Avalon, they might blow up something important. Also, sorcery makes one hell of a lot of noise, which pisses off tired witches who've just spent weeks in the field. I gather fighting terrorists makes them all a little twitchy."

Eva snorted. "Yeah, I can see how all those magical booms would trigger a nasty case of PTSD. I . . ."

Malevolence seemed to explode in her senses, a sense of sheer evil that made the hair rise on the back of her neck. She sucked in a breath to yell a warning, but Smoke had already thrown up a hand in a sweeping gesture.

Blinding light shot out of the darkness to rage around them as boiling blue energy. Eva instinctively threw her arms up to shield her face. Smoke grunted as if catching something massively heavy.

It took her a moment of stark terror to realize nothing hurt. Eva peered around her arms to find the attack had been blocked by a shimmering hemisphere of golden force.

Smoke's face contorted with effort, his teeth clenched, his blue eyes glowing. A second flaming ball slammed into the shield he'd cast, then another, then a whole pounding salvo of them, coming fast and hard.

Eva instinctively huddled into the shelter of his strength. He swept out an arm to push her behind him as if to give her the additional shield of his body.

"What the hell is going on?" But even as she yelled the question, she knew the answer.

"Warlock," Smoke snarled. "How did the bastard find us? Must have tapped into the elemental's—my—memories. He knows I love this bloody island."

"Can you cast a gate?" Eva shouted over the noise.

"I've already tried. He's got some kind of barrier blocking me. From the feel of it, he must have walked a spell circle around the whole island and keyed it to tell him when we arrived."

It felt as if ice replaced the blood in her veins. "It was a trap."

"And we walked right into it."

Eva slipped one arm around his waist as she looked past his brawny shoulder. She still couldn't see where the blasts were coming from.

Smoke swore. "I can't fire back at him because I'd have to drop the shield. And I can't do that because it would leave you vulnerable."

"But Gwen said werewolves are immune to magic!" She had to yell it over the sizzle and crack of the blasts.

"Yes, but you're not immune to lightning. Just because he uses magic to call down bolts, that doesn't mean the electricity won't fry you."

"And thanks for that mental image."

"I'm a little too busy for tact, Eva." Smoke grabbed her by the wrist and pulled her after him as he broke into a sprint. She pounded behind him, heart in her throat. Holding his free hand lifted, he sent power pouring from his palm to feed the shield.

Finally they reached the shelter of one of the massive rocks. Warlock's blasts splashed harmlessly against it. As if realizing that, he stopped firing.

"I think the bastard may have just outsmarted himself this time," Smoke whispered into the sudden quiet. "Between that barrier and these attacks, he's using a lot of power. If you can keep these rocks between you and him, I can take the fight to him. If I wear him down enough, he's dead."

"Those stones," Eva realized. "You said they're resistant to magic."

"Otherwise the baby witches would blow them to gravel," he agreed. "When you get the chance, I want you to shift to wolf form and run like hell. You'll be faster and more agile on four legs."

"Four—?" She stared at him. Even as a human, Eva could see pretty well in the dark. "You want me to turn into a regular wolf? But I've never done that!"

"You're a Dire Wolf, Eva, it's one of your transformations. Just imagine being a wolf instead of a werewolf. The magic'll do the rest."

"Then what?"

"Lay low—don't try to help me. In fact, stay as far away as possible. I'm going to cut loose with everything I've got, and I don't want you hurt in the process. Besides, we don't know if he's brought any of his thugs along, so you need to stay hidden."

Eva opened her mouth to argue, but another blast hit the block so hard, it rocked against their backs. She gasped.

"I'm going to run left," Smoke told her, then pointed out across the field. "You go straight. Put as much rock between you and that furry bastard as possible."

"Are you sure I can't help?"

"This fight is going to be too far out of your league." He popped his head around the block, then jerked back as something sizzled. "Go." When she hesitated, he barked, "I said *go!*"

Eva went, flinging herself out into the night, darting for the next block, then the next, concentrating on putting as much distance as she could between herself and Warlock.

At least until she figured out a way to help. Damned if she was going to twiddle her thumbs while Smoke fought for his life.

Suddenly every hair on her body rose, and she smelled the dry scent of ozone. Instinct drove her behind the nearest rock. Lightning shook the ground with a thunderous boom, shaking the earth under her feet. She looked toward the sound, her heart leaping in sheer terror. "Smoke!"

He bellowed, "How'd you like that, you bastard?"

Warlock responded with a roll of profanity, including a few terms Eva had never even heard before.

Smoke had thrown that bolt? The man she'd spent the afternoon making love to called down lightning? *Holy baby Jesus and all the saints!*

A chill crept over her, and Eva realized Smoke was right. She didn't need to get too close to this fish fry.

She was entirely too damned likely to wind up as one of the fish.

On the other hand, Eva did want to find a place where she could watch what was happening. What if Smoke got hurt and needed help?

The trick was to find a decent vantage point that wouldn't give Warlock an opportunity to take her prisoner.

She scanned the landscape of blocks, standing silver and black in the moonlight. Another blinding bolt illuminated a hunk of stone the size of a two-story building with three shorter cubes arrayed around it like steps. It looked like the perfect vantage point. The only problem was that she'd need to cross half the field to get to it.

Eva cast a quick glance over her shoulder, but she could see nothing of what was going on except flashes of light, Warlock's red and Smoke's gold. She broke into a run.

Her destination was still fifty yards away when she smelled a scent she knew too well. She slid to a stop, but before she could whirl to sprint the other way, a Dire Wolf stepped around the block ahead of her. He towered like a grizzly, massive and black as pitch. "Why, hello there." His grin flashed white with fang.

Eva whirled, then jerked back to avoid slamming into the second Dire Wolf, who'd slipped up behind her.

"You smell like sex," the pale wolf said. "Want to have a little fun before we kill you?"

Eva gave him a big grin. "Sure. Why not?" She made as if to start toward him—and called her magic. It spilled through her, yanking bone and muscle into burning streams of pain. The world grew as she sank, transforming her into a timber wolf.

Spinning left, Eva ran, zipping behind the closest block before darting around a second stone just beyond it, then making for yet another some yards away.

The two wolf thugs howled and thundered in pursuit. "Get her," one yelled. "If she gets away, Warlock is going to fuck us up!"

"It's an island, you moron!" the other snapped back. "Where the hell is she going to go?"

Which was a damn good point.

Doesn't matter. She had to give running her best shot and hope something else occurred to her before the bad guys caught up.

At least she was doing okay with the wolf thing. Eva had been afraid she'd trip over her own paws, but it seemed her body knew how to move in this form. Yet another werewolf mystery, like where her cell phone went when she shifted.

Don't think, Eva, run!

Smoke roared a wordless battle cry as he called down another lightning bolt. Raw exhilaration surged through him as black clouds boiled overhead with the forces he commanded. He hadn't cut loose like this in years. He'd almost forgotten how good it felt.

Lightning cracked out of the darkness, and he barely got a shield up in time to block it.

That one wasn't his.

He felt the nasty electrical jolt despite the shield, a painful jangle along his nerves. The bolt would have killed him if he hadn't blocked it in time.

Where the hell had Warlock gotten that kind of power? He no longer had access to Smoke's magic, so he shouldn't be capable of calling lightning. Yet he was doing it anyway.

It was almost as if he'd gotten his hands on another elemental. But very few had survived the Dark One invasion, and all those Smoke knew of would have been too much for Warlock to take on. Except for . . .

"Zephyr sends his regards!" Warlock called as if he'd

read Smoke's mind. He'd leaped to the top of one of the blocks as if daring Smoke to hit him. One clawed hand was wrapped around Kingslayer, the gem that tipped the great battle-axe lighting up the rocks around him with a searing red glow. "He was easy prey—just like your woman. Who's probably dead already, assuming my Bastards haven't taken the time to rape her."

Smoke stared up at him, feeling as if a stake of ice had been driven through his heart. Jerking free of the pain, he sent lightning forking down at his brazen enemy.

Warlock laughed like a loon as he leaped clear, disappearing behind another block ten yards away. "You're so easy, Pussycat," he called from its shelter. "All I have to do is dump her corpse at your feet, and you'll be too busy grieving to fight."

"What do you think Merlin would say of making war on women?" Smoke roared back. "I doubt he'd approve!"

Warlock said nothing, a silence that steamed with fury. *I'm not the only one with a weakness,* Smoke thought.

He just had to find a way to use it.

As for where Eva was or whether she was safe—he didn't dare even think about that, or he'd be no good to her. The only chance they had was if he finished the Dire Wolf fast. Then he could find her and make a werewolf-skin coat out of Warlock's pet dogs.

He let his power spill, reshaping his body into the form he'd worn to kill killers once before.

Then he leaped, leaped, and leaped again, until he arrived at the block he sensed Warlock hiding behind. He bounded over it, meaning to come down on the Dire Wolf feet first. Unfortunately, the sorcerer sensed him coming, twisted with incredible agility, and threw himself out of the way. Smoke hit the ground, bounced, and slammed into him anyway, clawed hands raking down the front of Warlock's body to grab his dick and jerk. The werewolf howled and tore away, magic dancing down his body to heal the mangled flesh.

Smoke followed and hit him with an uppercut that drove

his head back. Warlock fell flat on his back, and Smoke dove on top of him, snarling.

Finally—*finally!*—he was going to make the fucker pay.

Eva crouched on top of the two-story stone with the three steps, the one she'd first spotted all the way across the field. The two werewolves were casting around on the ground below, trying to untangle her scent. They'd finally assumed wolf form themselves when they realized that wolf Eva could run rings around them. Which she literally had, racing in great loops around the stones to muddy her scent.

Smoke had been right. She *was* faster and more agile in wolf form.

Something exploded. Eva instinctively flattened on top of the block. Her lover and Warlock were stalking somewhere out there in the darkness. She'd seen Smoke shift into the form of the huge werecat he'd used during the fight back at the complex. He was now every bit as big as his foe. Not that they were using all that muscle at the moment; they were too busy shooting bolts and fireballs at each other as they ducked in and out between the stones. Their attacks lit up the night and shook the ground with deafening cracks.

And I've been sleeping with that man. Or is "man" even the right word for him?

Eva pushed the thought aside. It didn't matter that Smoke was a borderline god, while she was a comic book geek in way over her head. *The point is to get through the night, and I won't if I don't pull my head out of my butt.*

She needed to take care of Fang and Fanger. Then maybe she could find a way to help Smoke with Warlock.

Another blast rattled her teeth. *Or not. Jeez.*

Concentrate on killing the nasty werewolves, Eva.

In that moment, she saw her chance. The pale wolf had paused directly below the stone she crouched on, head down as he breathed in her scent. He started to glance up, finally realizing where she must have gone . . .

And she landed on him, four hundred pounds of pissed-off Dire Wolf slamming him flat. She heard bones crack with the impact. He had time for one yelp before she grabbed his muzzle and twisted hard.

Another crack.

Eva hesitated, surprised at the sudden sick sensation killing him gave her. She knew he'd have done far worse to . . .

The black Dire Wolf exploded out of the darkness, knocking her off her victim. They both went tumbling. Her back slammed into one of the blocks, and her head cracked against it in an explosion of stars. She slid to the ground, limp and stunned.

"Oh, you little bitch," the werewolf snarled, "You're going to pay for that."

"You're going to pay for that." The voice of the were-wolf serial killer sounded in her memory, saying exactly the same words.

Eva saw a blur over her head as the werewolf struck, raking a vicious furrow across her breasts. She screamed as he grabbed her torn flesh and squeezed hard. "Nice tits," he growled. "I'm going to enjoy this."

Smoke had taught her a dozen ways to get out of just this situation. She tried to roll into a throw, but her body refused to obey.

With a chill, she realized she was completely paralyzed. Had the werewolf broken her spine?

Oh, sweet God. He's going to rip me apart. Just like before. Except this time I'm going to die.

Eva screamed.

The horror and hopelessness in the sound cut through Smoke like a razor slicing into his soul. Instinctively, he jerked away from Warlock's half-stunned body, in the direction of the cry.

The moment of distraction was damned near fatal. The werewolf sorcerer shot a blast right at his face. He barely got his shield up in time.

Another bloodcurdling scream sliced across the battle-field.

Smoke whirled and ran toward the chilling cry. He no

longer gave a fuck about Warlock or getting revenge. All he wanted was to save Eva from the creature that was killing her.

Unfortunately, Warlock had other ideas.

Smoke heard the thump of the Dire Wolf's big paws. Raw instinct sent him ducking left. A fireball roared past.

I can't help Eva if the fucking werewolf fries me. Summoning his magic, he spun the power around him into a suit of matte black plate armor big enough to protect his werecat form from Warlock's blasts.

Then he raced through the dark, praying he got to her in time.

TWENTY-ONE

"Oh, that's good," purred the dark werewolf. "Scream some more for me." His claws flashed down, raking another bloody furrow across Eva's belly. Any minute now, he was going to cut deep enough to gut her, just like the werewolf who'd torn her up all those years ago. Like that first attacker, he wasn't even bothering to hold her down. He'd realized she couldn't move, couldn't fight no matter how desperately she wanted to.

Her mind raged in the cage of her body. She should be fighting, but she couldn't make herself move. Was this some kind of spell? It wasn't a spinal injury, because she could feel the pressure of the Dire Wolf's weight across her legs, the pain of his raking claws. Her back wasn't broken, yet the only part of her she could control was her voice. So she screamed in another ringing shriek.

And Smoke answered. "Eva!"

Boom!

The dark werewolf laughed. "Sounds like your boyfriend is getting his ass handed to him." He grabbed her bloody breasts again and squeezed viciously hard, digging his talons in. The pain in her torn flesh was nauseating.

"You're Warlock's secret weapon, bitch. He told me all I had to do was make you howl, and he'd be able to take lover-boy apart." Baring his teeth, he added, "Let's give him a really loud one this time." His claws sliced her nipple.

This time Eva didn't even feel the pain. *Warlock's using me against Smoke?*

"Eva!" Smoke's voice rang out, hoarse with desperation. A lightning strike lit up the darkness with a deafening crack that shook the ground under her back.

Was that a cry of pain? She couldn't tell in the aftermath of the thunder.

Bastard. Oh, Warlock, you bastard. The blast of rage she felt exploded her paralysis.

Eva drove both hands straight upward, just as Smoke had taught her, clawed thumbs spearing into the werewolf's eyes. He fell back, roaring in agony as she flipped him onto his back. Now she was on top, and it was her claws doing the raking.

And she didn't fuck around with any teasing, shallow cuts.

He tried to fight back, but she'd already torn out his throat, and his strength bled away before she even noticed his claws.

Her fury seemed a separate thing, something that had grown for five years. Something that sent her ripping into him with talons and teeth and hot, animal rage that anyone would dare use her to hurt the man she loved. It mixed with an older, colder fury that anyone would attack *her*, bite *her*, rip *her* open, *infect her, make her something not human, make her lie to the people she loved.*

The dark werewolf paid for it all.

She finally realized he'd stopped moving. When she blinked the red out of her eyes and actually looked at him, he was very . . . wet.

Boom-CRACK!

Smoke. Her head lifted. Smoke was still fighting Warlock. Warlock, who had sent this bastard to make her scream, solely to destroy the man she loved.

Warlock needed to pay, too.

Eva rose, blood dripping from her claws and muzzle. The taste made her stomach twist. Some part of her recoiled in horror.

She ignored it. Smoke needed her, and Warlock needed to pay.

Where were they? Glancing around, Eva jolted as she glimpsed something white standing right beside her. She gasped and whirled, only to realize the figure was Zephyr. Not Warlock, thank God.

The big white stag stood watching her, his elegant head lifted with its impressive spread of antlers on display, sparks of magic dancing among the sharp tips. *"You are not prey."* His voice rang in her mind like a great bell, deep and resonant.

It took her a moment to notice she could see the block behind him through his milky white glow. But he'd been solid when she'd met him before. She took an automatic step back. "Are you a ghost?"

He tilted his head, considering. *"That's as good a word as any."* His sigh gusted through her mind. *"Warlock slew me and stole my power. Now he uses it against my friend."*

"And I've got to go save Smoke. I'm so sorry, Zephyr." She stared to turn away. His next words stopped her in her tracks.

"As you are, you will fail. And so will Smoke." The stag's voice sounded remorseless. *"Kingslayer amplifies Warlock's magic beyond Smoke's ability to fight."*

A chill lanced through her, but she shook it off. "That may be, but I've got to try anyway."

The stag instantly appeared in her path. *"I can help you. I can break Merlin's lock on the magic in your DNA so you can use it for more than shifting."*

Eva clenched her fists, sensing the remorseless race of time running out. "I don't have time for that. I've got to go."

"Not yet, you don't. Let me enter you as Smoke entered the Sidhe. Let me share your life and show you the way to magic." The stag's eyes ignited in a white blaze. *"Let me help you kill Warlock and avenge us both."*

Another boom rocked the ground.

Eva stared at him, knowing Zephyr was right. She couldn't help Smoke as she was now; she could only become a hostage Warlock would use to kill him. And she was tired of being used.

She didn't let herself think of all the reasons this was a bad idea. Smoke was all that mattered. "Do it."

The stag leaped. The impact of his charge rocked her back on her heels as he vanished into her chest. She looked down just in time to see his glowing hooves disappear between her bleeding breasts.

The magic Merlin used to create both Warlock and his people was exactly the same, his voice said in her mind. *But to make the Direkind immune to the Majae's power, he had to limit your ability to use your magic. But you can shift your DNA just as you do your bones and flesh . . .*

Eva's eyes went wide as Zephyr showed her the spell deep within her own DNA—a spell Merlin had created, that had spread to her by the the werewolf who bit her five years ago. The stag showed her the simple molecular shift in her DNA that would change the spell, so that she could reach into the dimension the elementals called home. So she, too, could call power in a torrent of magic.

So Eva called the magic and transformed, just the way she'd always done. But this time, with Zephyr's guidance, she shifted her DNA as well. To become a magic user.

Eva had stopped screaming.

But Warlock, damn him to all the hells, would not let Smoke past. Every time he tried to get by, Warlock sent lighting and fire to block his path. Smoke had managed to avoid every stroke, shield against every blast, but he hadn't managed to get by. And Eva might be dying.

Helpless fury filled his mouth with the taste of brass and blood. He was going to have to take the time to kill the fucker and pray Eva could hold on a little longer. As long as she remained alive, even if badly hurt, he could use his magic to heal her.

"Eva, I'm coming," he bellowed.

Warlock stepped out from behind a block and grinned at him in the smug way that was quickly driving Smoke insane. "No, you're not."

"Yes, gods curse you, *I am*." The sword materialized in Smoke's clawed hands, and he leaped forward, swinging the huge blade with all his werecat strength.

Warlock heaved Kingslayer up to meet the attack, and the two weapons clanged together with teeth-jarring force. Until Kingslayer's gem flashed and the magic roared, picked Smoke up, and tossed him through the air.

He hit rolling, lost the sword, and somehow rolled to his feet, shaking his spinning head hard.

"You can't beat me, Cat." Warlock stalked toward him, raising Kingslayer as he came. The axe burst into red flame. "You don't have the power."

"You know what I've noticed about you, Warlock?" The voice was female, but so deep, Smoke didn't recognize it. "You have a talent for biting off more than you can chew."

Magic sizzled through the darkness, a blazing white blast that caught Warlock in the side. The werewolf howled as it picked him up and tossed him like a Ping-Pong ball in a hurricane.

Gods and devils, what now? Smoke spun.

Eva stepped out from around a block. She was in Dire Wolf form, but a great glowing rack of ghostly antlers crowned her head. Sparks danced from point to point in a way Smoke recognized. "Eva," he whispered, "what did you do?"

She tilted her antlered head in a way that was painfully familiar, though it was nothing she'd ever done before. "Made a deal with what's left of Zephyr."

"Which couldn't have been much." Warlock vaulted a block to land directly in front of her. "I ate most of him."

"Yeah," Eva bared her fangs. "And he's really pissed about that."

Her fist swung. It must not have occurred to Warlock that she'd have the balls to hit him, because the blow rocked his head.

"You *bitch*!" He swung the axe at her, but the blade

clanged against Smoke's conjured great sword. The were-cat rammed his shoulder against Warlock's, driving him back a pace.

Smoke stepped in with a left cross that snapped the Dire Wolf's head around. In the same motion, the cat raked his claws down Warlock's belly, though the wolf jerked back so the blow didn't quite gut him. Pivoting, he rammed his elbow at Smoke's chin.

Smoke knocked the blow aside and struck, claws raking the Dire Wolf's throat. Blood flew, and Warlock stumbled back with a yelp, one hand covering his wounded neck.

"That's right, fucker." Smoke sneered at the flash of fear in Warlock's eyes. "You can die just like the rest of us."

Unfortunately, he hadn't caught enough flesh to really hurt the bastard—Warlock was damned fast. The werewolf sneered right back. "So can you, Cat. And you're going to—right *now*." He started to swing his axe.

Which was when Eva lowered her head and came up under Warlock's guard to drive her suddenly solid antlers into the Dire Wolf's gut. He roared in pain, the cry spiraling into a high, shocked yowl when she sent a spell crackling through her rack. The air filled with the nauseating smell of burning flesh.

Warlock grabbed for her antlers, as if to drag them out of his body, but his hand passed right through them.

Eva jerked her ghostly horns free in a spray of hot, red blood. Cursing her viciously, Warlock swung his axe at her head. Smoke surged forward meaning to block the blow, but Warlock was too damned fast, and he missed.

Eva leaped straight up, and the axe whizzed harmlessly past her clawed feet. She landed ten feet away with a neat, catlike thump. *"Zephyr says to get that damned axe,"* she growled directly into Smoke's mind. *"It amplifies his power. Without it, we can take him apart."*

"Ooooh, yessssss!" Smoke lunged forward, transforming his sword into an axe of his own. He hooked Warlock's blade with his, dragged it down, and punched the Dire Wolf with merciless force, right in his sensitive nose. The blow loosened Warlock's grip as Smoke twisted his axe, jerking both blades into a hard arc.

Kingslayer went flying. Eva reached up to grab the airborne weapon.

"Don't you touch my axe, bitch!" Warlock roared in rage and leaped, snatching the great blade out of the air before her fingers could close around the handle. Power boiled red around the blade as he drew it back. Smoke smelled the familiar reek of death magic, and knew if the blow landed, she was finished.

He leaped over Warlock's head and came down right in his path, both hands lifted as he reached for his magic and sent it all, everything he had, screaming into the Dire Wolf's face. Even as he fired, he watched the axe arc toward his head and knew he was looking at his own death.

Eva's slender hand reached past his ear. Far more magic than she should have had blasted from her palm, adding to his furious salvo.

The mingled energy hit Warlock like a freight train, smashing him backward right through one of the blocks. The thing shattered, but Warlock kept going, hitting yet another block, then still one more, before sailing over the edge of the cliff.

For a long, ticking moment, neither of them moved as they strained their ears. But there was nothing: no outraged curse, no roar of rage, not even a distant splash.

"I sure hope that got the bastard," Eva said in a faint voice, "Because I just used up everything I had."

"You're not the only one." Smoke limped toward the edge of the cliff to peer out into the darkness. Though he strained both his eyes and his magical senses, there was no sign of the Dire Wolf.

"You're bleeding," Eva said, walking up behind him. "There." One of her furred hands touched a deep cut in his ribs.

He had no idea when he'd gotten it. "I must've missed a parry."

"Not completely," she murmured. "Or you'd be dead."

Her big, dark eyes met his, lovely and familiar even in her lupine skull. "Just as I'd be if you hadn't stepped into his path. He was going to take my head."

Smoke gave her a tired smile and wrapped an arm around her shoulders. "No he wasn't. You wouldn't have let him."

Eva cuddled against his chest, her furry arms encircling his equally furry waist. "I don't know about that. He's damn fast."

They fell silent, clinging together like a pair of weary children, until she asked, "You think he's dead?"

"We're not that fucking lucky." Smoke wondered whether he had the energy to levitate out over the ocean and search some more, then reluctantly decided it was probably beyond him. He'd wiped out his energy reserves.

Fortunately, he was willing to bet Warlock was in no better shape.

When Smoke cast the communication spell with the last of his magic, he got through to Guinevere. Twenty minutes later, dozens of witches and vampires were combing the ocean and every inch of island beach. But they found nothing.

"Do you think you got him?" Arthur asked, as the healer worked over Smoke's collection of scrapes, bruises, and one of two really deep wounds. He was still in werecat form, since he'd been too drained to change. The healer looked tiny next to him, her hands trailing sparks as she gently traced his injuries.

Eva was already healed; Smoke had insisted the witch work on her first. Now she watched the Maja with quiet interest, as if absorbing her techniques.

Knowing Eva, she probably was.

"Frankly, I suspect he's back in that lair of his licking his wounds and plotting revenge," Smoke told Arthur bluntly. "He stole a hell of a lot of power from Zephyr."

"And he was formidable even before that," Eva put in absently.

Arthur cursed. "So basically we've still got to deal with the bastard. I'll have to talk to the Direkind Council of Chosen again, try to convince the idiots to give him up."

"That's not going to happen," Tristan said, appearing with a weary Belle at his heels. A light coat of sand covered his armor, and he looked tired and grouchy. Which was no surprise; he should be in the Daysleep now, but like Arthur, he'd woken when Belle had transported him to this night-shrouded hemisphere. "Those people really believe Warlock's a god."

"And they'll protect him to the death," Belle added, her expression grim.

Arthur growled. "Fanatics. Hate 'em. Every fanatic I've ever encountered has been a pain in my ass—including the ones who were supposed to be on my side."

"Yes," Smoke said, rising to his feet, the healer's work finished. "But I'd like to point out that you're still here, and they're not. We'll find Warlock, and we'll take him out, just like all the others."

"And we'll make him pay." Eva's eyes flashed white, and for a moment, ghostly antlers appeared over her head. "Get his axe and he's done. We almost had it today, but he was quicker than I thought."

"You do realize he's going to come after Excalibur just as hard?" Tristan said, lifting a blond brow. "Because that sword is just as important to you as the axe is to him."

"He's not going to get it." Arthur's hand fisted on the sword's hilt. "Trouble is, Merlin created those bastards to defeat us, and I've got a really ugly feeling they're going to give it their best shot."

Warlock swam in pain, his big body twitching and cold. It had taken everything he had left to create the gate back to his lair before he slammed into the ocean. He'd had just enough wit left to realize the impact probably would have killed him.

He still needed to shift to heal the burns that covered his body from the cat's final attack. Unfortunately, he didn't have the power. He was going to have to endure until his magic regenerated.

But until it did, he had plans to make.

He'd tried to resolve this fight with Arthur with a minimum of deaths. He'd meant to kill only Pendragon's son, which would have made the Celt easy prey. When that plan failed, he figured stealing the elemental's power would enable him to take Arthur out. But Smoke had proven to be stronger and more powerful than he'd anticipated. At least he'd obtained Zephyr's magic.

He drew Kingslayer close with bloody, swollen hands and glared at the rocky ceiling of his lair. The Celt had to be brought low. And the past weeks had taught Warlock there was only one way to do it, even if it meant his own people would suffer in the process.

"War," he said into the silence, his voice cracked and dry and weak with pain. "The Magekind must bleed."

TWENTY-TWO

Belle took a break from the search long enough to open a portal to the gateway pool for Smoke and Eva, since neither was up to it just then.

Then she went back to work on her new hobby—pissing Tristan off.

Exhausted to the bone, Eva and Smoke walked into the pool hand in hand. The softly glowing water swirled around their feet, then their calves and hips as they waded deeper. And with every step, their bodies drank more magic.

"Oh, God," Eva moaned over the sound of the waterfall thundering into the pool. Her maned head fell back as her eyes closed. "That feels almost as good as sex."

Smoke laughed, a delicious male growl. "Nothing's as good as sex with you."

She opened one eye. It had already started to glow white. "Well, it does depend on the partner."

"Doesn't everything?" Sucking in a deep breath, he released her and dove, then began to swim toward the waterfall.

Eva followed suit, her arms stroking lazily as she kicked her way through the shimmering water. Opening her eyes, she watched with lazy interest as fish swam past, each the size of a dinner plate, scales iridescent and bright as rainbows.

She lifted her head as she reached the waterfall. Smoke had climbed up on one of the great black stones that surrounded the tumble of water so that the steam pelted his cat face, slicking his fur to his massive body. As she watched, magic swirled around him, and he shrank back into Sidhe form.

Eva pulled herself up onto the rock beside him and gasped in delight. The water pounding on her head carried a rush of warm magic that stole her breath. It felt delicious, and she tilted her head back and opened her mouth, gulping both the water and the raw power it carried from the dimensional portal overhead. As she drank, she let the magic roll through her body.

The shift to human barely hurt at all.

Eva opened her eyes to find Smoke reaching for her. She went into his arms joyfully, slipping hers around his neck as he pulled her tight. Their mouths met under the pounding spray, lips pressing, tongues stroking in a hot and hungry kiss that burned with magic.

His hands found her bare, thoroughly healed breasts and cupped her, his fingers rolling and pinching nipples that had gone pert and eager under the pounding tingle. She threw back her head and gasped at the startling intensity of the sensation he created. It was as if the magic made it more, somehow. Hotter, fiercer, even more luscious. He grinned against her mouth as if sensing her reaction.

They stood there on the slick black stone, hands drifting over wet skin, stroking and sliding and squeezing, savoring each electric zing of pleasure, each falling drop of magic.

Smoke dropped to his knees before her and parted the lips of her sex. She sucked in a breath as his tongue slipped deep. He sent a stream of enchanted water sluicing over her clit, and she damned near jolted into orbit.

That boy always was creative, Zephyr laughed in her mind.

Shush, Fluffy told him. *I want to enjoy this.*

Good God, Eva thought. *I've got my own peanut gallery.*

But then Smoke gave her another hot mouthful of magic, and her mind went deliciously blank. His tongue swirled lazily over her clit, tracing a slippery figure eight. She fisted her hands in his hair and let her head fall back, rolling her hips against his mouth.

He reached one hand up and found a nipple, then began to play with it lazily as his mouth slowly drove her insane. Fingers pinched and stroked and played as he alternated licking her clit and spraying mouthfuls of magic across it.

Her climax thundered out of nowhere, quick and hard and merciless, and she screamed into the delicious pound of the waterfall.

Her knees buckled, but Smoke caught her hips with one hand, steadying her. Then he lifted one of her legs and draped it over his shoulder. And went back to eating her lazily as she gasped and moaned her way into another blazing orgasm.

Finally she fell back against the wet stone, limp as a drenched sock, weak from his ruthless pleasuring. Smoke pulled away from her and stood, one arm going around her waist, the other hooking under her knee to sling it over his hip.

Eva read his intention and grabbed his shoulders as she wrapped her other leg around his waist. He took her butt in both hands and lifted her just above the eager jut of his cock. The hard tip found her slick opening as he arched his hips and lowered her, pushing his width between her creamy lower lips, moving slowly, his eyes on hers.

Eva sucked in a breath, loving every inch of the exquisite penetration.

God, he felt incredible, his wet shaft beaded with magic, tingling and hot inside her.

Finally he was in up to the balls, and she let her head fall back, savoring him, loving his blazing length. His mouth found her throat, his teeth raking the sensitive cords of it, gently ruthless.

"God, Smoke . . ." she whimpered.

"That's right—Smoke," he growled against her skin. "I'm your Smoke, no matter who else I am."

She smiled as she tightened the grip of her thighs, hunching hard against his hips. "And I'm yours, period. As I always will be."

Smoke growled in pleasure, loving the heat of her slick grip, the way her hips rolled in his hands as he held her plastered against his pelvis, his cock buried to the balls. "Always," he gritted. "You do realize Zephyr made you immortal? Like me . . ."

Her smile took on a fierce edge. "Just like you." Digging her sharp little nails into his back, Eva hooked her ankles together and ground down on his cock.

The sensation of her slick cunt taking every inch of him nearly hurled him right to orgasm, but he held it off, desperate to ride a little longer.

He braced her back against the wet stone and stepped deeper into her grip, sliding that last delicious fraction into her cunt. The waterfall pounded down on their heads, drenching them in magic as they kissed again, licking, biting, tongues thrusting deep. Kisses that dizzied them as they ground together, cock in cunt, magic surging into magic, blending together in a blue-white glow that spilled over their skin, rolled from head to heels.

The orgasm tore through them both in a white-hot cascade that made them scream together in one long chorused howl of delight.

Singing their pleasure to the magic.

Naked and deliciously limp, Eva floated in the magical pool, the fingers of one hand twined with Smoke's as he floated with his head inches from hers, his body at an angle to hers.

"Damn," she purred. "I can see we'll be making a habit out of this."

He growled a deep sound of assent, his eyes closed, his expression relaxed. She could sense his emotions as clearly as his own, as if they'd linked somehow, and she knew he'd never felt this at peace. Neither had she, though she knew there was so damned much to do.

They were going to have to set wards around the comic shop as well as her parents' home and vehicles. If any werewolf got close, she and Smoke could gate there first and kick whatever ass needed kicking. They had more than enough power to take care of Warlock's henchmen.

Unfortunately, Warlock had gained power, too, and he'd use it, God only knew how.

"We'll stop him," Smoke said, reading her thoughts, his eyes still comfortably closed. Apparently the waterfall adventure had indeed linked them. And wasn't that luscious?

Better enjoy it now, Zephyr warned in his deep, ghostly voice. *Because there will be war.*

Then we'll fight, Fluffy told him. *And we'll win.*

Together. She couldn't tell who'd thought that, but it didn't really matter.

It was true.

EPILOGUE

Miranda bustled through the diner with two plates in her hands, the scent of fried eggs, pancakes, and bacon teasing her nose. She found the correct table and put the plates down in front of a middle-aged couple in their Sunday best, gave them a sunny smile and a "you're welcome" in exchange for their thanks, and strode to the next table.

"Hi!" She smiled at the family of four, also fresh from the Baptist church, and started scribbling their orders on her pad.

Miranda had not expected to be happy. True, there were moments when grief for her mother weighed hard, especially when she went home to her lonely apartment. But Randy had found that as long as she kept busy, she could avoid her darker memories and concentrate on the present. The present, with its new friendships and bright hopes.

She had not expected to like humans. Miranda had never known any, since Joelle had home schooled her, probably because Warlock had wanted to make sure she never complained to school authorities. That kind of attention would have been damned inconvenient.

Or maybe he was just a controlling bastard who wanted to make sure her every move was carefully supervised.

Miranda found the people she worked with almost restful by comparison, far less inclined to anger and casual violence than Dire Wolves. And in the event anyone did get violent, she knew she could defend herself, since her werewolf nature made her strong even in human form.

It was nice not being afraid.

And it was interesting, watching the way humans interacted, watching them eat and talk and tell jokes. Learning how to pass for human was the whole point of getting this job.

She had also created a whole new identity for herself, complete with school records, driver's license, and a birth certificate in her new name. It hadn't even been difficult. All she'd had to do was to go to the appropriate schools, the DMV, and the health department, then cast a spell or two on the right people.

Magic made officials very helpful.

So now she was Randi Crestfield, 28—she'd made herself a couple of years older than her actual age to make it more difficult for any of Warlock's hackers to find her with a casual search. A trip to the beauty shop had turned her red curls into a sassy brunette bob, and colored contacts had given her the eyes to match.

Of course, there was the possibility some Dire Wolf would catch her casting spells, realize who she was, and report her to Warlock. If that happened, she'd have to run like hell and start all over again. So Miranda had done everything she could to minimize the threat of discovery by picking a town that had no Dire Wolf population, at least according to the Southern Clans database she'd hacked into.

Morgan, South Carolina did have a decent community college, though, and she'd already enrolled there for the fall semester in the Radiologic Technology program. She should be a certified X-ray tech in a couple of years.

The medical field was ideal for her purposes. Werewolves avoided hospitals, since they could heal their own injuries and didn't get sick. On the other hand, certain medical tests could draw attention to their magical differences. Miranda, however, could avoid that problem with a few judicious spells.

So she had a future now, one which didn't include rape or violence. She had an apartment and a used Honda Civic, having sold her father's Lexus and its magically doctored car title. She'd become an ordinary human woman working her way through college.

Life was good—as long as Warlock didn't find her.

But if he did find her . . .

Well. She just wouldn't think about that.

Turn the page for a special preview of
Angela Knight's next Mageverse novel

MASTER OF SHADOWS

Coming soon from Berkley Sensation!

"*What do you* do when they order you to kill?"

The conversation instantly died as every witch and vampire in the room turned to stare at Davon Fredericks. Davon did not flinch under the weight of those incredulous stares. He'd been a trauma surgeon before becoming a vampire, and he'd never lacked balls. He just gazed at Belle, his chocolate eyes level and troubled.

Belle looked up at him from the plates of hors d'oeuvres on the coffee table, a stuffed mushroom halfway to her mouth. She'd cooked all day, and her efforts had turned out rather well. "Why do you ask?"

A muscle flexed in his dark, chiseled jaw, and he looked up at the "*Congratulations, Davon and Cherise!*" banner hanging across the back of the den.

Belle had designed the room especially for the dinner parties she loved to throw, with two big, white leather sectionals arranged around a low, circular coffee table. Davon's brooding gaze dropped to the table, flicking among the trays and bottles that crowded it. He chose a beer and opened it with a violent twist of one strong hand. "I was just wondering."

Now all twenty of her guests looked uneasy. Ten vampires and ten witches, all of them wet behind the ears. Though, like Davon, they were in their early thirties or late twenties, none of them had been Magekind for longer than a few months. Well, except for Cherise.

And Belle herself, who had been around one hell of a lot longer than that. She sighed and decided she'd better scotch this concern before they *all* started obsessing about it. "First off, none of you kids is going to be ordered to kill anybody." She dropped the mushroom on her paper plate and used a toothpick to stab a couple of cheese cubes from a tray. "If someone needs killing, Arthur will send one of the Knights of the Round Table."

Like Tristan, who had been avoiding her for the past month. She curled a lip and stabbed a cheddar cube through its cold, imaginary heart.

"But . . ." Cherise began, only to fall silent with a glance at Davon, who sat beside her on the sectional. Each promptly looked away from the other, as if they'd synchronized their chins.

Frowning, Belle eyed them. The two had just returned from their first mission a few days before, which was the whole point of this get-together. Belle always threw her boys parties to celebrate that first-mission milestone. *You're a real Magus now, kid.*

There was more to being a Magekind vampire—a Magus—than having a set of fangs. You had to save the world, too.

Whether the world liked it or not.

But Cherise was no green recruit; she'd been a Maja for several years now. A steady, intelligent young witch, she had just enough power to handle most jobs without getting dangerously cocky about it. Belle had been pleased Davon had been assigned to her.

So why were they acting so twitchy now, when Belle knew for a fact neither was the twitchy sort?

Eyeing them, she popped the mushroom in her mouth and chewed, absently enjoying the earthy, spicy taste. Definitely one of her better efforts. Being French, Belle loved to cook almost as much as she loved to eat. She swallowed. "Look, Arthur doesn't make the decision to kill humans lightly. You've got to be a career asshole along the lines of Osama bin Laden to make him decide to take you out."

Richard Spotted Horse looked up from pouring himself a glass from one of the bottles of donated blood each of the witches had brought. "But why not just cast a spell on Osama to make him give up the terrorist business?"

"Wouldn't work." Belle nibbled a meatball as she watched Davon, who was now pointedly avoiding her gaze. She'd have to pull him aside after the party and make him spill whatever was bothering him. Nobody had appointed her den mother to the men she'd recruited; she just couldn't help herself. "Once a murderous attitude becomes deeply engrained, you can't wipe it out of a subject's mind no matter how much magic you use."

"So why is he still alive?" Davon picked up a chocolate covered strawberry, then dropped it back on the tray as if he'd remembered he didn't eat anymore.

Belle laughed. "Oh, *chéri*, the fights the council had over *that* subject. We finally decided killing him would just make him a martyr, which is the last thing we need right now. There are enough psychos in that movement that the loss of one wouldn't even put a dent in it. I . . ."

A rumbling male voice interrupted. "I need you, Belle. Now. Let's go." Tristan loomed in the room's doorway, tall and muscular, his handsome face impatient. He was dressed all in black—black jeans, black polo shirt, black boots—and the dramatic contrast with his shoulder-length blond hair was striking.

Belle gave him a smile sweet enough to rot the fangs right out of his head. The kids, of course, were staring at him in hero-worshipping awe. "Come on in, Tristan." *Since you already let yourself in my house without knocking.* "We're celebrating Davon's first mission."

"Congrats, kid." Tristan didn't even glance over at him. "Look, Belle, I've got a pissed-off werewolf waiting for me. It's kind of urgent."

She bared her teeth. They weren't fangs, but they apparently got the message across; he flinched. "I'll be happy to open a gate for you to go meet your fuzzy friend, but I'm a little too busy to accompany you just now. I'll join you once the party's over." Damned if he was going to stroll into her house and start ordering her around. Not when he'd been treating her like a Black Plague victim for weeks.

"Belle, if you need to go on a job, we can clean up," Cherise said earnestly.

"I think we can all be trusted not to get drunk and trash the place." Richard gave her a lazy grin.

Tristan glowered at him, before turning the glare on her. "Look, I realize I'm interrupting fun and games with your . . . boys, but the Direkind needs us to investigate the murder of a seventeen-year-old kid. And they're convinced magic was involved."

Belle stared, making the instant leap. "Warlock."

"That's my thought."

Warlock and his daughter were the only Direkind werewolves who could work spells, and he was both immortal and incredibly powerful. He was also murderous and crazy as hell. Belle and Tristan had locked horns with him the month before, and had damn near died in the process. If he'd surfaced again . . .

Rising from the sectional, Belle looked around at the Majae she'd done all the cooking for. Unlike the vampires, they did eat. "There's more hors d'oeuvres in the kitchen, girls. Please finish them off. Stay as long as you want, everyone."

As Tristan stepped aside, she stalked past him through a chorus of good-byes. "All right, where am I opening this gate?" she said when he'd closed the door behind her. "And what the hell's going on?" *And why have you been avoiding me?*

Tristan shook his head. "Actually, I don't know many of the details myself. William Justice is my contact. He's the Wolf Sheriff—the top werewolf cop appointed by the Direkind Council of Clans. He's a good guy, not a nut-job like their aristocrats. I met him when he fought for us during the Dragon Wars." When they'd been ass-deep in alien demons and calling in every ally they could find, whether Sidhe, werewolf, or dragon. "He's been contacting me for help on cases ever since, usually when he needs me to bring in magical firepower." Like vampires, werewolves couldn't use magic beyond the limits of their own bodies; for spell work, they needed witch help.

"So where is this scene?"

"South Carolina. Some Podunk little town." There were a lot of werewolves in South Carolina, Merlin only knew why. He reached into a pocket to pull out an iPhone. "Hey, Justice? I found my witch. Tell her what she needs to know, would you?" He extended the cell, and she accepted it. The touch of his hand sent a flush of frustrated heat zinging up her arm.

Belle dragged her attention away from his stern, handsome face as she put the phone to her ear. Some Maja had enchanted it to carry inter-dimensional transmissions between Mortal Earth and the magical city of Avalon. She could sense the buzz of an active spell as she handled it. "Hello, Justice?" Good name for a cop.

"Look, you people need to get over here *now*," growled a deep voice with a distinct Southern drawl. "The kid's parents have called every wolf in the fucking county. The mood's getting ugly. I need to get you and the knight in and out before I have a riot on my hands."

"I'm sorry for the delay," Belle told him. "We're on our way."

"Do you want to gate directly to the scene?"

"Not if you want me to sense any magic cast by the killer," she told him. "A dimensional gate produces a pretty strong blast of magical energies that would destroy older traces. We're going to have to come in some distance from the scene if we don't want to contaminate it."

"You do realize that means you're going to have to walk through a pack of pissed-off family members?"

She shrugged. "Can't be helped."

"All right. Give me a minute to get far enough out." A minute or so went by as she listened to the rustle of clothes and the murmur of angry voices, then the click of boots on cement. "Okay."

Closing her eyes, Belle concentrated, using the phone's magical connection to home in on Justice's location. A flick of her fingers conjured a glowing point in the center of the hallway. A heartbeat later, it had expanded into a shimmering oval: an inter-dimensional gate.

Avalon, the Magekind's capital city, was located in another universe entirely, on a world that was a twin to Mortal Earth. Magic was a physical law in the Mageverse; both the Magekind and their werewolf cousins, the Dire-kind, drew on its energies to power their magic. Travel between the two Earths could only be accomplished with a magical gate, which meant Tristan needed Belle's help. Otherwise he'd probably still be avoiding her, the bastard.

Tristan ducked through the gate before it was even finished expanding. Belle followed, trying not to admire his ass as she went. Like the rest of him, it was a very nice ass.

Too bad she needed to stay the hell away from him *and* his very nice ass.

They emerged in a neighborhood straight out of a '50s sitcom—middle-class tract homes, all very similar, nestled in small yards surrounded by azaleas and oak trees. Crickets chirped serenely, and a black cat slinked past them in the dim light cast by a quarter moon.

William Justice must be the guy pacing the sidewalk, a big, muscular man dressed in a Windbreaker he didn't need in the hot summer night. Probably wearing a gun under it.

Justice carried himself with the self-confident wariness that told Belle he was either currently in human law enforcement or had left the field very recently. "Clock's ticking here," he told them after a quick round of introductions. "I need you to check the scene so we can get the boy to the funeral home before some human cop shows up and starts asking questions. Or before there's a riot. Could go either way."

"Tell us about this kid." Tristan frowned down at the sidewalk as though his vampire senses had detected something that worried him. Belle, being merely a Maja, heard nothing.

Justice rotated his shoulders, apparently resettling the straps of a shoulder holster. He was definitely packing. "Vic is seventeen years old. Name's Jimmy Sheridan. Just got through his transition successfully, so his mom and dad thought they were in the clear."

"In the clear?" Belle asked. "Of what?"

"A fifth of our kids don't survive their first transformation," he explained. "The magic runs rogue and burns them alive. Just incinerates them right to ash."

She stared at him in horror, having never heard that particular detail about the Direkind. "My God."

He shook his dark head. "Why do you think we call it 'Merlin's Curse'? It's hell on our families. Which is why we're a little nuts when it comes to our kids."

"Everybody's nuts when it comes to their kids." She cast a quick spell, opening a telepathic link to Tristan. *"This is going to get really, really ugly."*

"Yeah, I picked up on that."

"You are *quick."* Belle curled her lip at him before turning to Justice. "Please, go on. What happened next?"

"The Sheridans took their oldest son out to dinner. They left Jimmy at home because he had a term paper he'd been putting off writing. Paper was due tomorrow, so he was cutting it pretty close. Apparently, they had a little fight about that."

"And the parents are now suffering the agonies of the damned," Belle muttered. She'd been a parent once, a couple of hundred years ago. Never again. She had to deal with enough loss and grief as it was. Watching her mortal daughter die of old age had almost been more than she could take.

"That's certainly part of the rage factor," Justice told her. "The family headed to Outback at 5:40 P.M. When they got home at 8:20, they found the den sprayed with blood splatter. Boy's body was sitting in an arm chair with his Xbox controller in his lap. They found his head under the coffee table. Looked like he didn't even hear his killer walk up behind him. Sure as shit didn't put up a fight. He was just executed."

"Oh, shit." Tristan scrubbed a hand over his face.

"You haven't heard the worst of it yet. The weapon was obviously a sword, and the room stinks of magic." Justice eyed them, his face utterly expressionless. "Magekind magic."

They stared at him. Belle felt her jaw drop, and Tristan exploded in outrage. "Wait a minute—you're suggesting one of *us* decapitated a seventeen-year-old boy while he was playing a video game?"

Justice didn't drop his hard gaze. "The evidence is pretty damned clear, Tristan."

"Fuck that," the knight spat. "We don't murder children, boy."

"Any of us with that kind of mental defect is detected right after the first turn," Belle said, laying a calming hand on Tristan's tense shoulder. *I should know—I detect them.* "We have to kill them on the spot. It could not have been one of us."

"You're assuming the killer is crazy," Justice said. "The family thinks this could be revenge for the attempted murder of Arthur's son a few months ago."

"You think *Arthur Pendragon* butchered that lad?" Tristan's voice dropped to a furious hiss Belle found more unnerving than a shout.

"That makes no sense," she interjected hastily. Tristan's temper could be explosive. "Logan already killed the werewolves who tried to assassinate him. And in the process, he prevented the deaths of three hundred humans." Logan's fellow cops, gathered at a funeral home to mourn the death of an officer murdered by the werewolves' hired assassin. "Those wolves strapped suicide vests on the Sheriff's grandchildren. Everyone would have died if Logan hadn't disarmed the bombs." Which he then used to blow up the werewolves. *Pissing off a Pendragon is never a good idea,* she thought with a grim private smile.

"I'm aware of that," Justice said. "That's why I want you to check out the scene. I don't believe Arthur would kill a child either, but the family is pretty worked up."

"I don't bloody care," Tristan snapped. "Yes, Arthur has ordered deaths, but only terrorist leaders and military dictators. He's not going to murder an innocent boy to revenge himself on the Direkind. That's insane."

"But it's exactly the kind of thing Warlock would do," Belle said thoughtfully. "Especially if he's trying to trigger a war between the Direkind and the Magekind."

"Warlock?" Justice gave her a blank look. "There's no such thing as Warlock."

"Right, he's 'only a myth'—we've already heard that song and dance from every werewolf we've talked to." Tristan drawled, waving a dismissive hand. "Only your legend damned near killed one of my best friends last month, so please believe us when we tell you he definitely exists. And he's a psychopath, so if anybody is butchering seventeen-year-olds, it's Warlock."

"But . . ." Justice stared at him, shaken out of his cool professionalism. "If Warlock really does exist, he's as big a hero to my people as Arthur is to yours. Why would he kill that child?"

"Because he's a son of a bitch," Tristan snapped. "Why don't you let us check the scene and see what we can find out? If he's trying to frame Arthur, Belle will be able to work a spell to prove it."

Justice took a deep breath and blew it out. "Fine. Come on then."

The scent of Belle Coeur was driving Tristan insane. Some of that cock-teasing smell was expensive perfume—probably French, knowing her. She smelled like jasmine and moonbeams . . .

Merlin's Balls, what romantic tripe was that? *Great. She's making me think stupid shit.*

Then there was the scent of distilled sex, as rawly female as the swing of her ass and the sway of her breasts.

Tristan had spent the past month trying to dig Belle out of his skull. He'd worked out with Arthur, both with blade and hand-to-hand, until his skin streamed sweat and his legs shook.

Eventually even his best friend had enough. "You're

obsessed with that woman," Arthur had said after listening to Tristan bitch about his partner one too many times.
"She's worked her way under your skin all the way to
bone—and I hope she leads you a merry chase. Serves you
right for all those women whose dreams you crushed, you
stone-hearted bastard."

Tristan had next tried women as the cure for Belle,
banging every pretty young Maja he could seduce, the
older ones being wise to his habits. Unfortunately, those
green enough to be susceptible to his advances maddened
him with their awed stares. He could say any rude thing
he pleased, and all he'd get in return was a lip quiver that
made him feel like a prick.

Belle didn't quiver her lip. Belle gave as good as she got,
toe-to-toe and snarl for snarl.

And his mind was supposed to be on the murdered boy,
not on Belle's admittedly luscious ass. How did she do this
to him? He never had trouble keeping his mind on the job.
Distraction got you killed in this line of work. Worse, it
could get innocents killed. Like Belle . . .

. . . And Merlin's Balls, look at all the werewolves.

Tristan came to a stop in the center of the sidewalk, staring at the house at the end of the cul-de-sac. The brick colo-
nial had a bigger yard than most of those on the block, with
a long brick colonnaded porch, neatly trimmed hedges,
and a yard shaded by cedars and oaks.

Under those trees, standing in groups, clustered around
the open beds of pickup trucks, or sitting on lawn chairs,
were dozens of werewolves. The smell of Direwolf magic
rode the summer breeze, thick with the scent of fur and rage.

And beer.

Oh, great. The werewolves were getting plowed.

They were all still in human form, thank Merlin. The
men were dressed for the weather in T-shirts and jeans or
khakis, while most of the women wore sundresses or shorts
as they clustered together on the porch, gathered protectively around a woman who sobbed fitfully in utter despair.

The boy's mother, no doubt.

Every instinct Tristan had told him this was going to get

nasty. For a split second, he considered asking Belle to conjure his armor and sword. Then he realized that the sight of an armored knight would only light the tinder under the werewolves' rage. He simply couldn't afford to do that, even if it meant being seriously underequipped if things went south.

So instead he fell back a pace behind Belle, guarding her back as Justice led them up the walk toward the front porch.

Until one of the men stepped directly into the Wolf Sheriff's path. "What the hell are you doing bringing them here, Justice?" He glared at them past the other werewolf's shoulder, his gaze scalding in its fury.

Tristan was instantly aware of being the focus of enough rage-filled eyes to light a bonfire. This was the stuff of which lynch mobs were made.

Belle's voice rang out, cool and clear. "If one of the Magekind did kill that boy, I can work a spell to identify the source of the magic."

"Question is, will you tell us who it is—or will you cover it up?" a male voice shouted.

She turned and scanned every face in the yard. The Direkind was immune to magic, but Belle had another kind of power in her eyes—the kind that made even furious men remember she was a woman. And decent men protected women. "I swore to serve mankind when I became a witch. Anyone who would kill a child—especially from behind with a coward's stroke—deserves nothing but death. If it's one of the Magekind, I'll kill him myself."

"What if it's Arthur?" a hoarse voice shouted.

Tristan had had enough of hearing his friend maligned. "Arthur Pendragon is no child-killing coward. And any man who says so in my presence again had better be prepared to bleed!" The last word was a little too close to a battlefield roar, but damned if he'd back down.

Arthur might no longer be high king of Britain—he hated anyone calling him by that title—but he'd never be anything but king to Tristan. Even if Tristan would rather die than admit as much out loud. And he'd certainly never say as much to Arthur himself.

"Any more questions?" Tristan snapped.

Nobody said a damned word as the Wolf Sheriff led the Magekind toward the house. As they climbed the stairs, Tristan realized they had yet another gauntlet to run.

The werewolf women. They glared as the little group walked onto the porch, silent outrage in their eyes.

Finally one of them rose from the midst of the group. Her face shone in the dim moonlight, the tracks of tears glistening. Her nose ran, and she wiped it with a wadded tissue. "He was a good boy," she croaked in a voice hoarse from crying. "He gave me roses every Mother's Day since he started working. A dozen every single Mother's Day. Maybe his grades could have been better, maybe I had to ride him about doing his homework. But he cut the lawn every other Saturday without being asked. Somebody hit the neighbor's cat with a car last week, and he found it lying on the side of the road, all bloody and hurt. He took it to the vet himself and paid for it to be treated. He hates cats, but he said Bonnie—that's the neighbor's five-year-old—she loves that animal. And the cat made it because Jimmy took it to the vet." She was crying so hard by the time she finished that Tristan could barely understand her last wailing words. "He didn't deserve this!"

"I know, ma'am," Belle said gently. "I'm so sorry this happened. We'll find out who's responsible."

The kid's mother gave them a look so pitiful, Tristan felt his own eyes sting. "That won't bring him back."

"No, I'm afraid it won't."

"Could you . . ." There was a sudden horrible hope in her eyes. "They say you Magekind are really powerful. Could you bring him . . ."

"No," Belle interrupted, her voice catching. "If I could, please believe me, I would." She swallowed. "I had a daughter. I know how . . . I'm sorry. Sorry for your loss."

Breaking off as if realizing she was on the verge of losing it completely, Belle whirled and headed for the house's front door. Justice pulled it open for her, and she started inside—only to stop in the doorway, her body recoiling.

Tristan realized why as the smell of blood rolled out in

a choking wave. The boy's mother collapsed back in her chair and began to sob. The women around her joined in, voices a rising wail that made Tristan wish he was any other damned place at all.

Helpless. He hated feeling helpless.

Belle straightened her shoulders and walked into the house, her head high, her spine erect. The two men followed.

In the short foyer, Justice silently took the lead. Not that he had to. They could easily tell where the scene was from the bloody tracks on parquet floor.

When they stepped inside, it was every bit as bad as Tristan had known it would be. He was no stranger to the effects of a beheading, so he expected the blood spray. He'd expected the body, still sitting erect in the armchair.

What bothered him was the big screen television and the Xbox, which was still mindlessly running the kid's video game. Two characters in armor, swinging swords, the sound of thunks and cries. "Christ."

"Yeah," Justice agreed. "But take a deep breath. Under the blood—isn't that the smell of a Magus?"

Tristan frowned at him, but dropped to one knee and took an obedient breath right behind the armchair, where the killer must have stood.

He expected a generic scent, something Warlock had faked in an effort to trigger a war between Direkind and Magekind. Maybe even Arthur's scent, since Warlock hated the Magus with an insane jealousy that could have led him to frame the man.

But as he breathed in, Tristan recognized a scent he didn't expect. One he'd smelled just a few hours before.

Startled, he looked up at Belle, who was standing frozen at his side, her face pale as Wedgwood porcelain. "Merlin's cup, Belle—it's Davon Fredericks."

A BRAND-NEW COLLECTION
FROM BESTSELLING PROVOCATEURS
OF THE PARANORMAL . . .

BURNING UP

New York Times bestselling authors

ANGELA KNIGHT
NALINI SINGH
VIRGINIA KANTRA
MELJEAN BROOK

In Angela Knight's *Blood and Roses*, a vampire warrior and his seductive captor join forces to stop a traitor from unleashing an army of demonic predators on their kingdom.

Whisper of Sin is new in Nalini Singh's Psy-Changeling series, in which a woman in lethal danger finds an unlikely protector—and lover—in a volatile member of the DarkRiver pack.

Virginia Kantra continues the haunting tales of the Children of the Sea in *Shifting Sea*, the story of a wounded soldier rescued by a strange and enigmatic young woman.

Meljean Brook launches a bold new steampunk series with *Here There Be Monsters* as a desperate woman strikes a provocative—and terrifying—bargain to gain overseas passage.

M643T0210